Ryan Gawley was born and raised in Northern Ireland.
He lives with his wife Kira and their dog Tasha.
Escape To Survive is his first novel.

Escape To Survive

Ryan Gawley

Ryan can be contacted at
ryangawleyauthor@gmail.com

CHAPTER 1

Freezing wind and rain lashed Sam's face and stung his eyes as he pulled the hood of a faded army surplus jacket over his shaved head and pushed through the heavy windowless door. A stream of despondent souls trudged in line ahead of him and many more followed behind as he made his way toward the imposing factory gates to collect his final earnings from the bookish payroll clerk who wore an apologetic expression as he was forced one last time to do the company's bidding. It was a typically miserable evening for this time of year and Sam had just finished his final shift at Central Food Plant Three. The factory was one of several large processing plants where raw ingredients were ground and mixed to provide basic food supplements to the Dreg masses. It would now be decommissioned like plants two and five had been a few months earlier.

The clerk and his cash box were guarded by two surly, well-built men standing in close formation. They wore dark grey helmets with a clear polycarbonate visor lowered over their eyes and every inch of their body was protected by thick black leather and heavy black Kevlar body armour. Both held Mossberg 590A1 pump action 12 gauge shotguns and their red and black arm insignia proclaimed them to be Enforcers, the city's militarised guard force under direct command of General Curran. They were stationed to provide crowd control ensuring no one would dare argue about the measly sum handed to them in this final payoff. Sam took his envelope and paused to open the packet and check its contents.

'Move along,' barked a harsh voice.

Sam looked up to see an Enforcer had moved a step toward him. He opened his mouth to say something but quickly thought better of it before stuffing the thin packet deep into his inside jacket pocket and re-joined the procession of ex-workers, following them through the gate. Once out onto the wet, crowded streets Sam made his way through the hurrying masses, everyone trying to just get home or perhaps to a favoured bar or someplace else that suited their mood. Nobody looked at anyone else; everyone disconnected, all part the same crowd yet each of them alone. Sam always had a deep sense of anxiety in the city. Something always felt very wrong to him but since martial law had been enacted few Dreg citizens had any choice about their circumstances. What puzzled Sam was how most people seemed to accept their lot like they truly believed their confinement behind the oppressive city walls was somehow for their own well-being.

'Some people just aren't meant to live in the city,' he thought to himself and quickened pace to hurry his escape from the noise and chaos.

Most people used the remnants of the old underground transport system to travel in Rook City but Sam preferred to walk. It took longer to move around but cost him nothing and the exercise kept him in shape. He enjoyed being in control of his own journey and it also minimised exposure to the incessant advertising streamed live by Central Media from most places of public gathering. Sam was stubbornly independent almost to a fault and he found it hard to allow other people do things for him, only accepting help when he had exhausted all other options. It made life difficult at times but in a world where the Elites had control over many elements of his life Sam took pleasure in finding every possible thing he could do or provide for himself.

'Now. Hand it over! Just give me the wallet or your wife

will be crying over a corpse tonight!'

'Shit,' Sam muttered to himself as he walked past the scene with the hundreds of other citizens like sardines escaping a barracuda by staying with the shoal. They seemed oblivious to just another street attack and were only too glad it wasn't them this time.

'I'm not gonna ask again you old bastard. Money, now!'

The voice wasn't one Sam recognised but he'd heard the same intent in words from a time in his past that he cared not to remember. After just a few yards he ducked into a doorway and watched through the flow of passing commuters as an old man in a torn black duffel coat with what looked like a half bottle of whiskey in one pocket and a loose package of some kind of meat in his left hand reached nervously under the coat to his wallet.

'Damn it, this old guy's got nothing but he's probably going die for it all the same,' Sam thought aloud. He figured the attacker to be in his late twenties, tall, wiry and looked like any remaining muscle on his bones had withered. He held a rough, pointed scrap of iron wrapped in cloth as a makeshift knife, a stabbing weapon no less effective despite its crude construction.

'Probably a junkie needs a fix,' thought Sam noticing the red sunken eyes and clustered scabs on exposed forearms. His thoughts raced as quickly as his heart and he dived into the stream of human traffic before he had even decided what he would do. In a few seconds Sam was moving behind the old man toward the addict. He passed on by, not making eye contact, as if just part of the uncaring crowd but quickly he turned about to come up behind the attacker.

Sam darted forward as the ragged spike was thrust toward the old man's gut. He reached past the junkie's left side and caught the offending arm, pulling it back just as the weapon's sharp tip punctured the thick fabric of the would-be victim's coat. At the same time Sam wrapped his right arm around the attacker's neck and tightened his grip into a choke while dragging him backwards and off balance. Caught by surprise the assailant offered little resistance at first but quickly began to struggle.

Sam had an iron grip on the left arm which still held tight to the rough blade and while wrestling to maintain control of the writhing figure he saw a spray of blood erupt from the junkie's nose as the old man rammed the base of his whiskey bottle hard into his attacker's face. The knife made a loud metallic clank when it fell to the ground as the junkie stopped struggling and tried to bring his free hand up to protect his smashed nose. Sam took the opportunity to release the choke and heaved the attacker round, slamming his head into a lamp post leaving him crumpled on the ground and out cold. Sam knelt and checked the unconscious man's breathing and propped his head up with a discarded cardboard box before kicking the fallen knife into the opening of a nearby drain.

It wasn't an elegant rescue by any measure but no one had been killed and that was a result. The crowd continued to hurry past like a river of bodies as if unaware of the violent scene, none daring to risk involvement or draw attention.

'If that bottle's not broken I could really do with a drink!' Sam said to the old man who was visibly shaken but otherwise none the worse for his ordeal.

'No bother my friend,' replied the man, offering a sip from his bottle. 'I thought I was for the city furnaces there, thanks for stepping in.'

After a good pull on the bottle and feeling the warming liquid run down to his stomach Sam felt his nerves settle.

'We'd better get moving before an Enforcer patrol sees this, where's home for you?'

'It's just a few streets up and on the left, and the name's Arthur'.

'Okay, I'll see you that far Arthur then I'm heading for home myself, these bloody streets get worse every day,' grumbled Sam, mad at himself for getting involved but knowing he couldn't have done anything less.

The pair turned and walked quickly away as the downed man groaned and began to regain consciousness. They merged with the swiftly moving crowd to make their way toward Arthur's house before a bored cop spotted the disturbance on his surveillance display and dispatched a patrol wagon. The lobotomised Enforcer thugs sent from Central Command regularly rounded up trouble makers and brought them to one of the city's numerous detention centres for "processing".

'It's this left here,' said Arthur indicating that they'd reached his turn. Sam dropped out of the crowd to say goodbye to his temporary companion.

'Will you join me for another drink?' asked Arthur.

'Thanks but I'll pass. I appreciate the offer but I really need to get home.'

'Please, I insist. It's the least I can do after what you did for me.'

Sam thought about it, he had to get back and walk his dog Molly before it was too late to safely roam the streets. 'I suppose after the day I've had I could use a drink and sure I've come this far with you.'

The street here was like any other in the Dreg sector of Rook City. Once proudly maintained homes were now personal fortresses. Bars on every window, reinforced doors and those that could find and afford them had cameras monitoring their barbed wire topped boundary walls. At the door to his house Arthur didn't take out a key but banged two times fast, paused, then banged once more. After a few seconds an elderly but strong female voice shouted from behind the door.

'That you Arthur? I heard another voice, is all okay?'

'Yes love, it's me and this is Sam. He's a friend, he's okay. Come on now and let us in, I promised this man a drink.'

Sam could hear a heavy bolt or bar being drawn back and several locks being disengaged before the steel reinforced door swung easily back on its upgraded hinges revealing an old but still attractive lady, her shoulder length silver hair casually held back in a simple pony tail. Sam could tell she'd been through tough times as everyone had these past years but she hadn't lost the light in her soft blue eyes which sparkled when she welcomed him into their home.

Sam mostly kept to himself these days but still had a good intuition for character. 'These are good people,' he decided. He followed Arthur and his wife to the kitchen where he took the offered seat at a small table. The kitchen felt warm and cosy, a poor house but no less homely for it. An old wood burning stove radiated heat and on one of its two small hobs a pot of something thick and green bubbled gently filling the room with a faintly unpleasant but somehow still appetising aroma. Sam thought to himself how people used to remove these stoves for more modern appliances but this old couple seemed so wise now for holding onto their wood burner since most other folk couldn't afford black market drums of gas or heating oil and had to depend on the unreliable electricity service from Central Supply to provide their main source of power and heating.

'I'm Alice by the way,' said the old lady, throwing a mock scolding glance at her husband for failing to introduce her then hurried over to a cupboard to retrieve two glasses and a tall unlabelled bottle of amber liquid. 'I don't drink this stuff myself, gin is my sin!' she chuckled to herself while Arthur hung his wet coat on the back of the kitchen door to dry near the stove then gave Alice the packet of meat he had held tightly in his hand since before Sam met him on the street.

Unwrapped from his coat and scarf Arthur defied his aged appearance and retained quite an athletic build and seemed in good shape. His white hair, wild and crazy was still fuller than many men half his age. He would happily tell those that passed comment it was his dear Alice that kept him youthful.

Arthur unscrewed the lid of the bottle and poured two generous measures for Sam and himself. 'Get that into you, it's a distillation of my own creation,' he quipped proudly.

'Really? You make this stuff yourself?' asked Sam genuinely impressed before taking a long sip of the liquid and held it in his mouth for a few seconds to fully appreciate the flavour then swallowed it down. 'Well, that's a fine whiskey indeed,' he exclaimed enjoying the warmth and comforting aroma of the intoxicating liquor. 'I make a few gallons of beer from time to time and haven't tried my hand at spirits but this would encourage me to try.'

Arthur was visibly pleased at the compliment while Alice smiled to see her husband moved over such a trivial thing and she delighted in seeing him excited about something again.

Pouring another glass each Arthur appeared to come to some decision. 'Would you like to see my still?' he asked.

Sam, anxious to get home to take Molly for her walk knew this was a great gesture of trust on behalf of the old man since brewing or distilling was breaking numerous contraband rules and so, not wanting to offend, he agreed. Arthur grabbed his coat from the kitchen door and threw it loosely over his shoulders.

'Bring your glass, you can finish it in the shed,' he said gesturing for Sam to follow him out the rear door of the house.

Arthur led the way down a short path to a large block-built shed at the back of a well-kept garden. As far as Sam could tell from the light thrown out from the kitchen window the back of the house appeared almost old fashioned with its potted plants, neat lawn and wooden garden furniture. You just had to ignore the high iron fences and razor wire protecting each house from the next.

Arthur took a key from his pocket and unlocked a large well-greased brass padlock then slid open a heavy bar securing the shed door and stood aside to allow Sam to enter ahead of him. As he made his way into the pitch black interior Sam felt an oily curtain or tarpaulin to his left side and followed its length part way until Arthur hurried in behind to get out of the rain and turned on the dim single light bulb dangling from the ceiling.

'There she is,' said Arthur eagerly pointing to the right-hand wall of the shed about twenty feet from the entrance as he took Sam by the arm and directed him away from the dividing sheet which hung from ceiling to floor across the breadth of the room.

Set against a cleared wall beyond the workshop tools, gardening equipment, odd scraps of timber and the usual shed detritus stood an old copper hot water tank, an ancient looking oak barrel, propane burner and an assortment of copper tubing, pipes, glass jugs and bottles. The product of this home-made chemistry experiment was some of the finest whiskey Sam had ever tasted. Not that he considered himself a connoisseur given the poor quality liquor available in the city's bars and off-licence shops.

Arthur keenly began to explain the processes of his art but Sam really needed to be going as Molly would be eagerly awaiting her evening walk and it was dangerous to be out too late at night in this side of the city. Sam politely made his excuses and followed Arthur to the door but near the exit he absent-mindedly pulled back the soiled curtain and glanced into the gloom beyond. Despite the poor illumination from the low wattage bulb enough light filtered through rips and gaps to allow Sam to identify several rows of shelves loaded with canned food, bottled drinking water, reference books of various size and subject and all manner of camping equipment. On the floor in front of the shelves were two rucksacks, one large size, one medium and both apparently packed and waiting for an expedition as they had rolled foam mats and sleeping bags tightly secured to their exterior with straps. Apart from the distillation equipment the backpacks were the only thing in the shed not covered in a layer of dust and cobwebs.

'Do you go camping much these days Arthur?' enquired Sam casually. 'I used to really enjoy getting out in the mountains back home before my family moved here but it's not so easy to enjoy the wilderness when you're trapped in this damn city'.

'Ah my old bones find the cold too much for comfort these days...' Arthur replied irritably.

'I only ask because I see you like to keep your pack ready.'

Arthur glanced back at Sam but said nothing. He had opened the shed door to leave but now he pulled it shut again locking it from the inside. Suddenly he lunged at Sam driving a shoulder into Sam's chest which sent him reeling backward. As Sam's back slammed against the wall of the shed Arthur leapt at him in a flash and pinned his forearm across Sam's throat. The younger man had been caught by surprise but had superior strength and grabbed Arthur by the shoulders shoving him off then dropped low and punched him hard in the gut immediately winding the older man who doubled over, clutching a battered workbench to steady himself as he gasped for breath.

'What the hell's wrong with you?' shouted Sam keeping his distance but scanning around for anything he could use as a weapon, ready to defend himself.

'You shouldn't have looked back there, it's none of your business. Why so interested in my backpack?' wheezed Arthur. 'Why all the damn questions?'

Sam held Arthur by the shoulders again but this time to help him stand upright. 'I only asked because it looks very much like the one I have at home,' he said staring Arthur right in the eye with a conspiratorial look. 'You know, just in case.'

Arthur returned the stare, pausing to catch his breath and regaining his composure and poise. 'You're an interesting man Sam, I'll tell you that. I'm glad we met. Not least because you saved me from a stabbing today but I guess we've more in common than just rucksacks and a liking for whiskey'.

'I hear what you're saying; I think we've a bit more to talk about but I've to get going here, I need to get back to walk Molly. What if I stop in with you and Alice again next week? Besides, I dropped my glass when you tackled me and I'd like a chance to drink the next one.'

The two men laughed having found a common bond, shook hands and went back to the house where Alice had laid three places at the table. Sam noticed this before Alice extended a warm invitation to stay for dinner. It meant a lot to him that he was welcomed into this house despite being a stranger; something very rare in these dark times. He politely declined the offer, said his goodbyes promising to return after the weekend so he and Arthur could talk further. He pulled up the hood of his jacket and walked back out into the street hearing locks and heavy bolts being clamped in place behind him.

'Sorry Molly,' he spoke into the wind hoping his best friend in the world wouldn't be too mad at him for coming back late but he knew she'd forgive him. She always did.

CHAPTER 2

In a darkened boardroom high above the city streets flickering light from a projected display danced over the sombre faces of nine men as live feeds were patched in from surveillance cameras throughout the twin capital cities. The men betrayed no emotion as they sat around a massive marble topped table observing graphic horror in vivid detail as the sickening violence silently played out before them during the first update of the project.

After several minutes one of the nine from his seat at the head of the table discreetly clicked a faintly glowing button on a recessed console and the display faded while the room lights gently came up to full illumination. Eight figures wearing complexions as grey as their suits turned their timeworn executive chairs to face their leader, Victor Henderson. He was fifty-three years old and the only son of the city's former senior politician from a time before the Elites overtly grabbed power. Standing five feet nine inches tall and weighing two hundred and forty pounds with blotchy red complexion, almost permanent sweat on his bare scalp and a trademark dark blue double breasted business suit straining at the seams he was the object of mockery from his subordinates but only ever in his absence. His beady yet penetrating eyes, or more the sense of something dark and wicked behind them elicited fear and obedience from those around him.

Henderson surveyed the room waiting for hush and then

spoke in a deep but laboured voice. 'As you can clearly see gentlemen, the project has begun and the initial reports are somewhat promising. Higher volumes than expected have succumbed to our efforts for which we owe thanks to Doctor Follis and his development team.'

All eyes briefly glanced to a physically withered, balding man with a neatly trimmed ginger chinstrap beard who remained silent but crossed his fingers in front of his chest and nodded to acknowledge the compliment.

Henderson continued. 'Our agents succeeded in mixing the enhanced compounds with the regular ration supplements and these have been performing excellently. As a precaution we arranged for a small fire and an equipment malfunction to temporarily close down Central Food Plants in both Raven City and Rook City where the tainted rations were produced and distributed so as to ensure no chance of discovery until we can remove any residual evidence. However at this stage nothing could be done even if international agencies decided to investigate. The increased food shortages caused by the closing of the plants are an added bonus since they only serve to fuel tensions in the poorest areas of the Dreg sectors.'

A few quiet murmurs of approval resonated through the group before Henderson cleared his throat to signal he required silence once more. 'As you are all aware Mr. Yardley has been working for the past two years to perfect the triggering signal which has been slipstreamed by Central Media into the video feeds to Dreg sector channels. So far all cerebral programming appears to have been silently absorbed and nothing has been observed to indicate awareness of its presence.'

The expressionless faces glanced across the table as another member of the circle quietly accepted acknowledgement of his efforts while Henderson continued to address the meeting. 'Test patients were obtained through random abductions from Central Medical casualty wards and following extensive lab trials the combination of repeated exposure to loaded video streams and tainted food rations caused every test subject to become highly susceptible to elevated stress levels and prone to metabolic mutations when sufficient stimuli were provided although it has been found that the trigger event and level of background stress can differ between subjects. Again this serves us well in that it makes detection almost impossible. I will defer to General Curran for an update on security concerns.'

Henderson took his seat and attention turned to a tall heavily built man with tightly cropped grey hair who wore a thick well-groomed moustache and black military uniform with red insignia. 'Thank you Victor,' said the head of Central Command, the Elite's security division. The informal use of Henderson's first name visibly grated on the ineffectual leader as was the General's intention.

Curran continued with his report. 'I have briefed Enforcer Patrol Commanders to expect increased violence in Dreg sectors but as agreed I've not informed them as to the reason for this. I have stationed my most trusted men with carefully chosen squads to patrol and protect the Elite side of the sector barriers. I'm confident there is no serious cause for concern at this time and I feel it is not necessary to alert the Elite population.' The General brushed the ends of his luxurious moustache with a stout finger for a moment using the brief silence to focus his next point. 'However I would like to take this opportunity to voice my concern that despite increased indoctrination programs, recruitment levels among the Dreg sectors remain low meaning existing forces will be stretched and could well be overrun in certain areas. As a precaution senior personnel should instruct family members to remain strictly within Elite residential areas as there is still a small danger of violence breaking through the sector barricades.'

'Thank you General,' said Henderson quickly rising to speak, indicating he had heard enough and so reasserting his authority. 'I'm sure with you in charge at Central Command we have nothing to fear but none the less we should all encourage our families to stay off the streets as you advise. Your forces are capable of containing this problem I have no doubt.'

What Henderson didn't add was the other members of the Upper Council had agreed without the General's knowledge that while additional security forces would be required it would be wise to secretly restrict funding and via other channels hinder recruitment. Their efforts were to prevent the ranks of the military wing swelling to proportions that may lead the General to consider challenging the Council for leadership. It was Henderson's personal intention for troop numbers to be decimated.

'Well gentlemen I believe that brings us up to date. As you now know the project has begun and initial indications are that the Dregs will tear themselves apart as hoped. Those that do not turn will be destroyed by those that do. The panic and confusion will lead to many other casualties and whatever small number of Dregs remain will be easily gathered and forced to work in our service. After all we still need someone to do the dirty jobs.' Henderson laughed and was immediately but nervously accompanied by his colleagues. 'We'll meet here again in one week but further updates will be sent twice daily.' Henderson hoisted his bulk from his chair to indicate the meeting had ended. 'Until then gentlemen, good day.'

Once the session had concluded and the Upper Council members had filed out of the room Henderson pressed another button on his console. He placed a call to his driver requesting his car be brought to the underground garage from where he would be transported in secure luxury over the short distance to the tallest tower in Raven City, the top two floors of which Henderson enjoyed as his personal residence.

Like many of the Elites he chose to live in a tower block where the elevated position provided security but in Henderson's case it also massaged the ego of a man who believed in every way he should be seen as being above all others. The lower five floors of each building were reserved for exclusive shops or office space while the floors above these levels were occupied by the city's rich inhabitants with price and luxury climbing proportionately with distance from the street below. This hierarchy served to remind everyone of who was above whom in the social pecking order and of course clearly showed who was currently on top. Each of the nine members of the Upper Council lived in a different penthouse atop individual towers but the grandest of all was Henderson's only for as long as he retained his seat of power.

CHAPTER 3

Waking on the couch with Molly whining softly and licking his face Sam looked about his apartment in a bleary-eyed haze. The golden retriever wagged her tail excitedly upon seeing her master awake at last as she yearned for affection and some food for her empty dish.

'Breakfast time already girl?' Sam groaned sleepily, sitting up slowly, rubbing his face and stretching to try and ease the knots in his back.

Another night had passed and again Sam hadn't managed to stumble to his bed but instead had lain sprawled on the couch where he'd drunkenly slipped into restless sleep. A weak grey light shone through the thin fabric of cheap curtains silhouetting an impressive collection of empty beer cans and a mostly finished whiskey bottle which were strewn on the floor and across a low wooden coffee table.

Ignoring the throbbing in his head Sam stumbled to the back of the joint kitchen and living area. Checking the condition of a rusted can of dog food the faded details on the torn label were enough to identify it as chicken flavour. He peeled back the lid using the provided ring pull and scraped a third of the foul smelling contents into a metal food dish mixing the meat with dry kibble. With such a hangover it was close to unbearable but he'd not eaten yet and managed to hold his stomach while he wrapped the can in an old plastic bag and set it on the top shelf in the door of his fridge to save for later. While he was there he took one of three filter jugs from the bottom shelf, poured and immediately drank a large glass of cool water for himself then filled a bowl for Molly setting it down beside her as she hungrily chased the last few morsels around her dish. He poured another glass for himself draining the jug then refilled it with cloudy brown water from the kitchen tap and set it back in the fridge to slowly drip through the filter. He checked the salad drawer which was empty except for a single remaining filter cartridge. It was still sealed in its protective packaging but he knew he'd have to find something to trade soon or else clean water would be off the menu.

'I can't keep doing this Molly,' he said as the throb in his head continued to pound a painful rhythm. The dog acknowledged him by briefly looking up from her water bowl and cocking her head as if in understanding. 'A little celebration at leaving that hell-hole and it's lasted three days now, time to clean up a bit eh?'

He trudged to the bathroom sink and splashed water over the stubble on his head then began scraping the stubble from his face and felt slightly more human again. Back in the kitchen he fried the last of the fatty bacon and the duck eggs he'd bought from the market as a final luxury, washed them down with a large mug of strong black coffee then changed into his jogging shorts and stepped into the old running shoes he kept under his bed. 'Molly, get your lead, we're going out'.

Sam had saved Molly one freezing night when he found her under a bridge near his apartment. She had been abandoned but instead of allowing her to fend for herself some cruel bastard had locked her in a discarded shipping crate where she would have frozen to death had Sam not heard her whimpering and freed her. She followed him home that night and they'd been together since. She was a very clever dog and obedient but still liked doing things her own way at times which Sam found equally frustrating and endearing.

17

Molly got her lead from where it always hung over a narrow table in the hall and came to Sam, tail wagging wildly and looking up at him with the lead in her mouth.

'Only a short run today Molly, I'm not feeling too good just yet.'

Sam liked to get some exercise as regularly as he could and found the best way to clear a hangover was to sweat it out in the fresh air and to get the blood pumping round his body. Even if the idea seemed like hell at first it always made him feel better afterwards.

There was a park nearby that he liked to run in so he and Molly made their way toward it at a slow jog. It used to be a well-kept public space but now like everything else it had been abandoned to gradually decay. The carefully mown lawns were now meadows of tall grass and the manicured flower beds were overgrown with weeds and wild flowers. The benches had been broken up for firewood long ago and the paths were covered in moss and cracked where weeds had pushed up through the uneven tarred surface. Ducks, swans and rabbits among other native wildlife had returned and populated the more natural areas which was one of the reasons Sam liked this place, it felt real to him amongst the manmade forest of concrete and steel.

After running a loop of a few miles Sam was exhausted, the previous few days of heavy drinking had drained his stamina. 'This is kill or cure Molly but I think I'll live another day,' he gasped, struggling for breath as he steadied himself on a rusted railing at the edge of the park and stretched his calf muscles. He told himself he needed to clean up and get in shape again. He'd had a nagging feeling for as long as he could remember that he needed to stay fit, to be ready.

Returning home Sam found a letter in his mailbox, one of a vast wall of similar boxes in the entrance hall to the building. He hadn't received a personal letter since moving into his apartment but he was in the habit of checking the mailbox each day, just in case. He had however received a few letters from Central Control who issued fines and infringement notices in drab recycled grey envelopes and Sam's mood sunk upon discovering another official notification.

'What the hell is it this time?' he wondered aloud, slamming the door of his mailbox shut. He stopped short of ripping the letter to pieces knowing that settling the fine was better than an eventual visit from the Enforcers due to non-payment.

Once he and Molly were safely back in his apartment and the door secured Sam opened his windows to freshen the air and swept his arm across the living room table to clear a space, threw the letter down, got some water for himself and Molly then hit the shower to scrub off the rancid sweat he had worked up from his run.

He finished dressing in a clean pair of faded blue boot cut jeans and a plain black t-shirt and sat down prepared to deal with the dreary envelope but before opening it he was interrupted by a bang on his door. Sam didn't get many visitors and anyone calling would buzz the intercom at the building entrance. He ran to his bedroom and grabbed the old wooden baseball bat he kept by his bed and returned to the apartment door to look through the spy-hole. With a sigh he relaxed his grip on the bat, slid the locking bolt aside and opened the door to his neighbour from the apartment across the hall.

'Hi Pete, what's up?' asked Sam making no effort to hide his irritation.

Pete was an administrative manager for Central Distribution and his position led him to consider himself superior to most other workers but to the Elites he was just a Dreg like all the rest. Pete was also completely inept at household maintenance or any kind of technical repair. Sam knew both these things about Pete and could have chosen to ignore him considering Pete's usual condescending attitude but he was harmless all the same. Also the change in Pete's personality when he needed a favour amused Sam so he tolerated him.

'Ah, sorry to bother you Sam, I wouldn't ask except my recyc-chute is jammed and my rubbish is backing up in here and you know how long it takes to get Central Services out. I tried calling on you yesterday but it sounded like you were having a party or something.'

'Yeah, a party for one,' Sam muttered under his breath. 'Alright, let me get my boots on and grab my tools and I'll take a look for you.'

By the time Sam was finished with his repairs it was late, he needed another shower and to get something to eat. He also had to take Molly out for another walk and when he got back he was so tired he crawled into his bed for the first time in three days and slept a deep dreamless sleep until morning.

Sam awoke feeling clear headed and fed Molly before getting washed and making himself a simple breakfast of porridge made from oats and water washed down with black coffee. When he had finished eating he set aside his bowl and grumpily snatched the grey envelope from the table deciding just to pay the damn fine and try get on with his day. He opened the official paper and was surprised to find it blank but folded inside was a handwritten letter. He immediately recognised the writing as that of his girlfriend Lucy.

They had met years earlier at a mutual friend's thirtieth birthday party in a bar in downtown Rook City and that night they were intoxicated by each other more so than their drinks. They dated for a short while and then on a whim, seized an opportunity and sold nearly all they owned to go travelling around the world together for several months. They had the happiest time of their lives on that trip, fully embracing the freedom of hitching rides as it suited them, casually drifting from one place to the next, enjoying the adventure of the seemingly endless road and discovering more about each other as their bond deepened. It all happened just a year before Central Command had declared martial law and enclosed both their cities behind massive makeshift walls meaning it was now near impossible to travel even around their own small island country.

Their trip had been cut short when Lucy received word from her aunt Susan that her father had died. Lucy was devastated and upon their return she moved to live with her aunt in Raven City on the mid-west coast, the opposite side of the country to Rook City. Lucy had been mostly raised by Susan since her mother died when she was very young and her father had to work terribly long hours doing his best to provide for all three of them. Now her aunt was about the only family she had left so Sam understood why Lucy felt she had to go. He had planned to save some money and follow Lucy in a few months when she felt ready but the city had been barricaded and locked down shortly after their return and any unauthorised travel earned a trip to the labour camps far to the south.

Despite the difficult years that followed Sam and Lucy still cared deeply for each other and had vowed to remain in contact hoping one day they would work out a way to be together again. Since the collapse, mobile phone usage was limited to those areas where the network infrastructure was reasonably maintained. This meant only certain areas in the Elite sectors had access so Sam and Lucy had to rely on weekly coded conversations via the state provided multimedia screens which were mandatorily installed in every home and operated via remnants the old hardwired telephone network infrastructure.

This was the first actual letter he had received from Lucy in all the time they had known each other. He read slowly as she expressed how much she missed him and was so looking forward to when they could see one another again. She spoke of things they couldn't freely discuss online and Sam felt a pang of grief in his chest, longing to hold her and tell her how much he loved her and that everything would be ok. He clutched the letter tightly and savoured every precious word.

The tone changed now as she wrote of her concern for events she'd witnessed in Raven City. There seemed to be much more street violence where she lived, people were reporting disappearances of family and friends and there were greater numbers of Enforcer patrols than before. She finished her letter cryptically saying she had wonderful news but it was also terrible and she hoped they could meet in person soon so she could tell him all about it.

She sounded scared and Sam was worried about her. The times in which they lived meant a little paranoia was healthy for survival and he understood her reasons for taking the risk to send a written letter. While the net-screens were reported to provide secure communications the service was provided by a division of Central Media and so in reality every conversation was closely monitored. The traditional postal service was redundant now and utilised only by Central Control for official notifications. Citizens occasionally used the postal network to exchange private messages but it was dangerous and expensive. Bribes had to be paid in order for the message to be manually directed to the intended recipient meaning a letter often passed through several hands before it was discreetly inserted into one of the grey envelopes at Central Distribution.

Sam wondered what made Lucy so excited and yet so afraid she could only tell him in person. It was time to talk with Arthur.

'Molly, get your lead, we're going out'.

CHAPTER 4

'You'll find him at Kenny's Bar.' Alice whispered to Sam through a narrow opening in the doorway of her home. Although she'd met him the previous week and he seemed to be a good person she kept a heavy security chain on the inside of the door firmly in place and spoke through the gap.

'No bother Alice, thanks,' said Sam turning to leave. 'And be sure to bar your door again,' he added so as to indicate he took no offence from her caution.

Molly pulled on her lead and excitedly led the way forward as if she knew where they were going from hearing Alice speak the name. Kenny's Bar was a run-down dump but was also a real pub, one of the last in a city full of sterile, centrally sanctioned and operated Shot Joints which sold only sub-grade alcohol infused with a variety of synthesised flavours in pre-packaged vials.

Kenny's was located on the outer edge of the city and the nearest place to Sam's side of town you could go for a poured drink that wasn't illegally brewed in a shed or an attic. Sometimes you just need to sit at the bar with kindred spirits even if the only conversation is to order another round from the barman.

It was a clear sunny morning and the wet streets reflected the low sun dazzling Sam as he and Molly made their way to a dilapidated single story building which proudly stood alone among waste ground and piles of rubble, the sole survivor of a once prosperous area. Ken had stubbornly refused to sell his pub to developers and while the other buildings were bought and demolished around him he and his patrons sat in the dark interior listening to the roars of machinery clearing the way for a better future of which they had no interest in being a part. In the end the money dried up and nothing had been rebuilt in the desolate space so the old bar sat alone, depressed but for many still a refuge.

Sam pulled on the tarnished brass handle opening the door and vented a blast of fuggy air from the pub's dreary interior. He let Molly go in first but held tightly to her lead. Most places wouldn't allow dogs but Sam came here often enough and Ken didn't mind dogs in his bar so long as they were quiet, housebroken and their owners were putting cash in his register. As he stood at the door allowing his eyes to adjust to the gloom Sam looked around for Arthur but couldn't see him. There were three men spaced out at the bar which ran along the left side of the narrow room, all were apparently alone with their thoughts and their drink. A young couple in their early twenties were snuggled in a booth toward the back right corner and to Sam's immediate right on a table beneath the opaque front window were half a glass of some deep amber liquor and a battered novel laid open with its spine facing upward. The only sounds were quiet giggling from the young couple and a low mutter from a drunk sitting at the far end of the bar.

'Alright Ken, how's yourself?' Sam asked approaching the bar.

Ken Byron was a short man at five feet six inches tall but with wide shoulders, seemingly no neck and arms as thick most men's legs he was an imposing figure. His bullish stature helped him keep order in his bar single-handedly on many occasions but he'd gathered a collection of scars over the years the most striking of which was a raggedly healed gash on the right side of his face running in a diagonal curve from ear to chin where Ken had been just too late pulling back from a broken bottle slashed at his face. No one had seen the drunk who gave him the scar after that night and although he was probably smart enough not to come back it was rumoured Ken had more than evened the score and that the attacker was buried somewhere in the waste ground surrounding the bar. True or not it suited Ken to keep that rumour in circulation.

'Haven't seen you in a while, usual is it?' asked the bar owner and without waiting for a response he proceeded to pour a pint of dark ale for Sam and a small amount of the same beer into an old glass ashtray for Molly.

As he was paying for the drinks Sam heard a door at the rear of the bar creak open.

'Bloody hell Ken, the stench in there gets worse every time I go in.'

'Aye, well it's funny you say that because the air out here gets fresher when you leave.'

'You could at least throw some water down the urinals, smart arse!'

Ken and Arthur laughed heartily at the easy going verbal exchange although it was true the neglected plumbing required urgent attention. Carrying drinks for himself and Molly, Sam turned to greet the old man, his new friend, as he passed the bar.

'Ah Sam, it's good to see you. I take it Alice told you I was here? Come on, I'm over by the window.'

The two men settled at the small round table and Sam set Molly's dish of beer on the floor where she lapped thirstily at the cold liquid treat. It wasn't something she got often but Sam knew she'd lie down quietly and let him enjoy his pint if she got a drop too.

Arthur and Sam caught up on what had been happening over the past few days and spoke again of the night Sam had helped the older man. Both men knew they had more serious matters to discuss but neither at this point knew the other's perspective, only that it was likely one they both shared. Arthur got another round of drinks and Sam, leaving Molly to contentedly doze on the floor, walked over to the old jukebox and selected several favourite classic rock tunes. The machine was an antique but just like the rest of the bar it somehow stubbornly hung on and continued to entertain when called upon. He figured some music would provide cover for their conversation and besides, it was nearly midday and about time to wake things up a bit.

Taking his cue as the music filled the silence Arthur had a sip from his glass. 'So tell me Sam, the other night in my shed when you saw my, ah, my camping equipment. You gave the impression you used to be a bit of an outdoorsman yourself? Although I don't suppose there's many city folks have appreciation for nature anymore.'

Sam considered his reply as he took a long pull of his pint, carefully watching the old man's eye for a sign that would warn him to steer off the conversation and make a swift exit. Even though Arthur seemed trustworthy caution was needed here.

'Well, years ago I used to enjoy camping is all and it just seemed we might have something in common, you have a lot of gear and you like to keep your pack in good order, I know I do myself. But since the walls went up I've not been outside the city and I wouldn't have thought an old man like you would risk getting shot to go hiking.'

'Alright Sam, I think I can trust you and I think you want to trust me so let's cut through the bullshit.' Momentary silence returned as the jukebox shuffled between songs so Arthur swirled a melting ice cube in his glass with his finger, glancing around the bar until the next track played. 'I'm planning to escape the city. You've seen the increased patrols, right? You know it's getting worse out on the streets and conditions in all the Dreg sectors are getting really out of hand. You don't have to be my age to remember a time before the crash when things were better. Still bad but not like this. Something is coming Sam, I don't know what but it will be big and very bad. Me and Alice, we plan to leave, try and make it to the west coast, I have a cousin there and he has a house near a small harbour, practically deserted now there's no private fishing boats allowed at sea. If we can get there we might be left alone and maybe we'll have a chance. It sounds crazy but that's my story, so now, what's yours?'

Listening to the old man tell of his plans Sam knew he was right to seek him out and confide in him. 'Arthur, you're very direct, I appreciate that. After last week I knew I had to find you again, to talk to you and I'm glad I stopped at your house for that drink or we wouldn't be here now. I keep an ear to the ground myself and I've been preparing like you. Me and Molly can clear out if we need to. My family are from the mountains in the northwest. They abandoned the house, all got on the boats years ago when Central Control started to restrict marine traffic but I stayed. I don't know how many times I've wished I went with them but I stayed for Lucy. I've thought of just getting out of this damn city and trying to make it to the old house, maybe getting further from there but I guess you can also get trapped in a place by nothing more than habit and situation.'

Sam took another pull on his pint. 'I got a letter from Lucy the other day. I think it's about time to go'.

'What was in this letter?' asked Arthur and Sam explained how the same increasing sense of unease, the escalating violence and Enforcer patrols were happening in Lucy's city now too. It was getting serious and they knew those that stayed in the city would suffer the worst of whatever was to come.

'See Arthur, that's the thing, I plan to get out, same as you. I'm heading to the forest and mountains at home but I can't leave Lucy. I have to get to her and bring her with me but it means sneaking out of the city and hoping Lucy can get out of Raven City to meet me and Molly on the road somewhere. It'll be dangerous but we have to try.'

Arthur stared at the wet circles on the table-top for a moment, thinking things through and then suddenly slammed down his glass as he reached some conclusion.

'Well Sam, seems to me we're in this together now. It'll be safer if we travel together and for the most part we'll all be heading west anyway.'

'Aye, well that sounds like a good idea for sure, but what about Alice, will she be okay with it?'

'Don't worry, I'll talk it over with her. Alice likes you, when she hears about today I know she'll be on board and glad of the company. I'd say she'll feel safer for having you with us on the road.'

'Okay then, we'll make our way west together until you have to turn south along the coast, at least we'll be able to watch each other's backs till then,' said Sam. 'I say we don't hang about, we leave tomorrow, before it's too late, if that'll work for you and Alice.'

Arthur said he wanted to wait a day to speak with Alice and Sam agreed another day would be fine; it would give him time to contact Lucy, tell her the plan and make arrangements to meet on the road east of Raven City. The two men shook hands to cement their deal.

'This calls for another pint!' Sam exclaimed as he got up and walked to the bar. He was happy to have found a companion for the journey ahead and excited now at the prospect of seeing Lucy again. He was concerned however that his travel companions were an elderly couple and hoped they wouldn't be slowed down too much but Arthur could handle himself and he felt Alice would manage okay too. Molly of course would be her happy, excitable self.

'What's got you two in such a good mood?' enquired Ken from behind his bar, mildly interested to know what was cause for celebration.

'Ah, nothing really Ken, it's just that Arthur found twenty quid in his coat pocket and the wife doesn't know about it so we're making good use of it while we can!' Sam laughed hoping he sounded convincing.

'It's good with me, as long as you're spending it in my place,' said Ken grumpily and seemed to immediately lose interest again, much to Sam's relief. The escape from the city would be difficult enough without worrying who might have overheard their conversation and informed the patrols.

Ken poured a generous measure of whiskey into a rocks glass and began filling a pint glass from one of the two working beer taps when the front door to the bar crashed open with enough force to swing it hard on its hinges and bang against the wall shattering the opaque glass panel. At the same instant a four man Enforcer squad burst in, one covering any exit from the front door, one keeping his shotgun levelled at the heads of the sitting bar patrons as the other two rushed toward the bar. Arthur dived to the floor and thankfully held Molly tight on her leash as she was snarling and barking angrily. The young couple in the corner fearfully held tight to each other while the three men seated at the bar had nowhere to go and froze.

Hearing the door smash open Sam turned from the bar and found himself almost face to face with the first Enforcer and squared up raising his hands following an instinctual reaction to defend himself and was dealt a savage blow to the head from the butt of a shotgun that caught him in the left eye socket and cheek. Sharp pain instantly coursed through his face and sent him reeling into the bar as blood poured from the open wound. As bad as it was at least Sam wasn't the intended target and the two guards pushed past and grabbed the muttering drunk sitting at the far end of the bar, much to his horror and to the guilty relief of everyone else.

'Under Protocol Nine, section four you are hereby detained. You have no further rights,' shouted the Enforcer who had struck Sam as he and his partner grabbed the terrified man and dragged him from his stool and out through the shattered door while he screamed his innocence. The Enforcers withdrew as suddenly as they appeared leaving a trail of destruction in their wake.

An epic guitar solo wailed from the juke box as the remaining occupants of the bar took stock of what had just happened. Arthur righted his stool and sitting up again at his table calmed Molly while the young girl in the corner sobbed into her boyfriend's shoulder as he tried to steady his hand enough to take a drink and settle his nerves. Sam, groaning with pain, picked himself up off the bar and held his hand to his head trying and stop the bleeding.

'That's six fifty.'

'What?' asked Sam looking at Ken across the bar while blood seeped through his fingers and trickled down his forearm.

'Six fifty,' said Ken who throughout the whole episode had barely flinched, instead focusing on crafting the pint he had begun to pour.

'For the beer and the whiskey, six quid fifty. I suppose you'll be wanting a bandage or something, no charge for that.'

'Oh, well that's bloody generous of you!' said Sam incredulously as he slapped a handful of coins down on the bar. Ken rummaged in a drawer under the register and then slid a small first aid box over to Sam who tucked it under his arm and lifted two drinks back to the table to try and fix himself up.

Arthur helped Sam back to his seat while Ken dejectedly busied himself sweeping up the broken glass, splinters of wood and other fragments from his cherished pub while the remaining two men at the bar directed their gaze back to unfinished drinks and their thoughts back to whatever darkness had brought them here in the first place.

'Enforcer bastards!' exclaimed Sam as he took his hand away from his face so Arthur could tend to his injury. 'This bloody place is getting well out of order. I pity the poor soul they took away. If anyone even sees him after this he'll never be the same man again after what they'll do to him.'

Everyone had heard the stories but no one actually knew for sure what went on in the Central Detention Blocks. Most who were taken didn't return. Many were tortured before being sent to the prison farms in the far south and those who were released following intensive questioning were so psychologically damaged they were barely recognisable even to family and friends. They pathetically shuffled about like a ghost of their former selves with no apparent awareness of their surroundings, a hollowed out shell. They never lived long like that and it was widely believed that the only reason a few people were released was to serve as a warning to everyone else. The message was loud and clear - obey or you could be next.

'Okay, come on now, relax. Take a drink and then let me have a look at this gash on your face,' said Arthur wincing in sympathy as he saw the deep cut running down from Sam's forehead across the eye socket and down to the left cheek.

'Ah shit Sam, it's not good. I reckon there's enough in this med kit to patch you up or you could try the emergency ward at Central Medical.'

'We both know I'm not going up there Arthur. Who knows what crap they'll stick me with? I'm not going to be a lab rat, just do your best Arthur,' said Sam wiping the blood from his hand onto his jacket and taking a long pull of his pint.

Arthur set about cleaning the deep cut before using suture strips to hold the wound closed. He stuck cotton pads above and below Sam's eye holding them in place with surgical tape. Thankfully the eye wasn't damaged and apart from some bruising and a long deep cut the injury wasn't as bad as it first seemed.

'Well, you weren't pretty before but you're just plain ugly now!'

'Ha, ha. Ow!' Sam laughed with Arthur and pain pulsed from his wound. 'Damn it, don't make me laugh. I suppose every scar has a story but this is one I could happily live without.'

Molly rested her head on Sam's thigh and looked up at him with her big sad eyes as she did when he was feeling sick or hungover. She knew when he wasn't well and tried in her own way to console him. 'Ah Molly, always looking after me. Where would I be without you eh? Good girl,' he said reaching down and ruffling her ears to reassure her that he would be okay.

'Thanks for patching me up Arthur, I appreciate it,' said

Sam downing the rest his drink in a few large gulps. 'That's the last straw. We're right to get the hell out of here Arthur and we need to stick to the plan and get moving as soon as possible. We need to think about how we're going to do this and do it right. I'm going to the bar, I owe you a drink for the surgery and then we can figure out what we're going to do.'

Over their next couple of drinks the two men discussed plans for where they could meet, what route would be safest and the time of day most likely to allow them to slip out of the city without arousing suspicion from the checkpoints or patrols.

'I have an old Landover pickup in a lockup garage,' explained Arthur. 'It belonged to a friend but he got sick a few years ago, cancer or something awful like that. We never found out what it was as he couldn't afford proper treatment and wanted to leave this world from his own bed, not from the butcher's block in hospital. He'd not used the truck in years but always kept the tank full plus a couple of jerry cans of spare diesel, you know, just in case. I was about the only person who still came to visit him toward the end and I guess he wanted the truck to go to someone who'd thought as he did and so he passed it to me. Must be no one else knew about it since no one has ever come looking so I head out to the lockup every few weeks to crank the engine over and keep the battery charged.'

'You're full of surprises old man! But it'll attract a lot of attention won't it? I mean there's not many civilian vehicles on the road these days, especially among the Dregs. What are the patrols going to think?'

'She's a real wreck, looks like she's rattle herself to pieces but she's tough. With an old guy like me behind the wheel the Enforcers should believe I've had it most of my days, at least from before the crash anyway. It's believable enough and she's so beat up I'm guessing they're not likely to confiscate it. It's a chance we'll have to take. There's room for three in the cab but Molly will have to ride in the back.'

'Ah don't worry about Molly; she'll love it, her first ride in a truck. I reckon though we'd have more of a chance of getting through in smaller numbers. You and Alice take the truck through the checkpoints while me and Molly sneak out on foot until we're well out of the city. It will raise less suspicion that way and we can climb on-board when it's safe.'

They agreed they would meet again in two days outside the city, each travelling separately and rendezvous at the edge of the woodlands early in the morning while the city inhabitants were waking up and beginning the commute inward to their dreary jobs. This would ensure fewer eyes on the city perimeter and hopefully less attention paid to a couple of elderly travellers.

'I suppose I'll head home then Arthur, got a few things to do you know,' Sam said excitedly, feeling a bit drunk now but mentally listing some final arrangements before his last day in the city.

'No bother Sam, it was good to see you. I'll catch up with you another time eh? Take care of that scratch!' Arthur said loudly enough for others in the bar to hear while rising unsteadily from his stool for one last trip to the bar.

'Make it a double please Ken, one for the road.'

CHAPTER 5

An attractive brunette woman in her early thirties was loading basic provisions packaged in plain grey paper into a wire shopping basket. The supermarket was unusually busy since the typically empty shelves had been partially stocked with rations following an unscheduled delivery from one of the remaining food production plants. She was startled when a tall grey haired man in a dark blue store security uniform approached silently from behind and grabbed her by the elbow.

'Excuse me miss, please set the basket down. I'll have to ask you to come with me.' The security guard was used to stopping shoplifters and was actually sympathetic to most. He had often noticed the woman in the store accompanied by a child, a boy of about six years old he guessed. Today she was alone and the guard had watched as she slid several grey packets of processed meat inside a tear in the lining of her long wool coat. He had already decided he wouldn't report her but instead take her to the back office just to scare her a little. Still held tightly by the guard the young woman stared, unfocused and wide eyed as if completely vacant. She said nothing for a moment and made no attempt to run neither did she yield to the guard's gesture to follow.

'Come on now miss, there's no point pretending you don't know what this is about. Let's try to avoid making a scene here shall we?'

Suddenly a manic glare flashed in her eyes, her head

rolled heavily to the left and a stream of bloody saliva oozed from her mouth as she clenched her teeth, biting down on her tongue and the inside of her cheeks. She began convulsing where she stood, the shopping basket she had been holding crashed to the floor, glass jars smashed, cans spilled out and rolled along the floor. The guard leapt back in surprise. He'd never seen anything like this and had no idea how to react, whether to try to help or call for backup from his younger colleague who was on duty near the store entrance. Other shoppers turned toward the commotion and stared dumbfounded as the young woman shook violently as though in a seizure then stopped, her eyes glazed over with an empty yet utterly terrifying stare, her head still cocked sideways at an odd angle as she began tearing out lumps of her hair. Another shopper screamed in horror as the psychotic woman scratched her nails down her face gouging deep channels of flesh from her cheeks.

The stupefied guard snapped from his indecision and quickly but cautiously approached attempting to restrain the woman for her own safety but she immediately turned, throwing herself toward him with flailing arms, screaming, scratching and biting anything that came close to her. People had gathered from other areas of the store and were now crowded at each end of the aisle to witness the terrifying spectacle of this poor woman suffering some kind of breakdown then attacking the overwhelmed security guard. Upon seeing the wounds inflicted on the guard nobody in the assembled crowd dared to help but none it seemed were concerned enough for their own safety to leave, instead curiously watching with morbid fascination as the pale-faced guard, covered in both his own and the woman's blood, slumped against an empty freezer unit and fumbled with his radio urgently calling to his colleague. As the junior security guard appeared at the top of the aisle pushing through the mass of onlookers the older guard scrambled to join him and both began slowly advancing again with arms held wide and low.

'Now calm down miss,' said the older guard in as calm a tone as he could muster, 'there's no need for any more trouble. We can sort this out, just come with us and we'll get you some help, okay?'

The crazed woman looked to the two guards, and then turned to check the exit beyond the bewildered crowd. Without warning she darted down the aisle toward the door, shrieking as she ran, crazed and bleeding as the guards gave chase and terrified shoppers scrambled to get out of her path. In her rush to escape she failed to notice the glass door was shut and charged through it shattering the thick glass, lacerating her face, hands and legs as she fell to the pavement outside. She didn't stop but leapt to her feet and immediately ran out to the street into the path of a speeding bus where her body was smashed by the impact before she fell under the still moving vehicle to be pulverised under a massive tyre. She was dead before the shocked driver even got his foot on the brake.

The bus screeched to a halt and horns blared as other drivers swerved to avoid a collision. Many people who witnessed the accident glanced briefly at the horrific scene but most passed on by, caring little about just another victim of harsh city life. The people in the supermarket began returning to their shopping as if nothing happened. The show was over and what little food remained on the shelves would soon be gone if they didn't gather now what they could afford. The younger guard returned to his post while his older colleague looked out to the street for a moment shaking his head at the tragedy then left to tend his wounds when a store worker arrived to clear up the broken glass from the door.

On-board the bus confusion and panic spread as shocked commuters screamed when they heard the impact and saw blood splash across the windscreen, others were angry and shouted to the driver to move on or they would be late for urgent appointments, still others were up out of their seats, asking what had happened and trying to get the best view of the carnage. No one could leave the bus because the driver hadn't moved from his seat, he sat just staring through the blood streaked windscreen, his fingers tightly gripped around the steering wheel. He was the only person on the bus not moving or speaking.

One of the female passengers left her seat and tried in vain to release the front door using the emergency exit controls.

'Come on man, get moving or let us off this thing, I've no time to wait for you to get yourself together,' snapped a male passenger as he reached into the front compartment and shoved the driver's shoulder to get his attention.

For a few seconds the driver didn't respond but just as the impatient male passenger considered shoving him again the driver tensed, his arms shot straight and rigid, his grip on the steering wheel tightened, knuckles whitening with the effort and suddenly he began to shake violently. The female passenger frantically pulled and pushed at the emergency lever but the mechanism had long since failed.

'Ah, look, sorry about pushing you. Are you okay? Do you take any medication?' asked the male passenger in a loud slow voice but the driver just coughed and spat crimson froth over the instrument panel in front of him.

In a single explosive movement the driver leapt from his seat and lunged toward the female passenger as she screamed, too late to run. Catching the woman under her chin with an open hand he swiftly advanced, lifting her up and back with incredible force slamming her head through the narrow reinforced window in the door of the bus in the same instant shattering both the glass and the back of her skull. The driver then turned on the male passenger who had shoved him but the man reacted quickly, raising his left arm to defend the attack. He wasn't quick enough however to stop the driver gripping him by the throat with his other hand and stared helplessly into the depths of the driver's expressionless, glazed over eyes feeling his wind pipe being slowly crushed by large hands exerting an inhuman force.

In the few seconds it took for the driver to kill his first two victims the remaining passengers realised they were trapped in the bus with a madman and all panicked, scrambling toward the rear of the vehicle, desperately trying to open the rear emergency door. Someone found the only fire hammer and broke a window midway along the right side of the vehicle allowing a few people to tumble out onto the street but twelve passengers missed the opportunity and were cornered farther to the rear. All knew they would be murdered by the psychotic driver unless they escaped and quickly.

The crazed driver thrashed about the confined space wildly lashing out at anything within his range whether it was flesh or steel. As the passengers screamed in horror and fought with the release mechanism on the rear door the driver continued to destroy the interior of the bus and his own body by punching, kicking, tearing and biting anything with which he made contact. In a matter of seconds he had reached the rear of the vehicle and grabbed the hand of a teenage boy, biting off the index finger then spitting it to the floor as the boy screamed in fear and agony. A desperate struggle began between the driver, the teenager and an older male passenger who accepted he had no hope of escape. He tried to help by fighting off the blood soaked savage, pushing and stabbing with the pointed tip of his umbrella allowing the boy the scramble farther back to join the crush of bodies at the rear of the bus. At last the emergency exit was opened and just as more of the terrified passengers spilled from the bus an Enforcer squad pulled up sharply in a heavily armoured matt black Land Rover Defender, standard transport for all Enforcer teams. They jumped simultaneously from the front and back of the truck, quickly assessing the scene and disregarded the injured passengers instead focusing on their target.

Two of the Enforcers tore open the front doors of the bus using hydraulic tools and entered the vehicle while their two squad mates at the rear pushed the escaping passengers aside. Four shocked passengers who remained inside were trapped between the psychotic driver and the psychopathic Enforcers.

'Get down, get down!' shouted the squad commander as his men entered the bus from the front and advanced on their target.

A mother in her late twenties was struggling to get her young daughter out of the bus ahead of her but on hearing the order from the lead Enforcer she pushed her daughter to the floor and threw herself protectively on top. The teenager who had lost his finger was still screaming and stumbling about in shock but the older man who helped fend off the driver heard the shouts of the guards and grabbed the boy in a bear hug from the rear and pulled him backwards to the floor just as the two Enforcers on board each let loose a close range shotgun blast, both aiming at the head of the insane monster.

With two simultaneous deafening bangs and a thick spray of dark blood which painted a large section of the interior roof with a sickening fragment speckled red the driver's head simply disappeared. The body stopped moving almost instantly but stood swaying, dripping gore before falling forward like a felled tree onto the two male passengers still lying on the floor who now were desperately pushing themselves backward to escape, their heels slipping in the gruesome pool of bodily fluids seeping toward them from the rough stump between the shoulders of the fresh cadaver.

No attempt was made by the Enforcers to assist those shocked and injured passengers who hadn't fled the scene at their first opportunity. Unfortunately most of the city's inhabitants didn't care either so the survivors were left to tend their own injuries and irreparably damaged psyches. As the Enforcers withdrew the squad commander barked into his radio.

'Patrol twenty-seven to Command; reported bus incident now under control. Request clean-up crew and wagons for body disposal.'

'Report acknowledged Patrol twenty-seven.'

He had just finished speaking when almost immediately the radio on the commander's chest crackled to life again and an urgent message was relayed. On his signal the squad quickly boarded their armoured truck and the engine roared as they sped off to their next incident. Unnoticed by the Enforcers and busy crowd the young mother, one of the last survivors to escape the bus, stopped comforting her daughter, all expression melted from her face and a red drool ran from her mouth as she began to convulse.

Patrol twenty-seven had been ordered to join a battalion of Enforcer squads currently racing through the city to converge on a downtown high school. Their orders were to contain the scene and subdue troublemakers with any level of force deemed necessary. A teacher at the school apparently had gone on a rampage, killed several students and now a full scale riot had developed.

It had been an average day in the hell that was life for a relief teacher in secondary level education, Geoff Dalton had the task of trying to teach geography to 4C, a class like any other who had no interest in learning and even less interest in respecting the authority of the faculty staff, least of all that of a relief teacher. In a bout of frustration Mr. Dalton had thrown a plastic ruler at a particularly rowdy pupil only to find himself gasping for breath a few seconds later as the pupil leapt from his desk and pinned him to the wall, forcing the bone of his forearm across the teacher's throat closing off his airway.

As the pupil laughed, egged on by his classmates Mr. Dalton stopped struggling for a few seconds then began to spasm uncontrollably causing the aggressive pupil to back off, the game had turned serious. When the convulsions ceased the teacher stood before the now silent class, his head cocked sideways, lifeless eyes directed at the boy who had attacked him, limbs twitching involuntarily then suddenly he launched his body across the room parallel to the first row of seated pupils, arms outstretched, fingers spread but tips turned in like claws. Dalton targeted the teenager and with his momentum carrying him forward he grabbed the boy's head in both hands, forcing him backwards while violently twisting the neck with a sickening snap. The teacher landed, not gracefully but heavily on his right shoulder with a crunching thump then slid on the smooth floor tiles head first into the sharp corner of a supplies cupboard which split his skull open killing him instantly.

The mangled bodies of teacher and pupil lay at the front of the crowded room in full view of the class. A few seconds passed before the class erupted in a roar of cheers as the teenagers whooped and hollered, drunk with excitement at the scene that had played out in front of them. All but one was engaged in the drama. A slight built and naturally quieter boy sitting a few rows back to the side of the room began shaking although in the commotion was not noticed. His tremors subsided, life seemed to drain from his face and just seconds later he screamed an eerie wail which few heard among the din before he took a pen in his right hand and stabbed it deep into his own leg. Again and again he took pens and pencils and drove their points deep into his own flesh.

'What the hell are you doing Marshal?' shouted a fellow pupil jumping back in surprise and causing a circle to open around the boy as the others also backed away.

'Oh shit, are you okay Marshal?' another shouted more out of curiosity than concern.

The young boy looked up with a vacant stare and the other pupils recognised the same expression they had just witnessed from their dead tutor. They realised only too late they were in danger.

Young Marshal slowly rose from his chair, blood oozing from deep cuts in his legs, assorted stationary protruding from the wounds. With lightning speed he plucked a disposable pen from his leg, lunged forward and stabbed it through the throat of an unfortunate student who reeled backward clutching his neck and gargling blood as he collapsed backwards over a desk. Some of the boys now fearing for their own lives ran from the room in terror but others stayed intent on exacting revenge for the death of their friend. The manic boy focused his rage on the closing crowd ripping and tearing at anything his hands could grab. He dealt serious injury to several of the mob but was quickly overcome and thrown to the ground where he was kicked and stomped to a gruesome death.

Every classroom had a security camera installed and class 4C's geography lesson had been relayed to a control room where the grisly events were discovered all too late by a bored and underpaid guard who's reaction would have dire consequences. Instead of putting the building on lockdown and containing the problem until the Enforcers arrived the guard panicked and signalled for an emergency evacuation of the entire school. As the siren wailed the school's teachers and students alike assumed it to be just another drill and began casually filing out of classrooms into the hallways where they mixed with members of class 4C. A few boys who ran in fear into the corridors after the savage deaths of their tutor and friends were dispersed through the crowd now crammed into the narrow halls. Panicked but unable to escape through the tight slow moving crowd, each within minutes of one another stopped walking, slowing the crowd and causing a bottle neck. If any of the students or teachers surrounding them at that moment had witnessed the earlier horrors they would have ran for their lives as the afflicted boys in their turn began to shudder and manifest the symptoms that lead to the earlier deaths.

As each affected pupil turned killer a stampede of terrified students desperate to escape the terror triggered yet another victim to turn. As the fear escalated teachers and students lost any sense of order and ran in all directions trying to distance themselves from the bloody fury erupting around them. The school security guard realising his error and knowing the building control systems wouldn't allow him to initiate a lockdown once an evacuation was in progress called his own team back to the control room where they barricaded themselves inside. They sent a priority call to Central Control which was routed directly to Central Command and additional squads of Enforcers were immediately dispatched.

When the Enforcers arrived they surrounded the school with a four man squad stationed at every locked gate and as each new unit joined them a wall of armed Enforcers with riot shields formed and fought back the crowd while a second line working from behind launched gas grenades into the school yard to incapacitate those not overcome by the madness. Only the ultra-violent victims of the sickness seemed immune to the stun-gas and this tactic allowed the Enforcers to mercilessly gun down the most severe threats while minimising casualties. Those still in the building were left to fend for themselves and the Enforcers weren't concerned if a few innocents were killed in the process - they had their orders to contain the situation at all cost.

It was too late.

Scores of students and several teachers had made it to the gates and fled into the crowded city before the first patrols had been able to respond. Those that escaped ran for home or any place of safety but for many the fear and adrenaline acted as the trigger for their own transformation so a wave of panic and violence began to spread throughout the city.

CHAPTER 6

Victor Henderson's car passed swiftly through building security with a nervous nod between guard and driver. The luxury vehicle came to a gentle stop in front of the underground door to the private lift reserved exclusively for the residents of the upper five floors. Henderson dismissed the chauffeur and entering the lift he held his left wrist against a small black panel just inside the door which scanned the implanted chip in his arm and the lift automatically ascended to the top floor. There were no buttons on the control panel for the uppermost floors as each could be accessed only by authorised personnel using an implant chip or by thumbprint identification.

Since his wife had been dead for two years now the only other people with access were his trusted driver and Kathy, his twenty-two year old daughter. The driver was an intimidating figure but obedient and made no objection to being chipped. Kathy however was stubborn like her mother and refused to be implanted. It no longer mattered anyway since Henderson and had disabled Kathy's access to the lift controls effectively holding her prisoner in her own home.

The lift climbed quickly and smoothly and within a few moments the doors opened directly onto the entrance hall to the lower level of Henderson's private living quarters. As he disembarked the doors began to close behind him for the lift was being called by another of the buildings residents. Henderson was hanging his coat on a stand in the wide hallway when his daughter sprang from a store cupboard nearby and darted into the lift before the doors could close. She stared wild-eyed through the narrowing gap as the bloated figure of her father swiftly grabbed an antique walking stick from the coat stand and rushed toward the lift again. Kathy's hopes were dashed as Henderson shoved the tip of the walking stick between the doors just as they were almost shut forcing them to open again.

Kathy knew from bitter experience that fighting would accomplish nothing and just slumped to the floor with her head in her hands, her dark bobbed hair covering her face as she cried silently. She knew trying to escape was a futile effort, she had attempted and failed several times before but still she had to try.

'Why do you continue to try my patience?' asked Henderson testily. 'You know why I had to disable your access. After your mother died I need you here, I can't allow you to leave and you must learn to accept that fact. Come on, come out here now so I don't have to punish you, you know it makes me angry.'

Painful memories of lashes from her father's leather belt were the sole reason Kathy got to her feet and cautiously walked from the relative sanctuary of the lift into the luxury home that was her prison. Henderson stepped back from the entrance to entice Kathy to enter freely but as she passed by he grabbed her by the throat pushing her back hard into the wall. Kathy didn't struggle but tried with every fibre of her body to pull herself backward as if she could somehow melt into the plaster and concrete to distance herself further from the maniac assaulting her. Henderson held Kathy by the jaw now so he could force her to look at him, his flushed complexion and foul breath becoming her focus as he raged through wobbling jowls and gritted teeth.

'You know what happened to your mother; since you're aware of how she met her end it should suffice as a deterrent. If you ever disobey or disrespect me like that again I will ensure you suffer the same fate.'

Henderson maintained his hold on Kathy's jawbone for a moment and neither spoke, tears streamed from her eyes but she made no sound, her body limp, defeated. Satisfied his point had been made and sensing no further struggle Henderson's anger subsided and he relaxed his grip.

'Now, go and clean yourself up, put on a nice dress and make me that salmon dish you know I like. We'll forget this ever happened, there's a good girl.'

Kathy slid out from wall and kept her gaze on the ornate carpet as she made her way through the spacious main living area to her own room at the top of the left staircase. She felt the cold hard eyes of the monster who kept her incarcerated following her every step. Terrified yet angry at herself she knew she had no choice but to comply and swore she would never let her spirit be broken. She would continue to resist and one day make good her escape.

Once Kathy was out of sight Henderson leaned over, steadied himself with the walking stick and clawed at his collar to open the top button of his shirt. He gasped from the exertion and clutched his chest, fighting to control his breathing and heart rate, gradually the stabbing pain eased and he was able to stand unaided. The emotional and physical stress his daughter caused him exacted a heavy toll on his already overburdened heart.

Returning the walking stick to the coat stand he moved into his main living quarters. A huge space combining the two upper floors of the tower block into a single open plan living area with staircases left and right leading to the upper levels and with several other bedrooms and living areas adjacent. Thick luxury carpet, highly polished brass fixtures, opulent chandeliers and furniture constructed of exotic hardwoods and upholstered with the finest fabrics. No expense was spared to indulge Henderson's expensive tastes. The overall effect was so over the top and lavish it actually looked cheap, tacky; the sum of the parts combining to create a look that was somehow less than one may have expected.

From under the right-hand staircase in an antique walnut cabinet Henderson selected a bottle from his collection of rare scotch and other liquors and proceeded to fix a drink before reclining in his favourite chair near the centre of the room. He was annoyed at himself for losing control and letting his short temper push his daughter further from his life. He tried in so many ways to make her love him but she refused to show the respect he felt was his to command.

'No matter,' he thought as he sipped the warming liquid from his glass. 'She will never leave these walls and with time she will grow to love me.' This thought helping to calm the beast that dwelled deep in his soul.

Kathy slipped quietly from her room and down the left staircase wearing a pretty sky blue summer dress to appease her father and went to the kitchen to prepare the evening meal as he requested. Her obedience finally subdued any remaining anger Henderson felt and as he sat in the silence of the large open room he reflected on the past few years in his personal life as he often did upon returning home, finding it remarkably easy to dismiss from his mind the gruesome events he had set in motion earlier that day.

How he missed his wife. Claudia was a wonderful woman, beautiful and loved by all who knew her. She would light up a room when she entered, was respected by other women and led Henderson to be the envy of other men who saw her on his arm at the many social functions they were expected to attend. Of course the public face of their relationship was highly practised and did not reflect the darkness of their home life. Claudia was strong willed, independent and would often question and criticize her husband's decisions. Initially these were traits that Henderson found endearing and he loved her for them but over time as his soul darkened his patience thinned and his temper flared. One evening early in their marriage when he asked Claudia to fix him a fourth drink she dared to question if he'd not already had enough saying he became intolerable after even a single glass. The rage which always boiled below the surface broke free and Henderson hoisted his bulk from his chair, charging across the room at his wife then struck her face with a vicious backhanded slap. Claudia was knocked off her feet from the force of the blow and she fell to the floor crying out as Henderson threw his empty glass to the floor smashing it to pieces just inches from her head sending shards of glass all over her. He screamed obscenities at her, cursing her for disobeying him as the small cuts on her face began to bleed. It was the beginning of a long period of unseen abuse she would be forced to suffer at the hand of the sadist to whom she was married.

Henderson's mind drifted back to the present for a moment as he drained his glass and decided the earlier successes of the day and his current melancholy mood earned him another drink. He brought the bottle from the cabinet, sat back in his chair and half-filled a rocks glass with more of the expensive liquor before sinking back into the memories that haunted him.

It had been two years almost to the day that his wife had died here in this very room. He supposed that perhaps his awareness of this timing had led him to hurt Kathy more than necessary during their earlier altercation. The planning and development for the Project had taken so much of his energy that only now he remembered the significance of the date, the approaching anniversary of the death of his beloved Claudia. The truth of her betrayal had been too much for him to bear. She had been involved with another man for over nineteen years. Even now the memory hurt him tremendously, he still wondered how she could have done this to him for so long. Deep down he knew but could not admit to himself that he had been absent from the marriage for most of their time together and he had treated his wife as a mere stage prop to reinforce his public persona.

What Henderson did not know was in addition to suffering physical abuse Claudia had been incredibly lonely in the early years of their relationship and had sought the affections of other men whenever she could. In the tight social circles in which they moved she was well known among the Elites as the wife of the renowned Victor Henderson. She found it safer and also thrilling to cross into the Dreg areas, to drink with the common people and at times when her husband was away for business to invite strange men back to share her bed. Knowing how this would madden her estranged husband only added to the excitement and she delighted in the deception and sought her dangerous pleasure more and more until one night in a lively traditional bar in the Dreg quarters she met the man with whom she would fall deeply in love.

James was a kind man, ruggedly handsome, strong but gentle. His wife had died from a serious illness several years before Claudia met him and he had briefly been with only one other woman since his wife's tragic death. He didn't know anything about the Henderson's when they met and she had given him no reason to suspect she was the wife of a senior Elite. By the time she revealed the truth to him James already loved her and understood why she hid her true identity from him. He cared for her all the more upon realising the terrible life to which returned when not with him.

James had a young daughter whom Claudia had met one morning in James' home as Claudia hurried to leave after a steamy stolen night. James usually asked his sister to mind his daughter when Claudia was coming to stay but his sister had guests on this occasion. When the little girl had got up to use the bathroom she and Claudia met awkwardly in the narrow hallway but never saw each other again after that day.

James and Claudia's affair was passionate and they met depending on what time the business appointments of Claudia's husband allowed which in practice was quite often. Their feelings quickly deepened as they learned how much they had in common despite coming from opposite sides of the social divide. Both knew their forbidden relationship could never allow them to be together openly and they spoke of breaking it off in order to spare each other greater pain. On what was supposed to be their last night together Claudia seemed quite distant and although James expected she would have the same feelings of deep sadness and regret for their parting he was shocked when she explained the reason for her mood. She was pregnant. She was absolutely positive it was James' child and was terrified of what her husband would do if he learned the truth. Under other circumstances both lovers would have been worried at this news but their lives and that of James' daughter and now their unborn child were in danger. The hurt they had separately endured meant they could no longer bear the thought of being apart. They lay in bed and just held each other for a long time each silently vowing that somehow they would find a way.

During the next couple of weeks the pair met only once and decided on what they would do. An abortion was out of the question since the only place safe for the procedure was Central Medical and Henderson would surely be notified when the medical staff scanned Claudia's implant chip and discovered who she was. She felt confident she could convince her husband the child was his own, conceived one drunken night he had obviously forgotten.

Henderson's ego would cloud his judgement and he would never even consider the possibility of his wife with another man. James painfully swore to stay out of the child's life and to never reveal the truth about it to his young daughter for fear that word would get to Henderson and terrible retribution would swiftly follow. The risk was just too great to involve the children but neither James nor Claudia could bring themselves to stop seeing each other.

Years passed and James and Claudia's daughter grew up among the Elites while Victor Henderson believed her to be his own. Claudia and James kept their affair going and their love for each other never waned although now they met less often so as to minimise the risk of being caught. Claudia brought pictures and stories of Kathy and James was overjoyed to hear every word but it also was killing him to know he could never hold her, never be a father to her and could never allow his two daughters to meet.

For nearly twenty years Henderson's absence from his own personal life had allowed the deception to continue right under his nose. He cared nothing for the day to day events and feelings of his wife and daughter. As long as they were obedient to his demands and played along with the charade of a happy loving home when he presented them at various social gatherings he was satisfied to leave them to do as they pleased. His arrogance assured him they lived in fear of him and so would never disrespect him even when he wasn't around to keep them in line.

His suspicions were aroused late one evening when he came home earlier than expected due to a rescheduled meeting and found his penthouse living quarters were empty. In itself that wasn't unusual as sometimes his wife would visit the wives of other Elites, a routine part of their social arrangements and sometimes Kathy visited friends in the lower levels of their block. Henderson fixed a drink from his cabinet, slightly annoyed at having to perform this menial task for himself and as he replaced the bottle he noticed the level in the bottle was a few drinks worth lower than it should have been. Although he drank heavily he counted his drinks carefully since fine liquor was a rare and expensive indulgence even for him. Kathy would never have dared to touch the liquor cabinet and Claudia was an occasional drinker with a preference for vodka so he wondered who had drunk his scotch? He knew a fresh bottle had been opened only a few days previously and even allowing for occasionally generous measures there should have been more liquid remaining. Henderson cleared it from his head telling himself the stresses of the day and his irritation with his wife were making him consider the ridiculous was in fact probable. He reclined in his favourite chair to read his business reports but couldn't concentrate on them as thoughts of the scotch bottle wouldn't leave his mind.

When his wife returned she appeared flustered having not expected to find him at home. He asked her where she had been and she quickly explained she had been shopping for a dress for the function they were to attend on the following weekend. Henderson's suspicions were increased when he noticed she was carrying not a single shopping bag. Even if she had not found the dress she wanted he knew his wife would never return from a shopping trip without buying at least something she didn't need as he was only too aware of how she thoroughly enjoyed spending his money. He chose not to confront her immediately deciding instead to prove what he now knew was a lie. He had no idea at that time just how big a lie he was about to uncover.

Although his work schedule was typically full Henderson cleared a day of engagements to allow him the time he needed to confirm his fears. He didn't arrange to have his wife followed by anyone else since he could not suffer the disgrace of others knowing the idyllic family life he portrayed was nothing but a sham. No, if his wife was cheating he would deal with this personally. It would be a chore he would have to endure but his growing anger hardened his resolve and he became more convinced of her guilt even before he had gathered any proof. He left dressed for work as usual and waited in an upmarket cafe at the bottom of a block facing the entrance to his own choosing a window seat where he used an arrangement of condiments and menus to obscure any direct view of his face from the street. If the staff and patrons recognised him and perhaps thought it unusual for the head of the Upper Council to be present none dared to question him.

To occupy the time Henderson worked from his personal networked tablet with which he was able connect to and control much of his business affairs but he couldn't concentrate as he glanced up at the entrance to his block with every movement detected in his peripheral vision. As the hours passed his frustration grew and he was becoming convinced his wife had managed to slip out while he used the cafe toilet or that in fact she simply just wasn't intending on meeting her mystery lover today. Henderson was cursing himself for letting his anger and paranoia overcome his better judgement and leading him to waste a valuable day when he spotted his wife leaving their block so he quickly waved his wrist over a scanner by his table to make a payment using his implanted chip leaving not a single cent for tips. He hurriedly threw on his coat and carefully placed his network tablet in a hand-sewn calf leather case before leaving the cafe and walking after his wife in the direction of the nearest sector barrier gate.

The sector gates were always manned by two squads of Enforcers but Elites and Dregs passed in both directions since some Elites liked to shop for black market goods in the Dregs sectors and many Dregs were employed as personal assistants, barmen, cleaners, maids, drivers and for other tasks the Elites considered to be menial. So long as a valid ID chip or authorised thumbprint was scanned the Enforcers would allow you to pass unquestioned, except of course that the Dregs were subjected to frequent random security checks and many were "detained" for unspecified offences to ensure discipline of the lower class was maintained.

It was over a mile walk to the nearest gate and Henderson found it difficult keeping up behind his wife's casual pace. He was not used to walking for any distance further than from office to car to lift as he travelled from home to work and back again. He supposed Claudia walked so as not to be noticed taking regular high class cab rides back and forth from the Dregs sector. Although his personal driver could be summoned at a moment's notice he was glad of the opportunity to follow her personally and observe her movements, aware that this was probably the most attention he had paid her since their marriage began. He waited until Claudia was about two hundred yards ahead and tried to discreetly follow. He had no idea what he would do or say if she were to look around and see him, acting without a definite plan was something he almost never did.

The afternoon was bright and crisp so the Elite sector streets were full of people out browsing the expensive stores looking to find that new imported household gadget or item of clothing. The mass of people provided Henderson some cover but they were not so tightly packed as to mean he would not be seen if indeed she did glance back. Luckily his wife appeared to be in no mood for shopping and walked straight past several of the designer boutiques he knew she favoured. To Henderson this confirmed his notion that he should follow her as he could not imagine his wife passing up any opportunity to add another hanger to her extensive wardrobe.

When she approached the sector gate she withdrew a slender hand from a soft leather glove and placed her thumb on the scanner, flashing a smile at the hard faced Enforcer who just nodded when the ID scanner confirmed green status and let her pass without a word. Henderson paused for a moment to consider what he would do now knowing that if he followed his wife through the barrier into the Dreg sector the Enforcers would recognise him as an Upper Council member if not in person then certainly when his implant chip was scanned. He had absolute authority to cross the divide as he wished but to do so on foot and unaccompanied would at the very least elicit a series of salutes and snapping to attention from the guards. Claudia would surely be alerted that a senior member of the Council was near meaning she would abandon her meeting.

He decided he could not risk his wife discovering she was being followed so kept to his own side of the gate instead stopping at a digital sector map attached to the railing nearby and made a pretence of confirming his location and planning a route. As he stood beside the map screen he peered through the railings into the Dreg sector beyond the barrier and watched as Claudia stopped at a hot food stall only fifty metres beyond. Henderson rarely visited the Dreg sectors finding them offensive to his sensibilities and had never paused to observe the daily comings and goings of everyday life in the sewers of his city.

He correctly assumed the food stand was one of several operating by the gate to provide cheap meals to the Dregs workers who were on their way to or from work in the Elite sector. The stall was busy and the food seemed to be enjoyed by those who ate outside at the plastic seats and tables but the aroma of charred cheap meat and grease made Henderson queasy. He couldn't understand how his wife had developed a taste for such filth. It was so obvious to him then that he thought himself a fool for not thinking of it immediately. She was waiting here to meet her lover. This way she was in sight of the Enforcers should there be any trouble but before venturing further into the Dregs sector she would have her man to escort her through the troubled streets.

He realised his luck and knew all he had to do was to wait a short time and his proof would present itself to him. In readiness for what he knew was inevitable he forced himself to contain his anger and channelled his rage into imagining what he would do to this man when he finally got his hands on him. He waited with his mobile phone discretely pointed at Claudia and set the camera to record video. His wife's lover must have already been waiting close by for within a few moments he approached her and the two held each other in a long embrace seeming not to care who saw them but they quickly appeared to gather their senses and awkwardly looked about them to check for anyone who may have noticed. Apparently satisfied their secret was intact they walked off together and disappeared into the crowd.

Although the throng around them paid no attention to the lovers the pair failed to notice the figure watching from the other side of the barrier. Henderson stopped the recording and slid the device back into the inside pocket of his coat. His blood pressure skyrocketed, his face flushed as his chest grew tight and his breathing became laboured so he forced himself to remain where he stood until he had regained control of his body and temper. He couldn't think, mentally paralysed by the incredible fury burning in his heart. When his emotions had calmed enough he walked a few streets from the barrier to signal his driver to collect him and bring him back to his tower block.

The luxury sedan screeched around the corner and pulled up to the curb beside Henderson. The driver thought it unusual that his employer had left his building on foot but he knew better than to ask questions. As he held the car door open Henderson climbed into the back of the vehicle without exchanging so much as a glance, seething with the repeating image of what he witnessed as he was quickly transported to the familiar comfort of his personal living quarters high above the city.

Henderson knew his wife would attempt to explain in some way the encounter he had observed but to him there was to be no forgiveness, no quarter would be given. He would deal with his wife personally then have her lover tracked down, arrested and interrogated by the Enforcers after which this man would not even remember his own name never mind have any recollection of Claudia. He waited until his wife returned home to confront her.

***

Sitting now in his high-rise mansion recalling the events of that terrible day from his favourite chair with only a stiff drink and her memory for comfort he could still hear her gargled scream in his mind, still feel the life draining from her body as he tightened his grip on her throat and throttled the last of her breath from her lungs. As the final light faded from his wife's eyes he realised what he had done and for the first time in his life Henderson felt a deep sorrow. The feeling didn't last for more than a moment and was quickly replaced with arrogance, self-righteousness and empowerment. 'She deserved to die, she had to die. She made me kill her. How could she do this to me knowing what I would do when I found out? And she knew I would find out. Nobody goes behind the back of Victor Henderson, nobody. Not even you Claudia my love,' he had spoken as he knelt over the lifeless body of his wife.

Henderson remembered the next few moments of that awful day with painful clarity. In his mind's eye he could see himself standing over his wife, his body trembling with rage when his attention had been drawn by a noise at the top of the stairs and he had looked up in time to see his teenage daughter run from the balcony to her room, the door slamming, the screams of fear and wailing of disbelief. He realised Kathy had witnessed the murder of her mother and knew with absolute certainty the two women in his life would now be forever dead to him because of the violence he had unleashed in their home.

Despite threats and occasionally beating her he could never bring himself to grievously harm Kathy but he also could never let her leave. In some sense he loved his daughter despite being absent from most of her life. He needed her and could not allow her to speak of what she had seen. Thinking fast he moved from the living room leaving his wife's body on the floor and hefted his considerable mass up the stairs to his daughter's room as quickly as he could manage and threw all his weight against the door splintering the frame and crashed into the room convincing Kathy she would be the next victim of her father's rampage. She ran to the corner of her room and began throwing perfume bottles, hair brushes, jewellery and anything else she could find desperately trying to keep her father at bay.

Henderson however was not concerned, fending off the various projectiles and ignoring the bottles of expensive perfume which smashed and ran in pungent streaks against the wall behind him. He frantically searched her room, throwing to the floor drawers full of clothes and tipping out the contents of her handbag until he found what he was looking for. He flipped open her mobile phone and twisted the two halves apart before removing the SIM card and snapping it between his fingers. He lifted a stool from under Kathy's desk and gripping it by the legs swung it hard into the wall mounted net-screen smashing the laminated ply-glass in a shower of fragments thus ensuring she had no way to communicate with the outside world.

As he moved to exit her room Kathy ran at him, her eyes stinging with tears, screaming and cursing him. She jumped at him slashing with her long nails, hammering his chest with balled up fists, biting him as though she were a rabid animal. All the years of violence she had silently witnessed now erupted from her and she directed the keen edge of her rage toward her father. The rapid flurry of blows were ineffective and Henderson easily warded off most of her attacks but before he was able to throw her down she managed to claw the nails of her left hand into his scalp leaving deep bleeding tracks across the top of his head.

Throwing her to the ground he kicked her in the stomach and she creased into a ball holding her abdomen and used her legs to wriggle backwards to the wall. Henderson was almost shocked at what he had done and began shouting as his daughter lay on the floor sobbing uncontrollably.

'Do you see what you made me do? Do you see?' he roared.

As quickly as he could Henderson raced to his home office on the opposite side of the balcony. He sat at his massive mahogany desk and swiped his wrist chip to access the network terminal where he logged into his personal building security control panel and locked out access to several other network terminals throughout the house then disabled all but his own access to and from his home. Now nobody could enter or leave unless he permitted it. The maintenance people were security cleared and supervised by his driver when required and he would have to consider cancelling their services to guard his secret but it could wait until morning. For now he had a body to dispose of.

Henderson knew he had to manage the scene carefully. He ran this city, controlled the country from his boardroom and had powerful friends that could help him but the nature of such men meant they would use any advantage to take his seat as the head the Upper Council. If they knew he had lost control and killed his wife they may challenge his suitability for leadership. He considered how much worse it would be if General Curran learned of this knowing a perceived lack of judgement could be all he needed to force a military takeover. No, this situation was too volatile and he must exercise caution.

He couldn't dispose of the body without help but who could he trust? There was only one person with whom he dared to share this secret and that was his driver and bodyguard. Involving anyone else at all would be a huge risk but he accepted it was now a risk he had no choice but to take. With his daughter trapped in the apartment he decided he could deal with her later and anyway she had seemingly withdrawn to some inner shell and appeared to be in shock and thankfully relatively quiet. He placed a call via his office terminal asking his driver to come up to the top floor. When he ended the call Henderson re-enabled the driver's access allowing him to enter the towering fortress.

If the driver felt any surprise or shock at seeing the body of his employer's wife lying still on the floor of the living area he made no outward indication that it bothered him. Henderson had observed on other occasions how this man appeared to have less capability for empathy than even he did and it frightened him to be in the company of someone so clinical.

Henderson explained that an argument had gotten out of control, it was a tragic accident but he obviously couldn't have any involvement of the authorities. A large bonus would be in order for assisting with the disposal of his wife's body with no questions asked. The driver simply nodded in agreement making no further issue of it and took a pair of tight fitting black leather gloves from a jacket pocket then pulled them on as Henderson smiled approvingly, almost in awe of the cold manner in which his bodyguard handled the difficult situation.

Together they bundled the corpse of Claudia Henderson into two suit bags he had taken from his wardrobe, one pulled over her head and shoulders, the other pulled up from her feet and where the bags overlapped secured them by wrapping several layers of duct tape from a roll the driver kept among other tools in the back of the car.

'What about the girl?

'She is not to be harmed, do you understand? I will deal with her myself.'

The driver just shrugged and said nothing further.

They planned to use a contact at Central Disposal who for the appropriate cash fee would go for a break at a convenient time allowing discrete disposal of any package. Henderson knew the city's waste incinerators were in operation twenty-four hours a day and would destroy anything they were fed. While the driver descended in the lift to load the body into the car Henderson went to his office safe and removed a bundle of notes, enough to cover the disposal fee and the initial half of the promised bonus payment.

With a corpse wrapped in the boot and a large wad of cash in his pocket the driver moved off calmly as if running a normal errand comfortable in the knowledge that he would not be stopped by the Enforcer patrols who would scan the license plates and back off upon confirming the car's registered owner was a high ranking Upper Council member.

Meanwhile Henderson had returned to his penthouse feeling calm and in control, he was almost in the clear. From his office he accessed the Central mainframe and arranged and personally approved travel documents for his wife and daughter which would lend credibility to his cover story that they had both travelled together for an extended visit to see Claudia's family on the continental mainland. Since Henderson was increasingly busy with special projects and now Kathy had finished school it was a good time for them to travel and for mother and daughter to spend some time together. It was a believable explanation since it was common knowledge the Henderson's had no other family living in the country and no one would care enough to probe any deeper.

Within an hour Henderson had received a brief message from his driver. 'Package delivered.' He hesitated for a moment but knew he could not afford to leave anything to chance. Almost regretfully he made a direct video call to a trusted Enforcer Commander and reported the theft of his private car. The loyal driver protested his innocence as an Enforcer dragged him from the vehicle only minutes after he had sent his confirmation message to Henderson. The driver immediately understood he had been double-crossed and even managed to pull his pistol from a hidden shoulder holster before an Enforcer shotgun blast punched through his chest at close range, shredding his heart and lungs and opening a massive hole in his back, killing him instantly.

All that remained for Henderson to do was to eliminate the man who for nineteen years had sneaked around behind his back, using his wife, mocking him with his very existence. How often had this man been here in his home Henderson wondered? A personal visit to exact the vengeance he deserved would be most fitting but direct involvement was just too great a risk. As much as he wanted to witness the suffering for himself Henderson had to accept that the best way of cleaning this mess would be to once again use the Enforcers.

Sitting back at his office terminal it took him twenty minutes to make a screenshot of the video he filmed on his mobile phone and crop a clear image of the man who had met his wife earlier that same day. He typed a brief report and submitted the name he had beat out of his wife before killing her. He added the facial image to an interrogation order which he encrypted and sent to Central Command along with a special request for a video copy of the interrogation. The reason stated was simply "personal security concerns". He could not involve the Enforcer

Commander as before for fear he may connect the incidents so instead sent the order via direct channels knowing a personal request from the head of the Upper Council would be processed immediately. Only two hours and ten minutes had passed when he received confirmation that the suspect had been located at his home and detained under Protocol Nine before being brought in for questioning.

The following morning Henderson had woken to find a securely encrypted video among his new messages. He had started his day feeling satisfied as he sat at his home office terminal enjoying a cup of fresh ground coffee brought to him by his now broken and compliant daughter while he watched the horrific torture of his former wife's lover. The tormented soul had no answer to any question asked of him, had no idea why he was being made to suffer. It was clean but Henderson had taken little satisfaction from watching the interrogation since he did not inflict the pain with his own hands. He had to accept the matter was now dealt with and the man who for nearly twenty years had made a fool of the most powerful man in the city was dead.

As he once again pulled his mind back to the present Henderson sat up straight in his lounge chair taking a sip of rare whiskey from his glass then stared into the heavy cut crystal vessel remarking to himself how he could remember these scenes so clearly but without regret or remorse. To Henderson obedience was all and if he could not command respect in his own home then how could he expect the same from the cities he controlled.

It had been almost two years now since that terrible day and while attending some of the obligatory social functions that were a necessary part of his position of office other Elites at first politely enquired about his wife and daughter but the cover story held and was universally accepted. Henderson delighted in seeing how people beamed and thought how lovely it must be for mother and daughter to travel together and of course it's best that they are with family and oh how he must miss them terribly.

He was pleased that his new driver Derek Stone was working out well. Stone had been recommended to him from a fellow member of Henderson's exclusive club who had known Stone only for a short time but confirmed his excellent references and security clearances. He was a frightening figure with horrific scars on his face and hands and had lost his left eye apparently in the line of duty so he chose to wear a simple leather eye patch rather than opt for a prosthetic replacement. Henderson cared only that he was efficient and obedient.

Kathy remained the only personal problem for him to manage but since she was effectively held prisoner she had no choice but to comply with anything he asked of her. The arrangement worked very well with Kathy cooking meals and fetching drinks whenever he wanted while the driver would deliver household supplies when required and if occasional household maintenance was needed Stone would sedate Kathy and lock her in her room then supervise the workers until the task was completed. Henderson revelled in smug satisfaction knowing he could enjoy his daughter's company and the luxury of being waited on in his home without the inconvenience of a nagging wife.

Kathy had been traumatised by the death of her mother at the hands of her father and for the most part appeared to have psychologically shut down but still made a few attempts at escape in the years following including her failed attempt earlier that day but Henderson felt sure that his warning had been sufficient to break her will further and he sadistically enjoyed wearing her down.

'Yes indeed, everything has come around wonderfully,' he thought to himself as he swirled the remnants around his glass. The whiskey was relaxing him and Henderson was enjoying this self-congratulation when his thoughts were disturbed by the sound of his daughter's voice. He looked up to see Kathy standing in front of him holding a wide polished silver tray.

'Victor, your dinner?' she said, sounding frustrated like she had tried more than once to get his attention. When Henderson shot her a dark look she quickly changed her tone and said as pleasantly as she could manage. 'I made you your favourite like you asked, remember? I made the sauce from scratch and used fresh salmon from that deli you like.'

Henderson finished his drink, placed his empty glass on a small table next to him and motioned Kathy to place the tray on his lap. Since his wife died he no longer ate at the dining table and instead preferred to eat from his chair.

'Will that be all?' asked Kathy apparently subdued by his earlier reprimand.

'Yes my dear, that's everything. Thank you. You see how lovely things can be when you do what I ask? Let's not fight. I don't know what I would do without you my beautiful daughter,' he said with all the charm of a coiled viper.

'In that case if you don't mind I'll go to my room for the evening. Thank you Victor,' said Kathy turning away from Henderson as he tucked into the meal she had prepared for him, sickened by the words falling from her lips. She had to bide her time, be patient.

'I'm not going to let that bastard break me. I'm going to escape this nightmare or die trying,' she swore to herself for the hundredth time as she locked the door of her bedroom and tried to sleep after another day in trapped hell.

CHAPTER 7

Sam and Molly sat together on the sofa in Sam's apartment, the golden haired canine enjoying the rare treat of being allowed up on the furniture. It was late afternoon and the effect of the few drinks he had earlier with Arthur was wearing off and he felt now the ache from the facial wound caused by the strike of the Enforcer's shotgun butt. After leaving Arthur in the bar Sam had walked quickly through the streets, his mind racing with thoughts of the journey ahead and what difficulties and dangers they may encounter but he had to calm himself and think how best to contact Lucy. The pain from his injury was helping to clear his mind and help him focus. He needed to tell her of their plan and arrange to meet her on the road outside Raven City. With no time to organise sending a reply to her letter he had no choice but to risk using the net-screen knowing their conversation could be monitored and reported.

'Might as well get on with it Molly, I just hope she's home and understands the message,' Sam said aloud as his dearest friend sleepily lifted her head from his lap.

He got up and drew his hand across the scratched plexi-glass panel to activate the screen, as usual ignoring the vast stream of video ads that were immediately competing for his attention and swiped his hand downwards, the gesture clearing the screen so he could make a call. What seemed like several minutes had passed and Sam was about to disconnect when the screen lit up with Lucy's live video image as she accepted the call. His heart soared when he saw her smiling face. A petite figure and standing five foot six in her army surplus boots Lucy was several inches shorter than Sam but he felt they fitted together perfectly when they held each other close. Her dark wavy shoulder length hair, sallow skin, delicate features and deep brown eyes gave her an air of feminine mystery, an untold depth he would give anything to spend his life exploring and knowing he would love every single thing he discovered.

'She is so beautiful,' Sam thought, instantly forgetting the pain in his face and the troubles on his mind.

The spell broke suddenly as Lucy's smile quickly faded.

'Oh my God, what happened? Are you alright? Look at your poor face, tell me what happened?' Lucy gasped in shock at seeing Sam's bloody and bruised face from under the dressings Arthur had hastily applied.

Sam hadn't looked in the mirror since he'd arrived home and only now remembered he must look a real mess. 'Oh shit, sorry babe, I forgot to clean up before I called you. Don't worry, it's just a scratch, I'm sure it looks worse than it actually is. Really I'm okay, just an accident, it doesn't even hurt. I'm fine,' he lied hoping to spare Lucy any undue worry considering what he had yet to tell her.

The two distant lovers spent several minutes catching up, much of which involved Sam trying to convince Lucy his injuries were superficial.

'So, I was thinking, you know how we've talked before about you meeting my family?'

'Yeah, we'd talked about it and you know I'd love to meet your parents,' Lucy replied quickly catching the meaning as she knew Sam's entire family had emigrated years ago.

'Well, something has come up here through work and I've managed to arrange a temporary travel permit and a lift with a trucker as far as Raven City. I was thinking in a few days we could meet up, remember where we had the picnic the summer after you moved to Raven? I was thinking it'd be great to visit there again, it's a really nice spot, just the two of us, and Molly of course.'

'Oh Sam, I'd love that. It's a wonderful idea, you have no idea how much I'm looking forward to seeing you. Our picnic that day was perfect, let's do it again!'

They spent a moment saying goodbye and ended their call terminating the net-screen connection.

Sam knew Lucy had understood his message. They had many previous coded conversations and she knew as well as he did to be very careful. She understood Sam was leaving Rook City in two days and would meet her outside Raven City about three days after that. The picnic spot he spoke of was a lake several miles from Raven City where they had camped out one summer evening when Sam last visited Lucy after they returned from their travels and they had spent a miserable night being bitten by clouds of flying insects. They awoke covered in red bite marks on every inch of exposed skin and Lucy would certainly never forget it! It was a quiet place and well out of sight of the road plus now in much cooler weather would thankfully be free of the annoying insects. It meant she had around five days to get out of her own city and meet Sam and his travelling companions at the lake. One of the things Sam loved about Lucy despite her stunning beauty was that she was practical and resourceful. He could count on her to be there and she would wait at the lake for him if there was any delay. Lucy also trusted Sam completely and knew he was true to his word, he would meet her as he said, whatever it took.

Sam felt relieved that he had delivered his message. He desperately wanted to get on the road and although his pack was ready to grab and run at a moment's notice he had promised to wait for Arthur and Alice. The day after tomorrow he would meet them at the edge of the forest a few miles beyond the Rook City boundary so if he waited until morning he could get one last sleep in his own bed and then travel all the next day. It had been a hard day between forming plans of escape and having his face smashed in so some rest before the journey would be most welcome.

It was early evening; too early for bed despite his physical exhaustion so Sam took the opportunity to check through his pack. He knew everything would be there but for peace of mind he double checked anyway. Sleeping bag, bivi bag and ground mat plus an old army tarp for shelter; dried food, chocolate and water filter bottle provided his rations, basic medical supplies, spare dry clothes, torch, a stout knife for camping and hunting, a small crowbar for urban scavenging and several other items Sam had long ago listed, gathered and packed in anticipation of this day. There were a thousand other things he could have packed but weight was a consideration and finding many items even on the city's black market was difficult.

He added some extra dry food mix and a small aluminium dish for Molly and filled his water bottle then packed the last of the spare filters. From under a carefully cut section of floorboard hidden behind the bath side panel Sam took a tightly wrapped package from its plastic cover and counted out five hundred dollars in cash. It wasn't worth much but it was all he had and it might prove useful on the road.

The last thing he did was to take the old wooden baseball bat his father had given him from beside his bed and strap it to the side of his pack. The heavy end of the club sat in a low outside pocket with the shaft loosely held by an upper strap which kept it secure but also allowed Sam to reach back and grab it in seconds if needed, a move he had practised many times to be sure he could pull it off smoothly in case of trouble. In terms of defence his knife could be useful but dangerous and his trusty bat gave him more reach and was certainly more intimidating. He knew it wasn't as good as a gun but he didn't know much about guns and probably couldn't have got one if he wanted anyway so the bat was better than nothing.

With his pack rechecked and additional preparations completed he took Molly for a short walk before dark and then went to bed since the next morning he would have an early start and the road to a new life would lie in front of him, if he could make it that far.

While Sam restlessly dreamt of the adventures ahead Arthur sat at his kitchen table talking things over with his wife and explaining all that had happened that day. She didn't need any convincing that it was time to exit the decaying city and was only too happy for the chance to leave. Both Alice and Arthur would have left the city years ago but age and feeling settled in their modest yet comfortable home meant the years just rolled by until it got that Alice felt too unsure of their prospects to make the journey alone. Although she trusted and stood by her husband through all their life she was also realistic and when they had previously discussed leaving both knew their chances of making it were slim. Now that Sam would be travelling with them husband and wife felt this could be their last best shot at spending their remaining years somewhere other than the rotting metropolis.

As keen as Alice was to leave it came as a surprise for her to learn that the men planned to rendezvous beyond the city limits the day after next.

'I'm sorry love,' said Arthur softly. 'I know it doesn't leave you much time to get used to the idea but you know we have to go. Remember how it used to be, remember how happy we once were. Well maybe we can find something of that life again at the end of our long road. I know we have memories here in this place but you know as well as I do that there are more bad memories than good now, it's time to leave it behind, take our chances and find something new. We're not too old for that yet. Are we?'

Alice's eyes filled with tears and she wept as she and Arthur held hands across the table. He got up from his chair and came around to hold Alice to comfort her.

'Oh I'm so sorry my love, I wish it didn't have to be this way but it'll be okay, you'll see.'

Alice leaned back from her husband, drying her eyes.

'You old fool, I'm not crying because I'm sad we're leaving this dump, I'm crying because after all these years together you still want to take silly risks and make a go of it with an old girl like me. I love you Arthur and whatever the weeks ahead have in store I'm just happy I'll be with you, that's all that matters.'

Husband and wife retired to bed where they lay and just held each other affirming a bond that had seen them through times happy and sad for over three decades together.

As the elderly couple drifted off to a contented sleep Sam was startled awake by the sound of a door being smashed in and the tramping of several pairs of heavy boots and aggressive shouts from an Enforcer squad commander.

'Under Protocol Nine, section four you are hereby detained. You have no further rights.'

An icy fist gripped Sam's heart and he leapt naked from his bed, pulse racing, scrambling into his jeans and boots, and waiting for his bedroom door to be broken off its hinges at any second. Molly who had been asleep in her basket in the bedroom barked and snarled at the door. Sam had nowhere to go, his apartment was eight floors up with a single exit to the communal hallway. He was trapped.

His thoughts were of Lucy, he would never see her again. She would wait at the lake for him for days but realise eventually he was not coming. Would she think he abandoned her? No, she'd know something had happened but would she make it to safety travelling outside the city alone? His mind ablaze now Sam looked to the corner of his bed thinking to grab his bat and maybe take a swing or two at the Enforcers before they beat him senseless but he realised it was in the living room, strapped to his backpack. If this was to be his last stand he wasn't going down easily. As the seconds ticked past in what seemed like an eternity Sam heard shouts of protest coming through the thin walls followed by screams of agony and he realised then the Enforcers weren't here for him.

Adrenaline coursed through his body as Sam fought to bring his mind and heart rate under control. He settled Molly to stop her barking and then taking care to switch off all lights in his apartment ran to his front door and cautiously peered through the spy hole. The four man Enforcer squad were now withdrawing from the apartment directly across the hall, the commander in front, a single guard at the rear and two in the middle of the group dragging Sam's neighbour Pete out into the hallway. He appeared badly beaten but still had strength to struggle. Already blood ran from several wounds and his shouts of innocence were garbled as he attempted to form words through a badly broken jaw and split lips, spitting and drooling blood with every syllable.

'That poor bastard,' Sam thought to himself.

Whatever Pete had done or was suspected of doing he would most likely pay with his life but if by some luck he survived interrogation he would be exiled to the prison farms far to the south or released onto the city streets to die.

Sam waited nervously and watched as the rear guard Enforcer checked up and down the hallway covering the withdrawal with his shotgun in case anyone felt brave enough to help their neighbour. Sam cursed himself for allowing Pete to be taken but he knew he was powerless against armed Enforcers and would have been badly beaten or arrested for interfering. He had to think about Lucy and needed to stay alive and well if they were ever to see each other again.

'Sorry Pete,' he said quietly, feeling ashamed.

Once sure that the Enforcers and their captive were descending in the lift Sam backed away from the door wiping a cold sweat from his brow and started to feel sick from the adrenaline that had pumped into his empty stomach. Wasting no time he ran to the bedroom to let Molly out and checked the clock as he got fully dressed. It was ten past four in the morning, a good time to make a run for the city perimeter as when he reached the wall the city would be fully awake and the morning commuter rush would ensure fewer Enforcer patrols on the fringes. He didn't have to meet with Arthur and Alice until the following morning but he couldn't wait a minute longer after the scare he just had.

In the bathroom he checked the wound on his face and removed the old dressings, cleaned the dried blood from around the deep cut then applied antiseptic cream and fresh suture strips. There was no sign of infection and he was pleased to see the swelling around his eye had gone down.

Dressed in faded blue jeans, used army boots, grey wool jumper, battered black leather motorcycle jacket and a waterproof khaki army jacket on top Sam was ready to go. He put a dish of food out for Molly and she hungrily wolfed down the tinned meat as he snacked on a couple of raw carrots which were past their best but the only remaining edible food in his fridge. He stuffed a few sticks of dried meat into his jacket pocket planning to save them to eat on the road. When Molly had finished her breakfast he hoisted his pack and tightened the shoulder straps to ensure a snug fit then snapped closed the fastener on the kidney belt so everything was well balanced and would leave his hands free.

He took one last look around the apartment where he had lived for the past four years and caring nothing for the meagre possessions left behind he made for the door.

'That was too close for comfort Molly. Get your lead, we're going out.'

In the vacant hallway Sam peered across the gloom into the apartment of his neighbour and couldn't help but wonder what inhumane treatment Pete would be subjected to even during transport for processing. With Molly by his side Sam started down the concrete staircase not trusting the lift to deliver him safely to the ground without jamming and bringing about the end of his journey before it even began.

Once out of his building he clipped Molly's lead to her collar and flipped up the hood on his army jacket to keep out the cold but also to shield his face from any operational security cameras he would pass beneath as he made his way west toward the perimeter and the relative sanctuary of the forest beyond. He navigated the city's dark streets as the sky began to lighten with the approaching dawn. To keep off the main streets and avoid the scrutiny of passing Enforcer patrols he used back alleys as much as possible. The stench of filth and rot was all the more pungent and reminders of social decay more obvious where hordes of the city's homeless huddled to keep warm in makeshift shelters. Some slept clutching bags or suitcases of treasured possessions and when Sam saw a skeletal man removing his torn sports jacket to lay it as a blanket over his two sleeping children he stopped and looked on, rummaging in his pocket.

'Please, we don't want any trouble,' cried the man as he threw himself defensively in front of his young son and daughter. 'Everything we own has already been taken, they killed my wife because I wouldn't give up our last can of food. It was for the kids you see, I couldn't let the bastards take it,' he said as his eyes shimmered and tears ran down through the thick dirty stubble on his cheeks.

'I'm sorry,' said Sam kneeling to speak to the man face to face. 'Here, I won't be needing these anymore,' and he pressed the keys to his apartment into the man's hand and leaned forward to whisper the address.

The man quickly snatched the keys for fear someone else might see.

'Thank you mister, thank you,' he whispered emotionally in reply.

Sam could think of no words of comfort so just smiled and shook the man's hand then continued down the alley. When he reached the end he turned to look back and saw the man disappear around a corner carrying his daughter in one arm and leading his son with the other, their only possessions in a little knapsack on the man's back.

'Good luck,' Sam wished them quietly.

A few times an armoured patrol wagon slowed as it drove

past but to Sam's relief they didn't stop to ask questions. Molly of course took it all in her stride and simply enjoyed savouring the new sounds and scents in areas of the city she had never been.

Passing through an alley behind yet another row of abandoned and boarded shops Sam felt a chill as he sensed the eerie quiet in the narrow space, not a person to be seen even in the darkest corner. He decided to push on but was stopped in his tracks by two men who stepped from the shadows and stood menacingly flashing their blades and blocking his path. Their ragged clothing was in much better condition than that of the other street people Sam had encountered and their muscular builds suggested they ate better too.

'This is our patch, if you want to pass there's a toll to pay,' said the biggest of the two. 'That backpack will cover the charge but we aren't letting you go without a warning for trespassing.'

Sam looked back and saw that the way behind was clear but he would never outrun them while carrying his heavy rucksack. As Molly bared her teeth in a low deep growl Sam reached down and grabbed her collar leading her as he slowly stepped backward keeping his eyes fixed on the two men.

'We don't want any bother fellas, just passing through. Didn't realise this was your turf, no disrespect intended.'

'I'm afraid it's too late for that my friend,' sneered the mouthy one as he ran at Sam with his right arm held high, holding his knife ready to stab down hard as soon as he was in range.

Sam raised his arm to try to ward off the attack and in doing so his grip on Molly's collar loosened allowing her to break free. She ran forward snarling, closing the gap between Sam and the attacker then sunk her teeth deep into the calf of the man before he could react. With the shock and pain he hit the ground hard and dropped his knife which thankfully fell away from his reach. Molly didn't let go and shook and growled angrily keeping her jaws clamped firmly to the bone as the man began raining blows on the wild animal ripping at his flesh. Within seconds Sam reached her trying to stop the punches from hitting his dearest friend but before he could do much to help the second man had rushed in. The force of his momentum pushed Sam back hard so he stumbled and was brought down on his back by the weight of his pack. Still bound by the shoulder straps he struggled like an upturned turtle but just in time managed to roll onto his side and pulled his knees and elbows together to protect the front of his body from a vicious kick aimed for his ribs.

Another couple of kicks came; one caught Sam in the shins, the other he blocked with the fleshy underside of his forearms causing him pain but no serious injury as his vital organs were at least protected. Sam kicked out from his defensive position on the ground aiming for the groin but the backpack limited his movements and he managed only a heavy kick to the front of the man's thigh.

That their victim fought back frustrated the second attacker who still brandished his knife so he tried to run around behind Sam where he might get a better target for his blade. With all this strength Sam pushed and rolled his body up and over the backpack and onto his other side and in a single fluid movement he reached behind his head, pulled his baseball bat from the exposed side of his pack and swung it hard into the brute's knee smashing the kneecap and bringing the assailant to the ground where he lay clutching his leg and howling with pain.

Sam unclipped the straps and freed himself from his pack and scrambling to his feet he heard a whimper from Molly then saw her being thrown back against the alley wall. The first man had kicked with his with his free leg and ignoring the pain from the severe bite wound and the blood soaking through his jeans lunged toward Molly with his knife thrust in front of him intent on gutting the beast who had savaged his leg.

'No!' Sam shouted leaping forward to defend Molly and

with a mighty swing brought the heavy club down hard on the man's outstretched arm folding bone and muscle around the rounded sides of bat. With one more fast swing of his weapon Sam struck the back of the man's knee even as he was still moving forward buckling the leg and crumpling the attacker in a heap against the wall where Molly had been lying only seconds before.

'Molly, here girl, are you okay? Oh Molly, you're so brave, thanks girl,' said Sam fussing over his furry companion and quickly checking her for injuries. She was back on feet and licking Sam's face more concerned for her master than her own wellbeing. She whined a little when he gently pressed some bruises to her ribs but she appeared to be none the worse for wear. Molly turned and barked ferociously at both downed men in turn as Sam heaved his pack onto his back and then pressed the heavy end of the bat under the chin of the man who had kicked Molly.

'Okay you pricks, I'd say I've paid my toll so we'll be on our way.'

Leaving the two men groaning in pain Sam knew with a busted knee and a heavily bleeding leg between them neither man would be following.

'Come on Molly, let's go. Maybe we'll just have to risk the main streets from here to the gates eh?'

The pair made their way along the remainder of the alley and back out onto the relative safety of the street to continue the trek to the city perimeter.

'I can't take much more of this Molly!' Sam said as the pain from this latest beating throbbed in his arms and legs but he used it to harden his resolve and determination to leave the damned city far behind.

Pushing on through the quiet streets the first stirrings of daytime life were beginning to show as morning approached. At intervals between the boarded and burnt out shop fronts sellers were setting up their temporary stalls keen to tempt the first commuters. Sam ignored the smells of foul meat being roasted over homemade charcoal braziers and passed by the newsstands selling the latest printed propaganda but the rumble in his belly meant he couldn't resist stopping to treat himself one last time to a warm bacon and cheese bagel from a little barrow stall.

The stall owner was a small downtrodden man with only a thin threadbare overcoat to protect him from the cold but to Sam he seemed surprisingly cheerful. Despite Sam's scruffy appearance this little man just nodded and smiled as he wrapped the warm bread in a crumpled napkin and although neither spoke except for the minimum exchange required for their transaction Sam felt heartened to make a connection with someone whose spirit apparently hadn't been crushed by the weight of life in the city.

As he walked and chewed on his bagel Sam could see a short distance ahead the tops of the iron bridge leading west out of the city which spanned a stretch of water providing a shortcut across the peninsula. The early morning sun rising behind him was illuminating the top of the massive arches coating the flaking white paintwork with a golden light like a beacon calling him onward to freedom.

Before he could cross the bridge he had to walk several more blocks and over a few hundred metres of open ground toward the city perimeter wall. The wall was constructed of massive one metre tall and two metre wide reinforced concrete sections stacked six blocks high topped with razor wire. It was a hastily built barricade erected around the entire city when the Elites took power and was intended only as a temporary measure to allow them to contain and control the city population in a time of chaos. Combined with Enforcer patrols and checkpoints at each exit on the four main compass points the barrier had proved to be effective in keeping the poorer Dregs residents in line and reinforcing a feeling of security and superiority for the Elites so it had remained in place. For one side of the city population the wall was a prison, for the other it served as a defence but most believed they were at least protected from the terrors they had been told existed beyond the wall.

Sam expected little civilian traffic and hoped at this early hour there would be mostly a few supply trucks coming and going and therefore fewer Enforcers stationed to the west gate. He could see the heavy steel gates were open allowing trucks to pass once the long red and white stripped pole was lifted after a full vehicle search had been conducted. However over the years any Enforcers unlucky enough to pull gate duty had become complacent and if they recognised the regular supply drivers they often just let them pass without question. Travellers on foot were uncommon because according to stories regularly circulated by Central Media the roads beyond the city were extremely dangerous due to regular killings and kidnappings by outlaws.

As he approached the gates Sam reached into the inside pocket of his leather jacket and pulled out a folded official travel permit issued the last time he had been hiking in the woods far beyond the wall. The permit was a few years old and he knew that in light of the increased patrols to apply for a travel permit would have drawn Central Control's spotlight on him and this would surely result in his own arrest and interrogation. Hoping against hope that flashing the permit to an undoubtedly bored guard would allow him and Molly to pass through the gate unhindered Sam held the document up to the thick glass of the guard hut for a brief moment and smiled then nodded to the guard as he kept moving forward and folded the paper back into his pocket.

'Confidence is the key, just keep walking. Nothing unusual here, just me and my dog heading out of the city for a few days, all above board,' Sam thought to himself praying he'd make it through. As he had hoped the guard on duty was half asleep at this early hour and had his feet up on the desk, uniform jacket half unbuttoned and showed no interest in Sam once he flashed the officially stamped document. Counting his blessings Sam guided Molly through the gate as they shuffled through the creaky, barely used pedestrian turnstyle. Just a few steps from freedom and Sam walked straight into a young Enforcer recruit as the junior guard walked from behind the outer wall zipping up his fly after relieving his bladder.

The young guard was obviously surprised and embarrassed and to save face spoke in a sharp official tone. 'Travel papers please.'

Sam's heart froze and his stomach suddenly felt as though it held a lead weight. 'Oh, I ah, I've shown my papers to the other guard, thanks,' he said and walked on toward the bridge.

'Your travel papers, now,' continued the young guard, irritated at this disregard for his authority.

Sam knew he had no choice and could only hope on feigning ignorance. He presented the aged permit to the guard who took an agonisingly long time to read it even though it was obviously out of date and glanced from the paper to Sam and back several times insinuating more of an insult each time he read it. Sam's expression betrayed that the feeble attempt to intimidate him just wasn't working.

The young Enforcer was visibly angry now. 'You do realise travelling without a permit is illegal? I'll have to write this up and call for a wagon to take you in and unless you can show me your animal permit the dog will have to be terminated.'

'Hey, no way, you're not taking Molly anywhere, she's not done anything wrong. I don't care what you do with me but leave her alone.'

'No one's going to kill your dog son,' said a weary voice from behind Sam and he noticed the young recruit straighten bolt upright.

'Sir, this man has no animal permit and his travel permit has expired almost four years, sir,' blurted the junior guard.

'Is this true?' asked the senior Enforcer as he walked from the guard hut with his uniform still unbuttoned and rubbing his face to rouse himself from his doze.

Sam turned to face him and although in shadow Sam could see the tired expression on the older guard's face. He seemed like a man who had seen it all and more than once too often.

'Look, there's been some misunderstanding here and me and your colleague have got off on the wrong foot,' said Sam speaking quickly to seize the opportunity. 'I seem to have an old travel permit in my jacket and must have left the new one at home. Of course I have an animal permit for Molly as well but it's early and I guess I left a few things in my usual coat. I'll only be gone overnight and its quiet here, no one would know, maybe you can let us go on eh?'

'Sir you can't allow them to pass, I was just about to call Command for a wagon,' complained the recruit keen to prove himself and follow procedure to the letter.

'Shut your yap,' snapped the older guard grumpily. 'You're fresh from the training grounds and you've no idea do you? This is an easy number, I like it, it's quiet out by the gate, no trouble and I won't have you stirring up a hornet's nest over a tramp and his dog. Geez the paperwork alone would have me buried for half a shift.'

'Yes sir, very good sir,' the younger guard replied looking like he'd taken a physical blow, the wind knocked out of his sails he was crestfallen much to Sam's amusement despite his unease at his own predicament.

'Now,' continued the senior guard turning his attention back to Sam, 'I'm certainly not letting you through the gate without a permit but I'm not calling out a bloody wagon either. Get your arse out of here and if you get picked up on the way back into the city don't breathe a word about speaking with me or I'll be sure both you and your dog see an interrogation chamber. Now beat it.' He turned and walked back into the guard hut to continue his snooze leaving the sneering recruit the pleasure of escorting Sam and Molly back through the turn-style toward the city.

'And don't let me see you again either,' shouted the young Enforcer as Sam squinted in the low morning sun before being engulfed by the long shadows of the city he couldn't now leave.

'What an arsehole!' Sam said to Molly and she gave a little bark as if to agree.

CHAPTER 8

As Sam retreated from his encounter with the perimeter guards he was completely thrown but not for a second did he consider giving up.

'What do we do now Molly?' he asked his loyal companion. 'There's no way we'll make it through the city to another gate and they'll be guarded just the same anyway.'

Tail wagging and tongue panting Molly just looked up at Sam with her big brown trusting eyes as if to reassure him that it would all be okay and he knew no matter the outcome she'd never leave him.

'You know Molly.....,' he began but his thoughts were interrupted as in the corner of his eye he caught sight of something that gave him an idea and renewed his hope.

Roughly two hundred metres to his right in the open border of waste ground between the city buildings and perimeter wall, he saw a depression where there appeared to be a bank sloping down on either side to a narrow channel. From the distance and angle he couldn't be sure but it looked like an exposed section of a culvert draining out from the city and under the main wall to the river beyond. Aware that the overzealous recruit would probably be watching him all the way back to the city's edge Sam casually glanced behind him to his right and with the morning sun shining on the east facing inside of the wall he traced the channel to where it met the tall concrete barricade and sure enough there did appear to be some irregularity to the construction where the pipe outlet would have to exit.

'That's how we'll get out Molly,' Sam said with renewed determination as he walked further into the cold morning shadows of the city. Once back in the city streets he walked along a block of abandoned buildings then turned right and then right again and walked to the end of the street so he looked back out to the west across the waste ground toward the city perimeter wall but now further away from the gate checkpoint and almost opposite to where the culvert exited under the wall. Taking off his pack Sam opened a front pouch and pulled out a canteen and a small metal dish then poured out some fresh water for Molly before taking a few sips himself. He then unbuttoned another flap on the outside of the pack and took out a small pair of field binoculars his grandfather had given him on one of their many hikes in the north of the country during his childhood.

Sam looked around to be sure he was alone and with his side of the street quiet and still in shadow he took the opportunity to use this vantage point to check the route he planned to take. He estimated at about twenty metres from the wall the ground receded and a narrow channel did indeed open up to expose a large pipe which had been stained a burnt orange colour from years of exposure and rust. The pipe didn't run under the wall after all but ended roughly five metres short then whatever waste ran from it flowed across open ground and through a metal grille out to the river beyond. A long shot for sure but Sam knew he'd have to take it if he was to meet with Arthur and Alice and then get to Lucy.

He put away Molly's dish but kept out the binoculars then strapped on his pack in readiness to run when the chance presented itself. He knew from his time working in the food plant that supply trucks arrived every morning delivering raw materials from the prison farms in the south. Since the south and east gates led into Elite sectors of the city all shipments arrived via the west gate so it would be just a matter of time until a supply truck appeared at the gate providing the distraction he needed.

The shadows maintained the biting morning chill and despite sitting now in a darkened doorway to ease the weight on his back the straps of his pack made Sam's shoulders ache. To make matters worse, as the sun continued to rise he would soon be in direct sunlight making him more conspicuous. He was thankful that with his cut face, old green army jacket worn over his biker jacket and dirty ripped jeans he looked typical of many street dwellers in the Dreg sector so most passers-by preferred to avoid making eye contact.

While he waited and watched Molly lay and dozed beside him. Sam found the waiting worse than anything as it led to nervousness but thinking of Lucy kept him focused. He realised he looked forward to seeing Arthur and Alice again too which was unusual for him since he usually preferred to keep his own company.

An Enforcer patrol wagon shook Sam from his thoughts as it rumbled past mid-way between the outer city edge and the perimeter wall following a dirt track worn smooth and packed hard by countless circling patrols. It was the first he had noticed go by during the time he'd been watching the gate and confirmed his guess that the early morning rush hour would be a busier time for the Enforcers in the city centre districts meaning patrol numbers on the perimeter were reduced.

After a couple of hours as he stood for the third time to stretch his legs and move around a little to keep warm Sam noticed some movement at the distant gate. He quickly raised the binoculars and watched discreetly as the younger guard who he had nearly run into earlier demanded that the driver of an incoming supply truck get out of the cab and submit to a vehicle search. The driver appeared annoyed about the search and from the cab of the truck gestured wildly to the guard.

'I wouldn't piss him off if I were you,' Sam said as he

watched the young Enforcer open the driver's door to begin his search, starting with the driver.

'The old guy must still be sleeping with his feet up, come on this is our chance,' Sam whispered, quickly getting to his feet and grabbing Molly's lead.

Just about to make a run for the wall Sam heard the distinct rumble of a big V8 engine and looked in time to see another Enforcer patrol wagon approaching. He had no choice but to pull back into the doorway and wait, trapped between the slowly cruising vehicle to his left and the gate guards on the right. As the seconds ticked by and with heart pounding in his chest Sam felt as if his chance was slipping away from him yet he could nothing except endure the agonising wait.

'That Enforcer must moonlight as a hearse driver in his spare time,' Sam said to Molly as he watched the heavily armoured patrol wagon cruise on past the gate and eventually disappear around a curve and out of sight. Sam could see the supply truck was still stopped at the gate and a quick check through the binoculars revealed that the senior guard had become involved and was speaking with the driver while the younger officer looked on. The driver had his wallet out now and appeared to be making his feelings known about being robbed blind by the guards.

'That old bastard has quite a racket going on at the gate, no wonder he doesn't want to attract attention to himself,' Sam thought. 'Come on Molly, it's now or never,' and taking a deep breath he ran as fast as he could, crouching low, keeping a tight grip on Molly's lead and a sharp eye on the gate.

Halfway across the open stretch of waste ground he heard the supply truck's door slam shut and the engine start. Glancing at the guards he saw the older of the pair turn toward him as he walked back to his station but the guard's attention was on the handful of bank notes he had just fleeced from the unfortunate driver. The truck belched black smoke as it pulled away from the gate and the younger guard waved to clear the air in front of his face as the large vehicle lurched off toward the city streets. Sure he'd be spotted any second Sam broke into a flat-out run with Molly pulling on her lead alongside. He could see the massive exposed waste pipe now and where the ground sloped down around its open end. Letting go of Molly's lead and with all the strength he had remaining Sam dived for cover into the ditch where he crawled on his belly the last few metres until he could be sure he was lying low enough to not be visible from ground level. He quickly released the straps on his pack and grabbing hold of Molly by her collar to keep her head down he scrambled up the side of the gulley peeking through the wild grass at its edge to check if their frantic dash had been noticed.

As the young guard shouted a smug remark after the truck driver some movement to his right had caught his eye. He looked around sharply and thought he saw the tail end of a golden haired dog run into the culvert.

'Probably chasing rats; actually those bloody rats are probably hunting the dog,' he thought to himself and walked back to the guard hut, interested now in learning from his older partner all about life on the gate since he knew there was a cash incentive for the otherwise monotonous post.

Sam breathed a heavy sigh of relief.

'Well done girl, so far so good but we're not out of here yet,' and he slid back into the deep ditch careful to guide Molly gently to its base.

Sam could stand without being seen from above and if he hunched over slightly he could have walked into the pipe's massive circular opening. Thankfully the rain over the previous few days hadn't been heavy and the river level was relatively low meaning the noxious liquid streaming from the pipe was just ankle deep and Sam's waterproof army boots kept his feet dry although not knowing its origin he didn't fancy splashing about in the stinking foaming soup for too long.

Examining the channel through which the effluent from the pipe oozed Sam estimated it to be slightly larger than the diameter of the pipe itself. He guessed the original idea may have been to extend the pipe through the wall out to the river beyond but the work must never have been completed so instead a heavy cast-iron grille had been hastily placed over the opening to secure the gap under the wall. The grille itself was not one single piece but comprised of two parts hinged like a gate at their outer sides and secured in the centre by a large corroded padlock.

From his pack Sam retrieved the small twelve-inch crowbar he had taken from his toolbox before leaving his apartment. He thought it would prove useful to scavenge supplies from some of the boarded up shops and abandoned buildings on his journey through the city and was glad for his foresight now. The padlock securing the centre parts of the grille appeared to be thoroughly rusted and so he pushed the straight end of the bar through the shackle and levering it against a section of ironwork pulled down on it with his full weight. The short crowbar had no effect on the sturdy lock and despite a few attempts the lock simply refused to be defeated. Sam thought perhaps he could bash the lock with a large rock but couldn't risk the noise.

Molly sat nearby on the dry bank watching Sam with interest and when he turned and threw the crowbar across the gulley in frustration she ran after and brought it right back to him like she was playing fetch.

'You're not letting me give up eh?' said Sam gently taking the bar from the dog's slobbering jowls and ruffling her ears the way she liked.

He took a thin stick of dried meat from his jacket, broke it in half and gave a piece to Molly who took it carefully then chewed hungrily on the treat.

'Good girl Molly, I'll think of something,' he said as he took a bite from the other half of the meat and stared at the seemingly impassable obstacle.

As he ate Sam studied the mounting points of the huge

grille and observed how they were made of thick metal spikes sunk into the concrete supports. The spikes were formed into loops at the end through which pins in the grille were inserted to act as hinges allowing the grille to pivot open if required. Below the high tide mark the lower mounts had become heavily corroded over years of submersion in river water and toxic run-off from the waste pipe.

'Never give up, right Molly?'

He checked both lower mounts and seeing the right-hand side appeared to have more damage set about working the flat tip of the crowbar into the small gap in the hinge. There was just room for him to get enough of the tool against the iron to gain leverage but it was all he needed. Tugging the bar at first seemed to accomplish nothing but in desperation and muttering a few choice curses Sam kept working, pushing and pulling the forged steel crowbar, working back and forth applying force to the corroded metalwork.

Gradually, almost imperceptibly the aged hinge succumbed to Sam's efforts and soon the rusted surface of the hinge released flakes of rotting metal and where it entered the concrete support post tiny crumbs of debris rolled away. Feeling something loosen he changed tactic and using the curved end of the bar for greater leverage attacked the spike where it was anchored to the concrete post. With the crowbar wedged now between the grille mount and the support post Sam sat down and used both feet to push against the free end of the bar using the strength of his legs to lever it then suddenly with a sharp snap the hinge lost the battle and half the mounting pulled free from the wall leaving the right side of the heavy grille held by only the top mount and the padlock in the middle. This had the effect of causing the bottom corner of the grille to twist slightly outward leaving a gap underneath.

He almost shouted out with joy at this small but hard won victory and then realised he hadn't been checking the guards. He cautiously climbed the side of the gulley and checked around him. His timing was such that he saw the young recruit wave to a passing patrol wagon then turn back to the guard hut.

Sliding back into the gulley Sam took off his army coat and leather jacket then his jumper and strapping them on top of his backpack pushed the bundle through the narrow opening he had created at the bottom of the grille and encouraged Molly to go through next. Finally he lay down in the filthy water and crawled through then pulled the grille back into position as best he could so it would appear upon casual inspection to be undamaged.

He held Molly's lead so she wouldn't run off to play in the river and worked his pack onto his back before carefully edging his way to the outer side of the wall. Cautiously peeking out from the open face of the drainage tunnel Sam could see no traffic or sign of the guards at the west gate and bridge to his right so keeping close to the wall he tracked left for several hundred metres following the river upstream until he came to a section where the stony river bed was visible beneath shallower water. He cut a strong branch from a nearby tree and stripped the small twigs and leaves from it so he could check the water's depth as he forged the river and keep his balance against the current.

Satisfied they were far enough from the city gate he unclipped the straps on his pack so he could quickly free himself if he fell while crossing and then holding tight to Molly's lead ventured out into the cold water. Although only waist high at its deepest and with a gentle current Sam still fought in places to keep from stumbling on the slippery rocks underfoot. He stayed down river of Molly so he could be sure she wouldn't be carried away although he needn't have worried as she could swim much better than him and his companion was thoroughly enjoying herself.

Safely to the opposite bank Sam helped Molly up out of the river where she shook her thick coat showering him with freezing water. He dragged himself onto the shore then leading Molly ran to the cover of some thick bushes close by. He was shivering with cold and exhausted but he was happy.

He had made it out of the city at last and knew he deserved to feel proud of that. Looking through the bushes and back across the river he knew couldn't stop here and had to press on but he took a few minutes to pour the water from his boots and change his wet jeans and underwear for spare dry clothes from the plastic wrapped bundle in his pack.

An old pair of olive green combat trousers and some dry wool socks were a welcome reward for his efforts and a square of chocolate gave him some energy and boosted his spirits.

'We're out Molly, we made it this far. Let's get to the forest now and wait for our new friends eh? Good girl.'

And with that Sam lifted his pack once more and hurried away overland, hiking through lush green fields toward the forest that lay several miles ahead, with each step leaving the doomed city farther behind.

CHAPTER 9

'It's time my love,' whispered Arthur to his wife as the morning sun filtered through a crack in the curtains. 'We need to get a move on if we're going to meet Sam.'

Alice stretched, kissed Arthur and in spite of her age sprang from their bed like an excited child on Christmas morning.

'Let's do it,' she said. 'I'll get breakfast started if you gather my bags to the hall. Adventure awaits!'

Arthur knew she was putting a brave face on things, knew it would be difficult for her to abandon their home of so many years but knew also that for ages she had longed to leave. Mixed feelings but as always Alice chose to be positive and to start the day with a smile. She amazed him and gave him courage and hope that he would have lost long ago if not for her.

Arthur dressed, shaved and then busied himself gathering the various bags and cases Alice had packed. Once he had brought everything downstairs he passed through their kitchen and out to the shed at the back of the small garden to grab their pre-packed rucksacks and several other items from the modest store of emergency supplies Arthur had saved and gathered.

As he hoisted his bag onto his back and felt the weight settle it brought back memories of countless forced marches, blistered feet and some of the best and worst days of his youth. Knowing he wouldn't have met Alice had it not been for his discharge meant he had long ago accepted the injustice but he still missed his friends and the life. Dismissing the thought he glanced at his homemade still and the several gallon jugs of moonshine whiskey he had stored away.

'Ah sure why not make the journey a little more enjoyable!' he thought to himself and hooked the index finger of each hand through the ear of a jug and carried them to the house.

The welcoming smell of frying bacon and eggs delighted his senses as he entered the kitchen. 'Oh that smells fantastic love, bit of soda bread too if there's any?'

Alice half joked. 'Is that for you or for running the truck I wonder?' pointing a metal spatula at the large jugs of liquor hanging from each of his arms.

'It's too good to leave behind and sure we'll have something to celebrate with when we reach my cousin's place. Besides, who knows how long it will take me to build a new still,' Arthur replied as Alice rolled her eyes and turned her attention back to the stove.

Arthur went back and forth between the shed and hallway and in two more runs had lined up six jugs beside their other belongings.

He stood in the doorway between hall and kitchen massaging an ache in his lower back which served to remind him of his age and stared at the two large suitcases and a smaller bag Alice had assembled, both their emergency rucksacks and the six gallons of booze.

'Geez love it's just as well we're taking the truck! What have you got in those cases? There's enough in our packs to see the two of us right for the journey, what could you possibly need to bring all that stuff for?'

'Arthur Graham!' his wife scolded from behind and Arthur winced knowing what was coming. 'If you have room to take all of that hooch of yours then I have room to bring a few things of my own. I want to leave this horrible old town as much as you but this was our home regardless of what it has become over the years and I won't leave it all behind. A few small bits and pieces to remember better times and friends and family are worth the space don't you think? A woman needs more than one frock too you know or don't you want me to feel like a lady when we get to our new home?'

'I'm sorry love, of course you're right. There's plenty of room, it'll be fine. Let's have our breakfast and not fight on this last morning here eh?' said Arthur smoothing over his mistake. He couldn't bring himself to tell his wife that if the going got tough they might have to dump the lot by the roadside.

'Better to take a leaf from Alice's book and be the eternal optimist,' Arthur thought to himself.

After their breakfast Alice got to work checking their house over one last time for anything she might have forgotten, filled a cardboard box with food and treats for the road as if they were simply heading on a weekend trip to the seaside. As Arthur suggested she set timers on lamps in the front and back of the house which would come on and off at random intervals during the night and give the appearance they were at home. It wouldn't matter really but a few of the neighbours on their street still cared enough to look out for an elderly couple and might get suspicious when they came home from work that night and found Alice and Arthur's house in darkness. Anything that would avoid drawing unwanted attention was worth doing.

Meanwhile Arthur had walked the short distance to the lock up garages that were rented out to a few of the people in his area. As he approached his senses alerted him to the acrid stench of burnt plastic and metal and saw that a garage two to the left of his own was badly fire damaged, the roof had caved in where the wooden roofing supports had burned through but oddly the door was open and completely intact and the heavy wooden door frame was only lightly scorched. As he got closer he noticed the inside of the garage was a completely different story as everything had been incinerated.

The contents were now a pile of ash, melted plastic and twisted metal. There had been only light rain the night before but the inside of the garage was completely saturated, puddles of black water mixing with the noxious chemical stew left from the fire.

Arthur's concern was for the old Land Rover pickup truck in his own garage and he quickened his pace to check his lockup but to his relief found all locks intact, no signs of break in and apart from the overpowering smell of the neighbouring inferno his own garage was unaffected. He knew if vandals or burglars had hit one lockup they would have ransacked several if not all and the old truck would have been a great prize for a thief or arsonist. Opening the heavy creaking door the ancient springs protested as they took the weight and as the door rose up Arthur was relieved to see the heavy steel bumper and the faded red paintwork of the battered old truck.

He thought about the burnt out garage and the nature of the targeted attack and relatively controlled burn with obvious signs of the fire being extinguished when the job was done. He realised it could mean only one of two things. In the old days it was common for people to pull an insurance job for cash but since it was now a capital offence no one would dare risk their life for a few worthless dollars. That meant it had to have been a sanctioned incineration which in turn meant that someone had tipped off the Enforcers about stored contraband.

This thought worried Arthur more than any material concern for the old truck even though it was their ticket out. He regularly visited the garage to check the battery charge and to crank the engine over so as to keep the tired old machine from seizing up altogether. If someone had been watching his neighbour they could have just as easily reported him.

Although he owned the truck legally and had all his permits in order he knew the Enforcers would act first and ask questions later and a chill shivered though Arthur's bones imagining his poor Alice being dragged out to the street as the Enforcers raided their home while another unit raced to catch him with the truck. It was just a touch of paranoia he knew but suddenly he felt a sense of urgency and trusting his gut wasted no further time in thought and loaded a few tools and two five gallon fuel cans full of diesel into the rusted load area of the truck covering them with an oily canvas tarp to hide them from casual observation.

He jumped into the cab, inserted the ignition key, waited for the heater plugs to warm then fired up the old turbo diesel engine which after a few turns and a couple of dabs on the throttle started with a cough of black smoke then settled into a reassuring rhythm.

'That's my girl,' said Arthur patting the dashboard and he pushed the heavy clutch pedal down, engaged first gear and rolled out into the daylight. He looked out through the narrow windscreen to be sure no one was around then jumped out to lock the garage door and left the engine running to warm then quickly climbed back in the cab and drove off slowly, resisting the urge to race the aged machine back to Alice.

Although it only took a few minutes to pull up in front of his house and lock the truck it seemed like over an hour. He ran into the house and met Alice in the hallway then without saying a word pulled her close and held her tightly to him as if he hadn't seen her in a year.

'What's the matter Arthur? Is everything okay?' asked Alice picking up on her husband's anxiety.

Arthur pulled back from Alice but held her with a hand on each arm and looked into her kind eyes. 'All's okay my love; I just had a bad feeling is all. Now, are you ready? Let's hit the road.'

They worked quickly and in just a few minutes all the bags and cases and jugs of liquor were loaded into the flatbed at the back of the truck and secured with ropes and elasticated cords. Alice put on her thick wool coat and a warm hat and carried the food bag into the cab with her as

Arthur locked the front door of their house for the last time then climbed into the driver seat. Before he started the engine he turned to his wife.

'I love you Alice, you know that right?'

'Oh you soppy old fool, are we going to sit here all day?' laughed Alice but the sparkle in her eyes told Arthur all he needed to know and he fired up the truck and started on the road to whatever lay ahead.

Arthur drove quickly but carefully through the busy streets taking his time to get familiar with the nuances of the old truck, she was big and basic but handled well enough at the pace he was driving. It had been a several years since he'd last driven any vehicle and that had been a forklift unloading supplies at the docks during a few months' work he'd been offered. Even so it's a skill that never really leaves a person and both he and Alice were enjoying the thrill of driving around streets with very few other cars since private vehicles were rare now and most other vehicles were government supply trucks or public buses. The old Land Rover wasn't paid much attention since Land Rovers were the standard Enforcer patrol vehicle and people were used to seeing them daily. The dented body panels and smoking exhaust of Arthur's truck showed it to be just one more heap of junk running itself to the grave which meant it was relatively inconspicuous and therefore relatively safe transport for their journey.

It was mid-morning as they entered downtown and Arthur was glad they had avoided the rush where the streets would have been thick with pedestrians jostling and pushing each other to make it to offices, factories or schools.

'Where do they all come from, I mean if nobody has any money and everyone is supposed to be at work where do all these people come from?' asked Arthur aloud.

'They're just people Arthur, they're getting on with their lives as best as they can. It's depressing though isn't it, I'm so glad we're leaving. There's really nothing left for us here.'

The old couple drove on in silence staring out at the people who wore faces as grey and lifeless as the buildings they mindlessly populated, slaves to lives barely lived.

As they followed the labyrinthine traffic system Arthur fought to keep his sense of direction.

'It's no bloody wonder people don't drive anymore, we've gone further north than west but I can't make a turn anywhere to get back on the route to the west gate,' he said angrily, cursing the city under his breath.

'We'll get there, we're making good time. Just try to take it easy and watch your blood pressure. I don't want you having heart attack before we even get past the gate.'

'Oh great, now we're stuck behind a bloody bus. That's it, I'm taking the next left turn wherever it leads and getting off the main streets, I'll be better following my own bearings than the damn road markings.'

'Arthur, look out!' screamed Alice. 'Oh my God, Arthur, did you see? Oh that poor woman, is she alright, can you see?'

Before Arthur got a chance to make the next turn the bus in front of their truck suddenly braked hard and the rear of the long vehicle fishtailed across the road blocking their path. Arthur stood hard on the brakes almost slamming into the back of the bus as he brought the heavy vehicle to a stop just inches from a collision.

'What the hell? Never mind out there, are you okay? We nearly crashed. What's going on love, are you alright?' he asked more concerned about Alice than the incident on the street.

'Why is nobody helping her? Look, they're all just walking past like nothing happened! Arthur what's wrong with people?' Alice seemed to be in shock and staring out the windscreen at the bus but at the same time was scrabbling desperately for the door release and before Arthur could stop her she was out of the truck and running toward the accident.

Arthur shouted after her as he snatched the keys from the

ignition and jumped from the truck to follow.

'Alice, no, leave it alone. Alice! Come back, we have to get out of here,' but even as he shouted he knew he couldn't stop her.

Alice froze when she approached the bus, the carnage stopping her in her tracks she stared in disbelief. 'She's dead Arthur, she's dead.' Tears gently rolled down Alice's face as she sobbed quietly.

A young woman, Alice guessed maybe early thirties had been hit by the bus and her body lay half under it, twisted and broken, blood still pooling around the warm corpse as it ran from her mangled remains. Arthur quickly stood in front of his wife and held her close to him gently pushing her face into his shoulder to prevent her from seeing any more of the gruesome spectacle but it was too late, no one could ever wash this scene from their mind.

As Arthur took a few moments to comfort his wife he looked around, recalling the words Alice had shouted as she climbed from the cab of the truck and he thought to himself 'What is wrong with these people? Isn't anyone even the slightest bit concerned?' but he knew the answer to that.

'Hell, if it wasn't for Sam I'd be just another dead body queued up in Central Disposal myself,' he thought. He looked around and saw the only signs of any interest were a few street security cameras pointed toward the bus and a shop assistant nervously glancing at the twitching remains under the bus while he swept broken glass from the street outside a supermarket.

Alice regained her composure and Arthur looked from the street to the bus driver. Through the blood streaked windscreen he could see the driver hadn't moved and just sat staring blankly through the glass.

'Hey, you okay mate?' Arthur shouted. The driver didn't respond so Arthur tried rapping the side window. 'Hey, buddy?' but still nothing. As he watched he saw a male passenger approach the driver and attempt to communicate.

In the distance now Arthur could hear the sirens of an

Enforcer patrol heading in their direction. 'Alice, we can't get involved in this. If the Enforcers think we were involved in any way the truck will be taken, we'll be interrogated and you know there'd likely be worse to follow.'

'It's just so awful Arthur, I saw her run out from the shop there and then it was all over so fast.'

'I know love but we have to go,' said Arthur leading his wife by the shoulders as quickly but as gently as he could. He helped her up into the cab then reaching into an inside pocket of his coat pulled out a steel hipflask with a worn leather cover, unscrewed the lid and gave it to her.

'Take a good sip, it'll help.'

He ran round the front of the truck pulling the keys from his side pocket and jumped into the cab, quickly started the engine and shoved the gearbox into reverse. The sirens were so close now he knew he had little time to back up and turn. As the crowds continued to pass around them seemingly oblivious to all but their own thoughts Arthur selected first gear and was about to pull away in the direction they had come when an Enforcer patrol screeched to a halt beside them. There was nothing they could do and Arthur knew it so he grabbed the hip flask from his wife, kissed her and then took a large swig to ready himself for what was coming.

The Enforcers sprang from their armoured patrol wagon but ignored Arthur and Alice instead focusing their attention on the bus. Husband and wife turned to look at each other not sure of what was happening. Arthur could have driven off but that would certainly have compounded their appearance of guilt and besides, the tired old diesel in his truck was no match for the three and a half litre V8 petrol engines fitted to patrol wagons so they turned further to watch through the back window of the pickup.

Arthur thought it strange how the Enforcers arrived so quickly for an accident in the Dreg quarters but then didn't show interest in the cause of the accident at all yet had shotguns ready as passengers screamed, panicked and fled the bus through a broken side window. They pushed the passengers roughly aside shouting for them to get down. Whatever the reason for the Enforcers presence, the bus was their main concern. Suddenly the street echoed with gunfire and Arthur instinctively pulled Alice down behind the seat in the cab of the truck.

'What the hell is going on?' he said, his mind racing, fearing for Alice more than himself.

Almost immediately after the shots were fired the Enforcers made their way back to their patrol wagon and as he heard them approach Arthur looked up from behind the seat again. He heard the squad commander order a clean-up and then some garbled message came back over the radio. As the terrified husband and wife looked on from their truck all four Enforcers scrambled back into their vehicle and the driver started up the powerful engine, turned sharply then sped off with sirens blaring leaving wounded bus passengers, uncaring pedestrians and a bewildered elderly couple in their wake.

Arthur took another long drink from the hip flask and passed it to his wife. 'I don't know what that was about but it's a sure sign we need to get the hell out of here right now.'

'Arthur, get us away from this horrible place,' Alice said grimacing as she took another sip from her husband's flask.

The engine was still running so Arthur slammed the truck into gear and drove off fast, plotting his own route through the city and ignoring traffic signs. Alice held tight to the door handle and steadied herself with a hand on the dashboard as Arthur threw the old machine around corners as fast as he dared, conscious of the valuable cargo in the rear and the more precious cargo sitting beside him.

Soon Arthur could see the top of the west bridge and shortly after they were rumbling along the cracked concrete road leading across the stretch of waste ground between the buildings on the city's fringe and the oppressive perimeter wall. 'One more obstacle to overcome,' thought Arthur trying to suppress his less than optimistic feelings about their chances.

As he rolled the truck to a gentle stop in front of the red and white steel barrier hoping in a moment to see it raised he said quietly to Alice. 'Just leave the talking to me, I know what these type are like.'

'No you don't, you've no idea what they're like, what are you talking about. Did you see what they did back there at the bus? They didn't care about that poor girl and who knows who they killed on the bus afterward,' snapped Alice understandably upset about what she had witnessed shortly before.

The gate guard walked around the front of the truck and Arthur could see he was quite young, guessing he was probably a new recruit.

'Look, I know, I understand but we're in this together as always and shouldn't be bickering. Oh hell, and look at this snot nosed little shit. Come on we're nearly out now, try and stay calm until we're through the gate at least.'

'I know, I'm sorry Arthur,'

'I'm sorry too, sorry either of us had to see any of that but we're almost out now. Ah crap, here goes, just play along.'

'Travel papers and ID please,' snapped the young Enforcer as Arthur wound the interior handle to open the window on the truck.

'Yes sir, here you are,' said Arthur handing the guard his identity card and a folded document listing the warranty terms and conditions for an old dishwasher he and Alice had bought twenty years ago.

The gate guard looked incredulously at the document he had been handed and then back to Arthur's wrinkled smiling face.

'Is there a problem officer?' asked Arthur in his most charming manner as Alice realising her husband was up to one his stupid stunts cringed in the seat beside him.

'Is this supposed to be some kind of a joke?' asked the guard waving the meaningless document in Arthur's face.

'Eh, no, not at all officer,' answered Arthur taking back

the paper and making a show of squinting and holding it closer then further from his eyes as if trying to read it better. 'Well I'm so embarrassed, my apologies officer, these aren't my papers at all.'

'I'm well aware these are not your papers and can only assume you are travelling without a permit in an unlicensed vehicle while medically unfit to do so. And while we're on the subject, I believe I can smell alcohol on your breath.'

The new recruit could hardly believe his luck, so many offences in a single stop this would be his first major arrest.

'Under Protocol Nine, section four you are hereby detained. You have no further rights. Your vehicle will be searched and impounded prior to destruction and any further offences discovered will be added to your charge,' he snapped with a sickening arrogance. 'You are ordered to disembark the vehicle and obey all commands,' he barked pathetically while stepping back and aiming his shotgun from the shoulder through the open side window of the truck.

'Whoa, easy, take it easy,' said Arthur raising his hands and reaching slowly through the window to open the door using the outer handle. 'Just relax, we're cooperating here but we're old so it takes a little longer is all. See, I'm getting out, nice and slow.'

'Sorry love,' he said looking sheepishly at Alice as she opened her door and carefully slid out.

'Leave it to me, you said,' mocked Alice, rolling her eyes as she stepped carefully around the front of the truck.

As the young guard ordered the elderly couple to line up facing the wall they heard an older voice shout from the guard hut.

'Hamilton, leave whatever you're doing, you're needed in the city.'

'But sir, I have made an arrest and protocol dictates it is my right to process these criminals accordingly. I will attend to my duties in the city when I'm finished here sir.'

'Protocol dictates I can stick my boot up your arse for not following orders!' snarled the older guard as he stormed out from the guard house, his face reddening with anger. 'A call came over the radio, all patrols have been ordered to assist in a major incident downtown and Perimeter Patrol Delta is, ah, here they are now, that's your ride Hamilton, now get to it.'

A patrol wagon pulled to an abrupt halt by the gate and the rear doors were flung open as squad commander jumped down from the front passenger seat. 'You Hamilton?' he said gesturing to the younger of the two gate guards then without waiting for a reply. 'Well, get in.'

The new recruit was swept along with the momentum and dared not question the order of a squad commander so obediently jumped into the back of the waiting truck. The commander and older gate guard casually exchanged salutes and with that the Enforcer patrol wagon shot off at high speed toward the city leaving Arthur and Alice in the hands of the more experienced officer.

The guard circled the truck and eyeballed the old pair as he spoke. 'Well, what seems to be the problem? Not too common to see a civilian vehicle but not unusual either I suppose. One male, one female occupant, married I assume.'

Arthur just nodded saying nothing but relieved thinking to himself. 'Now this is the kind of guard I know how to handle.'

'And what have we here?' said the old guard pulling back the canvas tarp to reveal six gallon jugs of Arthur's bootleg booze. 'Oh, this is some serious contraband. You're in a lot of trouble now I'm sure you know. I'll need to see some ID and your travel papers.'

Arthur took a chance and spoke. 'Well sir, we gave our papers to your junior officer and I'm afraid he didn't give them back, he took them with him in the patrol wagon.'

The guard rubbed the back of neck and looked to the sky obviously believing his idiot apprentice capable of such stupidity.

Arthur continued. 'The truck is mine, had her years but she doesn't get much use these days. We're actually heading for Raven City, my sister's boy had a little girl and my wife and I have been asked to be godparents. That's the reason for the hooch, you know, something to celebrate with.'

'Sorry sir but I can't let you pass without travel papers and absolutely not with this illegal alcohol. Your truck will be impounded and I'll personally see to the destruction of this contraband. Since my partner confiscated your papers I'll be lenient and allow you both to return to the city on foot where you can apply for replacement documents.'

Arthur was taken aback, he'd managed to talk his way around problems before but now their chances lay in ruins. He knew they were lucky not to be arrested but they couldn't leave the city without stamped travel documents and without the truck they'd never make it across the country. He was weighing up the options of pleading or delivering a well-timed head-butt when he heard Alice speak in a smooth silky voice he hadn't heard since the last time they'd tested the bed springs.

'I know you're just doing your job officer, a man in uniform doing his duty,' she said walking slowly toward him, flirty eyes holding his gaze then shyly looking away. She looked ten years younger than her true age and she radiated a beauty that had not faded with time. The old guard was like a mouse mesmerised by a cobra as Alice used all the tricks she usually reserved for Arthur when she wanted to encourage her man to the bedroom.

'I'm sure your wife knows she has a real man for a husband, a man who knows how to take care of a woman. I'm right aren't I?'

The guard stammered 'Y-y-yeah, eh, that's right,' embarrassed, surprised and delighted by the attention all in the same moment.

'My husband here isn't a professional man like you but he makes some fine whiskey. Imagine how pleased your wife will be when you tell her you brought home some of the finest liquor in town. She could trade it for new shoes, a new dress, maybe something a little more delicate eh?' and she stroked his arm, leaning her head slightly to the side, looking into his eyes giving him a little smile.

The old guard flushed red now, he'd never been spoken to like this by anyone but he was clearly enjoying it despite his embarrassment. Arthur couldn't believe what he was seeing but knew to keep his mouth firmly shut.

Alice reached into the back of the truck and lifted a container of the liquor then pulled the stopper out with her teeth and with a finger through the ear of the jug rested it on her forearm as she took a swig.

'Oh that is good. Here, try a little, I won't tell,' she said giving the open jug to the guard and doing her absolute best not to scrunch up her face as usual while the powerful liquid ran into her stomach.

'Well, I suppose a little drop wouldn't hurt. Who am I to refuse a drink from a lady?'

'Bloody hell, she's got him,' Arthur thought to himself knowing it was only an act but still fighting back pangs of jealously.

'You have another drink; a hardworking man like you deserves it. I just hope your wife knows how good you are to her. She's a very lucky woman. What's your name soldier?'

'Um, Phillip, mam,' replied the guard completely intoxicated but not from the whiskey.

'Well, Phil, she's a very lucky woman, believe me. Why don't you have a seat, it must be hard work out here. We'll unload a few bottles for you and get out of your way.'

'Oh, no I can't let you do that,' protested the guard half-heartedly as he took another pull from the jug.

'Aw Phillip, we were getting on so well. Why would you want to bother yourself over a lady and her old man? I just want to see my godson, I'm sure if you told your wife how compassionate you were today she'd be very understanding.' Alice looked up seductively batting her eye lashes. 'I know I would be.'

The old guard coughed and nearly spat whiskey over himself, Alice had him so tied up he didn't know what to do but Arthur was following his wife's lead and already started unloading two more of his precious jugs. Seeing three gallons of the fine liquor lined out in front of him and struggling to control a growing bulge in his trousers the guard looked to Alice.

'Mam, I couldn't do you the disservice of delaying you any longer,' and he moved quickly to the guard hut to raise the barrier.

'Quick, get in the truck,' Alice whispered to Arthur who didn't need to be told and was already rushing to climb into the driver's seat. He started the engine and moved forward even as the barrier was rising and before Alice had even closed her door. As the guard came back to collect the remaining jugs he waved to Alice as she leaned out of the truck and blew him a kiss

'What an idiot,' she said still smiling back at old Phillip.

'What the hell was that?' asked Arthur shocked at his wife's award winning performance and still feeling a little jealous.

'Well you'd completely cocked it up so somebody had to get us out of there!' teased Alice.

'And it only cost me three jugs of booze and my wife's honour.'

Alice laughed. 'You're lucky, I was planning to give him a lap dance in his office,'

'Shut up,' said Arthur pretending to sulk but they both knew he was stunned by the amazing woman beside him.

Arthur floored the accelerator and the reliable old diesel quickened the pace and carried them over the dilapidated bridge out of the city and onto the road toward their new life.

CHAPTER 10

Lucy Nolan sat alone in her bedroom. The net-screen still flickered on the wall where she had muted the volume but not shut it off after checking her messages and an irritating flashing advertisement had caught her peripheral vision distracting her. She crossed the room to turn off the screen when notification of an incoming video call from Sam appeared. She accepted the call immediately and her spirits soared until she saw the fresh wound on his face.

During their call Sam reassured her he would be fine, she didn't believe him but knew he didn't like her fussing over him. He seemed distracted and during their coded conversation spoke of things that at first didn't make sense to Lucy but she quickly caught his meaning and understood the plan. Something had happened and they both had to meet urgently. She hoped he would not be in danger but Sam was tough and stubborn and whatever he had in mind she knew he'd find some way of making it work. She had so much she needed to say to him too but it would have to wait now. Before she ended the call she told Sam she loved him and that she would tell him everything when they were together.

She turned the screen off and sat again on the edge of her bed. It was all too much to take in, after such heartache and feeling absolutely alone it was all now happening at once. She was overjoyed that she would soon be with Sam again but first she had to find a way out of the city. Until two days ago she had no reason to stay but now what was she to do? She couldn't stay but she couldn't leave and she couldn't explain any of it to Sam until they could speak in person since any eavesdropping over the network would surely lead to both their arrests and swift disappearances.

As she sat in silence, her brain locked up and unable to think, the empty house still echoed with memories of her Aunt Susan who had died only six weeks earlier despite Lucy's best efforts caring for her and the limited medicines they could find and afford. At least her death had been peaceful and she passed away in her sleep, a final release from the pain she had been suffering for this past year.

Lucy wished her aunt were still here to offer her the sage advice that always seemed to make sense of even the darkest problem. At twenty-seven Lucy's short life so far had been full of tragedy beginning with the death of her mother when Lucy was very young. She still remembered how upset her father had been and the months where it seemed their life would never get past that terrible event but her father was strong and provided a good life for her and Aunt Susan who took care of Lucy after her mother passed. Although they were poor Lucy wanted for nothing.

Lucy felt as though she was going to lose her mind but was distracted from her dilemma as she stared at her dressing table, her gaze falling upon framed photos of happier times, the smiling portraits of her father and her aunt, a faded picture of Lucy as a toddler with her parents which was the only picture she had of her mother and she was glad it was one in which they were all together, they had been a normal family at least at one time. Her mother had been incredibly beautiful and passed her looks on to Lucy even though she was too modest to see that in herself.

The most recent picture from only a few years ago showed a happy couple standing waist deep in crystal blue waters posing for a photo while wearing snorkel masks. Clear skies and a pristine beach lined with palm trees and little beach huts were just visible in the background. One of

Lucy's last happy memories was preserved here in a photograph of her and Sam from when they travelled around the mainland together.

They returned home, cutting their trip short when Lucy had received a message from Aunt Susan that her brother, Lucy's father had been killed following his arrest and interrogation by the Enforcers. For Lucy the news had been devastating, she had cried herself to the point of numbness on the long road to Rook City. Sam had been wonderful and stood by her but kept to the background, giving her the space she needed to grieve and helped her find the strength to carry on.

She remembered when Aunt Susan had come back to Rook City to help clear out the family home when Lucy decided she couldn't live any longer with the haunting memories. Susan had sorted through personal belongings and documents while Lucy organised her father's clothing and anything that might be donated to some of the few remaining homeless shelters. Sam volunteered and made himself busy cleaning, making tea and carrying boxes and bags while also trying not to intrude in the awkward way people do when in other people's homes following a death.

When everything had been dealt with and the house boarded up pending its unlikely sale Aunt Susan arranged transport with a supply trucker back to Raven City. Sam was crushed when Lucy decided to move to live with her aunt but he knew Susan was her only remaining family and didn't try to hold her back. Lucy had explained to him how she needed to go by herself, to get grounded again and to heal. Sam just told her gently that he understood, he loved her and he'd wait for as long it takes.

They had kept in contact by net-screen and Sam had even managed to visit once for a couple of weeks. The couple savoured every precious moment together which made parting all the more heart-breaking, leaving a hole in both their lives deeper than it had been before. They both knew they loved each other and that although sometimes life got in the way if they could just hold on somehow it would all work out.

When Aunt Susan fell sick Sam offered to move to Raven City and help Lucy but she said it was something she had to deal with by herself. 'It's a family thing', she'd told him but in reality Lucy desperately wanted Sam by her side but felt she couldn't burden him further. She promised that when Aunt Susan recovered a little they could talk about Sam moving in or maybe they could find a place nearby so they would be close to Susan but for now she needed her space and Sam being Sam, he agreed.

She sometimes worried about him living on his own in Rook City but she knew Sam was one of those rare people who were actually happy in solitude, a natural born loner she called him. She knew though that Sam loved her and missed her as much as she missed him.

Since Aunt Susan had died she felt like she'd been hollowed out, her soul ached with despair. She hadn't told Sam yet and she put on a brave face when they talked over the net-screen enjoying their conversations as the only ray of light and comfort in her dark, cold life. She had felt her dear Sam was the only thing she had left in the world but what life could they have in either of the two crumbling cities. With the borders closed and no civilian travel to the mainland permitted for over three years now they were trapped but she knew if they could just be together that would be enough.

But now things had changed. During the weeks since her aunt's death Lucy had worked alone this time carefully sorting and packing and organising each detail of Susan's life giving each item due attention before putting it to rest. The process was helping Lucy to come to terms with things and slowly, piece by piece she said goodbye. Only two days earlier while clearing a top shelf in her aunt's wardrobe Lucy found an old cardboard shoebox with an elastic band holding the lid closed. When she lifted it down she was surprised to find a letter taped to the lid with the words 'To Lucy' written on the envelope in her aunt's handwriting. After reading the letter for the third time she began reading through the all the other letters her aunt had provided her in the shoebox. Her mind struggled to comprehend what she had discovered but her heart longed for it to be true.

How was she going to tell Sam that poor Aunt Susan had died but had left her with amazing news? Although she was raised as an only child Lucy had a half-sister! In the shoebox were scores of love letters written to her father. In her letter Aunt Susan had explained how she found them when sorting through her father's belongings and had wanted to spare Lucy the shock since she was still coping with her father's death. It was Aunt Susan's intention to tell her everything when the time was right but when diagnosed as terminally ill she didn't know how to break the news about her sickness and also tell of the secret she had kept so instead wrote a letter to Lucy telling what she felt she needed to know.

Aunt Susan's letter explained how after Lucy's mother died her father had become involved in an affair with Claudia Henderson, the wife of the head of the Upper Council. A child was born from the affair and the girl had been named Kathy. She had been raised as an Elite but she was the daughter of James Nolan, Lucy's father, making Kathy Lucy's half-sister. It was all there in the box, old love letters, photos of her father and Claudia together and many pictures of Kathy at different ages, the dates and her age written on the back of each photo allowing Lucy to see what her sister looked like and how she had grown. She was surprised to see that they looked similar to one another but realised there would of course be some family resemblance.

In the most recent picture taken about three years earlier Lucy could see that Kathy had her father's eyes. That was when she knew it was true and that she could not leave Raven City without finding her sister.

'What to do?' Lucy wondered to herself speaking into the silence as she had been doing for the past few weeks since Susan passed away. After a city disposal crew arrived to remove the body for cremation Lucy had been left alone with no one to talk to apart from occasional calls to Sam so even the sound of her own voice helped relieve the isolation.

'If I stay to find Kathy I'll not be there to meet Sam but if I leave how am I ever going to find Kathy? Oh Aunt Susan I wish you were here,' she said aloud to the empty rooms half hoping for some answer from beyond the grave but she knew this was one more dilemma she would have to work through on her own.

'Come on Lucy, think. You've got to do something or you'll turn into a crazy old lady living alone and collecting stray cats. How does Sam live like this?' she wondered, feeling the lack of human contact like a vacuum all around her.

Her mind in a spin and with only a few days until she was to meet Sam the approaching deadline drove her to make a decision. She left the letter from Aunt Susan and the shoebox of letters and photos on the bed and walked downstairs to the kitchen to make a cup of herbal tea to help her relax. The ritual of boiling water and brewing the hot beverage often helped her to feel calm and focus. As she stirred the last spoonful from a jar of a honey into the tea an idea crept into her mind that she almost immediately disregarded, the thought making her skin crawl but at the same instant she knew it was her best chance of meeting her sister and somehow explaining to her all she had just learned.

Lucy worked for a cleaning company from the Dreg sector which had operated for several years providing services to Elite office buildings and residential tower blocks. All of the employees had to pass a strict security clearance program as did all Dregs who were cleared to pass the sector barricades each morning to work in servitude to the Elites. The money was better than working in the Dreg factories and Lucy found that some of the customers could be pleasant enough if you did what was expected of you and did a good job. At least her crew were a good bunch of people;

some had even grown to trust each other, except for the boss, Andrew Harper.

Harper gave himself a higher than fair share of the earnings and kept the best contracts for himself meaning he skimmed off the biggest tips. He worked in all the best Elite buildings and sleazed his way to the top floors, finding some sick gratification from sucking up to the rich clientele. He never invited the male staff to clean these prestigious residences allowing only the prettiest girls to work along with him, something he turned to his favour by requiring a fee from the girls for this privilege.

The very idea made Lucy nauseous but she knew this would be her only chance to access Henderson's building and attempt to contact her sister. She had already asked Harper to allow her a few weeks off to manage her Aunt's funeral and even though she was obviously deeply upset and grieving he had made stomach churning advances toward her. Lucy knew the boss had a thing for her since she began working for him and felt she needed a shower after every moment in his presence.

One of Lucy's colleagues had warned her about him. 'You'll go far if you let him go far, that's how it works,' but she never accepted Harper's repeated offers which made him covert her all the more.

Lucy observed how a few of the girls who worked with Harper in the high rate apartments banded together in a clique seeming to consider themselves a higher class than the other workers but Lucy guessed it was how they justified what they did. If you met one of the girls alone the haunted look in their eyes told all, they were desperate like everyone else and doing whatever they had to in order to survive or provide for their family.

Staring into a mirror over the fireplace she fixed her hair and applied a little eye shadow to hide the tiredness before powering on the net-screen in the small living room and placed a call to her boss, half hoping he wouldn't answer but knowing she had no choice but to speak with him. Seeing her

ID appear on his screen Harper accepted the call immediately and greeted Lucy with a predatory smile.

'Well hello my gorgeous little lady, how are feeling? You know I've missed you. We've all missed you of course. Are you coming back to us soon?'

Fighting the urge to just hang up the call Lucy forced a smile. 'Hi Mr. Harper.'

'Come on Lucy, you know its Andrew, please.'

'Well, Andrew, I wanted to get in touch. Thank you for letting me have the time off but I was hoping I could come back to work, I was thinking tomorrow morning if that suited?'

'Of course Lucy, of course. I'll always have a place for a pretty little thing like you. I filled your space with a young man who Stephen recommended but I'll tell him he's out, you're back and that's all there is to it.'

'Oh I don't want to cause someone to lose their job over me Andrew,' Lucy paused while she composed herself and tried to affect a soft girlish voice. 'I was thinking, you've been very good to me and I'd like it if I could join you and the other girls, you know, in the special services team. Some of the girls tell me you even work in the Upper Council residential towers. I've always worked hard for you, I do a good job; you think I've earned it?' Lucy coiled her hair around her finger while she fawned over the screen playing to the fantasies of the pervert on the other end of the call.

'Sure you can, I'd be only delighted to have you join me, join us I mean. The girls won't be too happy about having you along, more competition for them but I'll see to it that you're welcomed in. Stay with me and I'll make sure you're well looked after.' Harper replied, practically drooling on his shirt. 'But why now, I always thought you weren't interested in making more money. I could never understand why you always seemed happier doing the dirty work with the regular cleaning crews in the factories and kitchens.'

'Well, I've had some time to think over the past few weeks and I realise now that you saw something in me and I should have taken you up on your offer a long time ago. Thanks for giving me another chance.'

'I'm just glad you've decided to join us at last. Well, you can meet me and the girls at the office at seven tomorrow morning. Just remember to wear something nice, something short. You know what I like, you've seen what the other girls wear and we have to look the good for the customer, present a professional image to keep their business. Very important you remember that. Okay?'

'Oh yes, of course, you're right. I'll see you in the morning then Andrew, and thanks again,' said Lucy ending the call feeling as though her soul had shrivelled with every word she had spoken.

Spurred on by necessity and a new found sense of purpose Lucy searched for something to wear for her new role at work then spent the rest of the day writing a letter to her sister. 'How do you tell someone you have never met that you're their sister?' she wondered but after several attempts and crumpled pages she had drafted the best explanation she could manage and slipped the letter into an envelope along with a photograph from the shoebox showing a teenage Kathy with her mother and another picture of Lucy with their father. She hoped it would be enough to allow Kathy to believe there may be some truth in the words she had written but Lucy knew she had only just begun to believe it herself.

Early the next morning with the envelope containing her letter and the pictures tucked into the small of her back under the waist band of her underwear Lucy waited for her employer to arrive. Many of the workers travelled directly to the sites they maintained but some arrived each morning at the supply depot where they trudged through the office to the stores beyond to gather cleaning supplies and other sanitation consumables which they loaded into trailers towed behind bicycles rickshaw style. Teams of three or four worked together and covered an area of the city each. It was an efficient system and with minimal overheads especially in factories where everything but the workforce was supplied. Among the teams was Lucy's old crew who were by now all good friends and when they learned Lucy had returned they showed genuine concern asking how she was bearing up after her aunt had died and enquired as to when she would be coming back on the crew.

Stephen who had been on the team for the longest and had recommended another of his friends to be Lucy's replacement was the first to comment.

'Hey Lucy, what's with the makeup and hair? A bit glamorous for blue overalls don't you think?'

'Shut up Stephen, she's only back from a rough few weeks; she just wants to feel good about herself, leave it be. You look lovely Lucy,' said Julianne, another girl on her old crew sticking up for her.

'Oh yeah, well I don't think she'll be scrubbing factory toilets and kitchen sinks in heels like that,' said Stephen pointing to black patent leather shoes with three inch heel. While not skyscraper stilettos they were certainly nothing like the old army surplus boots Lucy had always worn.

'Oh Lucy, you haven't?' said Julianne. 'Tell me you haven't signed up to Harper's tramp squad?'

'I'm sorry guys,' said Lucy feeling ashamed and wanting to explain to her friends the reasons for what she was doing but she knew she had to keep it to herself. Just a few days to get word to her sister, meet with Sam and then, well, then she'd see what happens next but they would all be together wouldn't they? She had no choice now.

'Look, it's not what you think, there's something going on, it's complicated. You'd understand if I could tell you about it but I can't, I'm sorry. It's just that,' but as Lucy spoke everyone turned to look through the office window as a dilapidated dark blue van with "Harper's Executive Cleaning Services" emblazoned along the side panels in flaking white lettering pulled up outside. The door slid back as four attractive girls in their mid-twenties, wearing short black low cut dresses, white pinafore aprons, high heels, too much makeup and too much attitude stepped out and were accompanied by Andrew Harper as he quickly hopped down from the driver's seat and raced ahead of them to greet Lucy.

'Lucy, Lucy, Lucy. So good to see you,' said Harper as he walked into the office pushing past the regular crew in their blue uniform overalls and pulled Lucy into an awkward hug. 'Now let's get a look at you my dear,' he said taking a step back and gesturing for her to remove her long winter coat.

As she unbuttoned the front of her black parka jacket she faked a smile for Harper and looked to her former workmates for support but not even Julianne attempted to hide her disgust at Lucy's selling out. Silently she implored her friends to please understand as she opened her coat to reveal a short black dress. It was one she had kept in her wardrobe from when she and Sam had been first dating and she had kept it for special occasions. It was a beautiful dress and Lucy looked stunning in it but now she felt disgusting, the most uncomfortable she had ever been as Harper's greedy eyes roamed over her body.

'When this is over,' she told herself, 'I'm going to burn this dress,' since now it had been tainted she could never feel good wearing it again.

'Oh yes, you look fantastic Lucy, yes indeed. We'll just need an apron for you and I have a temporary Elite sector gate pass for you. If you show the Enforcers at the gate along with your ID card they'll let you pass, as long as I vouch for you. You'd tell me if you've been a naughty girl wouldn't you?' Harper said with a crawling tone and a sickening glint in his eye.

As Lucy waited for her gate pass and uniform apron her old crew filed past her throwing filthy looks, the joy at seeing her again now turned sour.

Julianne paused and said to Lucy, 'I can't believe you're going to work with Harper. All those dirty old bastards grabbing your arse and watching you bend over to pick up their mess just for a few extra dollars. And what if they ask for some personal attention? Is that what you're doing now? Of all people Lucy I never thought you'd sell yourself over to that.'

'Julianne, it's not like that.'

'Then what? What is it like? You tell me what good reason you have for leaving your crew to whore yourself like a little dolled up maid for those rich bastards. What's worse is giving in to that pervert Harper; he's the biggest slime of them all.'

'I'm sorry Julianne, I wish I could make you understand but I can't tell you, I'm really sorry.'

With that Julianne left saying nothing further but banged shoulders with Harper as she passed him on his way into the office with the uniform apron and ID for Lucy.

'Watch it,' Harper shouted after Julianne. 'You're easy to replace, drop the attitude.'

As she walked away Julianne flipped the bird over her shoulder which amused her colleagues and angered Harper who made a mental note to deal with her later in private.

Lucy found her first day back at work absolutely demeaning. At the sector barrier gate her temporary gate pass caused an alert and she was ordered out of the van and patted down by two Enforcers each taking their time with her, removing their gloves to run their hands up her legs, groping her bottom and breasts while the other girls in the van coldly looked on.

Staring into the side mirror Harper felt a burning jealousy surfacing from the fantasies he had of Lucy, of how he longed to do the same and more. He knew he couldn't stop the Enforcers so said nothing but only his fear of being arrested forced him to exercise great restraint for if another man had done the same Harper would have killed him. As far as he was concerned Lucy was his now and he planned that someday soon he would have her all for himself. Until then he would share her only with the Elites and even then only with those who paid.

All day they drove through the Elite sector according to that day's schedule working in various personal palaces each one grander than anything Lucy had ever seen, the contrast between even the most homely Dregs sector housing and the cheapest of the Elite's quarters like night and day. Harper amused himself by making sleazy, smutty remarks any time he opened his mouth or spent the time as the girls worked trying to ingratiate himself with the rich men who paid to have their homes cleaned by a team of pretty girls in short dresses. He told the girls he was there to be sure the work was completed satisfactorily and to be sure the customer didn't get too "hands-on" with the help but of course he only laughed when one of the high powered customers got frisky and grabbed a handful of buttock or pretended to accidentally brush past a breast while reaching for something on a shelf the very moment one of the girls was there to dust.

It was all part of the game for Harper and Lucy figured it was just a way for these rich men to get a cheap thrill until half way through the job at the first Elite apartment the owner, a skeleton of a man with a sickly grey completion pointed a bony finger toward one of the girls as she wiggled her behind while dusting a baby grand piano in the luxury living quarters.

'That one,' was all he said and Harper immediately approached the girl who had been chosen.

'Lydia, you're up,' said Harper as he put an arm around the girl's waist and brought her to the thin man as he unsteadily made his way toward the staircase. The girl remained expressionless and made no attempt to show warmth or affection instead seeming to withdraw even further into herself.

Seeing the frail old figure lead the young girl to his bedroom Lucy knew what she had gotten herself involved in. She had known what went on before she agreed to join Harper's special inner group or at least she had told herself the rumours were exaggerated but seeing it happen now in front of her she no longer felt angry at the bitter reception she received from the other girls. She pitied them for the life they lived and at the same time a ball of fear grew in the pit of her stomach thinking how she could be chosen at random by one of these disgusting men. She wanted to drop everything and run, to get home and scrub herself in the hottest of baths but she knew this was her only hope of getting close to her sister.

'Sometimes they don't choose anyone,' said one of the other girls, 'sometimes they just like to watch us work. If you do get chosen its extra money for Harper and you get your share but if you refuse to take a client Harper has your details from the security clearance background check, he threatens to report your family for harbouring gang members or illegal weapons or anything else he dreams up. He threatened to have my little boy taken from me, said he knew the Enforcers were taking children into their training camps as young as four now.'

'He can't do that can he?' asked Lucy. 'Besides, what would the Enforcers want with children? There aren't enough resources to manage the streets as it is without raising kids in some special recruitment camp. It sounds more like he's just trying to scare you.'

'I don't want to believe him but I can't take the chance, my boy is only six and his father was sent to the prison farms just after he was born. He's all I've got, I pay the old lady next door to mind him while I work and I have to try to make enough to feed us both and give him some kind of life. What else can I do?'

Lucy knew desperation forced people to things they would never otherwise consider and her own situation was no better. At least it would be only a few days for her, not years like some of the other poor girls. 'I just need to get a message to Kathy them I'm getting away from all of this,' she thought as she heard the muffled grunts from upstairs and the knot in her stomach tightened.

For the next couple of days Lucy tried to keep out of sight of the customers while she worked in each towering glass fronted mansion. The other girls had been in the job long enough that they accepted what Harper described as "special duties" and actually worked their bodies seductively vying for the attentions of the rich clients hoping for the additional income it would earn them. For this Lucy was glad as it meant she could keep in the side lines, work in areas of the homes that kept her from view and minimised her chances of being selected.

By the third morning Lucy had been accepted by the other girls on the team since they saw she wasn't keen to move in on their racket. As long as they satisfied the customers Harper got his extra revenue and Lucy stayed safe by doing her usual excellent cleaning tasks and flirting with Harper when he made crude comments about her figure or suggested she should try to impress the clients. After two jobs had been completed and none of the girls had been selected Harper was anxious to up the game and make his earnings for the day.

As Harper drove the old van through the bustling streets the girls looked out at the exclusive boutique shops, the fine clothes and newest styles of the Elite society women. There were expensive salons, cafes, windows full of chocolate temptations and delicate fabrics in an array of colours and textures. The glamour of it all struck Lucy but she wasn't seduced by the facade of riches, she knew happiness couldn't be bought in a store but all the same she couldn't help imagine herself meeting Sam wearing one of the gorgeous dresses she saw in a window as they stopped at a junction.

'You'll have to take on a few private sessions with the clients if you want one of those,' said Harper glancing in the rear view mirror and noticing Lucy's attention on the dress. 'Even the old stock we get on the black market would cost you several weeks' standard pay but you could earn that in a few days if you applied yourself.'

Lucy looked into the sickened soul reflected through the

eyes staring at her in the mirror then quickly glanced down at her hands knitted together on her knees as she sat sandwiched between the other girls in the crew seat of the van. The glare from her new colleagues and the smell of bleach, damp mops and other cleaning materials brought her back to her current reality with a snap.

'I'll try Mr. Harper, I mean Andrew, I'll try,' said Lucy quietly hoping not to encourage Harper or antagonise the other girls.

'Okay girls, it's the big tower today,' said Harper as the traffic lights changed and he turned onto a wide tree lined avenue with malls and stores even more grand than the other streets they had passed that morning. Lucy could see through the windscreen ahead the gleaming tower block, a massive vertical monument to decadence and she leaned her head toward the van's side window trying to look to the top of the building. The big tower as Harper called it was the tallest most exclusive tower in the city and one for which Harper had fought hard against other pimps to secure the right for only his girls to work. Crowned with the massive penthouse where the Henderson's lived it was where Lucy knew she would find her sister.

The bored Enforcer on sentry duty at the barrier to the car park beneath the tower took a quick glance at the ID cards of the girls and accepted the hundred dollar note Harper passed to him before raising the barrier and allowing them to pass. The guard was used to seeing the same old van arrive each week at around the same time and accepted the weekly pay-off which Harper handed over to ensure no questions were asked about work permits or about the paraphernalia some of the girls brought with them.

Harper parked the van in a visitor space and the girls stepped out onto the concrete floor, the clicking of heels echoing around the cavernous structure. All around were high-end sports cars and luxury saloons and Lucy noticed many were covered with white cotton tarpaulins she presumed to protect the near priceless vehicles from dust or perhaps just from prying eyes. Few of the cars were ever driven now as the Elites rarely left their cities for fear of outlaws beyond the city walls so much of the more exotic machinery sat unused.

Lucy quickly set about unloading her cleaning cart from the back of the van to avoid another jibe from Harper about her earning potential with the rich clients. As she tied her apron she adjusted the position of the hidden letter she had written for Kathy so it sat comfortably at her back and she felt excited to think she might be passing it to her sister in just a few hours.

When the girls all had their individual carts ready, some with a spare bag of additional equipment tailored to their client's known fetish all made their way to the lift with Harper. He pressed the button for the first apartment on today's rota and the doors closed sealing them in the cramped metal box but the lift didn't move and instead a screen flickered to life displaying a hard, lined face and cruel eyes.

'Yes?' was the terse greeting over the intercom.

Harper spoke in a grovelling tone. 'Ah, Mr. Madsen, it's Andrew Harper for your weekly cleaning appointment. I have the girls with me if you could buzz us up.'

'I can see you have a new girl Harper, anything I should know about?'

Lucy looked around as discreetly as she could and saw the small black dome of a security camera protruding from the ceiling. As with other Elite residential blocks the upper floors could only be accessed by outsiders if they had thumbprint authorisation or were permitted access after visual identification by an apartment owner. If there were any problems the lift doors would be sealed until an Enforcer patrol arrived and removed the intruders for processing.

'Nothing unusual Mr. Madsen, just a new girl on the team but I can vouch for her, she has her papers and she passed screening as always,' Harper replied nervously.

Without another word the screen went blank and the carriage began to ascend rapidly until six floors from the penthouse the lift stopped and the doors opened onto a magnificent entrance hall. A plush emerald green carpet lined with expensive mahogany stands of various sizes holding priceless antiquities greeted guests upon their arrival. Being careful not to disturb anything the cleaning girls sauntered into the apartment in an orderly line looking more like a cabaret dance troupe and as they passed the client each greeted him with a husky 'Hello Mr. Madsen,' before setting to work in various areas cleaning, polishing, and dusting, all but Lucy ensuring to pull necklines down and hemlines up while they went about their tasks.

As Harper talked with the client briefly and the other girls got to work Lucy followed the tactic that she'd used so far and made straight for the kitchen. She would be out of sight of the client where she was able to get on with her job and leave the other girls to compete with each other for the attentions of the man with the cash.

'Harper, I'd like a little something extra today if you would be so good as to arrange it,' said Madsen from his reclined position on the leather sofa where he was watching the girls.

'Of course Mr. Madsen, and who has caught your eye?'

'The new girl, where is she? I saw her come in; she seems shyer than the others, a quality it might be fun to explore. Bring her to me Harper.'

'Ah you mean Lucy, she's just been with us a few days Mr. Madsen, perhaps one of the more experienced girls would be to your liking?' said Harper, uncomfortable with the thought of Lucy and another man together but knowing he had little influence over the request.

'Bring the new girl,' said Madsen in a voice that told Harper he would not tolerate having to ask again.

'Yes Mr. Madsen, I'll go and find her. Please forgive me, I'll not be long.' Harper knew the trouble he would find himself in for not complying with an Elite client wouldn't be worth keeping his prize to himself and so walked straight to the kitchen where he knew Lucy would be hiding. 'Lucy? Lucy? There you are my sweet. Come now, Mr. Madsen would like to meet you in person. This is your chance to earn something toward that pretty new dress.'

Lucy froze with terror, she couldn't do this. It was one thing to be leered at and even groped, she could find a way to live with that if it meant finding her sister but not this, she wouldn't have sex with a strange man for money, not for anything, not like this. Lucy had only slept with two other men besides Sam and she was even a little uncomfortable around him if the light was on.

'I can't Mr. Harper, please I can't,' she begged. 'The other girls would be better to look after him, I can't give him what he wants, please Andrew, ask one of the other girls.'

'Lucy Mr. Madsen is our customer and he's asked for you specifically, the customer is always right and he wants you. Now come on, just come out and talk with him, I'll come with you, it'll be fine, you'll see.'

Realising she had to go through the main living quarters again to get to the exit Lucy knew she had no choice but to walk past the hard faced man who planned to do who knows what with her.

'Okay, I'm coming, I'll follow you out, please go first Andrew,' she said trying to placate her boss. As Harper turned his back Lucy lifted a small kitchen knife from the sink and tucked it into a fold under the waist ties of her apron thinking at least it would allow her to fend off unwanted advances if she was physically forced to do things against her will.

Once in the main living area the other girls saw Harper leading Lucy from the kitchen and they knew she had been chosen by the client. Instead of the icy stares they had thrown before the girls now looked at her with sympathy knowing this would be her first time and remembering how hard it had been for them.

'Mr. Madsen, this is Lucy,' said Harper as matter-of-factly

as introducing his mother to an old friend, completely unaffected by the implications of what he was doing and thinking only of the cash reward that Lucy would earn him.

'Very pretty,' said Madsen rising from the sofa. 'Come with me Lucy, there's something I want to show you,' and he placed his arm around her shoulder to guide her toward the corridor leading to the master bedroom.

Lucy resisted, shrugging the arm from her shoulders and turning to face Madsen. She kept the knife rolled in the folds of her apron but spoke quickly and apologetically. 'I'm sorry Mr. Madsen, I'm not feeling very well. Please, I can't.'

Madsen grabbed Lucy's wrist and pulled so as to drag her toward the bedroom despite her protest and she cried. 'No, please don't do this. No!'

Harper who was visibly nervous and afraid of what this powerful man would do to his precious Lucy suddenly found some small measure of courage and stepped between them keeping his back to Lucy and facing Madsen.

'Please Mr. Madsen sir, as I mentioned this girl is new, she means no disrespect. Inexperienced and unwilling aren't qualities to satisfy a gentleman of your standards. Please allow me to make amends,' said Harper thinking fast and scrambling to find a solution he hoped would be acceptable.

Signalling to two of the other girls he called them over. 'Janice, Leanne, please look after Mr. Madsen and make up for this disappointment. I'm sure you will both take very good care of him. Mr. Madsen, the girls will look after you personally and with my compliments while Becky finishes the cleaning tasks. I will see to it that Lucy is disciplined and I assure you nothing like this will happen again.'

'I suppose on this one occasion I can overlook this outrage but see to it that this girl doesn't come back to my apartment. I don't suffer disobedience lightly,' Madsen said as he was led away by the two girls both knowing Harper would pay them well if they treated their client to something special.

Lucy looked to Harper with tears in her eyes, relieved that

he had saved her from Madsen but fearful for what he might expect in return. 'I'm so sorry Mr. Harper, I tried to do a good job for you. You know I tried but I just can't be with a man like that, I'm sorry, I didn't mean to embarrass you, really I didn't. Thank you for saving me, I really appreciate it, I'll work extra shifts to make up for it, I promise.'

'You can make it up to me by working double shifts with your old crew; I can't have you working with the girls anymore. If it was anyone else but you Lucy I'd have let Madsen teach you a lesson but I like you so your pretty little behind belongs to me now, understand? When I call, you come running. We're going to get to know one another very well.'

'Yes Andrew, thank you, of course I'll make it up to you,' said Lucy thinking she'd never come back to work for this creepy bastard again, thankful for her narrow escape but her heart sank realising she had lost her chance to get a message to her sister.

'Becky, finish off here will you and when the girls are done wait for us in the van,' Harper said to the girl who was left behind half-heartedly dusting book shelves. 'Now Lucy, while the girls are fixing your mess you're coming with me.'

'Where are we going?' asked Lucy as she quickly felt around her waist to be sure the little knife was still hidden in her apron.

'You're going to work in the Henderson's apartment on the top floor. He usually isn't home at this time of day but arranges for his driver Mr. Stone to supervise while the weekly clean is done. He never takes a girl so you can work there safely for the rest of the day then make your own way home. I'll arrange a space on your old crew so be there early tomorrow morning. Mr. Stone will keep an eye on you until you're finished.'

Lucy gathered her things into her cleaning cart and followed Harper to the lift where he used the intercom to buzz the penthouse. After a few tense moments during which Harper impatiently kept buzzing the intercom

Henderson's guard answered with a grunt and checked the ID's held to the camera before he granted access and the lift quickly rose again to the upper floor of the highest building in the city.

Stone greeted Lucy as Harper explained she would be working alone for the rest of the day and before stepping back and descending in the lift he reached forward and squeezed her bottom.

'See you in the morning my sweet,' Harper said with a wink.

CHAPTER 11

Derek Stone was well built, muscular and at forty-seven fitter and stronger than many men half his age. He may have been considered handsome at some time in his life but a horrific car accident had left him disfigured with several visible scars, terrible burns and only one eye.

When his predecessor couldn't settle a gambling debt the local mob discretely but painfully disposed of him allowing Stone to assume his role with little effort. He arrived outside his new client Mr. Patterson's executive club right on schedule and driving Patterson's car. Stone rather boldly presented his credentials and security clearance documents informing his new boss that he could either accept Stone as his new driver or suffer the humiliation of being left stranded outside the exclusive private club. Patterson was taken aback for a moment but appreciated the ruthless professionalism Stone displayed and agreed to take him on although he conducted a secondary security check of his own as soon as he arrived home.

Patterson's follow up checks confirmed the details Stone had presented that morning. According to records obtained directly from Central Control, during his time with the former police service Stone had proven himself a tough cop, although dedicated to the job and prepared to do whatever was needed to close a case he had occasionally crossed the line. He had killed men in the line of duty but information suggested not all deaths were reported; most likely some back street interrogations had gone further than he would have liked. When Patterson questioned Stone about his less than perfect record Stone had joked. 'Well, you can't make an omelette without cracking a few skulls.'

Stone explained he had been close to serving his twenty years on the force and cashing out with a reasonable pension to compliment the bribes and protection money he had accumulated when the crash happened and he lost everything. No pension to claim, bundles of notes he had stored for years now less valuable than toilet paper, he was angry and bitter but knew how to survive. There were dirty jobs to be done, loose ends to tie up and Stone had a reputation as a man who got things done.

As it turned out Derek Stone worked for Patterson for only a few months when Patterson one day told him he had taken a new position which required relocation to another country and as such would no longer require Stone's services. In an unusual display of gratitude Patterson recommended Stone to the head of the Upper Council, Victor Henderson who had been asking at the club if anyone knew a reliable driver and bodyguard as he had been having difficulty finding a suitable replacement since his long term driver had disappeared.

For over a year now Stone had been on the payroll of Victor Henderson as his personal driver, bodyguard and errand boy. The days had become routine, few dared to challenge Henderson's authority backed as it was by the threat of the Enforcers and so Stone had been reduced to more of a chauffeur than bodyguard. An easy gig with reasonable salary allowed Stone to gather up some semblance of a retirement package and still enjoy a few luxuries so it suited him for now.

Today was typically monotonous and Stone silently and obediently carried out the weekly task of collecting Henderson at his apartment, driving him to his office tower then returning to supervise the cleaning staff while they worked in Henderson's penthouse. It wasn't so much the cleaning crews that Henderson worried about but rather keeping his daughter Kathy contained during regular maintenance visits. Stone wondered why Henderson just didn't force his daughter to clean since he had refused to let her leave the apartment for over two years now but he supposed Henderson's sense of elitism led him to consider cleaning as menial work beneath the station of his immediate family members. Stone was sympathetic to Kathy's pleas to release her and although he showed no remorse about restraining her when necessary to ensure her compliance with her father's wishes he was gentle and as much as possible treated her kindly.

Earlier that morning Stone had dressed in his usual black trousers and suit jacket, white shirt and black tie. The standard uniform of his trade, easy to launder, easy to replace and allowed him to always appear impeccably dressed but understated and unremarkable among associates of the Elite client by whom he was employed. Upon his return to Henderson's residential tower he saw the old van belonging to Harper's cleaning crew as expected. Despite regular offers from Harper he never paid for sex with the girls and would not be drawn to compromise himself by giving Harper something that could be used against him.

Stone had refused to have an ID chip implanted in his arm so pressed his thumb onto the opaque surface of the scanner in the lift to access Henderson's penthouse. He knew an implant made sense from a security point of view but he was adamant that he would quit before being implanted, an ultimatum that greatly annoyed Henderson but Stone had come highly recommended and so Henderson reluctantly agreed to Stone's demand.

Stone had been in the apartment for only a few minutes and had begun searching the many rooms of the large living space looking for Kathy so as to restrain her as usual for planned maintenance visits when he was interrupted by the buzzing intercom system.

'It's that idiot Harper, what the hell does he want? He's far too early,' grumbled Stone testily. 'Kathy, get out here now, you know the drill. Come on, it's easier for both of us if you just do what your father wants.'

The intercom buzzed a few more times and Stone began to lose his cool. 'Kathy, I mean it, get out here or I'll have to sedate you. I know you don't like that stuff and I'd rather not do it but you're leaving me no choice.'

Buzz, buzz, buzz.

Stone marched toward a panel by the entrance to the apartment to answer the irritating intercom since Harper was obviously intent on getting his attention.

As he walked down the wide entrance hall he checked his reflection in the lift doors with his remaining eye and adjusted his tie and cuffs and suddenly caught sight of Kathy running toward him from behind with an expensive marble rolling pin holding it aloft by its wooden handle. She ran barefoot and silent then swung her weapon as hard as she could but the polished brass doors gave her away and Stone spun around at the last second catching the makeshift club in an iron grip before it caved in his skull.

'Just give it up Kathy, Henderson will never let you go,' said Stone releasing his grip on the rolling pin and Kathy in frustration threw it to the ground behind her then slapped Stone hard across the face with an open hand, the blood rushing to his face and highlighting his deep scars.

The intercom buzzed again and Stone looked at Kathy, saying nothing, just shaking his head.

'Fuck you Derek,' she screamed then turned to run to her room but in her anger and haste she slipped on the rolling pin and fell, striking her head on a small ornate table and knocking over a large decorative antique vase which landed intact on the plush carpet. Kathy however lay still on the floor where she had fallen against the table and appeared to be unconscious.

'Kathy? Kathy? Oh, shit!' exclaimed Stone rushing to her then kneeling over her limp body and checking her pulse. He was relieved to feel a strong beat and found no blood as he gently teased her dark hair apart to check where she had hit her head.

'The vase fared better than you I'm afraid kid; you'll have a sore head when you wake up. You should have just come out when I called, but no, you've got to have it your way.'

As the intercom buzzed again behind him Stone replaced the vase on the table and then carefully lifted Kathy, cradling her in his strong arms and effortlessly carried her up the left staircase to her bedroom. He lay her on the bed in the recovery position to be sure she wouldn't swallow her tongue and laid a soft blanket over her before closing the bedroom door and walking at his leisure to answer the intercom at a nearby remote panel on the upper floor.

'What?' Stone barked at Harper's video image in the access panel display screen. 'Only one cleaning girl. Unusual,' Stone thought to himself, his curiosity aroused by the earlier than usual arrival of Harper, the insistent buzzing of the intercom and now only a single girl to clean the entire place.

'Hold your ID's to the camera,' Stone requested.

'You know me Stone, how long have I been coming here with the girls? Come on we've been waiting long enough,' complained Harper.

'Hold your ID's to the camera,' Stone asked again this time in a more demanding voice.

Seeing the IDs were valid and wanting to get rid of Harper as quickly as possible Stone granted access and allowed the lift to travel the few floors up to the Henderson penthouse. Before he raced down the staircase to meet them Stone realised he hadn't locked Kathy's room so ran back and pulling a key from his pocket ensured the door was secure.

When the lift doors opened Stone was in no mood to talk as Harper usually tried to either persuade him to pay for alone time with one of the girls or he spent the entire time talking crap which always gave Stone a migraine. Harper stepped out of the lift and approached Stone with his arms held wide as if planning to hug an old friend he'd not seen in years.

'Mr. Stone, so good to see you, and is Mr. Henderson going to be with us today?'

Stone stood with arms folded and as motionless as his namesake.

'He's not here, he's never here and you know he's never here so shut up, stop brown nosing and get on with the job.'

As Lucy followed Harper out of the lift she walked backwards pulling her cleaning cart behind her and when she turned around she gasped at the sight of the tall imposing figure of Derek Stone. His disfigured features were frightening to most and he'd gotten used to the reaction. Lucy quickly composed herself and stepped forward to shake Stone's hand in greeting, a gesture he seldom received when not wearing his gloves due to the horrifically melted skin on his hands.

'Good afternoon, I'm Lucy. I'll just get to work now if that's okay with you,' she said pleasantly. 'Hello Lucy, I'm, ah, I'm Derek,' said Stone as he took her hand and held it delicately, covering it gently with his other hand. She had to pull away after a moment as he stood silently, just looking at her with his watery eye. Lucy was confused and a bit unnerved by Stone; she was still badly shaken from her ordeal with Madsen in the apartment a few floors below where the other girls were still working to make up for her refusing to submit to him. She took her cleaning trolley and made her way past Stone and Harper into the main living area.

'Well, sorry we're a bit early, something of an unexpected problem downstairs with Mr. Madsen. Unfortunately the other girls will be delayed for the afternoon now but Lucy here is a good worker, I'm sure you'll enjoy her company.'

'Yes, I'm sure she'll be fine.'

'She's a new girl Stone; I'm afraid I can't stay but I expect she'll still be as new when she returns to me tomorrow morning.'

'You know I don't mess around with your whores Harper, she'll be as pure tomorrow as she is today,' said Stone. 'For all that's worth.'

Hearing Stone confirm what Harper had said about him not touching the girls allowed Lucy to breathe a little easier. Stone came across as a dangerous man but he could be anyway he wanted as far as Lucy was concerned so long as he didn't touch her. She desperately wanted to run away from all of this and thought of Sam on his way to be with her and knew one of the rooms somewhere in this apartment belonged to her sister. If she could just leave the letter she had written for her she'd have to trust Kathy found it okay. Lucy knew she couldn't risk another day working for Harper after this. Now was her only chance.

Stone escorted Harper back to the lift and then stepped back to watch the doors close; glad it would be another week before he had to deal with him again. He turned to see Lucy standing with her cleaning cart looking around the massive apartment.

'Lucy isn't it? Well I guess you'd better get on with it,' he spoke in his usual curt professional voice.

'Yes sir, I'll start in the kitchen if that's okay with you.'

Stone escorted Lucy to the kitchen then returned to the main lounge area pausing briefly to pour himself a large cognac from Henderson's private bar and sat with his drink in Henderson's favourite chair while she worked.

Lucy reckoned the huge kitchen had a floor area almost twice the size of the living room in her Aunt Susan's house. She found all the surfaces to be in good order and generally little needed to be done except cleaning the shelves in the fridge and dumping a bag of waste into the garbage chute in the utility room located out the back of the main kitchen area. Most of the Elites preferred to eat out in expensive restaurants or ordered high quality catered meals so the kitchens in their homes were largely unused, lifeless places but what she found here in the Henderson's were racks of spices, bottles of various flavoured oils and vinegars, fresh and dried herbs and several types of cured meat. The larder was well stocked with cans of food and plenty of fresh produce which Lucy assumed was imported either from the continent or grown in the prison farms and the best creamed off for the Elites personal consumption. The whole room felt alive, lived in, almost homely compared with the staid main living area.

Since the most recent letter she had read from the box her aunt left her was dated two years ago she feared that perhaps Kathy had moved out or maybe even got married and lived elsewhere in the city. It was only now she realised how much she had pinned her hopes on finding Kathy still living here but being the only lead she had what choice did she have. Lucy doubted Victor Henderson would even consider cooking for himself and whoever ran the kitchen here obviously had a culinary passion. The decor and general look of the room had a feminine feel to it too and Lucy was excited to think she might be standing in her sister's kitchen; she began to allow herself to hope that this could be the first real contact with the sister she had never known.

Her nerves now more settled and her spirits rising again Lucy checked the little knife she had taken from Madsen's apartment was still concealed in the folds of her apron before she composed herself and re-entered the main living space and for the first time really looked at the room. She found it truly mind-boggling how a probably priceless collection of beautiful objects and furniture could be assembled and arranged in such a way as to appear cheap and tacky. Lucy's impression of the room was one that most people would have concurred with.

Pushing her cleaning cart in front of her she became aware of the oppressive silence broken only by the rattling of the various cans and bottles of cleaning products as the cart rolled over the deep carpet. As she came from the kitchen she glanced to Stone who had not moved. He just sat there, sipping his drink and stared at the wall as she walked through the room. Normally in other elite apartments there would have been the sound of a few other girls working and Harper babbling on but here with just Stone she felt the full weight of the silence which made her incredibly uncomfortable.

She worked hard and fast wanting to get this ordeal over with as quickly as possible. She felt more afraid Harper would come back than of the man watching over her but even so she still had to deliver her vital message and get home. However this played out she would not risk being alone with Harper or any of these men ever again and she wondered how the other girls lived every day with the fear and violence.

While she picked up and straightened and dusted she kept an eye on Stone but he said nothing and moved only once to fix himself another drink. As she explored the other rooms on the lower level of the vast apartment she discovered a games room with full size billiards table, a cooled wine store, two bathrooms, general store room and a huge cloakroom with both men's and women's overcoats and jackets divided into one side each for the different genders.

Finding nothing of her sister here she knew she now had only the upstairs area to search and therefore only that space remained for her to find somewhere secure to deliver her letter.

'What am I doing?' Lucy thought to herself beginning to feel she had set herself an impossible task. 'Even if she does believe me I'm expecting her to, what, leave all her money and fine living behind to follow her crazy sister on a wild path with a strange man she has never met?'

Lucy knew she was asking for the moon but she also knew she could never forgive herself for not trying.

'I need to vacuum,' said Lucy calling to Stone and interrupting him from his thoughts. 'Do you know where they keep it? I didn't find one in the utility room.'

Stone placed his glass on the coffee table in front of him and without saying a word crossed the room to the hallway and pointed to a decorative panel on the wall. Lucy followed him and looked but couldn't see what he was pointing at, there was no door or handle as for the other cupboards and storage areas she had found. Stone pushed the panel and it clicked then swung open revealing a large cylinder resembling a hot water tank connected to several large pipes. Coiled and looped over a bracket beside the cylinder was a long flexible hose with a brass tube on one end and shorter brass fitting on the other.

'You really are new aren't you,' said Stone realising that Lucy didn't seem to know what to do with the apparatus he was showing her. 'It's a plumbed in vacuum system, there's no separate cleaner so you just take this tube and plug the end into the circular port along the bottom of the wall and the system starts. All the junk gets sucked into this big tank and it's emptied every couple of months when it gets full. It's neater and easier in a place this big.'

Lucy tentatively took the hose from the bracket and looked around for where to connect it.

Stone looked at her sympathetically and shook his head. 'Here, I'll show you,' he said taking the appropriate end of the tube and knelt to slide a little circular cover back from a nearby brass outlet close to the floor plugging and twisting the brass fitting into place. Once connected the silence in the apartment was replaced with a low hum rising in volume as the vacuum system powered up.

'I'm surprised you haven't seen one of these before. There are more of these outlets around the apartment so you can work from one to the other as you need to. Well, the attachments are stored in the same place so I assume you know what to do with those?' said Stone turning and walking back to take his seat and finish his drink.

'You'd best get on with it, I have to collect Mr. Henderson and drive him to his club this afternoon so I can't sit around waiting on you all day.'

'I'll start upstairs,' said Lucy as she looked toward Stone who drained the last of the liquid from his glass and stared back at her with his frightening single eye as he did so.

She selected a few items from her cleaning cart and carried the vacuum tube and nozzle attachments up the right hand staircase above the kitchen and began cleaning and vacuuming along the balcony. All the while she kept checking on the man in the living area below but he showed no further sign of interest in her. As she moved from the balcony and down the upper right corridor she realised she was out of sight now. She moved the vacuum pipe to the next outlet and when she was sure the noise covered her movements she ran quickly from room to room hoping to find evidence of Kathy.

Peeking around the doors she found another huge bathroom, a couple of undisturbed guest bedrooms and at the end of the corridor she found what she assumed was the master suite. Henderson's own private chambers were lined with white marble floors, black satin curtains, black silk sheets and brass and gold fittings everywhere including a massive floor to ceiling mirror held within a heavy gold frame. An offensive musty odour hung in the air and clothes and soiled underwear lay about the floor. Lucy's mind suddenly flashed a disgusting image of Henderson admiring his own grotesque naked form in the large mirror.

'The Emperor has no clothes,' she thought aloud. 'Gross.'

Ignoring the mess and feeling time slip away Lucy left the vacuum running and keeping close to the wall peered around the corner over the banister to see Stone had his head stuck in a large book he had lifted from the coffee table. Taking the chance she took her shoes off and holding one in each hand ran across the upper level to the left side and darted along the left hand upper corridor before she was spotted. Breathing heavily she began searching room by room, looking over her shoulder for fear that Stone would get curious or come to check on her at any minute.

Almost a mirror of the right-hand side the left corridor led to immaculate guest bedrooms with dust covers over the beds and a slightly stale smell in the air suggesting no one had used the rooms or opened a window for some time. As she neared the end of the corridor she was breathing even more heavily, not with effort but with anxiety, fearing what Stone would do if he caught her sneaking around as she was doing.

The last door at the very end Lucy guessed would be the mirror of Henderson's master suite but nothing could match it for its ostentatiousness.

'This is it, it has to be Kathy's room,' she whispered to herself and taking a deep breath turned the handle but found the door locked.

'Damn it!' she said a little too loudly and checked again over her shoulder relieved to find the corridor behind her still empty. 'Think Lucy, what do you do now?' she asked herself. 'I can't just leave the letter, what if I'm wrong and she's not even here. Oh this is crazy, just go. No, stop girl, you've got yourself this far, don't quit now. And stop talking to yourself.'

She ran back up the corridor to check again that Stone hadn't moved and her heart nearly stopped when she looked down and saw the empty chair and the big book lying open on the table.

'Shit! Where is he?' she whispered. Just as she was about to dash back to the other side of the balcony she thought she heard a faint clinking noise over the drone of the vacuum and a few seconds later she saw Stone walk from beneath her carrying another beverage back to his seat.

'Oh, thank you! Wow, he really knocks them back,' she thought. She supposed nobody would arrest Victor Henderson's own man for drunk driving.

Seizing her chance she ran back down the corridor to the locked door at the end. She retrieved the little knife from the fold in her apron and tried wedging it in the door jamb hoping to prise the lock but there was no straight path to the latch. She wiggled and scratched the blade in as deep as she could get it but it was hopeless and the lock refused to co-operate.

'This is crap, why does it always work in the movies,' she said aloud, catching herself again and slapping a hand over her mouth.

'Who's there?' asked a groggy sounding female voice from inside the locked room.

'Shit!'

'What?'

'Oh, balls!'

'Who is that?' the voice asked again more urgently.

'Shhh! Keep your voice down,' pleaded Lucy. 'I'm just the cleaning girl, can you open the door so I can finish up?' she asked quietly, feeling excited but nervous to think she might actually see her sister in the flesh.

'I can't, the door's locked from outside but listen, you've got to get me out of here. You're the first person from outside I've spoken to in ages. Please, I'll give you anything. They keep me locked in this apartment and I haven't been outside in years. Please, find the key or break the door or something.'

'Kathy?'

'How did you know my name? My father told me no-one knows I'm here except for Derek.'

'Derek? Is he the tall angry man with the eye patch who let me in here?'

'Yes, that's him, he's an ex-soldier or cop or something. My father pays him to do his dirty work and he usually keeps me locked up or sedated while your people are here. Look, it doesn't matter; just find some way to get me out of here, please.'

'Listen Kathy, I'm sorry but I can't get you out, I'm here alone and I don't have much time but I have something for you.'

'What could you possibly have for me that would make any difference?'

'Kathy, please believe me, I so much want to see you free from this place. I didn't even know you existed until a few days ago and I've risked my life to be here talking with you now. I don't know how else to say this so I'm just going to say it. My name is Lucy Nolan and I'm your half-sister.'

'What the hell are you talking about? I'm an only child. Is this some kind of sick joke? Did my father hire you to twist my mind, play with my head? Well it won't work, you hear me? I'm not listening to any of your bullshit.'

'Please Kathy, keep your voice down. If Stone hears you we're both going to be in serious trouble and me more than you. Look, I know it sounds crazy, believe me I'm still getting my head around it myself but here, this is for you.'

Lucy pulled up the back of her dress then took the letter she had been carrying for the past few days from the waist of her underwear and slid the thick envelope under the door. She could see the end of it sitting there for several seconds before Kathy finally snatched it away from the other side.

'Kathy, you have to believe me. I wrote you a letter that explains it all but Henderson is not your father. We have the same dad you and me but different mothers. I know it's a lot to take in but look at the photographs. That's you and there's one of your mother and your real father, our father. His name was James Nolan and he and your mother were lovers. See on the back of the photos, your age and the dates are written. That's your mother's hand-writing isn't it? You see, I'm telling the truth Kathy. I am your sister.'

The silence from the other side of the door was agony for Lucy as she crouched on the floor at the end of the corridor. She had risked everything as she knew she had to and now she needed to know it hadn't all been for nothing.

'Kathy?'

'Yeah, I'm here Lucy.'

The sound of her sister speaking her name brought tears to Lucy's eyes but she stayed silent, waiting for Kathy to come round in her own time, longing for them to be able to see each other, to hug and for just a moment be together.

'I don't know what to think Lucy, this is, well, I guess it all seems real enough but I need to think. I need time to think about all of this and more than anything I need to get out of here.'

'Kathy, I need to go, I can't stay here. Stone is downstairs and if I don't get back to work soon he'll know something is up. Listen, I'm leaving the city tomorrow. I have a boyfriend; his name is Sam. I'm supposed to meet him outside the city in a couple of days' time. We're heading north to the mountains and we can take you with us but you'll have to get out of here on your own. Can you do that?'

'It's not like I haven't tried to escape but the only way out of here is in the lift and only Stone and my father, I mean Victor have access to the controls.'

'If you were to get out is there anywhere safe you can go? Somewhere you could hide? I'll not be able to get back in here again after today but maybe I could come find you. You have to try again Kathy, whatever it takes.'

'There isn't anywhere I know of, I was always driven with Victor and my mother from one stupid dinner or speech or event to another. I actually don't know my way around the city at all and things have probably changed a lot since I was last even outside this apartment.'

'Are you alone with Henderson at night? I mean I assume Stone doesn't stay here and lives somewhere else?'

'No, he leaves Victor here in the evenings, then goes home I suppose. Victor normally doesn't like to be disturbed when he comes back from the office so unless he's called in for something unusual Derek won't be back until the morning.'

'That's good; at least we'll only have to deal with him if Stone isn't around. I noticed on the way in here that the underground car park has loads of cars all under dust covers. If you could get that far you could hide there for a while until I come for you. If Henderson notices you're gone he wouldn't think you'd still be practically under his nose.'

'I suppose I could do that. I've tried before several times but I'm not giving in to that bastard. If I get out you have to promise to find me.'

'Don't worry Kathy; I'll come back in a week from today,

okay? I'll come back and we can leave together then but you have to find a way out. Remember this day a week from now; I won't be able to wait for you if you're not there.'

'I'll find a way Lucy, I'll think of something.'

'Right, hide that letter; don't let anyone see it or we'll both be killed over it. I have to go; I've been away too long already. See you soon Kathy and keep safe until then.'

'Lucy?'

'I'm still here, what is it?'

'This is real, right? I'm not alone?'

'You're not alone Kathy, whatever happens always remember that.'

Lucy crept back up the corridor and again saw that Stone had moved from his chair.

'Shit, where is he now?' she cursed under her breath. Waiting cautiously for Stone to reappear in the living area below she put her shoes back on so as not to arouse his suspicion if she was spotted and rolled the little kitchen knife back into her apron. Then in the corner of her eye she saw movement and looked across at the opposite corridor to where Stone had appeared from one of the other rooms. He noticed her at the same instant and realising she was caught Lucy walked confidently across the balcony toward him.

'Where were you? What were you doing over there? The vacuum has been running for some time but I noticed the pipe wasn't moving so came to check what you're up to. Looking for something to steal perhaps?'

'I just thought I'd check the other rooms for laundry, you know, gather it all together first. One of the doors is locked so I was looking for a key. That's all,' said Lucy as her voice trembled involuntarily.

Stone stared at her trying to decide whether to believe her or not.

'Yeah, well that room is off limits. It was Mrs. Henderson's personal chambers and it's been sealed since she died. No one but Mr. Henderson goes in there so you're to leave it alone, understand?'

'Yes sir, I was only trying to do my job, I'm sorry, I didn't know. I'll just finish off here then and I'll get out of your way.'

'No there's no time for that now. I have to leave shortly to pick up Mr. Henderson downtown so if he's unhappy with your work he'll be unhappy with your boss. I'm sure Harper will try and take it out on you but I'll cover for you this once. I'd suggest finding another line of work if you can.'

'What do you care what happens to me?'

'I don't, I just can't abide a man hitting a woman. I don't want to have to get physical with Mr. Harper. He wouldn't like it,' said Stone with a flash of anger in his eye.

As Lucy hurried away and gathered her belongings onto her cart and replaced the vacuum hose in the recess behind the panel in the hall Stone walked down the left hand upper corridor to Kathy's room. He took a key from his jacket pocket and opened the door to find Kathy lying on the bed where she stirred slightly but appeared not to be fully conscious. Satisfied that all was well he backed out of the room and leaving the door unlocked he joined Lucy as she waited at the lift.

Using the wall panel he pressed his thumb on the scanner to call the lift then again using the thumbprint scanner he selected the basement and accompanied Lucy down to the car park leaving Kathy imprisoned as always in the penthouse high above.

'Do you have a good life Lucy?' he asked, breaking an awkward silence.

'It's okay, I get by. What the hell has it got to do with you?'

'Nothing. Nothing at all,' replied Stone as the lift chimed and the doors opened onto the basement car park.

Stone sped off behind the steering wheel of Henderson's executive city car leaving Lucy standing alone among the museum of stationary vehicles. She took off her apron and stuffed it into a bag with some cleaning rags and wheeled the cart toward Harper's beat up van which was still parked where he'd left it since the other girls obviously hadn't finished providing their rich client with additional services.

She walked up the concrete ramp and past the wolf whistling guards, squinting in the bright daylight to begin her long walk home.

'Well,' Lucy thought to herself, 'I found my sister, now I just have to meet up with Sam and then come and find her all over again.'

CHAPTER 12

Hearing the lift doors close and the carriage descend Kathy knew she was once again alone in the grand apartment, trapped one-hundred and eighteen floors above the crowded city streets. She leapt from her bed and ran across the upper floor landing to one of the vacant guest bedrooms where she pressed her face against the heavy glass wall shielding her eyes with her hand. Far below she could see her father's executive car driven by Stone hastily exit the building car park then a moment later she could make out a figure in a black dress walk from the car park and heading vaguely in the direction of the sector barriers. She knew it had to be the girl called Lucy, the girl claiming to be her sister and tried to follow her as far into the crowd as possible.

'If she was a setup planted by Victor then Stone would have driven her away in the car,' Kathy thought to herself, trying to temper the rising hope in her heart with some rationalisation and logical thinking.

She returned to her own bedroom and examined the photos Lucy had passed under the door. She laid each one down on the bed when she had studied them, seeing her own face at different ages, her mother and this man she had never met but who was her real father. At least that was according to Lucy who apparently was her half-sister. It was all explained in the letter and now Kathy felt the same mental contortions that Lucy had experienced only a few days previously when she discovered the letter left to her by her

Aunt Susan.

Kathy considered that of course the photographs could have been faked but there was no doubt about the hand writing on the back being that of her mother Claudia. And why would this girl Lucy put herself at such risk to bring this to her? Although it made sense it was all too unbelievable and so she sat and read again and again the words Lucy had written which confirmed the story she had whispered through the locked door. Kathy so desperately wanted to believe it was true and decided that she would use the week she had ahead to prepare another escape although reflecting on her previous failed attempts she felt no more optimistic for her chances. She knew at least she could look forward to help if she could just get out of the damn apartment.

Feeling the swelling on the back of her head from her fall against the table in the hallway Kathy looked at her reflection in her dressing table mirror. Once again she was alone in the huge apartment.

'What the hell, it's not like I had a hot date tonight,' she said aloud, laughing and almost crying at the same time.

Lucy had agreed to come back this day one week from now and Kathy knew she couldn't risk leaving too early or she might be discovered before the rendezvous that would be her best chance of making it on the outside so for now she'd bide her time and be prepared for the chance when it came. Knowing in her heart that Henderson wasn't her real father and the rage she felt toward him for what he had done to her mother she was ready to do anything, whatever it took to escape and destroy the man who had ruined her life.

Her plan had always just been to get out of the apartment, thinking to run and disappear into the streets, maybe make it to the Dreg quarter and take her chances where she wouldn't be recognised and figuring it was the last place her father would think she would run to. She realised it wasn't much of a plan but someone would take her in wouldn't they? Someone would help her surely. She knew she was fooling herself but to be free on the streets would be better than living as a prisoner in luxury. Now though she had a chance for something better. She had someone who cared for her, people who would take her away from all of this.

Although she would never have given in she had to admit Lucy had given her new hope and it strengthened her resolve and determination. It was something worth fighting for and she would be ready when her chance came.

She worked with what she had and gathered some favourite clothes, makeup and sanitary products and some jewellery thinking perhaps it could be sold since she had no access to cash. She gathered up the photographs and the letter from Lucy into their envelope and carefully wrapping it inside a fine wool shawl she piled it on top of everything else she had laid out across the floor. She went downstairs to the kitchen and gathered some fresh fruit and some cured meats placing them in bags. She also filled a small thermos flask with fresh water from their filtered water system and brought it all back to her room placing it along with everything else.

Although the Henderson family was one of the wealthiest in the country Kathy didn't have many personal possessions but what she did have was of the highest quality money could buy. Her problem was that she didn't have anything she could imagine being useful for a trek to the mountains. Looking now at the piles on the floor she knew she wouldn't make it without help but told herself this was her time, it was going to happen and she would have her own life at last, whatever it was to be.

She took a small suitcase from an expensive set of matching luggage belonging to her dead mother and packed the little pile of belongings and food sealing it all with brass zippers. She extended the pull handle and dragged it around her bedroom testing the weight and felt excited at the notion she was now prepared as best as she could be. Perhaps just one small step but a step forward none the less. Now the hardest part lay ahead and her stomach flipped thinking of what she still needed to do.

***

The senior technician stood trembling in the boardroom, his shirt clinging to the cold sweat running down his back. He had been called to deliver a report to the Upper Council regarding the stalled progress of the Project. Using a network tablet he controlled a presentation playing on a large recessed glass display panel in the wall at the end of the heavy table.

'You see our initial estimates were for simultaneous psychosis events to occur in both Raven City and Rook City,' he explained as the tablet shook in hands, 'but it's nearly impossible to predict exactly when the first subjects will be affected.'

One of the Council spoke making no attempt to conceal his anger. 'It is simply unacceptable, we have had reports of Dreg communications between the two cities and news is spreading through the Dreg sectors in Rook of how subjects in Raven have been affected by the process. If people know what to look for they will try avoid those affected, severely diminishing the ripple effect that you so carefully explained to us was necessary for the spread of the psychosis.'

'Yes sir, my team is working to alter the broadcast frequency encoded with live video streams to the Dreg sectors. All street displays, business and residential area net-screens will stream our subliminal coding at the maximum intensity possible while still remaining undetectable.'

'Well why has this not been done from the beginning? Your incompetence is a grave disappointment.' It was Victor Henderson who spoke this time, his fat jowly face practically glowing red as his blood pressure spiked.

Being addressed directly by the head of the Council nearly caused the technician's knees to finally give out but he struggled on hoping to come out of this with his life.

'Broadcasting the signal at that rate, well it may cause some headache or nausea which may mean people stop watching the screens which is why we reduced the signal strength. On all test subjects force fed with non-contaminated rations the lower intensity proved to have minimal perceivable side effects.'

'So Mr. Albright, please tell us when we can expect to see positive results, for your sake it had better be soon,' said Henderson leaning forward in his chair and gripping the marble table top with his stubby fingers.

'Sir, if I may explain,' whimpered the technician, 'the Dreg factory worker we paid to deliver the chemical agent to the ration mix was not in work for a few days. His son was ill so he took some time off. I personally made the call to confirm if he had successfully added the compound to the ingredient vats and learned of the delay. I thought it wouldn't throw off the schedule by any significant measure.'

'Well then kindly explain to us why there is only a slow trickle of reports of the psychosis so far,' enquired another of the Council members becoming more irate.

'It was unavoidable sir, when the worker returned to the factory another man had been put on his duty station in his absence and it was few days until the rota pattern returned to normal. It was too late to recruit another worker so I made the decision to wait. I mean there was nothing else we could do,' said the technician, his voice quivering.

'I see,' said Henderson forcing a calm, controlled tone. 'Well, you did your best, I can see that.'

'Yes sir, I assure you the project will not fail.'

'And the saboteur you hired, what of him?' enquired Henderson

'He has been silenced sir, once I had confirmed the compound had been delivered I told the Enforcer squad you had stationed to take him for interrogation relating to crimes not linked to the Project. He won't be seen again I can assure you.'

'Excellent work Mr. Albright, you have our thanks for your efforts, now please leave us to discuss other matters.'

'Yes sir, thank you sir,' said the terrified technician and

with great relief he ended the presentation and slinked out of the room to return to the sanctuary of his lab.

When the boardroom door had closed Henderson tapped and swiped through a list of contacts on his tablet and patched a call to the Chief of Command, General Curran. The large display panel came back to life again displaying a head and shoulders view of the General as he sat behind his own heavy wooden desk.

'Ah General, I am sending you profile details for one of our senior technicians, I want you have this man discretely arrested before he leaves the building. I believe you have a special squad for more unusual tasks. Please arrange for his tongue to be removed as well as a hand, a foot and an eye but keep him alive. Then send the parts to his family and ship what's left of him to the prison farms. He'll be not worth much down there and won't last long but the guards will have fun with him.'

The General looked to the desk mounted screen beside him and acknowledged receipt of the request. 'Understood Victor, I'll dispatch a team now,' and with that he disrespectfully terminated the call before Henderson had a chance to do so, much to Henderson's annoyance.

'Sir, do you think that's a bit extreme? Albright is a loyal man; he has been with the Project from the start.' It was Doctor Follis, head of the Research team and member of the Upper Council speaking up for his employee. As with his colleagues he knew Henderson rarely listened to reason but this harsh punishment was beyond any he had handed down yet.

'Doctor Follis, as head of the Council I can issue any order I see fit. I will not tolerate incompetence and you would do well to ensure the rest of your subordinates know the consequences of failure.'

The other Council members shifted uncomfortably in their chairs, all knowing that together their majority had the authority to overrule Henderson but individually none had the courage to speak up after hearing how Follis had been reprimanded.

'Now gentlemen a reminder that effective immediately all sector barrier gates between Elite and Dreg sectors will be locked down. Elites are free to come and go from the city via the perimeter gates but the sector division gates are in lockdown to prevent migration of affected subjects into our areas. The same protocol will be in effect in Rook City so if any of your family are in the habit of crossing into the Dreg sector for black market goods or to pay for more intimate pleasures you should understand that they are at risk of being locked out home so to speak.'

From the end of the table the eldest of the Council members leaned forward to address Henderson. 'Victor, the contempt General Curran holds for the Council is obvious. Are you sure we can continue to trust him?'

'Don't worry Mr. McGlade, although General Curran commands his Enforcer troops we have authority to override any of the city's automated control systems. If he fails to shut the gates we can enter our access codes and do it remotely from here,' said Henderson gesturing toward the recessed control interface in the heavy marble table around which they sat. It is absolutely secure gentlemen and I am sure General Curran will perform his duties admirably but I trust you feel more at ease knowing we have this failsafe.'

The other men around the table looked to each other, all thinking the same thing but none daring to admit they had more faith in the renegade General than in their elected leader.

'Well, I think that should be all, I have an afternoon appointment so I will see you in the morning,' said Henderson indicating the meeting was over. He called up another contact on his tablet but kept the conversation to the built in display.

'Derek, meet me below the office in ten minutes would you. I'm going to the club.'

When the room was cleared and he had the darkened

space to himself Henderson looked out through the thick floor to ceiling glass as the wind drove streaks of rain across its surface. The irony of having the entitlement to the highest office and grandest home in the entire city yet that same position providing the best view into the decaying Dreg quarters and the distant perimeter wall was something that ate away at Henderson.

Every day he rose he from his bed, drew back the curtain to admire all that he commanded and every day in the distance saw a rotting blot on the landscape, the discarded remnants of the old society. Who were they to hang on so long, mocking him with their very presence? What the crash hadn't destroyed he had stamped out. Most of the schools were closed, the remainder were overcrowded and ineffective, over sixty percent of factories were closed, the hospitals were reduced to providing placebos and field dressings and the Elite controlled Central Medical service was just a front for experimental medical procedures. The street gangs were a result of sustained high unemployment, terrorising and destroying their own neighbourhoods. The Elites had given the Dregs their own sector, provided basic employment in the remaining factories manufacturing machine parts for export or processing raw materials from the prison farms into rations for the hungry masses. Did they not appreciate the opportunity for work?

All this had been carefully planned and operated in an effort to keep the Dregs dependent on the Elites but if the Dregs realised their numbers were so great they could rise up and take back the city for themselves, something Henderson could not allow to happen.

As he looked to the horizon toward Rook City he imagined the carnage unfolding. The Elites could no longer allow the Dreg scourge to fester on their doorstep. Without military backing from General Curran and with insufficient troops the Upper Council had approved the Project to cause the Dregs to destroy themselves. The Dregs would be annihilated and in the chaos General Curran's Enforcers would be so hugely outnumbered that they too would have their ranks greatly reduced.

The Elites would survive intact and when the remaining Enforcers mopped up the last of the trouble the Dreg quarters could be wiped clean. Any surviving Dregs would be pressed into service to clear and rebuild. A manageable number of servants would be all that was needed and the twin cities of Raven City and Rook City would be a shining example of everything the Elites stood for. It would be Henderson's greatest achievement, it would be his legacy.

A chirp from behind him woke Henderson from his musings and he looked around to see a message on his tablet which had been sent from his car by Derek Stone. 'Ah, Derek, thank you. I was just finishing up here, I'll be with you in a moment,' he said realising he had become distracted and was now running late for his meeting at the club.

'Is everything alright sir?' asked Stone as he opened the rear door of the car for his employer.

'Oh yes, thank you Derek, just a little setback but it's all in order now. Just round to the club please and don't delay, you're a little late.'

'Yes sir, the club,' said Stone closing the door and swallowing the urge to slam it on Henderson's skull.

'He's forgets I'm waiting for him and I'm the one whose late?' Stone muttered to himself as he walked around to the driver's door. 'He's definitely not paying me enough,' he grumbled inwardly.

Stone plotted an efficient route using his mental map of the city preferring to use his own skills than to defer guidance to the on-board navigation system and before long they pulled up outside the massive granite pillars of an ornate bank building. It was no longer an operational bank since most financial transactions were now electronic making costly high street branches redundant. The extravagant building had been acquired by a secretive organisation for use as its private members club. Henderson's father had enjoyed a membership but the rule was that no two family members could join at once so it was upon the death of his father that the exclusive membership passed to Victor Henderson junior.

Leading from the pavement up and over the worn stone steps a navy blue carpet held with brass fixtures welcomed the club members to the entrance. An elderly uniformed doorman shuffled forward to open the car door for Henderson but Stone stepped in his way throwing a hard stare and opened the door himself while checking the street all around. He knew the old man was just doing his job but Stone had a job to do as well.

Henderson entered the club and stood by the door for a moment to allow his coat to be taken to the cloakroom by the attendant. The club was staffed by lower ranking Elites for inside these walls no Dreg would ever be allowed to set foot. Derek Stone had to park the car across the street and wait in line with other personal drivers for their employers to return.

As his eyes adjusted to the dim light in the dark, high ceilinged space Henderson walked across the rich deep carpet which had been laid over the original marble floor to preserve the silence. He approached the former tellers' counters which had been replaced with a deeply waxed and polished mahogany topped bar behind which the many shelves were stocked with the best wines, spirits and liqueurs from around the world. Strictly no beer was served as it was seen as a working class beverage and something only the Dregs enjoyed. He asked for twelve year old single malt and ordered it on the rocks, oblivious to the barman's silent disapproval of watering the fine liquor with ice.

Without waiting for his drink Henderson walked through the quiet room, savouring the smell of pipe tobacco and the pungent aroma from expensive cigars. Small groups of aged green leather chairs were gathered together like clusters of islands in a sea of plush blue carpet. On the walls hung priceless masterpieces and ancient books were displayed on heavily laden shelves. A respectful hush was maintained at all times and only the occasional rustle of a newspaper or the gentle murmur of quiet conversation rose above the high seat backs.

Although the club had moved to this location only thirty years previously the appearance and ambience was one of high class, tradition and time-steeped heritage. It was a look Henderson had strived and failed to achieve in his own home although it seemed only he was unaware of how widely he had missed the mark.

Henderson loved coming to the club. He was a powerful man amongst other powerful men and his rise to office had been discussed and agreed in this very building long before he had taken up membership. His own ruthlessness and ambition had helped him gain his high seat on the Council sooner than expected but he was unaware the path had already been set out for him by those who knew they would find him useful.

'Victor, how are you?' asked an elderly man with a deep tan, jet black dyed hair and thin moustache as he set down a huge cigar in a large crystal ash tray. He had the appearance of an aging film star who had refused to grow old gracefully and was fooling nobody with his unconvincing attempt to maintain a facade of youth. He didn't try to get up from his chair but stuck out his wrinkled hand in greeting to the younger Henderson.

'I'm very well John, very well,' replied Henderson shaking the offered hand before sitting in the opposite chair.

'And how are things progressing I wonder. Can I assume you have everything in order?'

'Yes John, you needn't worry. There was a small setback but..,'

'Quiet,' said the older man as he watched a waiter bring Henderson's drink and hand it to him with a square napkin under the glass.

'Thank you. Now, um, oh yes, a small set back,' continued Henderson after the waiter had turned smartly and walked back to the bar. 'There was a slight delay in the delivery of the chemical compound to the main food plant here in Raven City but it has been dealt with and we should expect reports of the first cases within a few days. Indications from Rook City are that the ripple effect predicted by Doctor Follis is as expected and already major street violence is stretching the Enforcers thin but no reported Enforcer casualties as yet.'

'The delay is unfortunate but no matter. If Rook City is progressing as planned then it gives us an example of what we can expect here. It is General Curran that I am most concerned about. The Elites have control only for so long as the General acts as our guard dog, give him too much control and he becomes a serious threat. You have the system override we arranged?'

'Yes John, I have everything under control, there is nothing to worry about,' Henderson replied in a smug self-assured tone.

'Don't be so damn cocksure of yourself!' blurted the older man in a sudden rage and he began coughing into a handkerchief while around them other club members lowered their drinks and newspapers to look scornfully in the direction of the outburst. Henderson squirmed with embarrassment at the stern reminder that his position of power meant nothing in these surroundings.

When the elder of the two men regained his composure he leaned forward, pointing his finger at Henderson and whispered angrily. 'Remember we put you where you are and we can take the privilege away from you.' He leaned back again and continued. 'This is a huge risk we are taking but one which must be taken if we are to ensure the remaining resources of this country are used for the society which is entitled to them, not squandered supporting the filth beyond the barriers and outside the walls. Be careful and do as we planned or it could be very costly for you. Your fellow Brothers will only tolerate your situation for so long before they cut you off.'

'Yes John, I understand and I can assure you that your

trust has not been misplaced,' grovelled Henderson, the arrogant streak in him overcome by his cowardice. He threw back his drink and got up to leave. 'I'll be sure to keep an eye on the General,' he said but already the older man had turned his attention back to relighting his cigar and ignored the comment from Henderson.

'Take me home Derek,' said Henderson grumpily as he climbed into the back of the car. Stone knew the meeting hadn't gone well from the gruff manner in which Henderson treated the club doorman as he left so said nothing and drove speedily but carefully through the early evening shadows of the tall glass towers surrounding them.

In the underground car park of Henderson's residential tower Stone opened the door and Henderson huffed and puffed as he struggled out of the car and onto his feet. He walked to the lift without saying a word and was about to swipe his implant chip to order the lift to his penthouse when Stone appeared at the still open doors.

'Will that be all sir?' he asked.

'Ah, yes that's all for today Derek, thank you. See you in the morning.'

Stone turned and heard the doors close behind him as the lift began the rapid ascent to the top floor.

'She better not try anything today, he's in a foul mood,' Stone said to himself then took the car home wishing Kathy luck as he drove fantasising about the cold beers he had in his fridge.

As the lift climbed and he left the world far below Henderson's temper cooled but he was still angry with the old man at the club and angrier at himself for showing weakness. As he entered the apartment he was on his guard for Kathy, half expecting another escape attempt but he'd be ready for her. As he hung his coat he looked around to see she was approaching him but this time not running or holding a weapon. She was dressed nicely for once and actually met him at the door rather than having to be summoned.

He was surprised by his daughter's pleasant behaviour and allowed himself to believe he had perhaps finally broken her spirit.

'Pour me a drink and then make me something to eat, I'll be in my office,' and with that he marched up the right hand staircase toward his private study.

After Kathy brought a scotch to his office Henderson unlocked a deep drawer in the bottom of his desk and took out a box of modestly priced cigars. They weren't the best he could afford but the best available until another shipment came in from the mainland. He selected one then sliced the tip with a gold plated cutter his wife had given him for a birthday several years earlier and used a large marble table lighter to get it going. Enjoying the mix of the spirits and fragrant smoke Henderson relaxed in his comfortable padded chair then used the network terminal in his office to patch into the Central Control network and spent the next while brooding over the operational figures of processes for which he had no real understanding. Like many bosses he micro-managed everything, suspicious of everyone, seeing incompetence everywhere except with his own leadership efforts.

As he glared at the screen and toyed with the idea of ordering the entire research team to be sent to the prison farms his thoughts were interrupted by Kathy as she knocked on his study door. Henderson peered over the thin display screen with a scowl that could have burned holes in concrete.

Kathy entered the room without waiting to be called and carried a heavy bottomed rocks glass filled with whiskey and ice.

'Sorry to interrupt, dinner will be ready soon but I thought you might like another drink,' she said setting the glass at the edge of Henderson's desk. She glanced at the screen which Henderson immediately angled from her view but she was most interested in the unlocked desk drawer which she could see was open just a crack.

'Here, take this with you,' said Henderson as he lifted his first glass to his mouth and threw it back.

Kathy took the empty glass and turned to go back to the kitchen. 'I'll call you when the food is ready,'

Leaving Henderson to his work she prepared a simple meal of steak, creamed potatoes and asparagus then poured a generous glass of pinot noir to allow it to breathe and brought the meal on a large tray upstairs to the study. She laid the plate and cutlery in front of her stepfather and set the wine glass to the side as again Henderson downed the last of the whiskey she had brought to him earlier.

'Thank you, Kathy. You see how much better things can be when you do as you're told,' remarked Henderson feeling the warming effect of the spirits mellow his mood and placing his cigar in a marble ashtray to slowly extinguish and be finished later.

When she had cleaned up the kitchen and given enough time for Henderson to have finished his meal Kathy went to the bathroom in the penthouse master-bedroom and turned on the taps to begin filling the bath. She ran downstairs and filled another glass of wine before returning to the study where Henderson was reclining in his chair happily puffing of the remainder of his cigar.

'Some more wine? I'll take these dishes out of your way,' she said giving him the full glass of red and loading the tray with used crockery and utensils. 'I've run a bath for you, why don't you take a soak and relax, you seem so tense,' said Kathy hoping to encourage Henderson out of his study and trying to disguise the nervousness in her voice.

'I think I'll do that, what a good daughter you can be, I wonder if you've finally come to your senses, eh?' said Henderson sipping from the fresh glass and mildly curious at Kathy's compliance. He laughed cruelly in her face as he rose from his seat and stepped toward the door carrying his wine and smouldering cigar stub.

Kathy just smiled meekly and walked behind the desk to wipe crumbs of food from the surface. Henderson stopped in his tracks and raced quickly back to the desk pushing her out of the way with his elbow and with the cigar still between his fingers tapped an onscreen button on the display to lock access.

'Getting a bit careless so I am, can't have you poking around in there can we?' he said manoeuvring his bulk toward the door again and taking a large gulp from the glass. 'I'm going to enjoy a good soak, this is excellent wine, bring the rest of the bottle up to me would you?'

Kathy stalled for time rattling dishes on the tray for a few seconds until she was sure Henderson had walked off for his bath thankful that the alcohol had numbed his senses and he'd overlooked the unlocked drawer in his desk.

She slid the drawer open and taking a second to remember the layout of its contents she took out a thin box of cigars, some digital video data disks each with a name printed in capital letters and most likely containing some dirt Henderson had on the named men. Other items included an ornately framed picture of her mother which Kathy found upsetting to find locked away and a large stack of high denomination bills. Under the wad of cash she found what she was looking for, it was a small rectangular leather case fastened around the centre by a brass zip. It was an item she knew well and one she hated for on many occasions when she had refused to co-operate she had watched Henderson go to his study and retrieve the black case.

She unzipped it and folded it open revealing a collection of hypodermic needles, syringes and small vials of clear liquid all neatly slotted into several compartments. Listening carefully for fear Henderson would return unexpectedly all she could hear was the sound of her own heart thumping. Quickly she removed a syringe, needle and a vial of powerful sedative then zipped the case closed before replacing all the items in the drawer, careful to place them in exactly the same position as before then slid the drawer fully closed.

As she carried the tray from the room she looked back to be sure she had left no trace of her activity. Walking down the stairs back to the kitchen she could hear the muffled sounds of Henderson singing in the tub, murdering some classical piece but blissfully unaware that Kathy now had all she needed to ensure her next escape attempt should be successful.

CHAPTER 13

The main road stretching west from the city led past the edge of a small forest and Sam had trekked along a shallow valley leading from the river which followed the left hand side the road until he could see the tops of the trees on the far side. He had sprinted up the sloping bank and across the crumbling tarmac surface then ran roughly fifty metres into the woodland pausing to let his breathing return to normal and for his senses to adjust to the gloomy light and soft sounds. Satisfied he was alone he relaxed and set up a temporary camp where he could observe through the trees and watch traffic pass but he was also far enough under cover to remain hidden from view. In the distance he could see the outline of the tall city towers but from here both Elite and Dreg buildings were indistinguishable from one another. Both classes of citizen were prisoners of their situation and Sam felt relieved to know he would never return.

Sam squatted in front of a small meths-burning camping stove he had made from an old beer can and watched a pan of water gently come to a boil. Using a small folding shovel from his pack he had dug a shallow pit in the soft forest floor and set the stove into the depression so the faint light cast by the blue flames would not be seen from even a short distance. Molly stayed close by as she sniffed around and both man and dog enjoyed the scents of the fresh damp air, the silence and stillness of the forest broken only by occasional bird calls or the rustling of some small creature foraging nearby.

Sam always found the calming effect of the natural environment to be magical and on the few past occasions when he ventured into the wild he always promised himself he would come back more often. As the water in the pan rolled to a boil he dropped a tea bag into an old enamelled tin cup then poured on the water to prepare his beverage and left it to brew wishing he had a drop of milk but the hot black tea was a luxury in itself. He laid out a bowl of water and a dish of dried food for Molly and then sat on a spongy cushion of dry pine needles and moss and leaned his back against the base of a large pine tree. After his trials to date he found the tea delicious and to celebrate getting this far he allowed himself a chunk of his chocolate ration.

Enjoying his drink Sam sat back and casually looked about his temporary camp. He didn't know how long he would have to wait but he was still too close to the city to get comfortable so had most of his gear still loaded into his pack in case he needed to make a quick retreat further into the forest and beyond. The thick canopy high above provided reasonable cover even from heavy rain but all the same Sam had strung a line of strong cord between two trees and about a metre from the ground then hung his army poncho over the line holding the sides and corners taut with hooks he had cut from thin branches to use as makeshift tent pegs. Another line hung higher up between neighbouring trees served as a washing line and he had hung his wet clothes from the earlier river crossing to drip dry in the still air. With his ground mat and sleeping bag in place under the shelter and a hot drink in his hand it was enough to make Sam feel at home.

His shoulders and legs ached from carrying the rucksack and he was concerned about the wound on his face but had applied some antiseptic cream from his med-kit when he had stopped to set up camp. The chance to catch his breath and rest a while now was just what he needed but as he sat he thought of Lucy and wondered how she had taken the news and hoped she could make her way to meet him as they planned. He wanted to keep going, to push on but he had promised to meet Arthur and Alice here and he knew wouldn't be able to make it across the country on foot in time to rendezvous with Lucy so he needed to wait for the ride. It would work out, it had to. His arrangement with Arthur would benefit them both and now he had time to relax a little, to conserve his energy and rest.

Sam woke to the sound of Molly barking. Judging by the low orange sun and the near blackness in the forest undergrowth it was early evening. Molly was alert, ears up and nose pointed to the tree line and Sam scrambled from his spot by the base of the tree throwing the essentials back into his pack but leaving the shelter and sleeping bag knowing if he had to run they would have to be left behind. He grabbed Molly by her collar and smoothed her coat, calming her down.

'Quiet Molly, shhh, good girl, good girl, be quiet Molly. Who's there eh? Who is it girl?' Sam could hear the high revving of a powerful engine and from his vantage point in the dark interior he could see the boxy outline of a heavy vehicle following the eastern tree line where it had turned right off the road and was making slow but steady progress over the rough terrain lunging and bobbing from side to side as the driver traversed the natural obstacles in his path. As Sam watched the vehicle progress further he hoisted his pack and secured it to his back and held Molly's lead so he was ready to run. The profile of the truck was unmistakable as that of a Land Rover, the Enforcers standard patrol vehicle.

About one hundred metres further from the road the truck turned left into a natural clearing where the trees were less populated and allowed the driver to negotiate gaps between the trees until he was a safe distance into the woods. The stationary vehicle sat with lights off and engine idling for a moment before the big motor shut down with a knock and deep rattle and it seemed like absolute silence had returned to the forest.

For a few moments nothing happened. Sam stood his ground watching the truck through the trees. He couldn't make out much detail in the diminishing light but he could hear the pinking sound of contracting metal as the engine and exhaust cooled. Molly whined and pulled at her lead inquisitive as always and eager to investigate the new smells but Sam held her lead tight, waiting. The silence was broken by a loud creak then a door slamming shut as the driver or passenger dismounted from the truck.

'Quiet Molly,' Sam whispered to his companion and petted her head to reassure her. He crept slowly toward the truck being careful where he stepped ensuring to avoid dry sticks or twigs that might give away his presence if he snapped them underfoot. He knew it had to be Arthur, who else would be here at this time but all the same he had to be careful. He could see the truck was a Land Rover alright but it had sounded like a diesel engine not a petrol V8 and as he edged closer he saw the rear of the truck was pickup type body covered with a canvas frame, not a solid armoured truck like an Enforcer patrol transport. Sam could hear the cracking of dry twigs as the driver walked around near the truck but he must have been exploring on the opposite side as Sam couldn't see any movement.

Closer now Sam could make out a passenger sitting in the truck but the window was rolled up fully and in the low light he couldn't be sure if it was Alice and he wasn't about to give himself away until he could be sure who he was dealing with. Just then he heard a click and a creak as the truck door was opened again, the driver had come back.

'Ah that's a relief; I thought I was going to piss myself.'

Sam immediately recognised Arthur's gruff voice and laughed aloud breaking cover announcing himself. 'Arthur, it's Sam,' he said as he approached with Molly excitedly leading the way.

Arthur stepped around the front of the truck as Alice unlocked her side door and stepped out into the cool air. Sam let Molly go and she bounded up to Alice, her body waving from the middle and her tail wagging in delight as Alice greeted and fussed over her while Arthur stuck out his hand and Sam took it returning a firm handshake while looking Arthur in the eye.

'I'm glad to see you made it old man, you're here a day early but it's good to see you.'

'Same to you Sam, same to you. I see that cut on your face is healing okay, still a bit angry looking but it doesn't seem infected. You know for a while there I thought we weren't going to make it out, something going on in the city and then trouble at the gate.'

'Tell me about it,' said Sam. 'Some new prick on duty, all by the book, I had to turn back, thought I was stuck until I sneaked out through an old drainage vent.'

'Oh we met the same little bollocks, nearly had us arrested until he was picked up by a patrol wagon for some emergency duty in the city. I tell you Sam something bad is going on, I reckon we just got away in time. Luckily I was able to smooth things over with the other guard and we got through.'

'Hey, now maybe you'd like to tell Sam what really happened? Hello Sam, it's nice to see you again,' said Alice coming over and hugging Sam as Molly sniffed around Arthur's legs and nudged her head gently against him to say hello and seeking attention.

'This old fool thought he could sweet talk the guard and of course just made things worse so a woman's touch was called for, thankfully we got through okay,' continued Alice as Arthur looked at Sam with an embarrassed expression but then laughed and slapped Sam on the back.

'Were all together now, sure that's what counts eh?' said Arthur with a smile and they all laughed together letting the tension of the past few days melt away and fully embracing the joy of the moment.

'So what do we do now?' asked Alice directing her question to Sam who felt uncomfortable that she had deferred to him and not her husband.

'Well, to be honest, I had just planned to get out, get to Raven City to pick up Lucy before making a run for the north. It's all a big sketchy, I'm really more of a make it up as I go kinda guy.'

'Oh yes, Arthur has filled me in on the plan, of course we have to find your Lucy but I mean what do we do right now? It's going to be dark soon, should we maybe get moving?'

'Well Arthur, what do you think?' asked Sam. 'I have a shelter and sleeping bag set up as I wasn't expecting you until morning but if you give me a few minutes I'll have it packed up and ready to go. You're the driver so it's up to you.'

'We might be better to travel at night, less traffic I suppose and if we took the driving in shifts we'd have covered some distance by morning. The only thing I'd worry about are raiders, they're worse than the city gangs from what I've heard and we'd be more easily spotted at night with the headlights on the truck.'

'I'd have to agree with you, I'd like to hit the road and put as much distance between us and the city as possible but if we ran into trouble or had to leave the road at any time we'd be better off in the day time. What do you say we camp here tonight and move out at first light?'

'Alice, what do you think?' said Arthur turning to his wife.

'It makes sense to me, we've had a hard day and I think we could all do with some rest. A little sleep would be good but I would love some tea even more.'

'Right, it's settled then,' said Sam making the final decision. 'If you two want to sort out where you're sleeping my shelter is about thirty metres this way,' he pointed through trees. 'I'll boil some water for tea and then you folks get some sleep and I'll take first watch, Arthur you can take over after a few hours and we'll swap through the night as needed.'

'That sounds good to me Sam, except for one thing.'

'Oh, what's that?'

'Well, I just thought you might like something a bit

stronger than tea,' Arthur said with a smile as he reached under the canvas cover at the back of the truck and pulled out a gallon jug of his own liquor.

'Ha ha! Great stuff,' laughed Sam. 'Something to keep the cold at bay eh?'

After Alice had her tea and the men drank whiskey from tin mugs Arthur poured another shot for Sam to keep him company during the first watch before they retired to bed in the cleared out back of the truck. It wasn't comfortable but it was off the ground and sleeping in their clothes with a few wool blankets underneath and over them it was enough for husband and wife to drift off. Sam sat with his back to a tree by his own camp just a short distance away and pulled his sleeping bag around him for warmth. Molly lay across his legs and dozed while Sam sipped from his mug and watched the road as the light from occasional supply truck headlights streamed past and filtered through the woodland in long moving streaks.

It was a dry night with little wind, the quiet air in the forest so strange to Sam after the constant noise of nights in the city. The thin walls in his apartment block meant he often fell asleep listening to couples rutting or shouting, music or TV turned up too loud, gangs fighting and sirens screaming on the streets below, even using earplugs he could still hear it all. Here though, still within sight of the glow from the city lights he felt a sense of calm. He could have slept soundly until the next afternoon propped up against this tree and awoke more rested than he had felt in years but he maintained his vigil and only allowed himself to sleep when Arthur relieved him a few hours later.

Sam woke with a shock the following morning as his shoulder was gently shaken and a delicate hand offered him a hot cup of tea. He looked up to see Alice wrapped in a wool blanket smiling down at him.

'Wake up sleepy head, the sun is almost up and we've a big day in front of us.'

'Where's Molly?' asked Sam rubbing his face to clear his senses then took the steaming mug and wrapped his hands around it to help warm the chill from his fingers.

'Don't worry, she heard Arthur and me loading the truck and she's happily getting in his way. He makes out he's grumpy about it but he loves having a dog around so she's in good company. How are you?'

'Stiff and cold,' said Sam standing and arching his back to work out a kink before he took a long sip of the warming beverage. Alice was still standing with him, patiently waiting but not saying anything. He realised it had been years since he had company other than Molly and wasn't much of a morning person at the best of times. 'Thanks for the tea,' he said, trying to make an effort and genuinely appreciative of the gesture.

'No problem, it's only tea. Thanks for getting us this far Sam.'

'I didn't do anything, you got yourselves here. It's the next part we'll do together.'

'Well, if you hadn't helped Arthur that day he might not be with us at all now and I would be alone in that old house, stuck in that horrible city. Thanks to you we're drinking tea in the forest and have the open road ahead. I just wanted to thank you Sam.'

'I'm not really sure I did anything but you're welcome,' said Sam feeling a bit awkward. 'We've a way to go yet, let's just agree that we'll all look after each other eh?'

'Okay Sam, it's a deal,' replied Alice, her eyes smiling as she patted his arm.

They were interrupted as Molly ran up to Sam and butted her head against his leg wagging her tail and looking up as excited to see him as if he had been away for a month.

'Are you two going to stand around chatting all day or are we going to find this girl of yours?' said Arthur loudly as he followed Molly from the truck. 'We're all packed and loaded Sam, if you want to stow your gear we can get going.

CHAPTER 14

As the sun broke over the horizon the tired diesel engine pulled the truck back up onto the main road and the four friends continued their journey west. Sam drove as Arthur dozed in the passenger seat with Alice perched between them on the cramped middle seat and Molly enjoyed the ride in the back of the pickup under the canvas cover amid the assorted supplies and equipment.

The weak morning sun shimmered in the damp patches of road where the last of the previous night's rain had yet to dry off and the tyres splashed through the deeper ruts and potholes making for an uncomfortable ride but everyone was happy to be increasing the gap between them and their old lives. Alice chatted about how she used to travel up and down the coast as a girl and about friends she knew and times her and Arthur had shared together while Sam politely followed the conversation but didn't contribute much. He was concentrating on his driving since it had been several years since he'd last driven a car and the most recent vehicle he'd owned was an old Triumph motorcycle belonging to his uncle but that had been destroyed in an accident before he'd went travelling.

He was glad for Alice talking away without concern that she was the only one really saying anything. Sam was still getting used to having company and with Arthur half asleep in the cab it left Sam to hold the conversation and he felt it was much too early in the morning for it. He knew if Lucy was here she'd be jabbing him in the ribs trying to encourage him to get more involved but no rush, one step at a time he thought.

At this early hour there was little traffic but they did pass a few supply lorries heading east for Rook City, probably delivering raw materials for the factories. A little later three big rigs hauling forty foot containers sped past, all escorted front and rear by Enforcer patrol trucks and were most likely transporting new stock for the exclusive Elite sector stores. Deliveries to the island country were getting fewer and the goods shipped in were therefore all the more valuable to the gangs who hijacked and sold stolen merchandise to Dreg traders to support the thriving black market economy.

Thankfully none seemed to pay any attention to the small band and their old truck as it rattled and smoked its way along the motorway. They were making steady progress and Sam calculated they could make half the journey before evening. He planned to scout for somewhere off the road to camp for the night then complete the journey in the morning. They would arrive a day early to meet Lucy but could hide the truck under the cover of the woods by the lake and wait for her. When the fuel gauge was reading low Sam pulled over and woke Arthur. The two men jumped out and Sam set about tending to the truck while Arthur kept lookout for patrols or bandits or any other trouble they could expect to meet on the open road beyond the city walls.

After he'd checked on Molly and found she was her usual excited self Sam poured a dish of water for her then grabbed a jerry can of diesel to refuel the truck. With four full cans of fuel plus the full tank they had left with he knew they'd make it to Raven City and on to Arthur's cousin's place farther south along the coast. He figured however there wouldn't be enough to reach the mountains and Sam grew increasingly concerned about the logistics for the journey north with Lucy. They could make it on foot if necessary but food and water would be a problem unless they could scavenge and forage along the way so using the truck would be ideal if

Arthur would part with it and if they could find more fuel. Sam reckoned he'd deal with that when the time came and knew he was lucky just to have gotten this far.

Alice took a turn behind the wheel and now the day had warmed Sam said he'd rearrange a few things and sit in the back with Molly for a while to keep her settled but really it was just because he wanted some time away from Alice's friendly but incessant chatter. He enjoyed riding in the back staring out from under the canvas as the road stretched out behind them and Molly lay contentedly across his legs with her head in his lap.

It was mid-afternoon and only shortly after their second fuel stop when Sam still riding in the back felt the truck slow down and pull to the left. He heard the crunch of loose dirt under the tyres as the truck left the tarmac and then saw an old delivery van parked with the bonnet up and two men waving as Alice pulled the truck to a stop along the shoulder about forty metres ahead of them. It seemed the men had broken down and the husband and wife team had decided to be good Samaritans and help. Although Sam was apprehensive and pulled his baseball bat from the side of his pack leaving it easy to grab if needed before dropping out of the back of the truck he knew he wouldn't have driven past someone in trouble without at least checking if they needed assistance.

He heard the door of the truck open and Arthur stepping out from the passenger side.

'Keep the engine running Alice and wait here,' he said and slammed the door shut before joining Sam at the tailgate. 'What do you think Sam, we saw them up ahead and figured they could use some help.'

Sam looked up and down the road and couldn't see any signs of trouble or other vehicles and the land all around was flat and open. About a quarter mile back up the road they had crossed an old stone bridge over abandoned railway tracks but that was the only structure of any kind in sight.

'Well, I guess we should see what their trouble is; I know I'd appreciate it if we were in some kind of bother. Molly, stay,' he spoke into the back of the truck and then walked with Arthur a few paces toward the stranded van before stopping again.

'Having some trouble there fellas?' shouted Sam without approaching any farther.

'Yeah, we blew a radiator hose and the motor overheated. We've got water to top up the coolant but it just sprays out again when we start her up,' replied one of the strangers as his partner had returned to working under the raised bonnet.

Arthur looked at Sam and shrugged his shoulders. 'Seems believable enough but with no spare parts I don't know what we can do for them.

'Hang on, I've an idea,' said Sam returning to the truck and disappearing up into the back before jumping back down a moment later with a thick black roll in his hand.

'Good old duct tape, better than nothing eh?' he said to Arthur then shouted to the men at the van as he approached. 'Hey, we can offer you some duct tape. It's decent stuff and might be enough to patch your hose for a while, maybe get you where you're going?'

Arthur followed closely behind Sam keeping an eye on the two strangers as Alice sat nervously in the front of the truck watching all four of them in the side mirror.

When Sam and Arthur had passed half way between the two vehicles the biggest of the strangers shouted out. 'That's far enough,' he said threateningly as his companion spun around from the van's engine bay with a wicked grin on his face and brandishing an Enforcer riot shotgun.

Sam stopped dead in his tracks and Arthur stopped closely behind leaving Sam fully exposed.

'Whoa, hang on now,' said Sam raising his hands slowly and gesturing he meant no harm. 'We're just three people on the road trying to get across country without any trouble. We've nothing but a few basic supplies and an old beat up Land Rover that's worth less than that van you have there.'

'We'll take whatever you've got,' sneered the man with the shotgun as Sam and Arthur began slowly backing away in the direction of their own vehicle.

'Hold it, turn around, hands in the air, both of you,' shouted the first man.

Sam turned slowly and found he was facing Arthur who had stood his ground.

'I said turn around,' repeated the stranger.

Before Sam knew what was happening Arthur had darted forward and right pushing Sam back with his left hand while in the same fluid motion he pulled a Glock 22 .40 calibre pistol from the back of his waistband and fired two rounds at the man holding the shotgun. Arthur's shots missed their target but were enough to ensure a blast from the shotgun went wide also missing the mark.

'Run Sam!' shouted Arthur who had turned and shoved Sam in the same direction, both men now running for their life.

'What the hell was that?' shouted Sam sprinting to find cover.

'Just run!'

Alice watched it all in the truck's mirror and held her nerve, ready to speed off as soon as the men were on board. Arthur fired a couple more rounds behind him to cover their retreat causing the raiders to drop to the ground providing a few vital seconds. Sam ran to the passenger side to jump in and called to Molly in the bed of the truck to lie down. Arthur ran to the driver's door and shouted for Alice to move over. Before either of them had closed their doors a hail of shrapnel from a shotgun blast ripped into the light aluminium body of the truck sending a shower of coloured taillight glass into the air and punching holes through the bodywork. Molly barked and growled but didn't seem to be hit and Sam was in the truck now helping Alice buckle into the middle seat as Arthur slammed the engine into gear.

Just as they were pulling away Alice cried out in pain as an explosion of glass and blood hit the inside of the windscreen. Another blast from the shotgun had passed through the pickup's canvas cover and blown out the rear window of the cab seriously wounding Alice's right shoulder.

'Shit! Alice, hang on. Sam, do something,' shouted Arthur as he pushed the old diesel motor to its limits trying to get away from the men who were now running back to their van and closing the bonnet to give chase. 'Ah Alice, I'm sorry love. Stay with me, stay with me Alice.'

Alice slumped over onto Sam and groaned but she hadn't lost consciousness. He tore a large section from the bottom of her dress and working as best as he could in the cramped cab he held Alice upright with one arm while leaning her forward and tended to the wound on her back applying pressure with the wad of fabric.

'That's it Alice, you're doing great.' He heard Molly whine in the back as she must have been terrified. 'It's okay Molly,' shouted Sam through the broken rear window.'

'Never mind the bloody dog, what about my wife,' snarled Arthur.

Sam glared at Arthur but said nothing. Molly was family too but he knew Arthur could think only of Alice at this moment. 'She's doing okay Arthur, she's taken a bad hit to the back of her shoulder and it's bleeding heavily but apart from the blood I don't see any head injury. There's likely some shot and broken glass in the wound and we need to get her patched up soon but I think I can slow the bleeding for now. What about the men in the van?'

'They're not giving up, the breakdown was a rouse and they're not far behind us. This old wagon wasn't built for speed and she's seen better days, we'll not get far at this rate. How's Alice doing?'

Sam had leaned back into the corner of the cab as much as he could and was trying to hold the wound and feed a little water to Alice at the same time. 'She's conscious but weak, hasn't lost too much blood yet but the shock is probably not doing her any good. The window took a lot of the force but she's still hurt bad. Between us we probably have enough bandage and gauze to patch her up, I've some painkillers, they're a few years out of date but probably still okay. I don't know Arthur; she needs to get proper help. Anyway, where the hell did that gun come from?'

'Yeah, the bastard must have hidden it in the engine bay waiting for us to get close,'

'I figured that much, I mean where did you get the gun from?'

'Oh, yeah, well that's my old service pistol. I'm not supposed to have it but when I knew my discharge was coming up I reported it stolen and hid it. I just kept it in case I'd ever need it but it's been wrapped in an oily rag in an old biscuit tin for about twenty years now. I checked and cleaned it before taking it along; surprisingly it's still works like new. More than I can say for myself, I missed by a mile. Still, it gave us an edge.'

'It nearly got us killed. They'd probably just have taken the truck and left us by the road until you started shooting at them, now they're really pissed off.'

'Okay Sam,' snapped Arthur angrily. 'Say they did just leave us at the roadside which is very unlikely, how long do you think we'd last before some of their friends or a supply escort patrol picked us up? We'd be sure as dead by tonight on this main road.'

'Yeah, you're right, sorry. Thanks I suppose,' said Sam looking in the side mirror and watching the van closing the gap. 'Look Arthur, we're not going to outrun them and they still have us out-gunned. I reckon our advantage is we can go off road but that van can't get far, take the next gate you see and cross the fields; maybe we can make a track overland and lose them then join the road again later.'

About a half mile further Arthur stepped heavily on the brakes and swung the pickup off the road crashing through an old galvanized gate into a disused field. The heavy steel bumper of the truck made light work of such a flimsy obstacle and the old machine forged on over the rough ground, slowing down but taking the change of terrain in its stride. Molly whimpered as the cargo bounced around while she tried to keep her footing. Alice groaned as the uneven surface pounded the harsh suspension and Sam did his best to keep her held securely while Arthur stared ahead with steely determination.

The pursuing van narrowed the gap when Arthur had slowed down to swing into the field and the driver pulled hard on the wheel fishtailing the rear of the vehicle as it left the road and followed the trail left by the old Land Rover through the overgrown field. The man with the shotgun leaned out of the window and aimed at the pickup but the rough ground prevented a clean shot and he hesitated as his companion tried to follow in the wake of the fleeing truck.

Farther into the field the ground became marshy and more rutted. The truck slowed further as the tyres sunk deeper into the soft ground but Arthur shoved the throttle pedal to the floor and the tired old diesel dug deep for power sending it to the permanent four wheel drive transmission which pulled the pickup through the mire with seemingly little effort. Behind them the van was still closing, rattling and jumping its way over the rough ground as the bandits kept up their pursuit. Sam monitored the van's progress in the mirror as Arthur coaxed the heavy truck toward a gap in a stone-built boundary wall where a section had partially collapsed.

Even though the driver must have seen the Land Rover's wheel tracks lead to the soft mud he didn't lift off the accelerator. Sam watched as the van advanced several feet into the bog carried by its own momentum then quickly slowed before coming to a complete stop as the front wheels bogged down and spun rapidly spraying liquid mud up and back across the body panels infuriating the men riding inside.

'Looks like we've lost them Arthur,' said Sam as another shotgun blast was discharged in frustration but missed.

Arthur eased back on the throttle and allowed the engine to slow before something broke and left them vulnerable. 'How's she doing Sam?' he asked looking over at the ashen face of his wife.

'I'm fine,' a weak croaking voice came from between Alice's grey lips. 'Don't worry boys, I'm fine.'

'We'll get you fixed up soon, love,' said Arthur throwing a worried look at Sam who still cradled Alice as best he could in the cramped cab.

For another half hour Arthur pushed the pickup on over disused farm land and Sam helped to navigate by spotting for gaps in the rubble of fallen and forgotten stone walls or areas of hedge thin enough to be sure there was no deep ditch beyond and allowing the truck to pass through.

'Over there,' said Sam pointing to what seemed to be an old farm house and barn in the distance set in a shallow valley. 'Looks like somewhere we could pull in and let Alice lie down and rest.'

Arthur scanned from right to left checking for any other detail that might indicate reason for concern around the buildings.

'I can see a laneway leading to the house and we should be able to pick it up after the next field,' he said as he plotted a course to intercept the point where he expected to find the narrow road. 'From here it looks as if the house is in good shape, the roof is still on and the barn seems intact, we might be in luck.'

Sure enough before long the pickup rolled out of the tall grass through an overgrown gap where a gate once stood and turned left onto a single vehicle lane with weeds and grass growing in a wide strip down the centre and two clear tracks of cracked tarmac either side where passing vehicles had prevented the growth of new vegetation.

'By the look of this lane I'd say it's still in use or it would be much more filled in by now,' said Arthur studying the road ahead for any further sign of trouble.

'Well let's hope nobody's home,' said Sam. 'We can maybe stay the night in the barn and hide the truck there too until Alice is feeling stronger, maybe even find some fresh water to fill our reserves.'

'I think we used up the last of our luck getting out of the city. Here, take this,' Arthur said as he passed his pistol to Sam. 'Just keep it handy and be ready to use it if I have to get us away again quickly.

'I don't know how to use this,' said Sam taking the pistol and surprised by the weight of the cold steel. 'I've never fired a gun in my life Arthur, seriously.'

'It's easy Sam; you know which is the dangerous end so keep that pointed away from anything you don't want to shoot and when you need to, slide that little switch with your thumb to take the safety off. Then you're ready to fire, just point and squeeze gently, you've eleven rounds left in the clip.'

The way Arthur spoke Sam knew there was no point arguing and instead put the gun on the seat behind his back being sure to point the barrel down and out toward the door since he was nervous about handling it.

'You okay Molly?' asked Sam through the shattered rear glass. He was greeted with a little bark and excited panting as Molly lifted her head toward the broken window in response to hearing her name. She seemed in better spirits again and the relatively smooth ride now that they were back on a road meant she wasn't being jostled around so much.

'Good girl, nearly there Molly, nearly there,' soothed Sam as he worried about his dearest friend.

The narrow track straightened out now and only about a quarter mile remained on the approach to the farm buildings. They could see the bottom windows and doors had been boarded up but the upper floor remained in good condition with even the small window panes appearing intact. Closer now to the house they could see that some of the overgrown land had been cleared and rows of crops had been planted and were being regularly tended to. There were smaller temporary buildings behind the main house like large sheds and parts of the main barn seemed to have been recently repaired. What looked from a distance to be just another abandoned farm in the middle of a forgotten countryside appeared to have been reclaimed and in use.

'Looks like we might expect some company after all,' said Sam exchanging a worried look with Arthur and reaching behind his back again surprised to be comforted by feel of the gun despite his reluctance to use it. Arthur slowed the truck to a crawl as they approached the barn and studied the top floor windows of the house which was a hundred metres or so further along the lane. Some movement had alerted him but his eyesight wasn't as keen as it used to be.

'Sam, did you see...,' but before he could say any more the heavy barn door slid sideways on its rollers and four cruiser motorcycles roared out from the dark interior quickly turning toward the old pickup and accelerating hard toward them. The two lead bikes had female pillions, neither wearing a helmet, their long dark hair flowing back with the wind and speed, both holding pistols trained on the windscreen of the truck. Arthur immediately stopped and shifted into reverse but before he had a chance to back up the lane the two rear bikes overtook the leaders and shot past the side of the truck in the narrow gap coming to a stop twenty metres or so behind blocking the exit, the riders swinging automatic rifles from their shoulders training them on the truck as Molly barked and snarled from under the canvas cover. One of the pillions from the lead bikes had dismounted and the rider casually dropped the kickstand then swung his leg over the saddle and walked confidently to the front of the idling truck as several more bikers emerged from the barn, some with pistols and shotguns, others just standing back in a show of force, each one of them intimidating and mean looking.

'I guess we've had it now Sam, there's no way we're going to be able to outrun those bikes even if I backup up over the ones behind us,' Arthur said despondently and turned to look at Alice, gently brushing the hair back from her face. 'I'm sorry my love, this looks like the end of the road for us. Whatever happens I won't let anyone hurt you anymore.'

'You're just giving up? Just like that after we've come this far?' asked Sam incredulously as he kept an eye on the gunmen in the mirror and watched the approaching biker.

'I'm not quitting on you Sam but Alice is in no shape to run and we're old remember. If you get a chance to make a run for it, go. You need to find Lucy.'

'We're in this together Arthur, I'm not leaving,' replied Sam more concerned for Alice than himself but thinking also of Lucy, worried he may not see her again after all and hoping somehow she'd understand.

'Here take this back,' said Sam reaching behind his back for the pistol but as Arthur reached across to grab it a sharp tap on the driver's side window made them both look up to see one of the bikers standing there pointing a rifle at them and slowly shaking his head. It was too late to take any action and now the door opened and Arthur was pulled out by the arm at gunpoint.

'You bastards better not touch my wife, if anyone lays so much as a finger on her,' but he couldn't finish his threat as the butt of the rifle was rammed into his stomach knocking the breath from his lungs.

Sam saw in his mirror another of the gang was coming up the side of the pickup from the rear to drag him out too. He wound down the window and threw the pistol on the ground then held his free hand out. 'I'm not armed but I have an injured woman here,' he shouted as the door was abruptly pulled open. The man held a pistol to Sam's head but said nothing then gestured with the gun for Sam to step out of the truck.

'This woman is injured, she's been shot and she's weak. Just give me a minute, I'm not going to try anything, just let me get her propped up, okay,' said Sam looking the gunman in the eye and with slow deliberate movements slid Alice's frail body off his right arm and gently rested her head against the rear bulkhead trying to keep the saturated wad of material wedged between her shoulder and the seat.

The biker paused when he saw Sam's blood stained hand and the blood on his jacket and looked to his leader for direction as Molly growled low and snapped a few sharp barks from the back of the truck.

'She needs help, she's lost a lot of blood, we need to get her some medical attention,' pleaded Sam as Arthur fought to regain his breath.

'Take it easy men,' said the leader as he came to the front of the truck. He was a tall thin man with long thinning black hair pulled back tight in a ponytail. He wore a thick black leather jacket covered with various threadbare club patches, scuffed leather trousers and heavy boots. He wasn't pointing a weapon but a large knife hung in a leather sheath from his belt. 'These people don't look like raiders. Bring the men to the house and park their pickup round the back. Get the old lady out of there too, we'll figure out what to do with them later.'

'No, leave her alone,' coughed Arthur still catching his breath.

Sam stepped toward the truck again but a gun muzzle was brought to his temple and he froze. 'She's in bad shape, please, let me help,' said Sam again.

The leader nodded at the man holding the gun to Sam's head and the pistol was lowered.

'Alright, give me a hand with her,' said the biker as he tucked the pistol into the waistband of his jeans.

Sam helped ease Alice out of the truck and Arthur, now recovered came around and picked her up and carried her in his arms.

'Wait, let me get Molly, my dog, she's in the back.'

'Okay but don't get any stupid ideas.'

Sam threw open a flap on the pickup cover and stepped up to greet Molly who whimpered and nuzzled his leg, happy to see him and reassured by his touch.

While in the back Sam was tempted to grab his bat but thought against it, after all what good could it do him against semi-automatic rifles and handguns? He had his own camping knife on his belt and it hadn't been taken off him yet for all the help it would be but just having a weapon of any sort gave Sam some reassurance.

'It's okay Molly, it's okay,' he told her gathering her up in his arms and helping her to ground level where she began barking and snarling at the aggressive looking strangers. 'Shh, Molly, it's okay,' Sam repeated while petting her head and calming her down before taking her by the leash and following beside Arthur as he carried Alice toward the farm buildings.

They were led to the old farmhouse amid the thunder of bike exhausts and fumes of petrol and oil as the bikers rode their pristine machines back up the lane and into the barn and Sam kept an eye on the Land Rover as it was carefully reversed behind the barn and out of sight. He noticed nobody had made an attempt to loot their belongings or force them to turn over anything of value. Maybe they'd just be shot and disposed, out here in this secluded farmland what was the rush he supposed.

The rear door to the farmhouse was opened before they had reached it and an attractive woman in her early forties, standing tall on black high heeled calf length boots, long brunette hair and dark mascara spoke to the leader. 'Ah, hell Ronnie, what have you brought home this time?' she said, leaning on one hip taking a long drag from a cigarette.

'Just a few lonely travellers by the look of them, they'll be on their way soon enough Linda. Clear off the table and get Sarah, we've a gunshot wound to clean up.'

Linda led the way as Arthur carried Alice into the house and Sam looked around noticing the bikes had all disappeared and the heavy sliding door on the barn was being closed again. A couple of bikers were following behind them into the house which he assumed was for security but no one had tried to hurt them since Arthur had been struck in the gut.

Inside the house Sam passed through a small entrance hall littered with heavy armoured leather and cut up denim jackets decorated with assorted patches and a large rack resembling a shoe rack but bigger holding various types and sizes of helmet.

Linda turned looking down at Molly. 'Keep the dog out here okay.'

'Stay Molly, stay,' said Sam and Molly whined a little then sniffed the sleeves of a few of the leather jackets before laying down on a straw mat under the coat rack, disappointed not to be able to investigate the rest of the new scents she could detect around her.

The hall led immediately to a large farmyard kitchen which although quite dark due to the boarded over windows and dim flickering light from sputtering oil lamps was surprisingly homely and he could smell a rich broth or stew as it bubbled and steamed on an old wood-fired stove. The kitchen table had been cleared off and a white plastic backed table cloth was spread across it. Arthur was instructed to lay Alice down on her side so the injured shoulder could be examined. Arthur held her head until someone handed him a few rolled up towels as a makeshift pillow.

'She'll be fine, we've patched up worse than this for some of the boys,' said the Linda extinguishing the end of her cigarette in a mug of cold coffee by the sink.

Sam and Arthur shuffled around nervously looking to one another for a cue but neither really knew what to think except that instead of being robbed and beaten these people seemed to want to help so they both just kept their mouths shut and tried to stay out of the way. A young girl aged about nineteen entered the room, dressed in similar garb to the others but carrying a bulky shoulder bag loaded with medical supplies and instruments. She confidently assessed Alice's wound and began giving orders to everyone to hold this and pass her that.

'Here, put this between her teeth,' said the girl. 'We've only whiskey to numb the pain and I'd say she's a bit weak to be filling her with booze.'

The girl was helped by Linda who Sam figured to be her mother and the pair worked efficiently to remove debris and shot from Alice's shoulder and then stitched up the wound and bandaged it for support and to prevent infection. Alice grimaced a few times during the procedure but suffered the pain well.

When the work was done Sarah set about cleaning and sterilising her equipment while Arthur and Linda helped Alice to a spare bedroom upstairs in the farmhouse followed by one of the male bikers. Sam tagged along at the rear carrying water and a blanket Sarah had given him. While the ground floor of the old house was dark and gloomy with only thin shafts of dim light streaming through the boards on the windows the upstairs rooms although very rundown were bright and airy by comparison. The threadbare carpets scarcely covered the creaking timber on the floor and layers of ancient wallpaper were peeling revealing damp patches in the crumbling plaster but each room they passed looked comfortable and inviting all the same thanks to the efforts of the new inhabitants. This abandoned house was more of a home than any Sam had lived in for a long time.

Alice's quarters were a little box room in a similar state of disrepair and judging by the cartoon aeroplanes on the wallpaper it was previously occupied by a young child but the sheets were freshly laundered and the wool blanket Sarah had given to Sam was soft and warm.

'She's still very weak but with some rest and fluids she should pull through okay, this room isn't being used now so she can stay until she's fit to move again. You two men will have to stay outside but there's plenty of room at the back of the house if you want to set up your tent or whatever you have,' said Linda, her tone softening but still she made it clear she preferred not to have guests.

'Listen, I can't thank you enough for what you've done for my wife,' said Arthur, genuinely relieved to see a little colour returning to Alice's ghostly complexion. 'If there's anything we can do?'

'Just keep out of the way and move along when she's ready, okay.'

'No problem,' said Sam. 'We have to meet someone near Raven City in three days' time so we'll be leaving tomorrow.'

'I don't know if she'll be fit for travel that soon,' warned Linda as Arthur looked from Alice to her.

'Sam, I know you've to meet Lucy but Alice needs rest. She's a tough old girl but she's not as young as she used to be you know.'

Seeing how both Linda and Arthur looked at him Sam knew he was asking too much to expect Alice to be on the road again as quickly as he hoped. 'I suppose you're right, thank you for helping us, we'll be on our way as soon as you think she's ready,' agreed Sam but he was used to being by himself, going where he liked when he liked. It was hard for him to adjust to being around people again but he accepted he was part of a group on this journey and whatever happened they would stick together. He just hoped Lucy was doing okay and that she'd wait for him.

Arthur stayed with Alice and a male biker stationed himself on a chair just down the hall from her room to keep guard on the strangers in his house as Linda led Sam back to the kitchen where Ronnie the club leader was waiting for them.

'Well, since you're here now would you like some stew? You can work it off later but I can offer my guests something at least,' said Ronnie gesturing for Linda to get Sam something from the pot on the hob.

Sam took the steaming bowl and saw it was filled with a rich meaty stew with fresh vegetables and herbs. 'This is amazing, thanks. I haven't tasted real food in so long I forgot what it can be like.'

'Yeah, well, we look after ourselves out here, got to, no one else will. We have all the land we need here and grow vegetables out the front of the house,' said Ronnie showing a little pride.

'What about the meat, it's really good?' asked Sam.

Linda answered quickly. 'The boys set wire snares to catch rabbits and Ronnie here is a good shot with a crossbow so sometimes we get pheasant or duck for a change. That's rabbit you're eating now though,' she said tiredly looking at Ronnie suggesting he could perhaps go hunting again soon.

'Well, it's delicious, thank you,' Sam said interrupting the silent exchange.

'You're welcome; I'll send some up for your friend. The old lady needs rest but when she's awake she might be fit to eat something. It'll help her get her strength back,' said Linda.

'Can I ask you something Ronnie?' said Sam.

'Fire away,' replied Ronnie casually.

'Why are you helping us? You could have shot us or at least took our truck and sent us on our way but so far you've patched up Alice and gave her a bed and now you're feeding me at your own table. I really appreciate it but, well, why?'

'Maybe you've been in the city too long pal. We like to keep to ourselves out here, strangers don't often come this far from the main road but when they do we either help them or bury them. Lucky for you that you checked out okay or you'd never have stepped out of that truck but since you did, consider yourself our guest.'

'Well, I'm glad you took the time to think about it before shooting'.

'Ah, it's nothing personal but the road gangs around here often pose as civilians and hook a sucker or two, take them for what they've got and then kill them. We have to defend what's ours and we've built a home here. We'll not let anyone take that from us.'

'Yeah, you're talking to a sucker here. We got ambushed by two bastards faking a breakdown, that's how Alice got shot. If it wasn't for the four wheel drive we'd be cooling off in a ditch by now.'

'I didn't want to ask about how the old girl got shot up, seemed like that was your business so long as you didn't bring the trouble with you. Well, you know why we take precautions then.'

'I guess we do,' agreed Sam.

Linda set down three mugs on the table and poured out fresh ground coffee for her, Ronnie and Sam. 'I guess you're alright,' she said. 'I don't take too well to new people these days but Ronnie is a good judge of character and I suppose you all seem okay. Just so you know though, you try anything funny with me, Sarah or the other girls and I won't need to call the boys to take care of things. I'll take your balls off myself, you got that?'

'Hey, hey, there won't be any problem. If you can show me where to bed down I'll keep out of the way and we'll be gone before we're a burden,' said Sam understanding that Linda could and would keep her promise although he'd never give her reason to.

'I told Sam here that he and the old man could set up out back,' Linda explained to her partner.

'Maybe we could roll out our sleeping bags in the barn?' Sam asked deciding it worth trying his luck a little farther.

Ronnie shot Sam a cold stare but said nothing so Linda answered back. 'Well they're not staying in the house with me and the girls and the old woman can't be moved for at least tonight.'

'Listen, we don't want to cause any problem here, if the barn is off limits we can set up camp on some of your land, it won't be an issue, seriously, we're just grateful for your help with Alice. Anywhere we can pitch a tarp and sleeping bag will be fine,' said Sam realising he was caught in the middle of something and wanting to get himself out of it before his hosts changed their mind about how welcome their new guests were.

Ronnie smoothed his hair back and appeared to relax a little. 'There's some shelter out the back of the house under an old sycamore tree. It's near the house if you want to use the kitchen. You can fill up your water tanks too; the water is clean here, comes from a natural underground reservoir or something. There's an electric pump to run water to the house and we've hooked it up to an old petrol generator. Just don't run the pump after dark okay?'

'Sure, that's very generous of you. Well, thanks for the food and coffee. If it's alright with you I'll take Molly for a walk up the lane then set up camp by the tree. Maybe you can tell Arthur I'm out there when he comes down?' said Sam feeling uncomfortable since the atmosphere changed at mention of the barn.

'Yeah, that's fine, just don't wander too far up the lane and be sure to knock the kitchen door here if you need anything,' said Ronnie, suddenly back to his easy going friendly self again.

'Will do, thanks,' said Sam as he made his way into the little hallway where he was greeted by an excited Molly. He took her lead from his jacket, clipped it on her collar then stepped out into the fresh air of the farmyard before walking off toward the lane down which they had driven earlier, Molly panting and tugging the lead, eager to explore as usual.

'Let's go Molly, anywhere but the barn,' he said quietly and glanced toward the heavy sliding door which was firmly shut. He was glad to be on his own again.

The open air and feeling of security even among the group of strangers gave Sam a chance to relax and breathe a sigh of relief. He was still anxious with thoughts of Lucy but for now he knew he would be staying in one place for at least a night without having to stand watch or worry about the old couple who were sharing his journey. Surrendering to the situation allowed him to enjoy a sense of ease he hadn't known in many years. Molly had quietened down after the rough ride in the back of the truck and was enjoying the walk along the dusty broken laneway.

Just to look across green fields, feel the wind on his face and smell the clean air was a relief after the ordeals of the past several days and Sam felt some of the tension leave his body as he let go of past events. These people were cautious, didn't trust the strangers in their house and Sam understood. He had been burned too many times in the past to remember, it was one reason for his own reclusive nature, but now, here in this place someone had shown some compassion and trust. First Arthur and Alice and now this group, Sam thought perhaps the world hadn't completely gone to hell after all.

When he returned from his walk he saw Arthur standing by the door of the farmhouse and the biker who had been guarding him cross the yard and enter the barn through a smaller panel cut into the main sliding door. The bearded and long-haired man looked at Sam and nodded his head smiling in a friendly gesture before closing the door behind him.

'Well, how is she?' asked Sam.

Arthur looked terrible, the strain of the past few days had taken its toll on the older man but he also had a look of relief in his eyes. 'She's going to be okay Sam, she just needs her rest now. I'd say things would be different if we hadn't met these folks but she opened her eyes for a moment and I could see she's alright, just weak.'

'Ah that's great Arthur; I tell you I thought we'd had it. Aren't you staying with her a while?'

'No, the women said they'll keep an eye on Alice through the night. She should be able to sit up and eat something in the morning but until then they don't want me hanging around the house. The hairy fella you saw there threw me out.'

'Well then you can help me set up camp over by that big sycamore. Ronnie said we are free to come and go, just respect the house and stay clear of the barn.'

'What do you suppose they've got going on in there?'

'Arthur, I don't care. I don't want to piss these people off. They've taken us in for now but I get the feeling we'll wear out our welcome fairly quickly. Come on; give me a hand getting the gear from the back of the truck.'

Sam let Molly off her lead and she sniffed around the yard while the two men unloaded what they needed and walked to the cover of the big tree behind the house to begin setting up their temporary home.

With their camp prepared Sam and Arthur sat on rolled up sleeping bags with their backs to the wide tree trunk and Molly lay dozing beside Sam now as both men silently worried about the women in their lives.

'Here, have a drink,' said Arthur unscrewing the top of a dented steel hipflask and passing it to Sam. 'There's nothing more we can do now, might as well just try and relax and enjoy some rest.'

'Thanks Arthur,' said Sam taking the flask and knocking back a shot from the narrow neck.

As the men sat and talked idly passing the time they saw the small panel in the barn door open again and Ronnie stepped out. He looked around then saw Sam and Arthur and walked casually toward them, the sound of the wooden heels of his black boots amplified by an echo from the barn and house walls.

'I see you're settled in okay and I'm glad to hear that your wife will pull through,' he said genuinely as he approached and stooped under the tarp and squatted down to speak with his guests.

'Yes, she's a tough old girl my Alice. She'll be okay thanks to you. Here, would you like a drink?' said Arthur offering the flask.

Ronnie took the steel container and tipped his head back taking a long swig and holding it in his mouth to taste before swallowing. 'Not bad at all, thanks,' he said passing back the liquor.

'Just a little hobby of mine,' said Arthur happy to receive praise. 'I have a couple of jugs left in the truck; I'd like you to have one. It's the least I can do to say thanks for what you've done for Alice.'

'I appreciate your offer but there's no need, really. Besides, maybe you'd like to try some of mine,' and Ronnie reached into his back pocket and pulled out a narrow hipflask sheathed in a worn black leather case.

Arthur took the flask and tried a drink. 'That's a fine dram there,' he said and passed it to Sam who also took the offered drink enjoying the warmth in his belly and allowing his muscles relax a little further.

Ronnie smiled before taking a gulp himself. 'Well, I can't take the credit myself actually, one of my men is the alchemist behind this but I thought you'd appreciate it.'

'So is that what you do in the barn?' asked Arthur and Sam's stomach tightened.

'Well, you've a great set up here,' Sam said changing the subject.

Ronnie hesitated before answering but quickly relaxed. 'Yeah, we've worked hard to fix this place up and build something of a life here. We're well off the main road, we've land to grow food and we don't get too many visitors so it fits our needs very nicely.'

'How'd you end up here?' asked Sam. 'Nearly everyone who didn't leave before the final boats sailed fled to the city for protection but you all seem to be doing okay.'

'Don't believe everything you hear,' said Ronnie laughing. 'Sure a lot of people headed for the city but only after teams of Enforcers went through every small town and village looting any resource or thing of value. Anyone who was left had little choice but to take their chances behind the barricades in the big cities. The real bandits out here are the Enforcers, at least they were but now they just escort the supply transports across the country. Think about it, everyone packed into a couple of crowded cities where they can be watched makes it much easier for the Elites to exercise control.'

'And here you are right in the middle of the two cities and close to the main supply routes. Seems like a perfect strategy to me,' said Arthur staring Ronnie in eye.

Ronnie stared hard at Arthur who matched his gaze and wouldn't back off. Sam knew Arthur was getting at something but aggravating their host wouldn't do them any good and they could be made to disappear if Ronnie decided they were a threat to his operation.

'Look, we're glad to be here.' Sam interjected 'You've

taken us in when you could have turned us away. Whatever you do to support yourselves here is okay with us, no one is judging anyone and we've no love for the Elites or anyone connected to them. We'll be on our way and out of yours as soon as Alice is able to move. Okay? Arthur, isn't that right? We're leaving soon.'

Arthur answered Sam first then broke his stare. 'Yes, we'll be on our way soon. We'll be just fine.'

'We take care of our own,' said Ronnie easing down now Arthur had backed off first. 'That's how we got this far, that's how we're gonna keep going too.'

'You have a great place here Ronnie; we understand you want to keep it that way. Thanks for your hospitality. Here's to surviving and thriving,' said Sam raising Arthur's hipflask gesturing a toast with Ronnie who clinked his flask and they both drank as Arthur held his hand out toward Ronnie to shake.

'No offence meant Ronnie.'

Ronnie shook Arthur's offered hand. 'None taken,' he responded tersely.

'Well, I'll leave you two to get some rest. If there's any update on your wife's condition during the night Sarah will let you know. Otherwise you can come into the house and see how she is in the morning,' said Ronnie getting to his feet and stepping out from under the tarpaulin leaving Sam and Arthur as he walked toward the farmhouse to spend the night with Linda while the two men rolled out their sleeping bags.

'What the hell was that about?' asked Sam when he figured Ronnie was out of earshot.

Arthur looked indignant. 'Well, I want to be sure who we're dealing with here. They've got my wife in there while I'm sleeping out under a tree with you.'

'Seemed to me more like you were trying to get a rise out of him, besides, they've given no reason to think they mean us harm.'

'It's that barn that has me curious.'

'Forget about it. Get some sleep and hopefully Alice will be up and about tomorrow then we can get going again,' said Sam becoming increasing concerned about the delay and the potential for yet more trouble before they even got back on the road.

The next morning Sam woke to his shoulder being rocked sharply and he opened his eyes to see a scuffed leather boot and the frayed hem of faded blue jeans just inches from his face. He sat bolt upright and wrestled his arms out of his sleeping bag, throwing off the hood and feeling the cold morning air on his shaved head.

'What the hell?' he exclaimed, fully awake now but Ronnie held his finger to his lips indicating he should keep quiet and not wake Arthur who had stirred but not woken.

'Get the keys,' said Ronnie pointing to the truck keys that were just visible from under Arthur's boots to the side of his sleeping bag.

Quickly pulling on his jeans and boots Sam stealthily removed the keys from beside Arthur as he slept and then scrambled to his feet and followed Ronnie toward the barn as Molly tagged along behind eager to play now that Sam was awake.

'What's going on?' asked Sam rubbing his face to try and clear his head.

'You're going to earn your keep.'

'What about Arthur, we should tell him where we're going,' said Sam hoping to alert his partner and also to learn more of what he had gotten himself into now.

'Can you ride?' asked Ronnie.

'Yeah, I've not been in the saddle for years but I can ride. I had an old Triumph Speedmaster but I've not ridden since I ploughed the tarmac,' replied Sam feeling a twinge of pain in his knee as he remembered the crash.

'Good to know, for now though I need you to follow us in your truck. Here, take this,' said Ronnie handing Sam a Sig Sauer P226 nine millimetre pistol.

'Hey, hang on Ronnie, what the hell are you expecting me

to do here. I'm not going to shoot anyone.'

'Yeah, I figured that much when you didn't shoot at me when you all arrived. Your friend knows what he's doing but I reckon he's too old for this. Look, do you know how to use that or not?'

'Arthur showed me but I've not fired a gun before,' said Sam wishing he could back out of this somehow but knowing he was already in over his head.

'Right, you'll probably not need it but all the same its better you have it in case. Don't get any ideas of running, that truck won't outrun our slowest bike and we've more firepower than you so just follow along and do what I tell you and this will all be over soon.'

'Listen Ronnie, I need to know what I'm getting involved in here. I see that I don't have much choice but if I'm risking my life you need to tell me what for.'

'Alright, I suppose that's fair enough. We need to get supplies but in case you haven't noticed we're a few miles from the nearest supermarket. That means we have to take what we need. We lost our own truck in the last supply run so we need yours. Simple enough for you?'

'Well why do you need me? Just take the keys, we're not going anywhere without it and there's nothing we can do to stop you taking it.'

'I need a full crew and we're a man down since our truck got destroyed so that's why I need you. Now come on.'

Reluctantly Sam climbed into the cab of Arthur's Land Rover and wedged the pistol into the gap between the base and backrest of the passenger seat as he looked down to Molly who whimpered, wanting to come along.

'Go to Arthur, Molly. Arthur, go to Arthur.'

He closed the door and cranked the tired engine. While it warmed up the clattering of the old diesel was engulfed by the thunder from large bore V-twin engines roaring through open pipe exhausts as several bikes were coaxed into life. Ronnie pulled out of the barn at the head of the pack and pointed a gloved finger at Sam then pointed toward the lane leading from the farmyard.

As the bikes were started Arthur had been woken by the noise and lifted his head watching a streak of shining chrome, black leather and blue denim spewing from the barn. All the men wore full face helmets and had shotguns or rifles which were held securely in line with their bike's forks by a fabricated bracket custom made for the purpose.

As the noise continued to build he watched his own truck begin to move and saw a cough of black smoke as the old diesel cleared its throat while being driven hard after the group of motorcycles. Another six or so bikes followed in close formation behind the truck as it chased the first group.

He saw Molly barking after the truck and for a second didn't believe his eyes when it appeared that Sam was driving.

He turned to check for Sam but he had indeed gone, his sleeping bag unzipped and empty on the ground beside his own.

'My truck, the bastard's have taken my truck,' shouted Arthur shaking off the fog of sleep and realising the full extent of the situation but knowing it was already too late to do anything about it.

He squirmed around desperately trying to find the zip on his sleeping bag as Molly came bounding over to him and excitedly wagged her tail and pushed her wet snout into his face enjoying the sudden flurry of activity.

'Not now Molly,' he said pulling on his boots.

Up and running now Arthur sprinted toward the lane as quickly as his stiff joints would allow and was overtaken by Molly as they both ran after the truck and convoy of bikes but as he drew nearer the yard he saw Sarah, the young girl who had patched up Alice, pulling the large sliding barn door closed.

Realising he had no chance of catching his truck he changed direction for the barn. Sarah saw him dashing toward her and desperately pulled with all her might on the heavy door but she couldn't make it move any faster. With a few inches still open Arthur had nearly reached the door but he was too late to stop her from securing the latch and still breathing hard, without saying a word, he punched the corrugated iron in anger and frustration.

'Where the hell are they taking my truck,' demanded Arthur who had just about caught his breath and grabbed Sarah by the shoulder to turn her to face him. 'Where are they taking it?'

'Get you're shrivelled hands of me you old pervert,' screamed Sarah, prepared to give as good as she got if it came to that.

Arthur raised his hand to backslap her cheek but caught himself, controlling his anger.

'You can't just steal my truck, why was Sam with them. What the hell is going on?' Arthur heard a metallic click behind him and froze.

'Leave her alone you crabby old bastard.'

It was Linda. She had come from the farmhouse and was aiming a hunting rifle at his head.

'I don't want to use this but you can be damn sure I know how if you give me a reason.'

'Alright, take it easy,' said Arthur backing away and slowly raising his hands. 'Just tell me what's going on. Is Alice okay? Where is Sam going with my truck?'

'You okay Sarah?' asked Linda.

'Yeah, he didn't touch me, its fine,' she replied more calmly.

Linda relaxed a little but kept the rifle pointed at Arthur.

'The boys have gone on a supply run. They needed a truck and driver so your friend has gone with them. Alright, that's enough small talk; I was on my way out here to get you. The old girl is wake and she's taken some soup and is asking for you.'

Sarah nodded to Linda and went to tend the kitchen garden behind the farmhouse where Molly was busy sniffing around and keen to play with a new friend. When Sarah turned to leave Arthur saw she had a sheathed hunting knife tucked into the waistband of her jeans. These women were used to being around tough men and knew how to handle themselves.

Linda lowered the rifle and stepped around behind Arthur following him as he walked to the house. He was excited about seeing Alice and Linda could see that the news of her improvement seemed to have lifted a weight off the older man's shoulders. She was still cautious of him but she knew he wouldn't try anything when his wife was still frail. When they reached the open door of the little bedroom sure enough she was sitting up and despite her bandaged shoulder appeared once more to be her good natured and happy self.

'How are you my love,' said Arthur pushing through the door and pulling Alice toward him in a hug, realising too late that he'd hurt her when she winced in pain.

'Take it easy you old fool,' she laughed but Arthur could see she still grimaced despite putting a brave face on things.

'I'm fine,' she replied, 'just a little stiff and a bit tired but you'll forgive me that much I'm sure.'

Arthur rubbed the wetness from his eyes before it welled up and ran down his cheeks. His Alice was okay and the emotion filled him but he didn't want the other woman to see him like this.

Alice reached out slowly holding his head in her hands and drew him toward her for a kiss.

'I'm really okay,' she whispered softly to him and kissed him again.

'I'll see you two later,' said Linda deciding she could trust Arthur enough to give the couple a little space.

For the rest of the day Arthur stayed with Alice and sat by her bed in a small uncomfortable armchair talking with her about how good things would be when they got to the house on the coast and when she was too tired to listen any more he just sat and watched her sleep. When she asked about Sam Arthur just said he had gone off to help Ronnie and would be in to see her later. He just prayed Sam would make it back alive from wherever he was now.

CHAPTER 15

The peaceful silence of late afternoon was shattered as Molly alerted and ran to the top of the concrete lane barking loudly. Arthur who had taken Alice out to sit by the vegetable garden for some air came running after the excited canine. When he saw the vehicles approach he went back to help Alice as she slowly walked around the farmhouse, both of them anxious to see if Sam would return. A moment later the rumble of engines and exhausts filled the air as a convoy of motorcycles weaved their way down the rutted lane and Arthur was relieved to see his truck in the middle of the group. This time however there was a second Land Rover following in the rear and as they all came nearer Arthur could see the distinctive drab grey of an Enforcer patrol vehicle. It had a bulkier appearance when compared with his truck due to the heavy steel plate armour mounted over all external body panels.

Sarah who was working in the garden tending the precious crop had come to wait with the older couple. 'Oh shit, they've found us,' she said when she saw the Enforcer's truck at the rear of the group and turned to run toward the house to warn Linda.

'Wait, there's only one of them,' said Arthur, 'and look, they're flashing the headlights. It's okay; it's not a raid, the patrol truck must be with them.'

Linda appeared just as the first bikes were reaching the end of the lane and quickly crossed the yard to unbolt the barn. Arthur stepped in to help her slide the heavy door open and this time there was no attempt to stop him. As daylight flooded the cavernous interior Arthur was amazed to see a luxurious club house had been constructed at the rear of the building while the front area served as a combined parking area and fully equipped workshop for the bikes. There was a second level recently constructed inside the main barn above the living and kitchen space at the back. It served as the sleeping quarters and was kitted out with several army surplus bunk beds, more than enough to house the club members and some spare bunks to allow their ranks to increase.

A small bar was positioned under the staircase and despite its limited size it was well stocked with an impressive selection of bottled beers and spirits although most of the liquor bottles were less than half full. The walls were decorated with rusted garage signs advertising a range of motorcycle brands or service items, neon bar signs that were seldom illuminated now, naked pictures of beautiful women torn from contraband magazine centrefolds and a display of used helmets mounted reverently with a small hand-engraved name plaque beneath each in memory of fallen comrades. The air was thick with exhaust fumes, petrol vapour, stale beer, sweat and cigarette smoke.

'I can see why you'd want to keep this to yourself,' Arthur said respectfully.

Linda smiled. 'I guess your boy proved himself with Ronnie so you've earned a little more trust.'

Arthur turned and threw a hard stare at Sam who waved back from the open side window. Arthur was angry with him for stealing the truck but relieved to see Sam had come back alive.

Sam parked at the side of the house while the Enforcer patrol vehicle was parked behind the barn and a few men worked quickly to secure a large canvas tarpaulin over it hiding it from any casual observer even though no one would be likely to wander anywhere near.

Ronnie pulled his bike to a stop in front of the house and removed his helmet setting it on the fuel tank in front of him while he waited as the other bikers took turns to shut off their engines and roll their heavy machines backward into the barn. Linda went to her man and wrapped her colourful tattooed arms around his neck then kissed him passionately before leaning back and wiping a trace of her lipstick from his mouth with her ringed index finger.

When all the other bikes had parked up in the barn he reached forward and playfully slapped Linda's backside then backed his own machine in at the head of the pack so he'd be in position as usual to lead the next charge. He nodded to Sam then grabbed an offered beer before joining the other men to celebrate.

Sam could hear beer bottles being opened and clinked and the pool table being racked, the sound of backs being slapped and of loud laughter from stories being swapped as the drama was relived and tensions released. He didn't join the celebrations or rush to greet Arthur and Alice but helped some of the other men retrieve guns, ammunition, tools and supplies from the back of Arthur's truck and carried some of the haul to the barn where they would be hidden in a deep cellar accessed under a section of false floor in the club house kitchen at the back.

When he came out to the yard Sam was looking awkwardly at his friends and feeling the heat from Arthur's glare. Molly was excitedly bumping her head against his leg and looking up at him for attention so he half-heartedly petted her head.

'Sorry about taking your truck Arthur, I had no choice,' Sam apologised. 'It's good to see you up and about Alice, how are you feeling?'

'I'm feeling much better, thank you Sam. And don't worry about this old grump; we're just glad you're back safe with us. Arthur just told me you'd been pressed into going with the bikers on some kind of a raid, what happened?'

Arthur still said nothing but his expression softened as he

knew Sam genuinely felt bad about taking the truck and he could see something had happened on the raid that had affected him deeply.

'Well....,' Sam began and rubbed the back of his neck while thinking of how to try to explain his involvement in the capture of the Enforcer patrol vehicle when he saw Arthur look past him and then felt a hand on his shoulder.

'Here he is,' said Ronnie as he gave one of the two beers he held in his other hand to Sam.

'Get a cold beer down you, you earned it today, you're one of us now,' and he clinked his bottle against Sam's.

'Sam here saved my arse today,' continued Ronnie as he threw his arm around Sam's shoulder now and hugged him as if he were a lifelong friend. 'I nearly took a shotgun blast to the gut but Sam put a bullet in the bastard's head before he got the shot off. I swear if it wasn't for Sam the boys would be having a funeral now instead of a party.'

Sam's head dropped and Arthur immediately understood why he had been distant since he'd come back and knew now what caused the haunted look in his eye. Taking a life even in defence is a heavy burden to carry and something Sam would have to find a way to live with. It was a feeling Arthur knew only too well from his time in service but that was the job. Sam though didn't have that rationalisation to comfort him and it would be tough but at least he knew he killed in the heat of the moment to save another life.

Feeling ashamed Sam glanced up at Alice who met his gaze with sympathy and understanding. He couldn't bring himself to say anything to her so looked to Arthur.

'Don't let it tear you up Sam, you had no choice. You acted on instinct to protect somebody you know. That's a good thing, believe me,' said Arthur gently, knowing his words would sound hollow but he said them anyway.

Ronnie was in high spirits after a successful raid and the capture of the Enforcer patrol vehicle was a huge prize.

'I guess our secret is out now you've seen our new toy,' said Ronnie directing the comment to Arthur and his wife and indicating to the patrol truck now hidden under the tarp.

'Come on, you might as well have the tour.'

He stepped into the barn again and gestured for his guests to follow. All conversation stopped and they were greeted with icy silence as the other bikers looked to their leader for guidance.

'You all know what Sam here did for us and these people are his friends and our guests, make them feel at home,' said Ronnie reaching into a cooler and handing a chilled beer to Arthur then pulling a chair over for Alice who was still weak and needed to sit.

At this cue the crowd visibly relaxed and it appeared the newcomers had been accepted at least temporarily. One of the group, a tall heavily built man wearing a black bandana around his neck to cover a thick scar approached Ronnie and took him by the arm to one side of the barn where they had a heated exchange for a few moments before Ronnie returned and the other man stomped off angrily.

Ronnie explained the situation. 'You've checked out okay, you can stay another night but that's it, things will get a little uneasy around here if it's for any longer. In the meantime, help yourself to beer and relax.'

The following morning Sam woke early despite suffering a rough hangover from the previous night's celebrations. He had been accepted into the group and had enjoyed blowing off some steam, the opportunity to relax and laugh was a healing balm for his troubled spirits and although Sam usually avoided crowds at all cost he was thankful for the distraction from the gruesome images playing over and over in his mind of the shocked expression of the Enforcer he had shot during the raid then the vacant stare as the life faded from his eyes.

Today was the day they had to leave. They would outstay their welcome if they remained at the farmhouse any longer and Sam was getting worried about the time they had spent here, all too aware that Lucy would be making her way out of the city and would be waiting for him alone in the forest. She was brave and strong and he could not betray the faith she had in him.

Sam crawled out of his sleeping bag and nudged Arthur awake then thirstily gulped down some water from a container he'd filled the night before and poured some for Molly also setting out a dish of food for her then stretched his stiff muscles, deeply breathing the cool morning air. When Arthur had risen Sam got to work packing down their gear and loaded their meagre belongings into the rear of the Land Rover while Arthur knocked the door of the farmhouse and waited to be allowed in to see his wife.

He had helped Alice to bed early in the evening as she was still quite weak but colour had returned to her cheeks and the sparkle in her eye told him all he needed to know. She just needed rest but despite the hospitality they had received Arthur knew they had to get back on the road. He heard heavy bolts being drawn and Sarah opened the door and invited him in. To his surprise he found Alice in the kitchen standing over the wood-burning stove stirring a pan of scrambled eggs with her good arm while the injured shoulder was supported by bandage and a sling.

'I told her she needs to rest but she insisted,' explained Sarah.

Arthur just laughed. 'You'll never keep my Alice down if she has a mind to do otherwise,' he said and crossed the kitchen to wrap his arms around his wife's waist as she cooked.

'Go and get Sam, go on now, the eggs are almost done,' she said turning and waving a spatula at him.

Arthur turned to Sarah and shrugged. 'See what I have to live with eh?' he said jokingly then stepped out returning a moment later with Sam.

Both men sat around the table and tucked into eggs on toast as Alice fussed around pouring tea while Sarah tried to make her sit and rest and was glad when Alice finally agreed and allowed her own tea to be poured for her but only after she had poured everyone else's.

The morning sunlight streaming in through the gaps in the boarded windows and from the open door in the hall brightened the room and the good food and fresh air helped ease Sam's throbbing head a little. The conversation at the table was easy going and here now Sam felt almost like he was part of a family again and allowed himself to believe that perhaps someday he could be part of something good like this.

As Sarah placed an old tin kettle on the stove to boil water for more tea the inner kitchen door opened slowly and Ronnie shuffled in wearing only jeans and unlaced boots. His heavily scarred and tattooed body looking only slightly less punished than his face which was contorted with a combination of sleep deprivation, nausea, blinding headache and thick stubble.

'Morning,' was all he could manage to say with a deep gravelly tone as the others returned his greeting then fell silent and watched him as he went to the corner of the kitchen and scooped handfuls of cold water from a deep basin on the counter top, splashing it over his face before deciding to dunk his entire head.

He pulled his head out with a loud exhalation and smoothed his hair back then stuck his hand in the basin for a few seconds and fished out a bottle of beer which he immediately twisted open and took a long pull downing half of it before taking the bottle from his lips.

Seemingly refreshed he wiped the water still dripping from his face.

'That was a hell of a night eh?' he said laughing. 'Man, we must have drunk our reserves almost dry but it was worth it. It's not every day you're nearly killed and come away with a patrol truck. Any eggs left?'

'We're leaving soon Ronnie,' said Sam matter-of-factly as he stood then turned to walk outside. 'Thanks for breakfast Alice.'

'What's up with him?' asked Ronnie taking another pull

on his beer.

'He's just worried about his girlfriend, we have to meet her soon outside Raven City and he wants to get going,' explained Alice.

'There's also whatever went on between you two yesterday, it's been eating at him since he came back,' added Arthur but he decided not to say anything further about it.

'Yeah, I guess I can understand that,' said Ronnie casually as he stretched and yawned before downing the last of his beer. 'Maybe I can make it up to him; after all he did save my nuts.'

A little later that morning Sam had the Land Rover loaded and pulled it out into the yard ready to leave. The barn was open now and some of the casualties from the heavy night's drinking were beginning to stir. Some stumbled out into the morning light while others were still passed out on the floor or slumped over tables in a deep sleep where they had fallen only hours before.

'Hey Sam, you guys leaving already?' asked one of the group as he relieved his bladder against the side of the barn, squinting from the smoke of a cigarette hanging from his mouth. 'That was a night to remember wasn't it? Actually I can't remember much of it,' he joked and coughed as he laughed and dropped his cigarette at his boots then looked down in time to realise he'd just pissed on it. 'Shit, that was my last smoke,' he said disappointedly.

'Yeah Gene, it was a good night,' replied Sam without enthusiasm. 'We're heading off this morning, we don't want to wear our welcome and my girl is waiting for me.'

Arthur, Alice and Sarah joined Sam at the truck and Molly sensed it was soon time to go and seemed to be excited about riding in the back of the pickup again. Sarah had changed the dressings on Alice's shoulder and given her some spare gauze and bandage so she would be able to keep the dressings clean.

Ronnie and Linda came from the house a few minutes later. 'Hey, don't be leaving without saying goodbye,' said

Ronnie. 'Hold on a minute, I've a few things I want to give you,' and he strolled off in his casual way toward one of the older farm buildings further from the barn and signalled Gene to follow him.

As they waited for Ronnie to return Arthur and Sarah helped Alice climb into the truck and got her seated as comfortably as possible while Sam lifted Molly up into the rear and got her settled down on a folded canvas tarp. Linda leaned on the side of the truck smoking a cigarette and as usual made it clear she wasn't interested in helping. She blew out the last of the smoke from the end of her cigarette before crushing it out with the toe of her boot.

She rolled her eyes and motioned to her young helper. 'Sarah, give me a hand getting some food together, we don't want them starving on the road I suppose. Be sure and top them up with water from the well before they go.'

A few moments later as the travellers loaded the last of the fresh food and water Ronnie appeared pushing an old motorcycle and was followed by Gene who carried two large twenty litre military style fuel cans. Ronnie beamed with a huge grin, highly amused by his surprise.

'Here you are my friend, this is for you,' he said leaning the bike over on its kickstand and throwing the key to Sam who caught it in his big hand. It was just a single key hanging from a miniature eight-ball key ring.

'You said you used to ride, yeah?' said Ronnie still smiling as Gene set down the heavy fuel cans.

'Yeah, but I've not ridden anything since I crashed my old Triumph.'

'Well, now you can get back in saddle,' grinned Ronnie.

'I can't take this Ronnie, I appreciate it but I can't take one of your bikes.'

'It's a gift; don't offend me by not accepting. Anyway, it's an old junker and you'd be doing me a favour by getting it out of here.'

'Hell Ronnie, I don't know what to say. Thanks! This is amazing,' said Sam truly delighted and quite taken aback by the generosity.

'She's an old Kawasaki VN800 Classic; they haven't made these for decades now. Me and the boys prefer to ride American iron though. I found this old heap in one of the sheds when we got here, fixed her up a bit so she runs okay. She's not so pretty anymore and she's not fast but that old V-twin in her heart has plenty of life. She'll keep you right Sam.'

'Ronnie this is great, really. Thanks.'

'Well, you proved yourself out on the raid. You helped us take a patrol truck and you saved my life. It's the least I can do. Gene here has a few gallons of juice for your bike and we refilled the diesel cans and fuel tank on Arthur's truck last night.'

Sam threw his leg over the motorcycle and it felt good to be sitting on a bike again after all these years although he also felt slightly nervous about riding for the first time since his crash. The saddle sat low in the frame and the bike was well balanced with a low centre of gravity which helped his confidence. He reached out and held the custom grips which swept back to meet his hands in a natural position thanks to the four inch risers. It was a perfect fit for him. He wiped a layer of dust and dirt off the tank and saw his dull reflection in the original black paint which although faded had survived fairly well considering the bike's age.

He leaned over and put the key in the ignition, turned it on then pulled out the choke and twisted the throttle a couple of times to prime the carburettor before thumbing the starter button. After a few laboured cranks the engine caught and the yard was filled with the roar from the rusted exhaust pipes. Despite his thumping headache a massive grin spread across Sam's face and he looked to Ronnie who started laughing and knew exactly how Sam was feeling, like only a fellow rider could.

With a few twists of the throttle and a couple of backfires the engine settled down into a steady idle and the low rumble of the exhaust echoed around the barn waking several of the semiconscious bikers, a couple of others came to see what the commotion was, some rolled over to doze some more and a few just hefted themselves from the floor and went to find somewhere more comfortable to sleep off the rest of their hangover.

'Here, you'll need these,' said Gene handing Sam a heavily scratched black full-face helmet and well worn leather gloves. 'They're my old gear but still serviceable. That lid should fit you okay, it's better than hitting the road with your skull if you have another spill!' he laughed.

The sound of the Land Rover's diesel engine starting up made Sam and the other's look toward the truck where Arthur had climbed in and shut his door and was tapping his wrist suggesting it was time they got back on the road. Sarah and Linda were saying their goodbye's to Alice who was thanking them profusely for all they had done for her and her group.

'I guess we'd better get on the road then,' said Sam zipping his leather jacket and then pulling on the helmet and securing the strap. 'Thanks again Ronnie,' and he leaned out and shook the big biker's hand firmly before pulling on his gloves.

'Get out of here, you're going to make me cry,' mocked Ronnie, still laughing and full of life.

As Ronnie and Gene opened a couple of fresh beers they stood with the girls and watched while Arthur moved the truck toward the lane and paused a moment as Sam squeezed the clutch lever and engaged first gear with a grind and a clunk. With a gentle twist of the throttle he smoothly pulled away and followed his companions as they made their way back to the main road to continue on their dangerous journey to where they hoped to find a better life like their new friends had made at the old farmyard.

Sam quickly got a feel for the old bike and a wonderful sense of freedom came flooding back to him but his thoughts were always of Lucy as he negotiated the winding, potholed road leading back to the main route west.

CHAPTER 16

'She was supposed to be here,' said Sam returning from his second scout with Molly through the dense woods around the tranquil lake as he searched for Lucy. Molly appeared to be relieved to stretch her legs and explore again and had delighted in swimming in the lake and chasing a pair of startled mallards. Sam however was unable to enjoy the peaceful surroundings as he had expected to find Lucy waiting by the lake but was gravely concerned now to find no sign of her.

'I don't know what's happened, she should be here, she knows this place, she wouldn't have forgotten.'

'Relax, she'll be here,' said Arthur taking a small pot off the campfire he'd built and prepared a tin mug of hot coffee for himself and Sam. 'If Lucy said she'd meet you here I'm sure she will. If things are as crazy here are they are back in Rook City then she's probably run into a few delays but she'll make it. Here drink this,' and he handed a steaming mug to Sam who took it and forced himself to calm down, sitting sideways on his bike saddle and sipping at the beverage.

'How's Alice?' asked Sam trying to think of something else for a while.

Arthur looked around at the side of the truck where he'd laid out a temporary bed made of stacked sleeping bags and blankets where his wife was peacefully dosing. 'She's doing okay, she's tired and the journey has worn her out but she's strong. Just needs a little more rest is all. We'll change those dressings again before we move on.'

Sam glanced worriedly at Arthur.

'Don't fret Sam, we're not going anywhere without Lucy,' said the older man reassuringly. 'We'll wait here with you, Alice won't leave without meeting this lady of yours anyway!'

'Thanks for the coffee, it's good,'

'How's that bike working out for you?' asked Arthur changing the subject to occupy Sam's mind a little to help him relax.

'Yeah, it's been a long time but it never leaves you. I didn't realise how much I missed it, it's the only way to travel, the sense of freedom, the pull of the engine, the noise and feeling like a part of the world you're travelling in instead of locked up in a tin box. It's a lot of fun.'

'You looked like you were enjoying yourself anyway.'

'Ah it's great alright. Bloody cold though!' said Sam and both men laughed.

A snap of branches started Molly barking which ended their conversation abruptly. They looked to one another and Sam's heart raced in hope it was Lucy but they still had to be cautious. Arthur looked over at Alice and saw she was still sleeping peacefully. More movement alerted them and Molly stood, her gaze fixed in the direction of the noise as Sam drew his bat from the back of the truck and Arthur quickly checked his pistol before both men spread out to flank the approaching stranger.

They hadn't reached the tree line when a small dishevelled figure carrying a large rucksack stumbled out of the woods and fell face forward onto outstretched hands with a shriek.

'Bollocks!'

'Lucy?'

'Sam?'

He recognised the voice immediately, dropped the bat and ran to lift the heavy bag as the owner appeared as though they would be crushed by its weight at any moment. Arthur relaxed and tucked the pistol back into his waistband and discreetly walked back to wake Alice.

Sam lifted the rucksack setting it to one side and quickly turned to help Lucy to her feet but was stopped in his tracks. She sat there in the leaves and grass, mud on her palms where she had fallen, scuffed army boots, black leggings and a stretched grey wool jumper covered with a weathered army jacket Sam had given her that was much too big so she'd rolled the sleeves up. Her long straight brunette hair was tied back in a simple pony tail and her face was dirty from the journey she had just undertaken. She was a mess and she was the most beautiful thing Sam had ever seen.

'So what does a girl have to do to get a hug around here?'

Sam shook himself from distraction. He ran to her and with one arm around her shoulders and the other under her knees he effortlessly lifted her off the ground and held her in his strong arms for a moment, losing himself in her deep brown eyes before setting her gently to her feet. They looked to one another for a brief second then kissed long and passionately, the pain of their separation instantly forgotten, the joy of their reunion magical.

'Would you like some coffee dear?' croaked a frail voice.

Sam and Lucy parted from their embrace and looked rather embarrassed to see they were being watched from the lakeside by the elderly couple.

'Coffee would be great, thank you,' said Lucy squeezing Sam's hand and dragging him to meet his friends.

'Lovely to meet you at last, we've heard so much about you,' said Alice smiling and reaching to shake Lucy's delicate hand.

'Pleased to meet you Lucy, Sam never told us you were so beautiful,' said Arthur passing a tin cup of fresh black coffee but paused when he received an elbow in the ribs from his wife for his comment.

Lucy flushed. 'I'm filthy and I'm sure I look awful but you're very kind to say so. It's nice to meet some of Sam's friends, I didn't know he had any!' she joked and bumped hips playfully with Sam who was feeling very embarrassed.

'Well, you've met Lucy, Lucy, this is Alice and Arthur. We've not known each other long but I suppose you could say we're old friends now.'

'I was really worried about you,' Sam continued, turning to face Lucy. 'We were held up on the way here and I thought you'd maybe think I wasn't coming and had left or that you'd not made it out of Raven City.'

Lucy reached her arms around Sam and hugged him again. 'I wasn't sure I'd make it, it's so good to be here with you. There's something going on in the city. I don't know what it is but people are really scared and the Enforcers are shutting down the sector gates.'

'We saw the same thing in Rook,' explained Arthur. 'Whatever it is it's happening in both cities now, I'd guess that's no coincidence.'

The group moved closer to the lake and sat around the fire and coffee pot. Arthur added more wood and Sam arranged some improvised seating so they could all sit more comfortably and talk.

Sam and Lucy had so much to catch up on even though they had talked as regularly as possible over the monitored city network. They all decided to spend the night by the lake. They were fifteen miles out of Raven City and the secluded spot meant they could enjoy a relaxed evening together, allow Alice time to rest before the next stage of their journey and it would give Sam and Lucy time to enjoy being with one another for the first time in far too long.

Lucy knew she had to tell Sam about Kathy, had to tell him that she wasn't leaving with him to go north as they had planned. She knew he would help, that he'd never leave without her but for now she couldn't bring herself to break the news to him and spoil this wonderful night.

They all sat around the fire with Molly choosing to lie down beside Lucy who was besotted with the golden haired dog as soon as she met her which pleased Sam immensely to see the two he cared most for getting on so well together. The group ate and drank until they were full and merry from some of the supplies they had brought from the biker's farm and all exchanged stories with Lucy about their journeys and everything that had happened to bring them here together by the lake.

Arthur and Alice retired to bed early that evening and Sam moved a comfortable distance from the truck and set up a shelter making the best bed he could with the limited resources while Lucy washed in lake water she had warmed on the fire. They lay down together hugged and kissed softly then undressed each other slowly at first then quicker, then ripping clothes off as their passion grew so intensely they could no longer restrain it. They made love until they were both exhausted and held each other as they lay under a thin blanket sharing the warm glow. They said nothing and no words were needed as they stared up through the trees at the starry night sky, each hoping they would never be apart again.

The next morning they woke in each other's arms as Molly licked their faces in turn meaning she was hungry and decided it was time Sam was up and about.

'Alright, easy Molly, go on, go away,' said Sam at first petting her then pushing her away.

'Morning,' said Lucy rolling over to lie on her back. 'Do you always get woken by your furry alarm clock?' she asked jokingly as she rubbed her eyes and sat up to pull her hair back into a ponytail.

'Ah, she's usually okay but if I sleep much past her regular breakfast time she lets me know,' replied Sam sitting up now too and feeling the stiffness from several recent injuries but forgetting the pain as he heard Lucy's voice and woke with her for the first time in years.

Both he and Lucy got up and went to the lake to wash before following the water's edge toward the other camp where they found Arthur and Alice already up with a fire going and some oats boiling in a large saucepan and a coffee pot sitting in the embers keeping a fresh brew hot until it was wanted.

'You heard the breakfast bell then?' smiled Alice as she stirred the porridge. 'I was going to send Arthur to wake you. Sorry it's not bacon and eggs, porridge is all that's on the menu for now but I do have a little jar of honey Linda gave us if you'd like something to sweeten it up?'

'That sounds lovely, thank you,' said Lucy as she sat on a log Arthur had dragged into the clearing to use as a seat while Sam rummaged in the back of the pickup for some food for Molly who was eagerly following at his heels and getting in the way as she usually did when she was hungry.

'Morning Sam,' called Arthur from close by as he worked to pack down the shelter where he and Alice had spent the night.

Sam just waved and smiled back then joined Lucy and Alice by the fire where he was handed a bowl of steaming grey sludge and a tin mug of strong black coffee. Sitting here now by the lake with Lucy after all this time and after everything that had happened his unappetising breakfast may as well have been five star fare served on a silver platter for all he cared.

When all had eaten and the coffee had done its job of waking and warming tired bodies and minds talk turned once again to the road ahead.

'Well, I suppose we'll be going our separate ways now,' said Sam finally saying aloud what had been unspoken between him, Arthur and Alice as he poked the dwindling fire with a stick. 'We're not far from the city again and the road north should be just ahead. I'll have to leave the bike here and we'll make it on foot from now on, no room for all our gear and Molly on the bike but maybe you could give us a lift to the start of road Arthur?'

'Of course Sam, of course, no bother at all. One last trip together eh? We passed the turn for the southern coast road about half an hour back the way we came but we can go on ahead a little and track back, it won't take us long,' replied Arthur. 'I've marked the location of my cousin's house on your map and a few directions and landmarks to help you find us in case you ever decide to venture southward to visit a pair of old codgers.'

'Oh Sam, I wish you didn't have to go. I understand you have your own road to follow but I'm going to miss you. I've packed a few extra things for you and Lucy, I know you can't carry much but there's a few small luxuries that might make life a little more pleasant on the rest of your journey,' Alice said with a heavy heart.

'I know, I'll miss you both too. It's been a hell of a trip eh?' said Sam laughing, attempting to lift the mood. 'Well, me and Lucy have a long road ahead of us but with a bit of luck we'll soon be setting up a new home in the mountains far away from all this crazy shit.' He turned to put his arm around Lucy and noticed tears streaming down her face.

'What's the matter Lucy, what's wrong?' Sam asked, alarmed.

Arthur and Alice looked to each other not knowing what had happened or what they could do to help as Sam now knelt in front of his girlfriend holding her hands trying to look up into her sorrowful brown eyes.

Lucy who had been silent throughout the conversation now broke down, her body wracked with each heavy sob as wet dots appeared on her faded black leggings from the tears that fell freely now from her cheeks.

'I'm so sorry Sam,' she managed to get out and then began to cry more heavily again.

'It's okay Lucy; whatever it is it's okay. We'll be okay; we'll fix it whatever it is,'

Sam threw his arms around her and held her, rocking her gently until she calmed and the tears stopped.

Alice handed a clean cloth handkerchief to Lucy and she used it to dab her face and eyes, drying the tears and then took a deep breath before speaking. Lucy recomposed herself and strength seemed to flow back into her, her usual steel had returned but she was still quite upset.

'I can't go with you Sam.'

Sam was visibly stunned. A moment passed in which

nobody spoke, the forest sounds around them seemed to intensify and fill the void as Sam's mind raced to process what Lucy had said.

'I'm sorry Sam, I had to come and meet you here. I knew you would wait for me no matter what and I had to see you but I can't go further with you.'

'But why not, what have you got to go back for? Come with me Lucy, I'm not leaving without you.'

'It's my sister Sam; I have to go back for my sister.'

'But you don't have a sister!'

'I didn't, but now I do. I mean I always did but I didn't know until just recently. I'm not making any sense am I?' said Lucy as her eyes began to well up again with emotion and frustration.

'Hey, it's okay. Lucy, look at me. It's going to be okay. Do you hear me?' said Sam holding Lucy's shoulders and looking right at her. Her eyes were filled with sadness and pleading. 'It's going to be okay Lucy, we'll go together. We'll find her and she'll come with us. Whatever it takes, I'm not going to lose you.'

'I guess I better put on another pot of coffee,' said Arthur.

As the coffee brewed the friends all listened to Lucy's story of how she had learned of her younger sister, the affair between her father and the wife of the head of the Elite's Upper Council, how she had escaped from being pimped out by her former employer and how she had actually spoken with her sister through a locked bedroom door but agonisingly had not been able to see her face to face. She explained how she had arranged to meet Kathy and the risks both sisters would have to take to be united for the first time in their lives.

Sam listened to it all without speaking, trying to figure out how they were going to pull this off and escape with their lives, never mind getting Kathy out as well.

When Lucy had finished telling her story her shoulders slumped, her emotions were drained but she felt a huge relief from having opened up, telling her truth and sharing the burden she had carried alone until now.

Sam was the first to speak as he stared into the fire. 'Arthur, I need to ask you a favour.'

Arthur looked to Alice and she nodded in silent agreement. Arthur knew that he owed Sam a lot as neither him nor Alice would have made it this far alone but they would never make back out of the city again, Alice was too frail to make another run like the one they'd just barely survived. All the same he knew Alice would risk it and both would agree to go with Sam if he asked it of them.

'Arthur, I need you to look after Molly for me,' said Sam who had also weighed up the options and knew what it would mean for the older couple to accompany him and Lucy.

'She'll be riding along with all of us Sam, we started this together, we'll see it through together,' said Arthur with gutsy determination.

'Sam, you'll need help,' Alice agreed taking her husband's hand and holding it tightly between her palms.

'Thank you both, I can't thank you enough for all you've done but where we're going it'd be better if it's just Lucy and me. Besides Alice, you still need to mind that wound. Really, you two should get to the coast as you planned. If you can look after Molly we'll come and find you after we've got out with Kathy.'

Arthur knew that despite Sam's confidence and reassurance a formidable challenge lay ahead of them. He realised Sam was aware he may not make it back and so didn't push the matter any further. With the decision made the camp was broken up and the gear loaded into the rear of the truck with Molly. They took one last look at the picturesque lake as the morning sun cast a golden haze over the shimmering water. They hugged, shook hands, and exchanged sorrowful goodbyes and wishes of good luck, the group now separating perhaps never to meet again. Sam took a long time to fuss over Molly, ruffling her shaggy coat, he fed her all the remaining treats he had brought for her and gave her a long hug before closing the tailgate of the truck and signalling to Arthur he was ready.

Sam gave his helmet to Lucy even though it was huge on her small head while he wore just his black wool hat which would be useless in the freezing headwind or a crash but better than nothing. He started the bike and waited until Lucy was seated securely on the pillion seat with her arms clamped tightly around his stomach.

Arthur led the way along the overgrown track back to the main road where Sam pulled the bike to a stop alongside the truck. They all took one last moment to acknowledge each other before Sam put the bike into first gear and sped off west toward Raven City while Arthur, Alice and Molly headed back east to pick up the turn for the southern coast road.

Cruising at a comfortable speed in the crisp morning air on a vintage motorcycle with Lucy holding tight to him, this was a moment Sam had dreamt about many times. Except now up ahead the jagged outline of Raven City rose up from the horizon with the promise of turning his dream to a nightmare.

CHAPTER 17

'No further delays will be tolerated,' scolded Victor Henderson's mysterious superior through a thick cloud of cigar smoke as Henderson himself trembled not with fear but anger at being spoken down to like a disobedient child.

'What did they know,' he thought to himself. This was his country, his command. For the Brotherhood to send their messenger like this to rap his knuckles was humiliating but he knew they had the upper hand for now so he forced himself to swallow his pride and washed it down with the remainder of his brandy.

The Brotherhood member continued. 'Your progress report from Raven City shows promise but we had expected fewer Enforcer casualties and it seems the spread rate of psychosis in Rook City is far below your initial projections.'

Henderson knew there was little point in lying since all feeds from his own sources were in turn monitored by the Brotherhood. He attempted to explain although he barely understood the statistics he was regurgitating. 'We now calculate a diminishing effect once approximately one quarter of the Dreg population has been turned. This was unforeseen as all simulations predicted at least a seventy percent turn rate. Currently, the Enforcers are coming under attack from manageable numbers of psychotics but what we had not accounted for was that a staggering number of unaffected Dreg citizens are not cowering in their homes where they could be easily swept up but rather are taking to the street and looting, rioting and attacking the sector barriers. Our Enforcer patrols are already stretched thin and we risk break through into the Elite sector at some of the lesser defended areas.'

The huge room felt as though it had dropped in temperature by several degrees and even other club members seemed to sense a change in the atmosphere. Henderson's superior said nothing for a moment but made a pretence of needing to smooth out his thin moustache and then to bring the ember of his cigar to his satisfaction before continuing.

'Your errors in judgement and careless mistakes will not go unrewarded Victor,' he said calmly but loudly and with venom dripping from every syllable.

The two men locked in a stare as the other club members returned their attention to their newspapers or previous personal conversations. Neither man uttered a word. The icy confrontation stopped only when a waiter happened by at that moment to collect an empty brandy glass which provided an opportunity for Henderson to rise sharply from his chair and storm off toward the exit. He had allowed himself to be angered and had shown weakness which only served to enrage him further.

'Someone will have to take responsibility for this,' Henderson thought to himself.

Derek Stone was very experienced in Henderson's moods and knew now was not the time to engage in conversation so he remained professionally silent and focused intently on the task at hand which was to drive Henderson to his downtown office in the Central Control building as swiftly as possible. The sooner he could get his boss out of the car the less chance there would be of Stone being on the receiving end of his wrath. Although Stone in no way perceived Henderson as a threat he still didn't relish the thought of a raving psychopath roaring at him from behind his seat.

While en route to his offices Henderson used his personal network tablet to summon all department heads to an emergency meeting. When he arrived at the top floor office the lift doors opened to unleash an enraged Henderson upon a trembling staff. He crossed the open plan office area and entered the large boardroom, slamming the heavy glass door behind him before using a terminal on the wall to turn the electronic glass from clear to opaque, simultaneously providing relief for those staff now left outside and further trapping and intimidating the department heads waiting around the huge boardroom table. The Enforcer commander General Curran was not so affected by Henderson's bluster but rather extremely irritated at being called to this meeting when his men were fighting a hard battle on the streets. Even though he knew the real plan behind the strange events and agreed that the sacrifice of a percentage of his troops would be necessary he felt a duty to oversee the action, not to be summoned by this idiotic fat man in a poorly fitting suit. He was aware however of the power Henderson wielded and knew his attendance would serve his own best interests.

All eyes followed Henderson as he fumbled to open the top button of his shirt collar and loosened his tie which seemed to relieve some of the pressure in his swollen red face but the furnace burning behind his dark eyes only grew in intensity.

'Welcome gentlemen,' said Henderson attempting to restrain himself. 'Thank you for attending at such short notice.' He looked to each man in turn, daring anyone to utter a single word of complaint, disappointed that none did so he continued. 'As you are well aware the Project has been initiated in both our nation's cities and while your initial reports seemed promising I can assure you that your projections have fallen very short of my satisfaction.'

The men around the table all looked to each other for support, each waiting and hoping someone would speak but knowing none would. All feared for their lives now except General Curran who knew his role as Chief Military Officer gave him almost equal standing to that of Henderson.

Henderson continued. 'According to my own independent analysis,' by which he meant the report his superiors in the Brotherhood had forwarded to him, 'it would seem the dispersal of the psychosis inducing chemicals was over-concentrated in certain areas leaving other areas insufficiently saturated. This critical element was key to ensuring the maximum wave effect throughout the Dreg sector, a serious error that cannot now be corrected.' Henderson gritted his teeth to hold himself from descending into a fury, now turning his penetrating gaze on the unfortunate head scientist. 'Doctor Gillan, I believe your department were charged with calculating the dispersal patterns of the required chemical agents. Please correct me if I am mistaken.'

Gillan felt like a lamb facing a wolf as he sensed a void grow around him and all attention now focus on the sacrificial pawn.

'Please Mr. Henderson; such a thing has never been attempted on the scale we have achieved here. The variables and timing involved were always a factor to consider. We have achieved dispersal ratios in the higher margin of our expectations based on all simulations.'

'Your excuses mean nothing to me Doctor Gillan, I hold you personally responsible for the failure of your department. Our goal was clear and you have failed,' said Henderson relishing the power he wielded and savouring the fear emanating in waves from his chosen victim. He lifted his network tablet from the table and tapped in a command then paused for a brief moment until two armed Enforcers entered the room, snapped to attention and saluted. The fact they directed their salute to General Curran and not him greatly annoyed Henderson but he carried on as though unaffected.

'As I was saying Doctor Gillan, you have failed me. You are to be immediately exiled to the prison farms for the remainder of your life which I assure you will be mercifully short.'

'Please, no! No, I only did what you asked. I did my part, someone please tell him,' pleaded the doctor in desperation as the coldly efficient Enforcers violently wrenched him from his chair. 'I have a wife and three children, please reconsider, please I'm begging you.'

Henderson's face broke into a purely evil grin. 'Thank you for reminding me. I am a generous man Doctor Gillan, which is why I will arrange for your family to join you in the farms. I'll leave it to you to explain to them why they have been forced to suffer, I'm sure they'll understand. Guards, remove him.'

The other men sat in terrified silence around the boardroom table listening to agonising screams of protest as the unfortunate doctor was dragged to his fate.

'I think it only fair to warn you all that I treated the good doctor with leniency in this circumstance. If I have to deal with failure again from any department the punishment will be execution for those responsible, including the execution of their immediate family,' said Henderson in an almost giddy mood having massaged his wounded ego. The General was disgusted to see such weakness but kept his thoughts to himself.

The remaining Upper Council members were still reeling in shock at what they had witnessed and from the threat they had received. Such an abuse of power was unheard of but none the less each knew their elected leader had the right by law to carry through with any action if he felt he had due cause. They could have voted to overturn his decision and remove him from office but not a single man among them trusted another enough to risk facing accusations of treason.

'Since it is obvious to me now that I am the only person with whom such responsibilities can lay I am hereby demanding that full control of the Project be directed to me personally and for the short-term at least I shall be taking overriding command of all system functionality. I expect you can manage to do your jobs without need for me to intervene but never the less please all now enter your authorisation codes to divert high command of each of your sectors to me.'

Henderson stood up sharply from his chair and leaned heavily on the huge table, balling his fists until his knuckles whitened as he stared down each man in turn until they silently took out their tablets and entered the required codes to transfer command to their insane leader. All except General Curran complied.

'I'm afraid Victor I must insist that military control remains under my final command,' said the General in casual defiance of Henderson's order.

Henderson turned his head to look at the General with such ferocity that the other men thought his neck may have snapped there and then. The contest between the two leaders made for another uncomfortable moment but the General's relaxed demeanour in the face of Henderson's efforts at intimidation bordered on mockery and Henderson knew it so to avoid humiliation for the second time that day he acceded to the General's request.

'Very good General, I know your men are quite overrun at present so under the circumstances I suppose it best to defer tactical command to you. For now,' he replied feeling as though the comment had won him this bout.

With ultimate control of the entire city's surveillance network, sector gate controls, water and power systems all now transferred to central access from his personal tablet Henderson felt more relaxed knowing he had sole command and could now do as he pleased without consulting other members of the Council. The Enforcers would defer to orders issued by General Curran but since they had their hands full dealing with the civilian threat he felt he could safely ignore them for now.

His objective completed Henderson decided to return to his penthouse to consider his next move. The day had been taxing and a troubling pain in his chest told him he needed to relax for the remainder of the evening.

'Mr. Stone, I'd like you to accompany me,' he said as his driver pulled the car alongside the door to the lift in the underground car park beneath his penthouse. 'Please see to it that my daughter is sedated. I'll require her to be kept out of my way until morning.'

'Certainly sir, are you expecting company?' Stone asked since he was usually only requested to administer the sedative when Henderson planned to allow guests or service personnel into his private domain and wanted Kathy's presence to go unnoticed.

'Not that it's any of your concern Mr. Stone, I'm simply in need of some peace and quiet for the rest of today and I'm in no mood to deal with my troublesome offspring,' replied Henderson grumpily.

Stone silently released a long breath to control his patience and said nothing further as he stepped out of the car and opened the door for his employer. Both men entered the lift and Henderson slid his heavy gold watch a little up his arm so he could expose the subdermal chip implanted in his wrist and waved it over the scanner embedded in the lift controls.

'Be ready for her,' Henderson told his henchman in expectation of another of his daughter's repeated escape attempts.

When both men stepped out into the entrance hall they waited until the lift doors had closed before going further into the huge living area where they found Kathy hard at work rearranging Henderson's vast collection of tasteless antiquities. She looked up at her step-father and his driver but said nothing to either instead focusing more intently on positioning a gaudy gold figurine Henderson had brought back from some business trip or other.

'A pleasant surprise to find you behaving yourself for once,' said Henderson. 'I think you've been working hard enough for today, it's time for you to sleep. Mr. Stone, if you please.'

Kathy made no attempt to run; she knew there was nowhere to go and to do so would only result in angering Henderson which could wreck her plan. Stone clamped his hand gently but firmly around her arm and coaxed her reluctantly toward the stairs leading to her bedroom as Henderson looked on grinning before turning to fix himself a drink.

Kathy had been through this on many occasions and knew that although Stone was a forceful man he would not hurt her. She could see he didn't share the sick pleasure her father enjoyed from treating her badly. That was of little comfort now though as she sat on her bed behind the locked door and waited for Stone to return. A moment later she heard the lock click and Stone reappeared carrying the familiar black leather case containing hypodermic needle, syringe and vials of potent sedative cocktail.

'Please don't do this,' she implored. 'Just lock the door again if you must but please no more needles. I'll be quiet, I really will, you don't need to use that.'

Stone was impassive 'I'm sorry Kathy; your father wants you to be quiet for the rest of the night, you know I hate to do this but I promise I'll be gentle. You'll just have a nice sleep is all,' he said opening the case and noticing one of the syringes was missing along with a vial of sedative.

He looked to Kathy questioningly but just at that moment Henderson's voice boomed angrily from downstairs. 'Stone, I need to see you immediately.'

Stone rolled his eyes and shouted through the open bedroom door. 'One moment sir, I'm just seeing to your daughter.'

'I said now, Stone.'

'I'll be back in a minute, and please don't try anything silly,' said Stone zipping the case of sedative apparatus, tucking it into his inside jacket pocket and leaving the room grumbling under his breath.

Kathy's heart raced. She thought her theft of a syringe and sedative from the black case from Henderson's desk drawer earlier in the week had now been discovered. She'd hidden it carefully along with her prepared suitcase for the moment she planned to once again attempt escape but now what? Had Stone really noticed the equipment was missing?

What would he do to her when he returned? She felt sick now realising she had probably made a huge mistake and would be made to pay a terrible price.

She thought of using her stolen syringe on Stone when he returned but it usually took a moment for the powerful drug to induce a deep sleep and what if he alerted Henderson before he lost consciousness?

She sat on her bed waiting helplessly, thoughts of her sister flooding her mind. As the minutes passed she could hear what had started as muffled conversation between her father and Stone began to get louder and angrier. Both men were raising their voices now, almost shouting. She crept from her room and dared to look down to main living area to watch the confrontation. Stone looked like an attack dog straining at his leash as some inner force of iron will held him back.

'This is the last bloody time,' Stone snapped. 'I had a deal to take care of this evening and you know that. It's worth a lot of money to me but more than that I look like an idiot when I don't show up. It's very unprofessional and I don't like unprofessional.'

Henderson's fat bald head was glistening with sweat and glowing red with anger. He spat when he spoke but forced himself to lower his voice which gave emphasis to his words

'Derek, you have proven yourself as a loyal employee. For this reason alone I will overlook your outburst,' he took a short breath and began shouting again, 'but when I give you an order I expect you carry it out. Without question.'

Stone stood for a second and eyeballed Henderson. He opened his mouth to say something but though better of it then turned sharply and strode toward the lift. An awkward moment passed until the lift arrived during which Stone could see from the reflection in the polished brass doors that Henderson was boring holes in the back of his skull with a ferocious glare.

As the doors closed Stone shouted out. 'I'll not make it back until tomorrow afternoon so you'll have to find another driver for the morning.' He smiled to himself as Henderson shouted a string of obscenities but he couldn't make out many of the words as the lift had already started to descend.

Peeking from her vantage point at the top of the stairs Kathy watched as Henderson suddenly clutched at his chest. He bent over and steadied himself against the wall with his other arm. For several seconds despite her hatred for him she considered running to help but then he seemed to recover slightly and stumbled to his favourite worn leather chair in the centre of the living space where he sat heavily and slurped a mouthful from a drink he had left on the coffee table earlier.

Kathy realised Henderson must have assumed Stone had administered the sedative as instructed and that she was now deep in a drug induced slumber. As she watched he massaged his chest a while until he had regained full control of himself and then began to work at something on his tablet. She crept quickly back to her room and eased the door closed, propping a chair under the door handle since she had no lock on the inside.

At last she'd gotten a break. Stone was gone and she reckoned with her stolen syringe and a full vial she had enough sedative to knock Henderson out cold for a week. Finally this would be her chance to get free.

CHAPTER 18

Kathy knew it was now or never. Lucy promised she would return but it would be dangerous for either of them to hide for long in the car park beneath the massive tower in which she had been imprisoned for the past few years. Since the previous week when she had crouched on the other side of her locked bedroom door and heard her sister's voice Kathy had dreamed of meeting her true family and escaping her life of confinement and servitude from the cruel and increasingly volatile Victor Henderson.

She had to resist the urge to make another attempt at breakout during the days leading to this moment as if she failed Henderson's inevitable overreaction could cost her any further opportunity of gaining her freedom. Now though Kathy dared to hope she had a real chance.

From under her bed she pulled the wheeled travel case she had prepared and checked it through one last time. She had little in the way of personal belongings despite the obvious wealth of her father and knew not what to expect beyond the limits of the city's Elite sector but she had packed as best she could. She had no cash but thought some jewellery she had kept to remember her dead mother may be worth something. Although she was loathe to give it away she would trade almost anything for her freedom. Along with the most practical clothes she owned and some basic toiletries she was ready. Anything else just reminded her of the life she longed to leave behind and she knew Lucy would take care of her if she could only escape.

Wearing her oldest designer jeans, a pair of barely worn blue and white vintage converse shoes and a deep red cashmere jumper for warmth under an expensive tailored brown leather jacket she was as dressed down and casual as her wardrobe allowed. She packed a small framed photograph from her dressing table that showed Kathy together with her mother. It had been taken just a couple of years before Claudia Henderson had been murdered by her husband. Packing this treasured possession into her bag she fastened the zips and took one last look at the room where she had spent so much of her life.

Glancing out the window across the tops of tall city buildings to the high perimeter walls and beyond Kathy was often struck by the fear that she may never live to see the real world outside of the life she had been forced to live all these years. She had dreamed of nothing else but now when it seemed she might really get her wish Kathy felt scared that she might actually succeed. How would she cope, where would she go, and what kind of life could she make for herself? She knew anything was better than living as a captive and besides, she would have Lucy now. She'd never be alone again, she had a sister and that gave her the courage she needed to push on with her plan.

She stared at the syringe and vial of serum lying now on her dressing table. It looked so innocent and doubts crept into her mind about whether her plan was foolish. She picked up the syringe and it felt too small and fragile an implement with which to confront her stepfather. Thoughts then rushed into her head of how she had been a victim for so long, suffering at the hands of the cruel bastard who had also murdered her mother. This steeled her will and hardened her determination to succeed. As she visualised what she knew she must do the small instrument began to feel like it truly was a weapon with which she could defeat her demons.

She decided to take no chances and inserted the needle

tip into the sealed top of the glass vial and drew back the plunger filling the syringe completely then upturned it and tapped the side while squeezing out any air bubbles so it was primed and ready. Kathy estimated it was roughly four times the dose she usually received but considering Henderson's massive bulk she wanted to be sure he'd go down.

Taking a few deep breaths to ready herself she carefully opened her bedroom door and carried her case along the corridor to the top of the stairs and peered around the corner to the main living quarters below. Henderson hadn't moved from his chair and seemed to be fully engrossed with whatever he was doing on his network tablet. Leaving her case she took the syringe in her left hand, holding it carefully and when Henderson turned his head away to lift his drink she dashed across the landing to the top of the opposite staircase so Henderson was now sitting with his back to her.

Kathy held her breath as he stood and turned, walking toward her she was sure that he had detected her movements or that she had made some noise that had given a sign of her presence. Henderson walked past the bottom of the staircase and after a few seconds she heard the clink of ice being dropped into a glass and the slosh of liquid as he fixed himself another drink. She was relieved to see him shuffle back to his seat and take a long sip from his beverage before settling his attention to once again tap and swipe the screen of his tablet.

'Come on girl, you can do this,' Kathy said to herself letting out a long slow breath to steady her breathing before stepping out from cover and creeping down the first few stairs. Countless times she had used these very steps but now the short descent felt like she was climbing down from a mountain, exposed on an open hillside where she would be spotted immediately if Henderson were to just glance around.

Seconds seemed like minutes as she placed a toe on the next step and eased her weight down slowly. Left foot here, now right foot a few inches from centre on the next step, careful with the left foot on the following step again, she silently mapped her way down, skilfully avoiding any stair that would creak, hardly daring to breathe until she had made it safely to the lower level.

She paused to compose herself for a brief moment then holding the syringe high with her thumb on the plunger she advanced quickly toward the unsuspecting Henderson, her feet swiftly and silently dancing across the gap. Standing directly behind him now she swung her arm and hammered the needle deep into his shoulder at the base of his neck and pressed the plunger down hard and fast injecting a massive dose of the powerful sedative. She let go of the syringe and backed away in terror as a shocked and enraged Henderson pushed himself to his feet and turned to stagger after her, the needle still embedded in his flesh leaving the syringe wagging about on top his shoulder.

'What have you done? I'll kill you, you little bitch, just like I killed your whore of a mother,' snarled Henderson as he charged at Kathy with arms outstretched and fingers grasping for her throat but his words had already begun to slur and his vision was tunnelling. From her own experience she knew it took a moment for the sedative to take effect but the huge dose she had given Henderson mixed with the liquor he had consumed began to do its job almost instantly.

Kathy continued to back away but Henderson's anger kept him fighting, driving him forward even as his legs began to fail him. He clutched his chest in agony but this seemed to anger him all the more and he charged at her with all his remaining strength, the hate boiled in his heart and Kathy would know the full extent of his wrath. She found herself backed into a corner with nowhere to go but the kitchen. There was only one entrance and now Henderson was blocking it, holding himself upright with a hand gripped tightly on each side of the door frame, his eyes glazed and searching for focus, sweat pouring from his bald head and soaking through his shirt but still he refused to fall.

Frightened that the dose she had given him was not

enough and that she made a terrible mistake Kathy knew she had no choice, if he got hold of her now she would die at the hands of her mother's killer. She ran to a drawer and desperately rummaged through its contents while keeping her eyes locked on Henderson. Her fingers found what she wanted and she pulled out a large kitchen knife, prepared to do now what she had never before allowed herself to consider.

Brandishing the knife she stood with her back to the rear wall of the kitchen facing Henderson as he swayed in the open doorway. Her defiance was too much for him to bear and he launched himself toward her at surprising speed for his size and condition. Kathy was poised to fight for her life but as he passed an island counter in the centre of the room Henderson stumbled catching his hip on the corner which spun him around and as he lost his footing he landed heavily on his back with a slap, banging his head on the hard tile floor as he fell.

Kathy watched as he squirmed slightly trying to get up but the sedative was really kicking in now and try as he might Henderson could not prevent himself from fading into unconsciousness. As she watched his pupils roll back under his eye lids she heard him stammer. 'I'll...kill...you...you...bi...'

She waited several moments to be sure he wasn't going to move again then still clutching the knife she moved to stand next to him, tapping his forehead with the flat of the blade. He didn't move or even groan but she could hear his raspy breathing. Not trusting that he wasn't faking it she parted his legs with her foot then kicked him squarely in the testicles as hard as she could manage but still there was no movement. She kicked him again. 'Take that you bastard,' she screamed, venting some of the pain he had caused her over many years.

Knowing that there was only one way to summon the lift and leave the penthouse Kathy prepared herself for a gruesome task. Quickly she gathered gauze and bandage from the small first aid kit mounted on the kitchen wall and knelt beside the unconscious mound of flesh on the floor.

237

She removed Henderson's watch and located the small vertical scar on the underside of his wrist. Using a smaller knife from the kitchen drawer she made an incision using the faint scar as a guide and taking care not to cut an artery with the point of the blade she dug out Henderson's implanted chip which resembled a large grain of rice made of glass.

Blood ran freely from the open cut so she quickly pressed gauze to the wound and wrapped bandage around the wrist several times to hold it in place. Using another piece of bandage she made a rough sling to hold Henderson's arm on top of his chest to help minimise bleeding. At the sink she scrubbed the blood from her hands and placed Henderson's ID chip in a small kitchen food bag so she wouldn't lose it then bundled up an apron and slid it under his head. She checked the dressing on his wound and satisfied herself it wouldn't bleed through. She tried rolling him into the recovery position but he was too heavy for her to manoeuvre so she had to trust he'd not swallow his tongue until he regained consciousness. Although she hated her step-father she wasn't a killer like him.

Hurrying now she ran from the kitchen to the top of the far staircase to grab her case then raced back down and along the entrance hall to the lift where she swiped Henderson's chip across the sensor in the control panel and was rewarded with a cheerful ding confirming the carriage was rising. As she waited she suddenly remembered Henderson's tablet had fallen to the floor when she had stuck him with the syringe and realised the device was still lying by his chair. Thinking that perhaps he could use it to track her she ran back and picked it up and glancing at the screen she was shocked to see a patchwork display of grotesque live images seemingly from security camera feeds showing a city on fire, crazed people tearing each other to pieces as others ran in horror, Enforcers fighting a battle on the streets against civilians armed only with sticks, bottles and rocks.

She swiped the top of the screen to close the video viewer and with her mind still reeling at what she saw Kathy wondered was this what the world outside had become. For a brief moment she considered maybe this was why Henderson had kept her locked away so long, to protect her from the dangers she could not see on the streets far below. She didn't hesitate for long and her fear of Henderson shook her back to the present. She slid the tablet into its leather case then stuffed it inside her zipped jacket and returned to the lift just as it came to a stop and doors the opened.

She stepped into the empty carriage and swiped the small bloody food bag containing Henderson's ID chip across the sensor then pressed the button for the basement level car park. As she waited for the doors to close she half expected to see Henderson bounding toward her, to thwart her escape at this final moment but he was deep in a dreamless sleep so she rode the entire way down without hindrance.

Disembarking the lift her senses were assailed by a blast of cold air and the smell of concrete, damp and exhaust fumes as is the same in any such place across the globe. Not having been this far from the apartment in years she was overwhelmed with anxiety and almost panicked but she wasn't going to blow this now. She looked ahead and saw the exit ramp leading up to the daylight above. The guards at the rising barrier were casually standing around; one was smoking and appeared to be half-heartedly listening to his partner animatedly recounting some romantic conquest.

She could see to her left a long line of cars were parked with their rear to the wall and about half way along the overhead lighting was turned off as from that point most of the vehicles were protected under dust covers. She knew Henderson had several classic and vintage cars and assumed the remainder of the vehicles must have belonged to other residential occupants of the prestigious building. They were collector's items and would rarely if ever be taken out on the road so she knew why Lucy had told her to wait here. It would be a safe place to hide and if Henderson regained consciousness sooner than expected he would never imagine that Kathy was hiding right under his nose.

Checking to be sure the guards were still preoccupied she made a dash from the lift behind the row of the parked cars keeping her head low so she wouldn't be seen until she reached the unlit section of the garage. She worked her way along now, gently lifting the covers so as not to disturb anything and tried the door handles but found each was locked.

With just three cars remaining on this side of the wall she found a 1958 MGA Roadster stored with the convertible top removed. Pushing her case in ahead of her she slipped up under the cover and made herself as comfortable as possible in the passenger seat, listening carefully for any sound that would indicate she had been discovered. After a few moments she was satisfied she had gotten to relative safety undetected so she allowed herself to relax a little and even congratulated herself for getting this far. She had actually escaped from him after all these years. Now she just had to sit tight and hope against hope that Lucy really would come back for her.

CHAPTER 19

The bike's left side mirror exploded in a shower of broken glass as a hail of gunfire from an Enforcer's pistol shot past Sam and Lucy as they sped into the Elite sector through the southern perimeter wall.

Knowing time was of the essence they had to get to Kathy as quickly as possible and couldn't afford to get stopped at the outer city barriers. They had waited by the roadside concealed in a shallow ditch with the bike leaned over on its side until an empty supply lorry rolled up to the barrier from inside the city. It would return to port without an escort since its valuable cargo of merchandise for the Elite stores had been delivered.

As the lone guard casually strolled from his hut and inspected the driver's papers Sam righted the bike and pushed it silently onto the tarmac. When Lucy was on board with her arms wrapped tightly around his waist Sam started the bike and slowly advanced to the gate. Neither the guard nor truck driver heard the approaching bike over the sound of the lorry's large diesel engine echoing in the concrete gateway.

The guard entered his hut again to activate the barrier allowing the lorry to move out and Sam seized the opportunity he had been hoping for. Quickly dropping a couple of gears with his left foot he twisted his right wrist back, sharply grabbing a handful of throttle and felt the surge of power as the old bike leapt forward. The heavy cruiser

241

with rider and pillion would win no races but was fast enough. As the lorry cleared the gateway the driver looked ahead to see the motorcycle speeding straight toward him. Sam held his nerve and waited until the last second to see which direction the driver would swerve then leaned the bike hard to the opposite side before correcting course, just narrowly avoiding the tail of the long vehicle as he raced toward the descending barrier. Sam leaned forward until his chin rested on the speedometer and Lucy pulled herself tight into his back, turning her head sideways to stay as flat as possible and watched as the underside of the barrier dropped just inches from her face as they barely cleared the gate.

The guard was taken completely by surprise and took a moment to react but then raced out of his hut, pistol drawn and stood in a wide stance firing multiple rounds toward the speeding intruders. As the bike thundered closer to the city's edge the Enforcer's best shot tore through the side mirror but neither rider nor pillion was hit. The guard was forced to cease fire as stray shots now were skimming off buildings ahead of the moving target, something permissible in the Dreg sector but the accidental shooting of an Elite resident would mean the his own execution. As Sam and Lucy disappeared into the city streets the guard ran back to report the incident, cursing himself for leaving his radio on his desk. It didn't matter anyway since all additional Enforcer squads had been detailed to sector barrier defences or to frontline duty in the developing chaos of the Dreg sectors.

Sam gunned the bike through tree lined residential streets, confidently passing the occasional luxury car as the occupants stared incredulously at the speeding machine tearing loudly through their neighbourhood, some lifting phones to dial for emergency services that would not come, others clutching their children back from the road or waving a fist in protest at this outrage.

Constantly scanning the road and occasionally checking the remaining mirror Sam felt sure now that they weren't being pursued so after zigzagging through several streets he eased back on the throttle and slowed to a comfortable forty miles per hour, the exhaust quieting to a low rumble. He spotted an alleyway between two rows of impressively maintained townhouses and killed the engine completely allowing the bike to roll silently from the street into the alley where he coasted as far as he could under momentum and pulled the bike to a stop behind the cover of the cleanest dumpster he had ever seen.

Still straddling the bike he leaned the over on the kickstand and took off his gloves setting them on the fuel tank in front of him. Lucy still tightly gripped her arms around his waist.

'Are you alright Lucy? Were you hit? Lucy?'

He held her hands and gently teased them apart then dismounted and turned to help Lucy climb down from the rear of the bike. Long strands of dark hair fell across her face as she removed the helmet and he carefully brushed them aside looking into her wild eyes as she spoke.

'I was really scared Sam, I thought we were going to crash or get shot or maybe both. I'm okay though, really, I'm okay. I just need a minute.'

'Okay,' he replied and allowed himself a moment now to gather himself and leaned against the wall to rest as his heart rate slowed again.

They had made it into the city in one piece. Finding Kathy and getting out again would be another matter but Sam wasn't about to quit now, not when they'd come so far.

'I think we'll have to abandon the bike,' said Sam. 'I hate to have to leave her so soon, I'd not realised how much I missed riding.' The thought of leaving his bike was like cutting off an arm, such is the way a motorcycle becomes a part of you.

'And I thought you'd miss me the most,' said Lucy jokingly.

'You know what I mean. Besides, it draws too much attention and we'll not be able to take Kathy on the bike anyway.'

He sat for one last time in the saddle but didn't start the engine, just laid his hands on the grips and then patted the fuel tank as if saying goodbye to a loyal but lame horse that had to be mercifully put down.

Sam pocketed the keys as a keepsake and they left the bike concealed behind the dumpster, prepared themselves and then ventured out of the alley into the streets of the Elite sector in Raven City.

'Look, you can see the masts on top of Kathy's building,' said Lucy easily identifying the tallest building among the high rise structures as the one in which she had risked everything to contact her sister several days earlier.

As they made their way toward Henderson's tower Sam couldn't help but notice the facade of riches was crumbling here too although not yet in the advanced state of decay endured by the Dreg sector inhabitants. He had heard stories of the opulence and excess of the Elites from those Dreg workers in service jobs in the Elite sectors in Rook City but had not set foot in the Elite sectors in person. Now that he was here he could see the standard of living was far in excess of anything he had ever known but all the same, the cracks were beginning to appear.

As they passed by boutique shops and exclusive bars and cafes the everyday Elite residents looked scornfully at the two scruffy, downtrodden Dregs walking through their streets but none reacted in such a way as to cause Sam or Lucy any concern. Most Dreg workers were uniformed in some fashion or another whether dressed for serving, maintenance or cleaning and were rarely seen on the street except for when bussed to their jobs early each morning and returned to exit at the sector barrier in late evening. Sam and Lucy stood out all the more in their torn, dirty clothing but it seemed no one wanted to engage with them as though it might somehow lead to contamination.

The ever watchful eye of security cameras seemed to follow their movements, the feeling that they would be stopped and arrested at any moment never left them. At one point a convoy of three Enforcer patrol wagons sped up behind them, sirens blaring but all continued in the direction of the sector gates much to the couple's relief.

Turning a corner their attention was immediately drawn to the pulsing blue lights from a blockade of patrol wagons lined up several hundred metres to their right. They had entered a long street a few blocks from one of the main sector barrier gates and could see that the Enforcers were attempting to reinforce the barricade with their vehicles.

Quickly the pair crossed the road and stood briefly behind a gathering crowd who were excitedly speculating on the unfolding drama.

'I heard the Dregs are protesting against unemployment,' said a young man in a fine tailored blue suit to his female colleague as he sipped coffee from a large mug on which was printed the words "The Boss Of Me".

'No,' replied another man who stood in front but turned to respond. 'Keith from accounts heard from his wife that the Dreg's are being rounded up to be taken to work camps, that's why they're rioting.'

'Well, it'll help to clean up that awful side of our city. Just so long as some are kept to pour the coffee and mop the floor,' said the female colleague and all three laughed heartily.

Sam and Lucy looked at each other silently acknowledging their disgust and discomfort.

Just then a volley of shots rang out and the crowd gasped as one and shrank back but relaxed as they heard a reassuringly authoritative voice boom into the well of silence which had followed.

'Disperse immediately! You will not be warned a second time. Return to your homes and await instruction.'

An Enforcer squad commander was using a loudspeaker to address the unruly crowd on the Dreg side of the barricade. A roar of voices rose up followed by a hail of bottles, stones and various other projectiles and people could be seen scaling the barrier fences beyond the row of armoured vehicles. More warning shots were fired into the air as Enforcers standing tall on the front of their patrol wagons began clubbing anyone who attempted to breach the barrier fence. Shots were fired into the seething crowd now and screams were heard over the roar of angry voices but still the stones and bottles flew and people continued to try to push up and over the steel wall. The gathering of spectating Elites grew as more office workers descended from their glass towers to brace the cold air and witness the drama unfold, watching with interest from a safe distance as if it were nothing more than a celebratory firework display, confident the authorities would protect them.

'Come on, we need to go,' whispered Sam as he gently pulled Lucy through the crowd and along an adjacent street. 'What the hell is happening? I know things are bad back in Rook but people throwing themselves at the Enforcers, that's something else. What could have made people so desperate?'

'I don't know Sam. When I was trying to get out to meet you, people were scared. There were patrol wagons racing around and a lot of people running in the opposite direction. Of course that happens sometimes but this was different, it was something more, you know?'

'Let's just keep going. Once we have Kathy we can get the hell out of here and never come back. Whatever's happening it won't matter to us anymore.'

'You can't say that Sam, it does matter, what happens to those people I mean.'

'Look Lucy, I feel bad for them, I do but we can't help them. We've barely made it this far ourselves but we've got our plan to try and make a life somewhere else, it's up to them to do the same if they want it badly enough. Sitting around complaining about Central Control cutting jobs or cutting rations or about the lower quality crap for sale on the black market these days, what kind of life is that anyway? It's no life held behind fences and walls, hiding from gangs or the government. Whatever lays ahead for us is better than waiting for someone else to come and save us from ourselves.'

They walked on in silence for a while noting the blurring distinction between older residential and newer office buildings until they were now in the main business district of the Elite sector and had to crane their necks to see the tops of the towers high above them. Sam was thankful the Enforcers seemed to be more concerned with the disturbance at the sector gate than with any reports of two Dreg workers walking alone through the Elite sector.

'Kathy's building is just a couple of streets along now,' said Lucy.

'Great, there's just the small matter of getting past the guards and leaving again with Kathy,' said Sam feeling increasing anxious about their chances.

Lucy stopped and turned to Sam, taking his hand and holding it between both of hers.

'I was thinking about that and I have an idea but I'll have to go in alone.'

'No Lucy, I can't let you go in there by yourself, what if something happens, how would I even know you were in danger? I have to go with you,' said Sam. He knew she could look after herself but the thought of leaving her to attempt the most dangerous part of Kathy's rescue alone sickened him.

'Sam, it's the only way. You'll never get past the guards and even trying to would make them more suspicious. We'd likely both be arrested on the spot. They're all the more cautious here since Victor Henderson is the penthouse resident.'

'Well, what makes you think you'll have any more luck than I will?' asked Sam.

'I have my feminine charm; even in my army boots and combat jacket I think I could wrap them around my little finger, or don't you think I'm pretty?' she said with a wry smile.

'Come on, quit messing with me, you're gorgeous but seriously, you can't just walk in there by smiling at the guards.'

'I know, but I also have this,' and she reached into her inside jacket pocket and winked as she took out her ID badge from Harper's cleaning crew which gave her authorization to work in many of the Elite buildings, including Henderson's.

'Clever but still risky, what if they don't accept it?'

'They should but we have to wait a little while.' She drew back the rolled cuff of her army jacket and checked a delicate silver watch. 'It's too early yet but in less than an hour from now my old boss is due to start work here, unless he's changed routine in the past few days but his customers like to see the girls regularly.'

'What do you mean, see the girls? What kind of cleaning company is he running? And you worked for this guy?' Sam teased her.

'Yeah, well, luckily nothing happened and I burned my bridges when I left that job.'

They walked closer to Henderson's building and darted into a delivery area at the rear of another office tower which gave them a view across the street to the entrance of the underground car park where Kathy would be waiting.

'I hope she's okay. She must be terrified,' said Lucy worrying about her younger sister and feeling increasingly nervous about meeting her face to face for the first time. The waiting had been so hard during these past days but now they were so close time seemed to slow even further.

'What if she's not there Sam? I didn't want to think about it but what if she wasn't able to get out? I can't leave her behind Sam, I can't.'

'Hey, come on now, she'll be there,' said Sam pulling Lucy into a hug which always reassured her, whatever the situation. 'If she's anything like her big sister, she'll have made it, believe me.'

'I love you Sam.'

'I love you too Lucy.'

They waited and watched as Lucy checked the time every

few minutes expecting the hands to have swept further around the dial than they had done. The usual time Harper and his crew would have arrived had passed and there was still no sign of him. Lucy was feeling despondent and Sam fought the urge to comfort her as he knew it would have the opposite effect when she was agitated like this.

Several more minutes had passed when a tatty old van screeched around the corner and pulled to a sharp halt in front of the red and white pole blocking vehicle access to the car park below.

'That's him, that's him, see I knew he'd be here,' Lucy said squeezing Sam's hand excitedly. Sam bit his tongue, now wasn't the time to jibe at her.

'Okay, take my jacket,' she said and took the ID card from her pocket before handing the jacket to Sam. Glancing nervously from around the corner at the guard hut and up and down the street she worked quickly, pulling her hair back into a neat pony tail and wrapping it up into a neater bun secured with a hairclip from her pocket. She tucked her black low cut t-shirt into the waist of her leggings and arranged it so it pulled tight accentuating her figure.

'How do I look?' she asked.

'Beautiful as always,' said Sam reaching to hold her head in his hands and kissing her softly. 'Be careful Lucy, I'll be here. I won't go anywhere but if you're not out in twenty minutes I'm coming in after you.'

'Trust me,' she said smiling but Sam could sense how nervous she felt.

She clutched her ID card, kissed Sam quickly for luck and ran across the street. The guards had returned to their hut and hadn't seen her but she kept running hard toward them stopping only when she crossed in front of the entrance barrier.

She held her ID out for one of the guards, a lower ranking Enforcer, to inspect. As she stood breathing heavily from the sprint the guard turned to his partner and passed the ID card to the more senior man.

'Sorry for running up like this, I'm late for work. I missed the van at the sector barrier this morning and just made it here now. Has Mr. Harper arrived yet?' she paused and looked up to the senior guard with big doleful eyes. 'I'm in so much trouble.'

'Your ID checks out okay but you don't look like you're dressed for work, who let you through to the Elite sector without approved escort and where's your uniform?' asked the junior officer keen to show his superior he was paying attention.

'Oh, one of the other nice men at the gate let me pass if I promised to come straight here. I'll be able to borrow some spare clothes from the other girls, they always bring a change. You know we like to look nice for the customers,' she said shyly but seductively and looked up again to the senior guard who had begun to blush.

'Well, I don't see that there's any reason for concern here,' said the older guard addressing his subordinate. 'Now then, Lucy,' he said checking her ID badge again to confirm her name before handing it back to her with a smile. 'It's your lucky day, Mr. Harper and the other girls just arrived a few minutes ago. They've gone up to the executive suites already but I'm sure you could slip in. Go on now but don't make a habit of it.'

Lucy nearly hugged him, just for effect but decided against it and instead grabbed his hand and held it while thanking him. 'Thank you so much, I really appreciate it. You're so kind; you don't know what it means to me.'

The junior officer appeared jealous and the senior guard blushed again. Lucy walked off down the concrete ramp into the gloom of the dimly lit parking area, turning half way and rippled her fingers in a wave and flashed a smile at the two guards who realised they'd be caught watching her arse as she left. Sufficiently embarrassed for one day the senior guard ushered his partner into their guard hut as Lucy carried on to the lower level.

Near the main lift sat Harper's rusted van which he

always left open since it was common for one of the girls to need fresh cleaning materials or sometimes to discretely retrieve another item they needed to satisfy a client's more unusual fetish. What she had also learned was that he kept a spare key in the ashtray for times when he needed to send a girl on an errand.

Biding her time and concerned that the guards may still watch her Lucy opened the back of the van and gathered some cleaning materials into a plastic caddy. She quietly closed the door again and slid the caddy under the van then darted to the wall opposite the van and out of any line of sight from the guard hut. Crouching behind the line of parked cars she crept up beyond the point at which the overhead lights were extinguished and whispered into the dark at each covered car desperately hoping to hear her sister's reply.

She had reached the end of the row and crossed over to begin working her way back along the wall toward the lift. At the second car from the top she heard a faint call.

'Lucy? Is that you?'

'Kathy? Yes it's me. I came back for you.'

'Is it safe?'

'Yes, but we have to go, where are you?'

Lucy detected some slight movement in the dim light from the next car down as a slender figure appeared from under the dust sheet. She rushed to hug her sister immediately but stopped short. It was overwhelming for both girls, they had only recently learned of each other's existence and until now had never seen one another. They couldn't even be sure each was who they claimed to be but here now some deeper instinct told them the truth.

Crouched in the dark, unseen between rows of stored antique cars the two sisters held each other and silently wept tears of joy. Both had known great pain and now that pain dissolved as a family bond that had never been was forged for the first time.

'Great place for a family reunion eh?' said Lucy laughing

off the emotion.

Kathy wiped the tears from her cheeks. 'I knew you would come back for me but now you're here I don't know what to say except thank you.'

'Don't worry, we'll have plenty of time to catch up soon but first we've got to get out of here. I have a friend waiting for us and he'll be getting pretty worried by now. Come on.'

They scurried along between the wall and rows of cars, feeling exposed as they entered the fully lit section of garage but kept going, time was short and they had to keep moving. Pausing by the last car Lucy looked to the guard hut at the top of the ramp to check for signs for movement but there were none so she took Kathy by the hand and led her across the open gap to Harper's van.

'Get in the side door and lie down between the seats,' said Lucy climbing into the driver's seat. As Kathy clicked the sliding door closed as quietly as possible Lucy pulled open the ash tray in the van's dash console.

'Shit, there's supposed to be a key here.'

'What's the matter, don't you have the keys already?'

'Does this look like my van?' asked Lucy beginning to panic.

'Well, how would I know, I've only just met you,' snapped Kathy.

Lucy took a moment to compose herself. 'Sorry, bickering like sisters already eh? It's just that this is my boss's van, well, ex-boss. He was supposed to have a spare key and it's not here.'

'Maybe you could hotwire it or something? Isn't that what people do in situations like this?'

Lucy anxiously checked the van's side mirrors and glanced at the lift, her gut tightening, expecting at any minute for a guard or Harper to appear and find them. Then she had an idea and got out and opened the back of the van franticly searching for a tool kit she had seen Harper store in the load space. She found it and unfastened the lid, rummaged around and selected a long narrow flat bladed screw driver.

Back in the driver's seat she slotted the point into the worn ignition and slapped it hard with her palm but it only slipped in a little way and hurt her hand. She looked around for anything she might use to encourage the screwdriver deeper when a claw hammer appeared from over the seat behind her.

'Would this help?' asked Kathy handing over the tool to her sister.

'Perfect, thanks,' said Lucy taking the hammer and striking the handle of the screwdriver and driving the shaft between the grooves of the ignition lock. The noise echoed around the concrete space and drew the attention of the junior guard who was standing out of the hut smoking a cigarette. He stood looking at the van but didn't see any movement.

'Pray this works Kathy,' said Lucy grabbing the handle of the screwdriver and turning the shaft. It turned freely and the dash lights came on. Another turn and the engine fired into life and Lucy could feel a cold sweat trickle down her back as her heart pounded in her chest.

She reversed the van then drove slowly up the ramp toward the guards.

'Hi, remember me?' she said to the junior officer who quickly dropped his cigarette and ground it under foot.

'Yes miss, leaving already?'

'Well, Mr. Harper asked me to run back for some supplies. I'll miss making my tips but if it keeps the boss happy maybe I won't lose my job, you know?'

'Sounds like you might just get away with it,' said the older guard as he appeared at the doorway of the hut.

Lucy smiled and batted her eyelids at him. 'Yeah, I think I just might.'

The barrier was raised and she slowly drove out. The guards watched as she stopped a short distance down the street and pulled into the loading area of a nearby building before reappearing a moment later and passed them this time driving in the opposite direction and waving as she went by. The guards cheerfully waved back as Lucy, Kathy and Sam sped off into the maze of streets never to return.

CHAPTER 20

'You must be Sam,' said Kathy when they were a safe distance from Henderson's building.

The big scruffy stranger flashed a friendly smile and thrust a large rough hand toward her in greeting. 'Hi Kathy, nice to meet you, let's hope we live long enough to get to know each other,' laughed Sam as they both bounced around in the rear of the van with cans of cleaning products and disinfectant falling on top of them from the narrow wooden shelves lining the sides of the load space.

'Excuse me a moment, I just need to speak to the driver,' said Sam stepping over Kathy and trying to steady himself as he made his way toward the front and peered out from between the seats through the cracked windscreen to the city streets ahead.

'How're you doing up here?' he asked Lucy. He knew she would be fine but she was gripping the wheel so tightly her knuckles were white.

Lucy felt nervous, scared and excited all at once. 'So far so good,' she replied, 'except I haven't driven in years so this old heap is a bit of a challenge.'

'You're doing well, just keep the speed down and hopefully we'll make it to the gate without being stopped. Head back to where we stashed the bike; I'm not leaving it behind now.'

'Why don't we just keep going? We're on the road now, let's get out of the city and away from here. You don't need the bike anymore do you?'

'I'm not leaving my bike, it's on the way anyway and I might never find another. Besides, it looks like we'll need to get some fuel.'

Lucy glanced down at the fuel gauge and saw Sam was right, they had only about a quarter tank left and that wouldn't get them too far when they got past the city perimeter. After a few streets more Lucy pulled the van to a halt by the kerb under a tree adjacent to the alley where she and Sam had ditched the motorcycle.

'What's happening?' Kathy asked nervously as she poked her head forward between the seats.

'Are you okay Kathy?' asked Lucy suddenly feeling guilty for excluding her sister. 'We have to pull in for a little bit but we won't be long. Sam wants to pick up his bike and we need to find fuel for the van before we leave.'

'But what if my father orders the Enforcers to come looking for me, they'll find us and he'll have us all killed. I'd rather die than go back but I don't want anything to happen to you two.'

'I thought you'd sedated him?' asked Lucy

'He's out cold, I gave him a huge dose but I don't know how long it'll last. I suppose he can't get out of the apartment without this,' said Kathy holding up the little plastic bag containing the blood smeared RFID chip from Henderson's arm implant.

'What the hell is that?' asked Sam

Kathy handed the bag to Sam so he could examine it more closely. 'It's a little chip from my father's arm; he uses it to access the controls for the lift to his apartment.'

'I knew it!' exclaimed Sam. 'Didn't I tell you they were experimenting with chipping people? I figured they'd chip the Dregs for tracking and control but I guess they have other plans for us if the Elites are beginning to implant themselves. Do you have a chip as well?'

'No, I was never implanted and he disabled my access after he killed my mother. The door to the lift won't work without a chip or an authorized thumbprint, that's how he held me captive.'

'What a bastard,' said Sam shaking his head.

'Come on, we can't sit here for too long, we're already getting attention from the locals,' said Lucy returning the stares of some passers-by who were obviously more accustomed to a better pedigree of vehicle on their streets than the rusty van in which the trio were riding.

Sam began to rummage through the equipment and supplies in the rear of the cleaning van and set aside several five litre cans of industrial cleaning solution which were simply marked as solvent. He pulled a long length of clear tubing from a carpet cleaning machine and coiled it before stuffing it in his jacket pocket. Finding the small tool kit Lucy had used in the parking garage he searched through it but couldn't find what he needed.

'Damn it, I wish I had the crowbar from my rucksack now. I need something to use as a lever but there's nothing useful here.'

'What about this?' asked Lucy passing back a large screwdriver.

'Yeah, that might work thanks.'

'Just don't lose it, that's our ignition key.'

Sam slid open the van's side door and stepped out onto the pavement as Lucy hopped down from the front seat and joined him.

'Kathy should come with us,' Lucy said to Sam as he unscrewed the metal lids from the solvent cans and worked quickly setting them on their sides spilling the noxious smelling liquid under the van where it ran along the kerb and began to pool in a dipped section of road that was long overdue for repair.

'If anything happens I don't want to get separated from her,' she said smiling at her sister who was sitting in the side opening of the van and covering her mouth and nose with her sleeve to try to avoid the powerful fumes rising from the solvent.

'Okay,' agreed Sam, 'but we all stick together, and everyone has to carry a couple of cans each. Here, take these,' he said screwing the lids back onto the first two empty cans and handing them to Kathy.

When they each had two empty cans they shut the van doors and hurried off along the street in the direction of a long line of residential buildings. The grand structures were four stories tall and large enough to house several families but each occupied by only one. Outside many of the homes were expensive cars, high-end models all of which had been preserved from destruction by their owners who had paid a huge fee to Central Control for the privilege of ownership. Now they were like trophies, gleaming but mostly unused, a status symbol proudly displayed on the driveways of those rich enough to afford the luxury.

As Kathy, Lucy and Sam walked quickly along the streets they would have raised suspicion from anyone who cared to notice but it seemed anybody they met was in a great hurry to be somewhere else. Several people rushed by with panic on their faces, some could be seen shooing their children inside before slamming and locking doors and closing blinds and drawing curtains. Sirens from Enforcer wagons wailed along the neighbouring streets but none passed by the three figures as they scurried from house to house, stopping out of sight for several moments alongside expensive Audi, BMW, Mercedes and Jaguar vehicles before moving to the next.

Sam spat a mouthful of petrol on the ground as the fuel ran freely from the tubing he had inserted in the tank of a silver Mercedes S65 AMG after prising open the fuel filler cap. He quickly moved the open end of the tube into the neck of an empty solvent can and coughed as his throat and nose burned from the taste and fumes of petrol.

'Oh, what I wouldn't give for a packet of mints now. Thankfully this is the last can. That's makes four gallons of diesel and two of petrol. I'll take the petrol for the bike, you girls take the diesel for the van and we're set'.

As they sat crouched between the car and a thick border

hedge lining the garden waiting for the trickle of fuel from the thin tube to fill the remaining can they heard the slap of leather soled shoes on pavement and heavy breathing as a man approached the house at a run. Sam and the girls froze, sure they would be found out but the man ran past and up the driveway to the front door. He was out of breath by the time he reached out and began repeatedly pressing the doorbell.

Eventually an attractive middle aged woman wearing a light blue dressing gown and with wisps of her blonde hair poking from under the white towel wrapped around her head opened the door with a scowl. Before the man could get a word out she began scolding him.

'Robert, what are you doing here? I was in the bath and it's freezing out here. Look at the state of you, what's this about?'

'Shut up Patricia!' said the man firmly while still struggling to regain his breath. 'Where are the kids?'

'They're upstairs in bed, Kevin came down with some bug and Sarah wasn't feeling well either so I thought it best to keep them home. What's this about? If this is some stupid attempt to get to see them you can forget it, you know you're only allowed to see the children every other weekend.'

'Patricia, listen to me. I have to come in. There's some kind of trouble in the Dreg sectors. I don't know what it is but it's serious. I haven't seen so many Enforcers on this side of the barricades in years. We were watching it all from the office window this morning. They're trying to get over the walls, the Enforcers are keeping them back but it's like a warzone along the sector barriers.'

'Look Robert, I'm sure that Central Control knows what they're doing. There has been no mention of any disturbance on the news feeds and you said yourself that the Enforcers are at the barriers and are keeping them back. A few angry Dregs are nothing to get so worked up about. I honestly don't know how I put up with your silly dramas for so many years.'

'Alright Patricia, have it your way, I'll go but please, for the sake of the kids, please, lock all the doors and windows and close the curtains. Keep a low profile and don't go anywhere until all this has been sorted out.'

As the three friends hid behind the car they heard the conversation end with the door slamming and the man turning to walk away quickly. 'Stupid bitch,' he muttered angrily before running back the way he came.

'Do you know what he was talking about?' asked Kathy remembering the distressing images she had noticed on Henderson's tablet screen when she grabbed it before leaving the penthouse.

Sam and Lucy looked to each other and knew the trouble they had witnessed at the sector gates earlier was escalating and their time was running short.

'We saw some rioting or fighting earlier and our friends Arthur and Alice mentioned they saw some horrible things begin to happen in the Dreg sector in Rook City just before they got out. Whatever it is we need to get moving,' answered Lucy.

Sam felt cold fluid run over his fingers and looked down to see the last can had overflowed so he secured the lid and pulled the tube from the car's fuel filler. They lifted their full cans by the handles on the tops and moved as quickly as they could while being careful not to spill too much fuel from the poorly fitting lids.

Spooked by the story they had overheard from the worried man they understood the urgency of the people they passed as they weaved their way back to the van. Some people obviously hadn't heard of the trouble or perhaps felt assured that their leaders had everything under control as they continued to walk their dogs, casually stroll with shopping bags or jogged along in sports gear just as they might do on any other day. If anyone found the trio to be suspicious and reported their presence to the Enforcers they would have been wasting their time. Even though security cameras had detected their movements the operators in

Central Command were more concerned with the images being fed to their surveillance systems from the Dreg sector and from along the sector barriers.

Back at the van Sam found a small plastic bottle and cut it in half to form a makeshift funnel which they used to pour three of the four gallons of diesel into the van's fuel tank. He took one of the cans of petrol into the alley way and found his motorbike hidden behind the dumpster just as he'd left it. His helmet and gloves were stashed between the bike and the wall and he was almost as happy to see the bike again as he was to see Lucy but of course he'd never tell her that. He topped up the tank and left the can in the alley then rolled the bike out into the street without starting it so as not to draw any more attention than necessary.

He found the sisters standing by the van hugging and with tears streaming down both their faces. 'What happened? Are you okay?' he asked, worried something else bad had happened in his absence.

'We're great Sam, really, we are. It's just not every day you get to meet your sister for the first time,' replied Lucy smiling.

Kathy wiped tears from her cheeks and laughed. 'I must be making a terrible first impression.'

'Ah, there's nothing to worry about and we'll have plenty of time to start over later,' Sam assured her. 'Are you ready to go?'

'I've been ready to leave this town my whole life.'

Sam pulled on his helmet and gloves as Lucy jammed the screwdriver into the van's ignition and started it up with a loud rattle and puff of thick black smoke. He started the bike and pulled up to the driver's window indicating for Lucy to wind it down.

'I'll ride out in front; I'll choke to death before we reach the gate if I've to follow this heap of junk. Stay close; we don't know what's ahead of us yet. Let's go.'

With Lucy and Kathy following close behind Sam plotted

their route toward the southern exit but a thought nagged his conscience and he turned away from the gate.

'What's he doing? This is taking us back into the city,' Lucy exclaimed as she turned the wheel sharply and followed the bike as Sam increased speed, quickly navigating the streets, easily weaving around the occasional car or startled pedestrian. He checked the bike's remaining mirror and saw that Lucy was dropping back since the van wasn't nearly as manoeuvrable.

Blue flashing lights of Enforcer patrol wagons were visible up ahead now and along both sides of the street people were running from offices and shops fleeing in all directions from the sector barrier and the lines of Enforcers who battled to maintain order.

Sam pulled the bike to the kerb a few hundred metres from the front line and removed his gloves and helmet as Lucy and Kathy pulled in behind.

'Are you mad? We need to get out of here, come on Sam, we need to go,' Lucy spoke with great urgency as she and her sister jumped down from the van.

Staring at the chaos, hearing cracks of gunfire and orders being barked through megaphones and screams of fear and panic Sam felt sick to his stomach.

'I wanted Kathy to see this for herself. So you know Kathy this is what we are so desperate to escape. Where we are going and the road that lies ahead will be difficult and dangerous but remember what you're leaving behind. The Dregs are caged and enslaved then beaten like animals if they dare to fight the hand that holds them down.'

Lucy put her arm around Kathy. 'That's enough Sam, I know what you're saying but none of this is Kathy's fault, it was that monster Henderson and his friends that brought this about. Leave my sister out of it.'

'It's okay Lucy,' explained Kathy. 'I understand why Sam came back here, I was locked away for so many years and what life I did see outside of that apartment was fake, none of it real, I know that. I see the city now for what it really is.

Don't worry Sam, this isn't my home, it never was'.

'I just wish there was something we could do about it, all those people in Rook City too, they're being massacred. There's no way we can help though. Sorry I brought you here Kathy, come on, let's move,' said Sam as he leaned to turn on the bike's ignition while another Enforcer patrol raced past them to join the outnumbered ranks at the barrier ahead.

'Wait!' shouted Kathy. 'Maybe there is something we can do. Look, I have this, maybe there's something on here we can use to help?'

She unzipped her jacket halfway and tugged Henderson's tablet free from the layers of clothing and held it out for Lucy and Sam to see. Lucy took the device and slid it from its leather case then swiped across the screen as Sam dismounted his bike again and joined the girls to see what Kathy was so excited about.

'It's locked,' said Lucy, 'and Kathy, it's wonderful you want to help but you heard what the woman back there told her husband, the news feeds aren't showing anything about the riots. Even if we could watch the feeds what could we learn from them that would be of any use to us?'

'No, you don't understand, this is Henderson's tablet,' explained Kathy, her eyes bright with excitement. 'He was watching something like this before. I saw it on the screen when I took his tablet after drugging him, I didn't know why he would be watching stuff like that but he was. He might have some other files or information or something, anything. Maybe it could help us get out or help those poor people?'

Sam though aloud. 'Well, it makes sense that if the news feeds aren't showing anything of this then Henderson's tablet must be tied into the security feeds directly. He's bound to have all kinds of high level access.'

'Well it doesn't matter anyway because as I was telling you, it's locked, see,' said Lucy turning the device to show Sam the screen with red capital letters "SECURED" against a black background. I've tried tapping the screen and pressing the buttons but nothing happens.'

'Let me see it a minute,' said Sam taking the tablet from Lucy. He swiped the screen again but all that appeared was the same "SECURED" message. He turned the tablet about in his hands and tilted it in various angles looking for a switch or button they hadn't tried, maybe something that would indicate a key would be needed. 'A key, yes, that's it. Kathy, have you still got that chip you dug out of Henderson's arm?'

Sam took the plastic bag containing the RFID chip and waved it over the screen which came to life again but this time a green message stating "ID CONFIRMED" briefly appeared before dissolving away and revealing a complex three dimensional arrangement of electronic screens that could be rotated into position as required and tapped to enlarge and activate.

'Ha, ha, we're in,' laughed Sam and he climbed into the van to sit down while he familiarised himself with the interface.

'Budge over,' said Kathy pushing in to sit on the other half of the long passenger seat beside Sam.

'Let me see it too,' said Lucy who had climbed into the driver's seat again and was leaning over to see what secrets might be contained on the glowing screen.

'It's similar to the net-screens we have in the tower blocks but this is much more advanced. A completely new operating system and seems to be capable of much more than just communications and entertainment,' said Sam, genuinely excited to tinker with the expensive device even though he rarely used the net-screen in his own apartment except for calling Lucy.

'Typical man, it's not a toy Sam,' Lucy mocked and winked at Kathy who smiled back. 'See if you can find anything useful so we can get the hell out of here.'

Sam swiped the screen and flicked through several of the active panels Henderson had previously selected. 'Wait a minute, what have we here?'

'What, what have you found?' asked Kathy as both she and Lucy snapped their attention to the tablet screen just as Sam covered it with his hand.

'You don't want to see that,' said Sam laughing, just some hot naked chick giving Henderson the time of his life. He must have set up a camera to record the action. Gross!'

'Ow,' yelped Sam as Lucy drove her elbow into his ribs.

'Stop messing about and find something or I'm driving us out of here now,' snapped Lucy even though she could see the funny side and appreciated the break in tension.

'Okay, okay, I'm looking. It seems like he's plugged into everything; there are live security camera feeds from both cities, direct contact channels for all department heads in Central Control, there's a load of emails sorted into a folder marked "The Brotherhood" but that name doesn't seem to be mentioned in any of the actual email addresses. They talk about lab reports for some chemical compound; I mean this is all just the stuff he had opened on the screen.'

Lucy was glancing from the screen to the street outside and getting more nervous with each passing minute. 'Come on Sam, we need to get going. Is there anything useful in there at all or just a bunch of emails?'

Kathy spoke up hoping to shed some light on the search. 'I overheard some conversations he had with other men when he used his tablet in his study. I only heard his side because he talks very loudly after he's had a few drinks. He often mentioned "The Project" and I heard him say "Clean Slate" a few times. I figured it was some new product he was developing.'

Sam tapped a few commands into the screen. 'Yeah, I just searched for Project Clean Slate and it's returned several results. Mostly emails from the same Brotherhood folder and a few of the lab reports. There's an email marked "Update" that he sent. I'll have a quick scan through that.'

For a few moments Sam read the emails and documents on Henderson's tablet quickly flicking from one file to another. He knew time was running out but couldn't risk leaving the city and breaking the uplink between the tablet and Central Control. As the din from the violent clashes at the sector barrier continued to grow in intensity so did the feeling of vulnerability and imminent danger.

'Holy shit! We have to get out of here now!' exclaimed Sam.

'I know, that's what I've been saying for the past ten minutes,' Lucy said exasperatedly.

'What have you found Sam?' Kathy asked, sure she didn't want to know the answer.

'This is bad, I mean really bad,' Sam answered still staring at the screen.

'What is it?' the sisters shouted simultaneously.

'Okay, from what I've read here, and understand I've just skimmed through a few things, but basically, Henderson and his Brotherhood friends plan on wiping out most of the Dreg sector so they can clear the city and build a new country when we're gone.'

'That's insane, why would anyone want to do that?' Lucy asked incredulously.

'Whatever their motives are it says here they've been working on it for some time. The outline of the scheme says they introduced some mind altering chemicals into the welfare food rations and then combined that with neural programming hidden in regular broadcasts over the net-screens to trigger some kind of psychological breakdown. Henderson reported to this Brotherhood group that testing on human subjects they rounded up from homeless shelters and hospitals resulted in involuntary pathological violence.'

'What does that mean?' asked Kathy.

'Well, I'm not sure,' said Sam, 'but it sounds to me like they infected as many of the Dregs population as possible and then when the time was right triggered the outbreak so we'd destroy ourselves. They probably planned for the violence to be contained behind the gates so they can walk in and mop up the survivors afterwards. I'm sure they figure they'd still need a few of us to pour their coffee and wash their cars.'

Kathy shook her head. 'I can't believe my father was involved in something so evil. He's a bastard and he murdered my mother but that was in a fit of anger. He's a bad man but he's not capable of this, he can't be,' she sobbed, not because she felt sorrow for her step-father but because she felt her connection to Henderson meant she was somehow a part of this.

'We all make our own choices and we all follow our own path. You're my sister Kathy, remember that. He's not your father, you have no ties to him and anything he does is not your fault,' said Lucy trying to comfort Kathy and feeling as though the words helped to further cement the bond between them.

'Hang on, I think I have something,' said Sam readjusting himself on the seat. 'Okay Lucy, start the van and get ready to drive. Fast.'

'What have you found?' Lucy asked turning the screwdriver and cranking the engine into a rough idle.

'I've got into the city gate access controls. Henderson is hooked into the entire city network, he can do pretty much anything he likes from this thing,' replied Sam.

'What are you going to do?' asked Kathy

'I'm going to open every gate and sector barrier in both cities. If the Elites want to start a riot then it's only fair they share the damage.'

'But what about all the innocent people in the Elite sectors, they'll be caught up in it too, you can't do that,' pleaded Kathy.

'There are a lot more Dregs than Elites living on the other side of those barriers and they're innocent too but with nowhere to run. At least opening the gates will give them a fighting chance and maybe even the playing field a bit'.

'You better move over and let him out Kathy, he's going do it and then we'll really need to run,' advised Lucy as she fastened her seatbelt.

With the girls ready in the van Sam pulled on his helmet

and started the bike. He slid the tablet inside his jacket and raised his hand making a horizontal circular motion in the air then rode the bike in a sharp U-turn so he faced away from the barrier and waited until Lucy had done the same and pulled up along the kerb in front of him.

Accessing the tablet again he drilled down through various submenus until he found the command module he was looking for labelled "Sector Barrier Master Override". He tapped on the button and selected the option labelled "Emergency Release and Open" but was presented with another black screen displaying capital red letters saying "LEVEL 6 AUTHORISATION REQUIRED".

'Shit,' muttered Sam realising that of course such a weighty command would be locked to prevent accidental execution. He was about to abandon the plan and make a break for the south gate when he remembered the ID chip and pulled the little bag from his pocket. He pressed the Emergency Release and Open button on the screen again and when asked for authorisation waved the chip across the screen and was rewarded with a cheerful message in green lettering "AUTHORISATION ACCEPTED – THANK YOU."

Almost immediately the battle at the sector barrier grew more intense as the shocked Enforcers looked on helplessly when heavy electromagnetic locks popped open on the massive vehicle access gates. The screech of grinding metal filled the air and a gaping chasm widened as powerful hydraulic rams pulled a section of the huge barrier aside allowing the seething Dreg crowd to pour through en masse as a stampede of terrified citizens ran from the carnage in their own sector into a withering heavy fire from Enforcer shotguns and rifles. Not all of the surging crowd could be stopped and within seconds the defensive line was breached as hundreds of people stampeded over the bodies of the fallen and began to run freely in all directions into the Elite sector streets.

Sam waited as the gate opened and felt a terrible pain in

his chest as he watched the first wave of Dreg citizens slain mercilessly then felt hope as the growing stream of people broke through to either fight or run.

'At least now they have a chance,' Sam said to no one but himself.

He pulled on his gloves then threw the tablet on the ground beneath him stamping the heel of his boot hard into the screen, destroying it. He slipped the bike into gear, revved hard and popped the clutch launching the old bike forward, swerving past the van as Lucy pulled out in his wake and followed close behind. They sped through the city as chaos erupted around them and easily cleared the open gate in the south perimeter wall leaving the city to ruin.

CHAPTER 21

As blackness gave way to light a sharp pain in Henderson's arm began to insist on his fuller attention. He lifted his arm to check the source of his discomfort and saw the makeshift sling and bandaged wound above his left wrist. His mind was still muddled by the powerful cocktail of sedatives he had been administered and the sight of the injury served only to confuse him further. Feeling the cold tile under his body and focusing his clearing eyesight on the chrome lighting fixture on his kitchen ceiling he realised he was lying on the floor and so attempted to sit upright but found the task a huge effort; more than was usual even for a man of his considerable bulk. He managed with much grunting and sweating to manoeuvre himself to a sitting position on the floor with his back to a nearby cabinet for support. Initially suspecting he had fallen after perhaps one too many brandies he looked about for a stool or something else that might help him to his feet when his eyes cast over the bloodied short bladed knife lying on the tiles beside the kitchen island in the centre of the room.

'Kathy!' he shouted, remembering with sudden clarity the events of the previous evening. 'Kathy you little bitch, get in here and help me up or I swear you'll feel my hands around your throat.' He listened intently for a moment and heard no sound other than the soft hum of the motor in the refrigerator and a distant tick from the antique grandfather clock in the main lobby of his living quarters.

Burning rage was a familiar feeling for Victor Henderson but a new intensity of fury began to rise in him fuelling his body and driving the fog further from his mind. On his feet now with legs barely responding he staggered to the sink and ran the cold water at a gentle flow while he unwrapped the bandage on his arm not wanting to see what he knew he would find. Holding his exposed arm under the trickling water the fresh blood washed away clearly showing the small ragged incision where his implanted chip should have been.

Henderson exploded with a malice that spilled from a well of hatred deep in his soul. He roared with animal emotion and grabbing the first thing to hand threw a heavy iron skillet across the kitchen smashing it through the glass door on the front of the oven then continued to pull apart and throw down anything he touched until his hand found grip on the handle of a large kitchen knife. Breathing heavily from exertion he ran his thumb along the blade slicing a clean opening and savoured the feeling of the cold steel parting his flesh. A crimson line slowly tracked its way down the blade's edge and turned to small red circles on the floor as his blood dripped freely while he lost himself in a private vision of retribution.

Regaining some control he steadied himself then still carrying the knife charged out into the main quarters, scanning for signs of movement. He ran from room to room, searching for Kathy yet knowing she would not be found. All the same he searched, growing madder as the reality of his situation fully dawned on him. After checking the wardrobe in the last of the guest rooms and confirming that indeed he was alone Henderson knew he would need the services of his driver and personal guard Derek Stone.

Before leaving the room he impatiently swiped a finger along the net-screen mounted on the wall. The sleek black screen was activated at his touch and glowing red letters requested ID authentication to continue. Out of habit he waved his left wrist across the screen but nothing happened. He waved again but still the glowing red message mocked him. Shards of plexi-glass and chunks of plaster fell to the floor as Henderson violently stabbed the knife through the screen then ripped the device from the wall and threw it across the room, destroying it as it struck and disfigured a priceless heirloom chest of drawers.

As quickly as he was able he descended the right hand staircase and returned to his favourite chair where he remembered working when Kathy had surprised him with the sedative. He searched frantically for his tablet and realising it was not where he expected he knew it was pointless to search further. It was gone too but between Kathy and the tablet the small device was infinitely more valuable to him.

He lumbered groggily along the grand entrance hall to the lift controls and tapped the button to summon the carriage but the panel remained infuriatingly dormant. He waved his left wrist frantically in front of the sensor but without his implanted chip it was a futile gesture. His ego demanded that everyone and everything should answer his command so he waited, fully expecting the inert electronic circuits to come to their senses and surrender to his will. Eventually he was forced to acknowledge that no matter how much he swore or shouted neither lift nor net-screen would respond without his authorisation chip. Worse still he had to accept he had been imprisoned in his own home.

Resignedly he began to walk back along the hall to sit in his chair and brood but turned again as he heard the pinging of the thick cables in the lift shaft as they took the load of the ascending car. It had worked after all he thought, perhaps his implant was still working and he had merely sustained an injury during a struggle with Kathy. She would still pay for her disobedience but he felt now at least he wouldn't be made to look a fool.

As he waited impatiently, despite his dishevelled appearance he admired his own reflection in the polished brass doors. Sure enough the lift arrived at his penthouse apartment and the doors parted silently on well-maintained runners but to Henderson's surprise the car was occupied.

'Afternoon Mr. Henderson,' said Derek Stone, as always punctual and simply but impeccably dressed in his usual black suit and black tie over plain white shirt. As was normal since he had downright refused to be chipped he had scanned his thumbprint on the reader beside the floor selection buttons in the lift and now stood casually radiating confidence, a hint of a smile in his remaining eye as he quickly assessed his employer's appearance and knew something was amiss. Although it would most likely mean more hassle for him Stone enjoyed any opportunity to see his egotistical boss in a more vulnerable moment.

Henderson rallied himself and snarled. 'Where the hell have you been? Do you know what time it is? Do you realise what has happened due to your incompetence?'

The lift doors began to close and Stone was tempted to allow them but thought better of it and pressed the door open button before stepping into the hallway to look down into the red face of Henderson as he unleashed a tiresome tirade to which Stone had long since become immune. As he listened Stone filtered out the abuse spewing from the intolerable fat man and analysed the fragments of actual information. It was serious indeed, Henderson had been drugged, his implant chip had been removed and Kathy had escaped with his networked tablet.

'You're lucky I don't have my tablet Stone or I would summon an Enforcer squad to take you for special interrogation. Well, don't just stand there, explain yourself,' demanded Henderson.

Stone remained outwardly stolid but internally fought to control an urge to grab Henderson by the lapels of his suit jacket and smash his nose with a head butt.

'Yes sir,' Stone managed to say after a deep controlled breath. 'If you remember I said I would see you this afternoon following the errand you insisted I attend to, which by the way is all taken care of. The delivery was confirmed and I have a case in the car to use for transfer of cash funds as you requested.'

Henderson opened his mouth to vent another stream of obscenities but realised both men knew who was responsible for the current situation and so decided to change tack. 'You can redeem yourself Mr. Stone by putting your talents to work in finding my errant daughter. She may have gotten out from behind these walls but I will show her she cannot escape my reach.'

Stone hesitated as he decided how to answer. 'I can certainly locate Kathy Mr. Henderson but I think you should know there is another more pressing matter that I guess you are not yet aware of, seeing as how you're out of the loop at the moment.'

It was Henderson's turn to listen as Stone efficiently delivered a verbal report about the breached sector barriers; the Dregs running amok, rioting and looting in the Elite sectors; the Enforcer's ongoing battle to suppress the surging masses spilling from the opened gates and of the horrific acts of violence committed by many of the Dregs who Stone described as seeming as if possessed. Henderson listened and understood clearly what had happened. Everything was unfolding as it should except now that the sector barrier had been opened the Enforcers hadn't a hope of containing the problem. He knew the Elite sector was in danger of being overrun and the thought of the Dregs desecrating Elite areas dealt a blow that his heart struggled to overcome causing him to clutch at his chest while scrabbling to loosen his collar.

'We have to locate General Curran; he has to get this under control. I cannot have Dregs running amok in my city, I will not tolerate it. I will not,' he ranted as his face grew redder and sweat streamed down his forehead while the vice around his heart tightened its grip. Stone half-heartedly stepped forward to steady the ailing man but was pushed aside.

'Leave me be', Henderson croaked. 'We have to get to Central Command. I must speak with the General,' he said stumbling toward the lift, chest heaving as he fought for breath.

Knowing there would be no reasoning with his employer Stone scanned his thumbprint once again to open the lift doors and rode with Henderson to the basement level car park. The brief journey provided a few moments to calm down and the cooler air seemed to help the older man's condition as he stormed ahead opening his own door in the rear of his luxury transport rather than wait for Stone to dutifully open it for him. Out now on the city streets Stone expertly guided the large sedan through fleeing pedestrians and several privately owned vehicles as he raced toward the dominating tower of the Central Control building. At Henderson's request he navigated a route as far around the sector barriers as possible, the failed leader unwilling to risk getting caught up in the devastation and carnage he had helped design and unleash.

Showing his ID card and lowering the darkened rear window a few inches to allow the Enforcer guards to confirm the identity of his passenger Stone was waved through the retracted pneumatic bollards and raced on screeching tyres into the underbelly of Central Control. Henderson's clearance level permitted unrestricted access through the outer layers of security but they were both stopped in their tracks upon reaching the heavily guarded inner sanctum, which was Central Command.

'Don't you know who I am,' spat an infuriated Henderson as two armed Enforcers stood guard, impassive and staring directly ahead, completely ignoring any threat Henderson imagined he posed to them.

Stone remained poker faced throughout but immensely enjoyed watching the panicked Henderson become increasingly agitated and desperate as he surely began to realise how little real power he wielded. After a few moments Henderson had quietened to huffing and puffing as he leaned against the wall clutching his chest. A buzzer sounded and the two guards stepped apart seconds before a heavy steel door raised up on hydraulic rams into a recess in the wall above.

General Curran marched out and intentionally ignored the sharp salutes of the stationed guards.

'What do you want Victor? Can't you see I have a situation here?' the General snapped although he was already aware of Henderson's predicament after keenly observing the fresh stitches on his wrist which answered the question as to why he was out here bothering the guards when he would normally have barged straight in and shouted at Curran directly.

'Perhaps you're having some difficulty gaining access Victor? Well, why didn't you say so,' said Curran relishing the opportunity to further humiliate his old adversary. 'You're lucky I stepped out for a moment or you could have been here all day.'

'Show me what's going on out there.' demanded Henderson. 'Mr. Stone relayed some of what he witnessed but I need to see the full extent of this disaster. You will allow Mr. Stone to accompany me, I have mislaid my daughter and he is helping me locate her. I give authorization for him to view any information that helps find her.'

'I don't like it Victor, as you know, civilians are not permitted to enter the command centre but since you insist I'm sure Mr. Stone will remain an unseen observer and stay out of my people's way,' Curran replied tersely.

Stone simply nodded and followed Henderson and the General as the heavy steel door closed quickly behind them with just a faint hiss which belied its great mass. They walked along a dark corridor lined from floor to ceiling with black marble slabs. Dim illumination was provided by a strip of green LEDs set into the wall at waist height which ran the length of the narrow space. They approached another heavy steel door identical to the first and Curran extended his left arm waving his wrist in front of a sensor which immediately responded and raised the door. As the door opened Henderson saw the General's smug grin lit up from the glow of display screens shining through from the next room.

Stone was surprised to see the command centre was not the cavernous space he imaged to be populated with hundreds of technicians staring intently into hundreds more screens. Instead there were ten uniformed Enforcer guards stationed in front of a transparent projected screen which appeared to be touch sensitive. From here they could observe a grid view of what seemed to be one hundred or more screens. Individual screens could be selected and enlarged so as to view in more detail. Each view appeared to allow control of the camera providing the feed and from this each Enforcer could scan and highlight areas for priority action then dispatch ground forces as required. One enormous central screen displayed a grid of ten screens, each showing what the ten guards were viewing at that moment and in such a way the General could keep abreast of the overall situation and issue commands as he felt necessary.

For Derek Stone the advanced technology would have been fascinating except for the sickening images currently displayed. They were of scenes he had witnessed first-hand when driving to Henderson's residential building earlier that afternoon but here, seeing so many at once, so much suffering, the massive scale of the city wide violence, across both capital cities, it was shocking and numbing all at once. From the live footage he could see that many of the first people to rush across the sector divide had been cut down instantly by relentless heavy fire from the Enforcers but the immense thrust of the crowd was proving too great. All across the city at each open barrier hundreds of terrified souls pushed forward, trampling the bodies of those that fell before them, many more were shot dead or grievously injured as they ran in fear or were driven forward by the huge crowd surging behind. Still others appeared invulnerable to the raining fire from Enforcer weaponry and despite seemingly lethal wounds continued to assault Dreg and Enforcer alike, ripping and tearing hair and flesh from any warm body they encountered until they too fell underfoot.

Would-be survivors fought hand to hand with Enforcers

pitting sticks, petrol bombs and rocks against powerful shotguns and rifles. Many Dregs died a gruesome death but they outnumbered the Enforcers who were rapidly overcome. The armour, weapons and ammunition of injured or dead Enforcers were stripped from the bodies and turned against their comrades in increasing intensity until they were forced to make a tactical retreat and the beginning of a massive street war blazed across all sectors of the city. Most Dregs who broke through unscathed began running for their lives to seek any place of refuge. Some who had reached a safe distance into the Elite sectors began looting; breaking shop windows, grabbing armfuls of the luxury items they had been denied for so long and fighting to defend their bounty while terrified Elites joined the fleeing Dregs and tried to run to find sanctuary. Many of those not gunned down in the initial onslaught suffered convulsions before turning on their own kind, the lust for luxury goods forgotten, only a compulsion to savage and eviscerate remained and the sight of the blood strewn carnage served to turn yet more of the terrified city inhabitants to mindless killers.

As he watched the events unfold rivers of sweat ran from Henderson's bald head and trickled down to wet his shirt collar while veins swelled and pumped as his blood pressure climbed to an unhealthy level. It wasn't supposed to happen like this, he had given assurances to the Brotherhood that he would personally oversee the successful execution of the final stages of the project.

'General Curran, your men are incompetent', he shouted but only one of the battle hardened Enforcers glanced over his shoulder fixing Henderson with a glare as if confirming his target for later.

'Do you see what they have allowed to happen?' Henderson continued. 'It seems General that I should have insisted military command authority was transferred to me. You will answer for the mistakes made here today. As highest ranking Upper Council member I order you to relinquish your command.'

General Curran didn't respond immediately but instead took a moment to casually walk to a desk at the rear of the room behind the rows of guards and retrieved a sheet of paper from a vintage printer that he insisted on continuing to use despite having the most advanced touch screen visualisation technology at his disposal. He crossed the room again to stand uncomfortably close to Henderson causing the shorter man to involuntarily step backward. Curran took a breath before he spoke and when he did it was in a low, controlled tone as he employed iron will to rule his emotions.

'Do you know what this is Victor? This is a report from my senior security analyst. I asked why my barriers were opened. Why my men are being beaten to a pulp with sticks and stones. Why hundreds of Dregs are now running free beyond any hope of containment. Do you know what this report tells me Victor?'

Henderson just stared blankly, he knew he was losing ground with every second and could do nothing but wipe the sweat from his face with a damp, stained handkerchief as the General leaned further into his face to eyeball him hard, the stare feeling as though it would burn through the back of his skull.

'This tells me Victor that it was you who issued the gate override command. It is you who has put my men in this situation and it is you Victor who will answer for the mistakes made here today.'

Henderson retorted in indignation at being falsely accused. 'Don't be ridiculous General, I never issued any such order. Why would I do that when we were so close to completing the project. This is preposterous; you cannot fabricate such a story just to retain your command. I gave you a direct order and I order you to follow it.'

Curran turned to a guard stationed inside the huge metal door. 'Sergeant, Mr. Henderson has not confirmed his identity. No civilians are permitted in the command centre. Please escort him and his driver off the premises. Immediately.'

The sergeant saluted sharply and grabbed Henderson by the arm and led him struggling toward the exit while another officer opened the door and directed a compliant Derek Stone to leave ahead of his humiliated employer.

'You can't do this, I am in charge here and I order you to stand down. General Curran you no longer have command authority. Sergeant, release me immediately. That is an order Sergeant.'

As the heavy steel door closed behind him Henderson heard Curran shout. 'You had your chance Victor. This is my city now.'

Stone rode the lift down to the basement car park under the Central Control building with his boss and the Enforcer sergeant who had maintained a secure grip of Henderson until shoving him, still spouting hollow threats, out into the parking bay as the lift doors closed and the soldier returned to his duty station. Henderson was dumbfounded and Stone had never seen him in such a state of confusion and panic. The over-confident bluster had disappeared and the feeble reality of Henderson's true character was all that remained.

'Where to now Sir?' asked Stone as he opened the rear door of the car.

Henderson gasped for breath and composed himself attempting to save a scrap of his tattered dignity. 'Take me to the club; I have to speak with a friend there who will help get this all straightened out.'

'Is that wise sir? You saw what's happening on the streets, it's not safe to be driving around out there. An expensive motor like this is a huge target for an angry mob. If we run into any obstacles I can't guarantee your safety.'

'What do I pay you so much for Stone if not to drive me and ensure my safety? If you can't do that then what use are you to me? Take me to the club. Now,' snarled Henderson unleashing his anger on Stone who said nothing as he fired the engine and sped out onto the streets hoping to make the journey to the exclusive club without incident.

There were more people on the road now than earlier and

all were running wildly in various directions, some running for home and some not knowing where they ran to except that anywhere would be better than the developing nightmare behind them. Stone drove expertly swerving around most pedestrians with precision until one young Dreg girl who Stone estimated was no older than Kathy ran straight at the car and repeatedly changed course to match Stone as he tried to avoid her. There was nothing he could do. She folded over the bonnet and her head smashed into the bodywork but she still reached forward, grasping toward the windscreen with a terrifying crazed look in her eyes and blood running down her cheeks from self-inflicted wounds scored deep using her own fingernails. Stone's gaze was fixed on her as she was carried forward on the front of the car until he stamped on the brakes sending her crushed body flying forward where she landed and rolled further breaking her damaged limbs and opening her skull as it impacted on the kerb.

Even Derek Stone who had witnessed and learned to live with many terrors was stunned by what he had seen. He sat frozen for a brief moment staring forward at the mangled corpse as people continued to run screaming past the car. A Dreg man in his mid-forties who was further along the street behind the girl stopped to see if the she was alright and Stone guessed maybe he recognised her or was by chance related to her because the man dropped to his knees apparently overcome with grief.

'Why have you stopped?' shouted Henderson from the back seat. 'We can't stop, move man. Drive. Stone, do you hear me? I said drive.'

Stone snapped back to his senses and slammed the car into gear. Accelerating past the scene he saw for a few seconds the man kneeling over the girl had leapt back to his feet and begun to shake violently. Glancing in the rear view mirror Stone could have sworn the man had now ripped out chunks of his hair and was waving them high over his head, screaming and shaking all the while.

'What the hell is going on? This is no riot. What have you done Henderson? What was the General saying about a project?'

'I pay you to drive Stone, now get me to the club,' Henderson snarled as he stared coldly into Stone's reflected glare.

Pulling up sharply outside the old bank building which was Henderson's club Stone left the engine running.

'I'll wait here as long as I can but I might need to circle around the block if things get a bit dicey.'

Henderson stepped from the rear of the car and hurried to the old wood framed revolving door which served as the club's entrance but found it wouldn't move. He pushed and pulled but couldn't move it an inch. He frantically looked about the street to check for signs of danger from the advancing crowd but the trouble hadn't spread this far into the Elite sector just yet. He tried the door once again and was about to give up and return to the relative sanctuary of his car when he heard a click and watched with relief as the door began to move freely on its axis. Slowly emerging from the doorway appeared the tired, wrinkled face of Maurice Hastings, the ancient doorman wearing his dark grey uniform contrasted by woven embellishments of silver cloth which complimented his thin silvery hair.

'Ah, Mister Henderson sir, I was just locking up, seems there's a spot of bother and we've to batten down the hatches eh?' said Hastings with a chuckle obviously unaware of the full extent of the situation unfolding only streets away.

'Excellent timing Maurice. Tell me, is Mr. Cartwright still in the club?' Henderson asked with urgency as he bolted to the door.

Hastings thought a moment; so many faces had passed through the club over the decades he had difficulty remembering who had died and who was still alive but suddenly a wave of clarity flit across the old man's face.

'Oh yes, of course, Mr. Cartwright. Yes, I believe if you hurry you may just catch him.'

Henderson looked puzzled. 'If you're locking down the club won't he be staying for the evening?'

'Oh my no, Mr. Cartwright was in quite a rush. He received a telephone call on his little screen thingy and seemed agitated. He actually asked me how to get to the roof. Can you believe that? I haven't been up there since, oh, now let me think. Yes it must be over twenty years at least, why was it now that I had cause to go up there I wonder?' the old man rambled as he lost himself in memory.

'Maurice, listen. It is very important that I speak with Mr. Cartwright. Can you tell me how to get to the roof?' asked Henderson in as patient a tone as he could manage knowing that getting rattled would only delay him further.

With rough directions Henderson squeezed his way through the revolving door and jogged as quickly as his bulk and weakening heart would allow. Puffing and sweating he ran across the entrance hall to the lifts drawing stares of disapproval from his fellow members for his appearance and ungainly behaviour.

For the first time this day chance favoured him and one of the two lifts sat empty and waiting at the ground floor. He rode it to the top level and again jogged as quickly as his tiring legs would carry him to a service door at the end of the corridor where he found the staircase leading to the roof access just as Hastings had described. Bursting out of the door onto the roof the rotor wash of an executive helicopter buffeted Henderson as he watched Cartwright being guided to the waiting craft by a dark-suited bodyguard.

'John!' shouted Henderson. 'Mr. Cartwright,' he shouted again as he advanced toward the helicopter. This time he was heard by the bodyguard who alerted his boss to Henderson's presence.

Cartwright paused, briefly considering whether to even acknowledge his subordinate.

'Henderson, what are you doing here?'

'Please Mr. Cartwright; you have let me go with you,' Henderson shouted over the roar of the twin turbine engines. 'The project has been sabotaged and General Curran has taken command of the city. I need to speak with you and make arrangements for reinforcement troops loyal to the Brotherhood. We can regain control. I can turn things around, I just need more time.'

Cartwright looked him hard in the eye. 'Henderson, this experiment was your responsibility and you have proven how wrong we were to assume you could be as efficient as your father. You have failed us and failure does not go unrewarded. I will speak with the Brotherhood and recommend you are exiled here to live or die by your own hand.'

With that Cartwright turned and climbed into the waiting helicopter which promptly lifted off from the roof of the club taking Henderson's life of entitlement with it. His only hope now was the loyal Derek Stone. Hurrying back down to the lobby and through the revolving door once again he was relieved to see Stone had been true to his word and waited dutifully outside the club entrance.

'Derek, my good man,' said Henderson patronizingly using Stone's first name. 'I appreciate you waiting; true professionalism.'

'Well, as you pointed out, that's what you pay me for,' replied Stone not rising to the baited compliment. 'Where to now, sir? Might I suggest you return to your apartment until this situation has been cleared up?'

'No, Derek. I have unfinished business with my daughter. You said you could find her? Then I want you to take me to her immediately.'

'I'll find her Mr. Henderson,' Stone replied confidently. 'I guarantee it. I'll find her.'

CHAPTER 22

Sam slowed and turned the bike into a rarely used fire road as the evening sun began to descend behind the tall evergreens stretching the length of this section of the southern highway. Closely followed by the girls in the old cleaning company van he rode slowly, careful to keep the bike in the left side of the rutted tarmac since a heavy growth of grass and weeds had sprouted along the centre line. They continued down the twisting lane for about a quarter mile until the trees gave way to clear flat land gently sloping off toward tall cliffs on the left and to lower land leading down to a small sandy inlet to the right.

The smell of the sea was inviting and as they drew closer they watched the warm orange orb of the sun sink low on the horizon. High on the dunes overlooking the beach at the far side of the inlet stood the only visible man-made structure, fragments of broken windows shone gold as they reflected the late evening rays. As the lane narrowed the cracked tar surface transitioned to broken concrete then to a wide track in the sand which meant Sam had to slow the bike to a crawl to maintain balance and traction in the soft uneven surface.

As they approached they faced into the sun so the building was in silhouette with much of the detail lost in shadow. Sam could see a section of the roof had collapsed and what perhaps was once a well-tended garden had been reclaimed by the wilderness. Tall coarse grass grew in thick clumps around the remaining posts of a fallen timber fence and wild flowers and short stunted grasses covered the sandy soil. Skeletal blackened joists peering out from under the scorched roof on the right side of the house were an ominous sight as were the sharp teeth of broken windows hanging from charred and blistered frames. The front door in the centre of the house had been painted white many years ago but coastal weather and neglect meant it was cracked and peeling although it seemed that it had been reinforced with newer timber more recently. One window in the left side was intact except for a broken pane which had been covered up with old fence boards.

Sam pulled up to the front of the building and killed the engine as Lucy parked behind the motorcycle and both she and Kathy stepped out of the van to stretch their legs. Sam approached removing his helmet then arched his back and rolled his shoulders to relieve cramp from the long ride.

'Are you sure this is the place Sam?' asked Lucy

'I think so, Arthur was very specific about the directions he marked on my map but I don't see any sign of life and his truck doesn't seem to be here.'

'It's so beautiful,'

'What, this old shack?' Sam said turning to question Kathy.

'No, the ocean, it's beautiful. I've never seen the ocean before.' She had walked to stand by the left side of the house and look out over the panorama before her.

Sam and Lucy joined her and held hands as Lucy put her arm around her sister's shoulder and they all stood in the cool breeze for a moment listening to the rhythm of the pounding surf.

'We'd better have a look around, it'll be getting dark soon and at the very least we need to sort out somewhere to sleep tonight, not to mention get something to eat. I don't know about you but I'm starving,' Sam said breaking the spell of the moment, anxious that his friends weren't here to greet them as he had hoped.

Lucy wiped the sleeve of her jacket on a window pane and pressed her face against the glass, shielding her gaze with her hands to try and see through to the gloom inside.

'Do you see anything?' asked Kathy

'No, not really, it looks like there's some old furniture like this was the living room. It doesn't look like the fire got to this part of the house though.'

'I'll check the door,' said Sam stepping up to the door and trying the handle but it wasn't the type that turned from the outside needing a key to open the latch lock. He tested the lock by butting his shoulder against it but the only thing to give way were flakes of the crumbling paintwork.

'It's pretty solid; I'd guess it's been propped up from the inside. We can always break that window if we need to but let's check around the far side first.'

An empty window frame blew open slowly as it caught a breeze passing through the missing upper floor and roof as they walked past the burnt section of the house. Sam pushed it closed and looked into the room. He could see the remains of an iron bed frame and some wooden furniture that hadn't been fully destroyed in the flames. The door was closed and although it had been badly scorched it hadn't burnt through completely. Somehow someone had managed to contain the fire and get it under control before it consumed the entire building. Turning the corner at the gable end which hadn't been visible from the road Sam was greeted with a familiar and welcome sight which lifted his spirits. There, parked neatly and facing him was a dilapidated red Land Rover pickup, the rear canvas cover flapping loosely in the wind.

'Look, its Arthur's truck,' he said excitedly. 'This is the right place for sure, come on, let's check around the back.'

'Why aren't they here then?' said Lucy nervously

'Do you think something might have happened to them?' Kathy asked picking up on her sister's concern.

'If the truck is here they have to be here,' replied Sam confidently as he strode forward and around the corner to the rear of the building. He tried the back door and found it unlocked so pushed it ajar and stepped inside. 'Wait here, I'm going to have a quick look around first.'

He searched the small kitchen finding it surprisingly neat and tidy with clean dishes stacked in the rack by the sink. Faded wallpaper with an old fashioned nautical theme still hung on the walls but sagged in the corners. A clock with a surround in the style of a ship's wheel was mounted above a worn wooden table top but the motionless hands incorrectly gave the time as four minutes past three since the battery had long since been removed. A dented aluminium whistling kettle sat on one of the four gas burners of an ancient stove. As Sam crossed the room to check if by some miracle any gas was left in the cylinder Lucy leaned in through the door and whispered urgently.

'Sam, come here, quick! I think someone's coming.'

Suddenly feeling trapped Sam ran out to Lucy and Kathy. 'Where are they? I can't see anyone.'

'I heard voices, Kathy heard them too.'

'I did Sam, it was faint but we both heard them,' Kathy confirmed.

Sam turned his ear to the breeze and listened carefully but couldn't detect anything other than the roar of wind and waves. Not trusting his luck Sam thought quickly on the best course of action.

'Go to the Land Rover, the lock on the driver's door is broken. Lift the base of the passenger seat, you should see the battery compartment, Arthur hides the keys there. If we need to we'll have a better chance of getting out fast along that lane if we have four wheel drive. If I come running start the engine and be ready to floor it.'

The sisters went to the truck and began checking for the keys as Sam bent low and crept quickly to the edge of the dune at the rear of the back garden where a narrow gap gave access to a set of crumbling concrete steps and a heavily rusted steel banister. He lay flat and tried to position himself where he might get a glimpse of the approaching strangers before they caught sight of him. Creeping forward on his belly to better see the beach directly below he saw a flash of shaggy golden hair running up the steep sand bank toward him immediately followed by excited barking and within seconds he was rolled over onto his back ruffling Molly's ears as she yelped with excitement and licked his face then bounced around him before returning to give and receive more affection.

'Molly, good girl, it's good to see you too,' laughed Sam as he rolled around on the grass getting reacquainted with his best friend. 'Lucy, Kathy, it's okay come on back here,' he shouted to the girls as he saw the tops of two familiar heads come into view through the gap in the dunes.

'Sam, is that you?' an older male voice asked.

'Of course it's Sam you old fool, don't you recognise him? Sam, come and help an old lady up these steps.'

Pushing Molly back so he could get to his feet as Lucy and Kathy joined him again behind the house Sam walked to the top of the steps and stretched out a hand to a spritely lady who gladly accepted despite being in no need of the assistance. She bounded up the last steps and threw her arms around Sam's waist and reached up to kiss him on the cheek.

'Oh Sam my boy, it's so good to see you alive and well. I've not slept a wink with worry about you and Lucy. And this must be Kathy, yes?' she said releasing Sam and striding quickly to embrace both sisters. 'Thanks for looking after him Lucy; I've grown fond of your Sam I must say. Hello Kathy, so nice to meet you, I'm Alice and that old codger dragging his heels behind me is my husband, Arthur,' she said looking over her shoulder and smiling as Arthur steadied himself on the railing as he reached the top step.

'Hey, less of the "old" comments eh? You're making me look bad in front of these gorgeous girls,' said Arthur catching his breath.

'Never mind about these young ladies, you can't even keep pace with me,' teased Alice and she turned to chatter with Lucy and Kathy.

'Well Sam, you made it back in one piece. Good to see

you lad, really good to see you,' said Arthur extending a hand which Sam shook firmly then both men engaged in a brief hug and slapped each other on the back before both felt mildly uncomfortable and separated.

'It's good to see you too Arthur.'

'What happened to the house?' asked Sam indicating the burnt section of roof. 'We thought maybe something had happened to you.'

Arthur rubbed the stubble on his cheeks as he considered the damage. 'It was like that when we got here Sam. I'd hoped I'd see my cousin and his wife but they've long gone by the looks of things. I guess someone stumbled across the house and tried torching it, probably just vandals. Thankfully it didn't take the whole building. We worked to save what we could and patched the place up a bit. It's too not bad really and I reckon in time I can repair the worst of it. Besides, the ocean view is amazing.'

'It sure is Arthur, you have yourself a great spot to retire,' laughed Sam.

'Well, this calls for a celebration don't you think?' said Arthur changing the subject and rushing off toward the house leaving the women talking as Sam knelt to rub Molly's belly.

'Here we go, there's one each,' said Arthur carefully carrying an old tin bar tray from the kitchen on which he had three small jam jars, a plastic beaker and a chipped china cup with no handle. 'The ladies get the glasses,' he said referring to the jam jars. 'A drink from the last bottle of my own whiskey and a toast to friends found safe.'

They all drank the toast and Kathy coughed at first not being used to liquor which made the others laugh. She took it well and enjoyed the rest of her drink and the company of more new friends, especially Molly who had taken a real shine to her. Arthur brought out the bottle and topped up everyone's drinks while they sat, legs dangling over the edge of the dune and watched the sun melt into the sea.

The sea air and a few drinks had everyone quite sleepy so

as Arthur cleared up Alice led their guests inside by the light of an old paraffin storm lantern they had found in the tool shed along with a half full bottle of fuel. Sam and the sisters followed Alice along the short hall to a room facing the rear of the house. In the dim flickering lamplight they could see the blistered paint on the door at the end of the passage which was the farthest room in the house and had sustained the worst damage in the fire. They were thankful to find their room was intact and even seemed welcoming given how tired they felt.

'I thought perhaps you girls wouldn't mind sharing the guest bed and since Sam is such a gentleman I'm sure he's happy to take the sofa in the living room.'

Lucy and Kathy agreed they would share and Sam pretended not to be disappointed at missing the chance to spend the night with Lucy. He knew it was the right thing to do and besides, the couch would provide more comfort than he'd had most nights of late.

As everyone settled down and the house grew silent Sam found even though he was exhausted he couldn't switch off. He reached down and stroked Molly's coat as she whimpered softly and twitched a leg, lost in a dream. Reflecting on how good it was to be here with everyone he cared about and listening to the calming rhythm of the ocean eventually his eyes grew heavy and a peaceful blanket of sleep fell over him.

Kathy awoke with terror as a gloved hand was clamped over her mouth and lean muscular arms dragged her from the bed. She tried to scream but a strong hand held her jaw tight. She could smell leather and sweat from the glove as she fought for breath and in her struggle she kicked out and struck Lucy who sleepily turned to adjust her position then sat bolt upright as she heard Kathy's muffled protests and she detected two large figures in the room.

Molly pricked up her ears and barked loudly waking Sam. 'What is it girl, what's wrong?' he asked knowing not to doubt his loyal friend for she had saved him from trouble many times before.

As Molly barked and scratched at the door leading down the hall Sam raced to pull on his jeans and boots then lifted his baseball bat which Arthur had left along with his pack and other gear in the corner of the room. He ran down the hall noticing the charred door at the end was lying open and the light of the near full moon was flooding through the missing section of roof.

'Lucy, are you alright?' he shouted as Molly reared up on her hind legs and clawed at the girl's bedroom door ahead of him.

'What are you waiting for?' snarled a breathless angry voice. 'Kill her and then let's get out of here'.

Lucy felt a sickening coldness creep into her stomach. 'Sam, help!' she managed to shout before she was struck hard across the face by a vicious backhand from Henderson that stung but also brought her fully alert only too late to react.

Arthur opened his bedroom door rubbing his eyes as Sam raced past. He didn't need to ask and immediately slammed the door shut, woke Alice, pulled on his boots and a tattered old dressing gown then grabbed his pistol from under his side of the mattress. He had only two rounds left but two was better than none.

He burst from his bedroom closely followed by Alice who kept tight behind her husband. They entered the hall just as Sam emerged from the guest room, backing out slowly with hands held high and commanding a snarling Molly to back up with him. Arthur froze and steadied his aim over Sam's shoulder but he couldn't fire without risking hitting Sam.

Next Kathy appeared still wearing only her night dress and walking barefoot. She was held tightly by Derek Stone who gripped the terrified girl around the neck from behind and used her to shield his withdrawal as he pointed a silenced pistol at Sam then quickly shifted his aim to Arthur who posed a greater threat now he also held a weapon. Stone paused in the narrow hall as Lucy was led out next in a similar fashion by Henderson who seized the opportunity to ensure his safe exit. His restraint technique proved to be less effective and Lucy sidestepped driving an elbow deep into his stomach then stamping her heel hard onto the small bones in the top of his foot. Henderson yelped in pain and Lucy fought her way free then ran to Sam who held her close but kept his eyes locked on the killer.

'How did you find us?' asked Kathy.

'You forgot about the chip, it was a simple matter of using a GPS locator coded for the chip and it led us straight to you,' answered Stone as he motioned with his raised pistol for the others to move along the hall toward the front door.

'I didn't know you could track my chip,' said Henderson as he followed Stone, suddenly wondering how many times before his personal guard had spied on his movements.

'Oh yes, it's a security precaution sir in case of a kidnap situation,' but what Stone didn't reveal was that he had acquired the GPS tracker to locate the chip implanted in his own lost dog years earlier then discretely coded the device for Henderson's arm chip allowing him to know his boss's location at all times in order to keep one step ahead of him.

Sam checked his pockets and found the plastic bag containing the tiny device. He realised his mistake and knew he had forgotten to destroy the chip when he had smashed Henderson's network tablet.

They all moved slowly up the hallway, Kathy struggling occasionally but Stone's iron grip was unbreakable. Alice led Arthur backward as he kept his own pistol trained on Stone while Sam and Lucy stayed flat to the wall to keep out of the line of fire as best they could as Molly continued to bare her teeth and growl at a heavily sweating Henderson. Clearing the corridor Henderson bolted to open the front door and stepped out onto the sandy lawn where he waited for Stone to provide cover for their retreat to the car which he was relieved to see still parked in gleaming moonlight farther down the rutted lane.

'That's far enough, stop there,' shouted Henderson now

that everyone had moved outside into the cold night air. 'Tell them Stone, no further,' he shouted again since his command was ignored.

'Okay, hold it there folks,' said Stone turning the pistol to Kathy's head and all froze except Lucy.

'No, leave her alone,' she screamed and ran toward Stone and Kathy in spite of her fear and the painful red welt rising in her cheek.

'Lucy, wait,' shouted Sam as he moved to follow her but Stone instantly aimed the pistol at Sam halting his advance.

'Arthur, shoot him,' cried Alice.

'I can't, I'll probably hit Kathy,' he said feeling his arm tiring from aiming the pistol for so long.

'You little bitch, you caused all this trouble. You and your pathetic boyfriend, you don't know what you've done. Do you know who I am?' Henderson snapped and launched himself toward Lucy as she ran to help her sister. He drew back and flung his fist round hard catching her on the cheek, the blow lifting Lucy from her feet and landing her on her back with a painful groan.

Henderson dropped to his knees in front of Lucy, forcing her legs apart and beginning to unbuckle his belt.

'This is what you'll get too Kathy, before I kill you myself. It's what you deserve but first you can watch what I do to your friend here. You can all watch,' he said wheezing with stinking breath as a semiconscious Lucy fought in vain to free herself from Henderson's massive bulk.

Instinctively Sam sprinted forward to help Lucy as both Stone and Arthur turned to shoot at the same moment but both men held fire for lack of a clear target. Sam dived low and ran into Henderson throwing all his weight into the charge ramming his shoulder into Henderson's side cracking several ribs and tumbling them both into a heap a couple of metres from Lucy. Alice ran forward to help Lucy and took her back toward the house where Arthur maintained cover. Sam was quick to his feet and seeing Lucy was safe stepped away from Henderson keeping behind him on the right while watching Stone and Kathy on his left.

Henderson grimaced as his broken ribs protested his movements but it served only to fuel his growing rage. He raised himself to his full height and bellowed into the night. 'You're all dead, do you hear me? You're all dead. Nobody does this to Victor Henderson, nobody. I'll kill you all.'

'No Victor, it's you who's dead,' said Stone icily as he turned the gun on Henderson. 'I'm so sorry Kathy, are you okay?' he asked as he released her. She didn't answer but tears erupted from her frightened eyes as she ran past Sam to Lucy who held her close as the group looked at Stone in disbelief.

'Stone, what the hell are you doing? I made you, I can break you. Without my money you're nothing, just a filthy Dreg for hire, a whore like my bitch wife and my traitorous daughter. I'm ordering you Stone; kill her then kill the rest of them. Now Stone!'

'My name's not Stone and Kathy is not your daughter. She's mine.'

'Shut up and do what I tell you or, wait, what the hell are you talking about Stone? If you're not Derek Stone then who the hell are you? What do you mean Kathy's your daughter?'

Stone stepped closer to Henderson and kept the gun trained on him.

'It's your turn to shut up and listen. My name is James Nolan and I was in love with your wife. Claudia kept our affair secret from you for years. Think about it Henderson, your wife was pregnant with my child; she knew you would kill them both if you discovered the truth so she convinced you the child was your own. She gave birth to a beautiful little girl and named her Kathy. I stayed away at first to keep her safe but me and Claudia, we were so much in love we risked everything to continue seeing each other.'

The friends listened in shocked silence as the former Derek Stone circled around Henderson as he spoke, his voice turning as cold and hard as the steel of the pistol aimed at Henderson's head.

'When you murdered Claudia you sent your Enforcers to arrest and torture me. When they'd finished their work they left me for dead in the streets like a dying rat but I couldn't leave my girls. I crawled on my belly to a back alley bar. A friend found me outside on the step, unconscious and bleeding. He took me in, got me patched up enough that I was able to walk again. The scars on my face and my missing eye helped hide my identity. I used that to my advantage and I sought you out. I bought fake papers and work references from a mob forger and earned the trust of one of your club friends to get one step closer to you. It was only by chance that I became your driver so quickly but it was Kathy I was protecting all along. I had to get close as it was the only way I could protect her from you.'

As he processed the information Henderson's jaw flapped open and closed but no sound except his laboured breathing was audible. He froze, a shocked expression crossed his face and he gripped his chest which felt to him like someone had rammed an ice pick into his heart. Driven by a raging fury and burning hatred for everyone that had betrayed him Victor Henderson willed his failing body back under his control. With an intense burst he leapt forward much faster than anyone could have thought possible and in a second had closed the gap between himself and James Nolan who with trained reflexes managed to get off a couple of shots before Henderson was on top of him. The first bullet ripped through Henderson's left shoulder, the second went higher and took off his left ear also gouging a track of flesh along the left side of his head but in his murderous rage Henderson felt nothing except intense anger and hatred. He pinned James to the ground, landing heavily on his chest with a massive weight advantage forcing the air from his lungs then clamped his chubby fingers around James' neck, tightened his grip and began to squeeze. James struggled for a few seconds trying to smash Henderson in the head with the butt of the pistol he still gripped but quickly weakened as he fought for breath.

'Help him!' cried Lucy.

'Keep back Sam,' shouted Arthur running forward aiming and firing the first of his remaining two rounds. His first shot was wide and missed the target. He took a deep breath, held it and fired again but Henderson moved at the last second and the shot passed clean through his arm, partially loosening the strangling grip but not enough to have any real effect. As James began to lose consciousness the pistol fell from his grasp. Sam darted forward and dived for the gun sliding on his belly, grabbing the weapon just as Henderson lunged to take it. Sam rolled onto his back as the red eyed Henderson stood and focused his attack on him.

'Look out Sam!' shouted Arthur.

Still lying on his back Sam brought the pistol up in both hands and fired five rounds into Victor Henderson, three in the chest and two in the face blowing the back and top of his head to pieces and raining blood, brains and bone over the sandy lawn. Arthur ran forward to Sam who was still aiming at where Henderson had been standing and took the gun from him.

'It's okay Sam, you got him. It's alright now my boy, it's alright.'

When Molly bounded over and pressed her wet nose into his cheek and licked him gently Sam relaxed a little and Arthur helped him to his feet.

'He would have killed Stone, I mean James. I had to Arthur.'

Arthur put his hand on Sam's shoulder. 'It's okay Sam; he would have killed all of us if he had the chance. You did good and we're safe now. You did good Sam.'

Lucy and Kathy knelt beside their father who was alive but coughing and fighting for breath. Alice came from the house with blankets for the girls who were still in their night wear and brought a glass of water for James.

'Daddy, is it really you?' said Lucy in shock, still recovering from her injuries and her father's revelations.

'Aunt Susan told me you had been killed. Why didn't you

come back for me daddy?'

'I'm so sorry Lucy,' croaked James through his damaged throat. I thought if Henderson knew I was still alive he'd come for me through you. It was the only way I could protect you.

Kathy was wary of the man she had only ever known as the ruthless Derek Stone.

'If you're my real father why did you help that monster keep me locked up? Why couldn't you have just taken me away or let me go free?'

'I'm sorry Kathy, I truly am. Henderson was a very powerful man with dangerous friends. I had to be sure you were safe and that he'd not come looking for you. I stayed close and kept you safe the only way I knew how.'

'Well, won't they come looking for him now? I mean the Enforcers and all, they'll never stop looking for him,' Lucy worried.

'I was there when he lost his seat of power, believe me. What's left of the military will be under better command now Victor and his cronies are gone. They have enough work to do in the cities and the General has no love for Henderson. Don't worry; I don't think anyone is going to miss him.'

James shed a tear of emotion; something Kathy had never seen him do.

'My beautiful girls, you found each other and now I have found you both. Can you ever forgive me?'

Lucy leaned in and kissed her father on the forehead and after a hesitation Kathy did the same. They helped James to his feet and led him to the house where Kathy helped Alice tend to his and Lucy's injuries.

'Go to the house Molly. House,' said Sam sending Molly in so he and Arthur could deal with the final gruesome task of the night.

'Burial at sea I reckon,' said Arthur.

'What, you think this piece of shit deserves that?'

'No, I say we bring him up there and throw him off the cliff,' laughed Arthur pointing to the rocky outcrop.

Sam and Arthur discussed the options and finally agreed they would drag the body to the beach and bury it in a shallow grave above the high tide line. Henderson might have been a monster but they weren't. They worked in silence covering the body with the sand they dug from the pit then built a mound of large smooth stones from the beach leaving the burial site unmarked. If anyone ever did find the final resting place of Victor Henderson no one would know who he was, or who he had been.

A few weeks later in the isolated north-western corner of the country, Sam rode his motorbike on winding roads through dense pine forests high into the mountains. He was followed by a father and his two daughters in an expensive executive saloon car and an old man and his wife in a battered truck with a golden haired dog excitedly sticking her head out from under the canvas cover in the rear.

They reached a large wooden cabin set into the side of the mountain and surrounded by woodland. The front of the cabin looked out over the valley and to the deep crystal lakes far below. As the others stretched cramped limbs and gathered some of their belongings Sam found the key under a small rock on the porch right where his grandfather used to keep it. He went inside and found things just as he remembered. The stone chimney and natural wood floor, a worn brown leather couch and a huge multi-coloured rag rug his grandmother had made lay on the floor in front of the hearth. Pieces of simple furniture his grandfather and father had built together still sat in the rooms and even the beds in each of the four bedrooms were made up with old patchwork quilts and thick wool blankets to ward off the cold mountain nights. Everything except for a few treasured keepsakes and photographs was left as it had been when his family hurriedly moved away.

Forgotten memories flooded back to him and Sam knew he was finally where he belonged. As his companions busied themselves moving into their new home he stood on the porch, savouring the scent of fresh pine as a cool mountain breeze sighed through the boughs of ancient trees. He watched a solitary hawk soar high above the valley and Sam felt he knew how it was to be so free.

Printed in Poland
by Amazon Fulfillment
Poland Sp. z o.o., Wrocław

54779255R00181